The jackals had been busy with the body . . .

Three of them lay dead, mounds of rancid fur, and Keith was at a loss to account for their condition. He played his flashlight up and down the corpse, inspected the flesh at which the jackals had been tearing. He bent closer, frowning in puzzlement. A peculiar pad of specialized tissue lay along the outside of the thighs, almost an inch thick. It was organized in orderly strips and fed plentifully from large arteries, and here and there Keith detected the glint of metal. Suddenly he guessed the nature of the tissue and why the jackals lay dead . . .

Those pads of gray flesh must be electro-organic tissue, similar to that of the electric eel, somehow adapted to human flesh by Russian biologists. Keith felt a sense of oppression. How far they exceed us! he thought. My power source is chemical, inorganic; that of this man was controlled by the functioning of his body and remained at so high a potential that three jackals had been electrocuted tearing into it . . .

THE AUGMENTED AGENT
AND OTHER STORIES
by Jack Vance

JACK VANCE

THE AUGMENTED AGENT AND OTHER STORIES

edited by
Steven Owen Godersky

ACE BOOKS, NEW YORK

This Ace book contains the revised
text of the original hardcover edition.
It has been completely reset in a typeface
designed for easy reading and was printed
from new film.

THE AUGMENTED AGENT
AND OTHER STORIES

An Ace Book/published by arrangement with
the author

PRINTING HISTORY
Underwood–Miller edition published 1986
Ace edition/September 1988

ISBN: 0-441-03610-4

Ace Books are published by The Berkley Publishing Group,
200 Madison Avenue, New York, NY 10016.
The name "ACE" and the "A" logo are trademarks
belonging to Charter Communications, Inc.

PRINTED IN THE UNITED STATES OF AMERICA

10 9 8 7 6 5 4 3 2 1

Contents

Shape-Up

JARVIS CAME DOWN Riverview Way from the direction of the terminal warehouse, where he had passed an uncomfortable night. At the corner of Sion Novack Way he plugged his next-to-last coin into the *Pegasus Square Farm and Mining Bulletin* dispenser; taking the pink tissue envelope, he picked his way through the muck of the street to the Original Blue Man Cafe. He chose a table with precision and nicety, his back to a corner, the length of the street in his line of sight.

The waiter appeared, looked Jarvis up and down. Jarvis countered with a hard stare. "Hot anise, a viewer."

The waiter turned away. Jarvis relaxed, sat rubbing his sore hip and watching the occasional dark shape hurrying against the mist. The streets were still dim; only one of the Procrustean suns had risen: no match for the fogs of Idle River.

The waiter returned with a dull metal pot and the viewer. Jarvis parted with his last coin, warmed his hands on the pot, notched in the film, and sipped the brew, giving his attention to the journal. Page and page flickered past: trifles of Earth news, cluster news, local news, topical discussions, practical mechanics. He found the classified advertisements, employ-

1

ment opportunities, skimmed down the listings. These were sparse enough: a well-digger wanted, glass puddlers, berry-pickers, creep-weed chasers. He bent forward; this was more to his interest.

Shape-up: Four travellers of top efficiency. Large profits for able workers; definite goals in sight. Only men of resource and willingness need apply. At 10 meridian, see Belisarius at the Old Solar Inn.

Jarvis read the paragraph once more, translating the oblique phrases to more definite meanings. He looked at his watch: still three hours. He glanced at the street, at the waiter, sipped from the pot, and settled to a study of the *Farm and Mining Bulletin*.

Two hours later the second sun, a blue-white ball, rose at the head of Riverview Way, flaring through the mist; now the population of the town began to appear. Jarvis took quiet leave of the cafe and set off down Riverview Way in the bright sunlight.

Heat and the exercise loosened the throb in his hip; when he reached the river esplanade his walk was smooth. He turned to the right, past the Memorial Fountain, and there was the Old Solar Inn, looking across the water to the gray marble bluffs.

Jarvis inspected it with care. It looked expensive but not elaborate, exuding dignity rather than elegance. He felt less skeptical; *Bulletin* notices occasionally promised more than they fulfilled; a man could not be too careful.

He approached the inn. The entrance was a massive wooden door with a stained glass window, where an emblem depicting a laughing Old Sol shot a golden ray upon green and blue Earth. The door swung open; Jarvis entered, bent to the wicket.

"Yes, sir?" asked the clerk.

"Mr. Belisarius," said Jarvis.

The clerk inspected Jarvis with much the expression of the waiter at the cafe. With the faintest of shrugs, he said, "Suite B—down the lower hall."

Jarvis crossed the lobby. As he entered the hall he heard the outer door open; a huge blond man in green suede came into the inn, paused like Jarvis by the wicket. Jarvis continued along the hall. The door to Suite B was ajar; Jarvis pushed it open, entered.

He stood in a large room panelled with dark green sea-tree, furnished simply—a tawny rug, chairs and couches around the walls, an elaborate chandelier decorated with glowing spangles—so elaborate, indeed, that Jarvis suspected a system of spy-cells. In itself this meant nothing; in fact, it might be construed as commendable caution.

Five others were waiting: men of various ages, size, skin-color. Only one aspect did they have in common; a way of seeming to look to all sides at once. Jarvis took a seat, sat back; a moment later the big blond man in green suede entered. He looked around the room, glanced at the chandelier, took a seat. A stringy gray-haired man with corrugated brown skin and a sly reckless smile said, "Omar Gildig! What are you here for, Gildig?"

The big blond man's eyes became blank for an instant; then he said, "For motives much like your own, Tixon."

The old man jerked his head back, blinked. "You mistake me; my name is Pardee, Captain Pardee."

"As you say, Captain."

There was silence in the room; then Tixon, or Pardee, nervously crossed to where Gildig sat and spoke in low tones. Gildig nodded like a placid lion.

Other men entered; each glanced around the room, at the chandelier, then took seats. Presently the room held twenty or more.

Other conversations arose. Jarvis found himself next to a small, sturdy man with a round moon-face, a bulbous little paunch, a hooked little nose and dark, owlish eyes. He seemed disposed to speak, and Jarvis made such comments as seemed judicious. "A cold night, last, for those of us to see the red sun set."

Jarvis assented.

"A lucky planet to win free from, this," continued the round man. "I've been watching the *Bulletin* for three weeks now; if I don't join Belisarius—why, by the juice of Jonah, I'll take a workaway job on a packet.''

Jarvis asked ''Who is this Belisarius?''

The round man opened his eyes wide. ''Belisarius? It's well-known—he's Belson!''

''Belson?'' Jarvis could not hold the surprised note out of his voice; the bruise on his hip began to jar and thud. ''Belson?''

The round man had turned away his head, but was staring over the bridge of his little beak-nose. ''Belson is an effective traveller, much respected.''

''So I understand,'' said Jarvis.

''Rumor comes that he has suffered reverses—notably one such, two months gone, on the swamps of Fenn.''

''How goes the rumor?'' asked Jarvis.

''There is large talk, small fact,'' the round man replied gracefully. ''Besides, have you ever speculated on the concentration of so much talent in so small a room? There is yourself. And my own humble talents—there is Omar Gildig— brawn like a Beshauer bull, a brain of guile. Over there is young Hancock McManus, an effective worker, and there—he who styles himself Lachesis, a metaphor. And I'll wager that in all our aggregate pockets there's not twenty Juillard crowns!''

''Certainly not in mine,'' admitted Jarvis.

''This is our life,'' said the round man. ''We live at the full—each minute an entity to be squeezed of its maximum; our moneys, our crowns, our credits—they buy us great sweetness, but they are soon gone. Then Belisarius hints of brave goals, and we come, like moths to a flame!''

''I wonder,'' mused Jarvis. ''Belisarius surely has trusted lieutenants. . . . When he calls for travellers through the *Farm Bulletin*—there always is the chance of Authority participation.''

''Perhaps they are unaware of the convention, the code.''

''More likely not.''

The round man shook his head, sighed. ''A brave agent would come to the Old Solar Inn on this day!''

''There are such men.''

''But they will not come to the shape-ups—and do you know why not?''

"Why not then?"

"Suppose they do—suppose they trap six men—a dozen."

"A dozen less to cope with."

"But the next time a shape-up is called, the travellers will prove themselves by the Test Supreme."

"And this is?" inquired Jarvis easily, though he knew quite well.

The round man explained with zest. "Each party kills in the presence of an umpire. The Authority will not risk the resumption of such tests; and so they allow the travellers to meet and foregather in peace." The round man peered at Jarvis. "This can hardly be new information?"

"I have heard talk," said Jarvis.

The round man said, "Caution is admirable when not carried to an excess."

Jarvis laughed, showing his long, sharp teeth. "Why not use an excess of caution, when it costs nothing?"

"Why not?" assented the round man, and said no more to Jarvis.

A few moments later the inner door opened; an old man, slight, crotchety, in tight black trousers and vest, peered out. His eyes were mild, his face was long, waxy, melancholy; his voice was suitably grave. "Your attention, if you please."

"By Crokus," muttered the round man, "Belson has hired undertakers to staff his conferences!"

The old man in black spoke on. "I will summon you one at a time, in the approximate order of your arrival. You will be given certain tests, you will submit to certain interrogations. . . . Anyone who finds the prospect overintimate may leave at this moment."

He waited. No one rose to depart, although scowls appeared, and Omar Gildig said, "Reasonable queries are resented by no one. If I find the interrogation too searching—then I shall protest."

The old man nodded, "Very well, as you wish. First then—you, Paul Pulliam."

A slim, elegant man in wine-colored jacket and tight trousers rose to his feet, entered the inner room.

"So that is Paul Pulliam," breathed the round man. "I

have wondered six years about him, ever since the Myknosis affair.''

"Who is that old man—the undertaker?" asked Jarvis.

"I have no idea."

"In fact," asked Jarvis, "Who is Belson? What is Belson's look?"

"In truth," said the round man, "I know no more to that."

The second man was called, then the third, the fourth, then:

"Gilbert Jarvis!"

Jarvis rose to his feet, thinking: how in thunder do they know *my first name*? He passed through into an anteroom, whose only furnishing was a scale. The old man in black said, "If you please, I wish to learn your weight."

Jarvis stepped on the scale; the dial glowed with the figure 163, which the old man recorded in a book. "Very well, now—I will prick your ear—"

Jarvis grabbed the instrument; the old man squawked, "Here, here, here!"

Jarvis inspected the bit of glass and metal, gave it back with a wolfish grin. "I am a man of caution; I'll have no drugs pumped into my ear."

"No, no," protested the old man, "I need but a drop to learn your blood characteristics."

"Why is this important?" asked Jarvis cynically. "It's been my experience that if a man bleeds, why so much the worse, but let him bleed till either he stops or he runs dry."

"Belisarius is a considerate master."

"I want no master," said Jarvis.

"Mentor, then—a considerate mentor."

"I think for myself."

"Devil drag me deathways!" exclaimed the old man, "you are a ticklish man to please." He put the drop from Jarvis' ear into an analyzer, peered at the dials. "Type O . . . Index 96 . . . Granuli B. . . . Very good, Gilbert Jarvis, very good indeed!"

"Humph," said Jarvis, "is that all the test Belisarius gives a man—his weight, his blood?"

"No, no," said the old man earnestly, "these are but the

preliminaries; but allow me to congratulate you, you are so far entirely suitable. Now—come with me and wait; in an hour we will have our lunch, and then discuss the remainder of the problem."

Of the original applicants, only eight remained after the preliminary elimination. Jarvis noticed that all of the eight approximated his own weight, with the exception of Omar Gildig, who weighed two hundred fifty or more.

The old man in black summoned them to lunch; the eight filed into a round green dining-saloon; they took places at a round green table. The old man gave a signal and wine and appetizers appeared in the service slots. He put on an air of heartiness. "Let us forget the background of our presence here," he said. "Let us enjoy the good food and such fellowship as we may bring to the occasion."

Omar Gildig snorted, a vast grimace that pulled his nose down over his mouth. "Who cares about fellowship? We want to know that which concerns us. What is this affair that Belson plans for?"

The old man shook his head smilingly. "There are still eight of you—and Belisarius needs but four."

"Then get on with your tests; there are better things to be doing than jumping through these jackanape hoops."

"There have been no hoops so far," said the old man gently. "Bear with me only an hour longer; none of you eight will go without your recompense, of one kind or another."

Jarvis looked from face to face. Gildig; sly, reckless old Tixon—or Captain Pardee, as he called himself; the round, owlish man; a blond, smiling youth like a girl in men's gear; two quiet nondescripts; a tall pencil-thin black, who might have been dumb, for all the words he spoke.

Food was served: small steaks of a local venison, a small platter of toasted pods with sauce of herbs and minced mussels. In fact, so small were the portions that Jarvis found his appetite merely whetted.

Next came glasses of frozen red punch, then braised crescents of white flesh, each with a bright red nubbin at both ends, swimming in a pungent sauce.

Jarvis smiled to himself and glanced around the table.

Gildig had fallen to with gusto, as had the thin dark-skinned man; one or two of the others were eating with more caution. Jarvis thought, I won't be caught quite so easily, and toyed with the food; and he saw from the corner of his eye that Tixon, the blond youth and the round man were likewise abstaining.

Their host looked around the table with a pained expression. "The dish, I see, is not popular."

The round man said plaintively, "Surely it's uncommon poor manners to poison us with the Fenn swamp-shrimp."

Gildig spat out a mouthful. "Poison!"

"Peace, Conrad, peace," said the old man, grinning. "These are not what you think them." He reached out a fork, speared one of the objects from the plate of Conrad, the round man, and ate it. "You see, you are mistaken. Perhaps these resemble the Fenn swamp-shrimp—but they are not."

Gildig looked suspiciously at his plate. "And what did you think they were?" he asked Conrad.

Conrad picked up one of the morsels, looked at it narrowly. "On Fenn when a man wants to put another man in his power for a day or a week, he seeks these—or shrimp like these—from the swamps. The toxic principle is in these red sacs." He pushed his plate away. "Swamp-shrimp or not, they still dull my appetite."

"We'll remove them," said the old man. "To the next dish, by all means—a bake of capons, as I recall."

The meal progressed; the old man produced no more wine— "because," he explained, "we have a test of skill approaching us; it's necessary that you have all faculties with you."

"A complicated system of filling out a roster," muttered Gildig.

The old man shrugged. "I act for Belisarius."

"Belson, you mean."

"Call him any name you wish."

Conrad, the round man, said thoughtfully, "Belson is not an easy master."

The old man looked surprised. "Does not Belson—as you call him—bring you large profits?"

"Belson allows no man's interference—and Belson never forgets a wrong."

The old man laughed a mournful chuckle. "That makes him an easy man to serve. Obey him, do him no wrongs—and you never need fear his anger."

Conrad shrugged, Gildig smiled. Jarvis sat watchfully. There was more to this business than filling out a roster, more than a profit to be achieved.

"Now," said the old man, "if you please, one at a time, through this door. Omar Gildig, I'll have you first."

The seven remained at the table, watching uneasily from the corners of their eyes. Conrad and Tixon—or Captain Pardee—spoke lightly; the blond youth joined their talk; then a thud caused them all to look up, the talk stopped short. After a pause, the conversation continued rather lamely.

The old man appeared. "Now you, Captain Pardee."

Captain Pardee—or Tixon—left the room. The six remaining listened; there were no further sounds.

The old man next summoned the blond youth, then Conrad, then one of the nondescripts, then the tall black man, the other nondescript, and finally Jarvis, where he sat alone.

"My apologies, Gilbert Jarvis—but I think we are effecting a satisfactory elimination. If you will come this way. . . ."

Jarvis entered a long dim room.

The old man said, "This as I have intimated, is a test of skill, agility, resource. I presume you carry your favorite weapons with you?"

Jarvis grinned. "Naturally."

"Notice," said the old man, "the screen at the far end of this room. Imagine behind, two armed and alert men who are your enemies, but not yet aware of your presence." He paused; watched Jarvis, who grinned his humorless smile.

"Well, then, are you imagining the situation?"

Jarvis listened; did he hear breathing? There was the feel of stealth in the room, of mounting strain, expectancy.

"Are you imagining?" asked the old man. "They will kill you if they find you. . . . They will kill you. . . ."

A sound, a rush—not from the end of the room—but at the side—a hurtling dark shape. The old man ducked; Jarvis jumped back, whipped out his weapon, a Parnassian sliver-spit. . . . The dark shape thumped with three internal explosions.

"Excellent," said the old man. "You have good reactions, Gilbert Jarvis—and with a sliver-spit too. Are they not difficult weapons?"

"Not to a man who knows their use; then they are most effective."

"An interesting diversity of opinion," said the old man. "Gildig, for instance, used a collapsible club. Where he had it hidden, I have no idea—a miracle of swiftness. Conrad was almost as adept with the shoot-blade as you are with the sliver-spit and Noel the blond youngster—he preferred a dammel-ray."

"Bulky," said Jarvis. "Bulky and delicate, with limited capacity."

"I agree," said the old man. "But each man to his own methods."

"It puzzles me," said Jarvis. "Where does he carry the weapon? I noticed none of the bulk of a dammel-ray on his person."

"He had it adjusted well," said the old man cryptically. "This way, if you please."

They returned to the original waiting room. Instead of the original twenty men, there were now but four: Gildig, old Tixon, the blond young Noel, and Conrad, the round man with the owlish face. Jarvis looked Noel over critically to see where he carried his weapon, but it was nowhere in evidence, though his clothes were pink, yellow and black weave, skin-tight.

The old man seemed in the best of spirits; his mournful jowls quivered and twitched. "Now, gentlemen, now—we come to the end of the elimination. Five men, when we need but four. One man must be dispensed with; can anyone propose a means to this end?"

The five men stiffened, looked sideways around with a guarded wariness, as the same idea suggested itself to each mind.

"Well," said the old man, "it would be one way out of the

impasse, but there might be several simultaneous elimina-
tions, and it would put Belisarius to considerable trouble."

No one spoke.

The old man mused, "I think I can resolve the quandary.
Let us assume that all of us are hired by Belisarius."

"I assume nothing," growled Gildig, "Either I'm hired, or
I'm not! If I'm hired, I want a retainer."

"Very well," said the old man. "You are are, then, hired
by Belisarius."

"By Belson."

"Yes—by Belson. Here—" he distributed five envelopes
"—here is earnest-money. A thousand crowns. Now each
and all of you are Belson's men. You understand what this
entails?"

"It entails loyalty," intoned Tixon, looking with satisfaction into the envelope.

"Complete, mindless, unswerving loyalty," echoed the old
man. "What's that?" he asked to Gildig's grumble.

Gildig said, "He doesn't leave a man a mind of his own."

"When he serves Belson, a man needs his mind only to
serve. Before, and after, he is as free as air. During his
employment, he must be Belson's man. The rewards are
great—but the punishments are certain."

Gildig grunted with resignation. "What next, then?"

"Now—we seek to eliminate the one superfluous man. I
think now we can do it." He looked around the faces.
"Gildig—Tixon—"

"Captain Pardee, call me—that's my name!"

"—Conrad—Noel—and Gilbert Jarvis."

"Well," said Conrad shortly, "get on with it."

"The theory of the situation," said the old man didactically, "is that now we are all Belson's loyal followers.
Suppose we find a traitor to Belson, an enemy—what do we
do then?"

"Kill him!" said Tixon.

"Exactly."

Gildig leaned forward, and the bulging muscles sent planes
of soft light moving down his green suede jacket. "How can
there be traitors when we are just hired?"

The old man looked mournfully at his pale fingers. "Actually, gentlemen, the situation goes rather deeper than one might suppose. This unwanted fifth man—the man to be eliminated—he happens to be one who has violated Belson's trust. The disposal of this man," he said sternly, "will provide an object lesson for the remaining four."

"Well," said Noel easily, "shall we proceed? Who is the betrayer?"

"Ah," said the old man, "we have gathered today to learn this very fact."

"Do you mean to say," snapped Conrad, "that this entire rigamarole is not to our benefit, but only yours?"

"No, no!" protested the old man. "The four who are selected will have employment—if I may say, employment on the instant. But let me explain; the background is this: at a lonesome camp, on the marshes of Fenn, Belson had stored a treasure—a rare treasure! Here he left three men to guard. Two were known to Belson, the third was a new recruit, an unknown from somewhere across the system.

"When the dawn was breaking, this new man rose, killed the two men, took the treasure across the marsh to the port city Momart, and there sold it. Belson's loyal lieutenant—myself—was on the planet. I made haste to investigate. I found tracks in the marsh. I established that the treasure had been sold. I learned that passage had been bought—I followed. Now, gentlemen," and the old man sat back, "we are all persons of discernment. We live for the pleasurable moment. We gain money, we spend money, at a rather predictable rate. Knowing the value of Belson's treasure, I was able to calculate just when the traitor would feel the pinch of poverty. At this time I baited the trap; I published the advertisement; and the trap is sprung. Is that not clever? Admit it now!"

And he glanced from face to face.

Jarvis eased his body around in the chair to provide swifter scope for movement, and also to ease his hip, which now throbbed painfully.

"Go on," said Gildig, likewise glaring from face to face.

"I now exercised my science. I cut turves from the swamp,

those which held the tracks, the crushed reeds, the compressed moss. At the laboratory, I found that a hundred and sixty pounds pressure, more or less, might make such tracks. Weight—'' he leaned forward to confide, ''—formed the basis of the first elimination. Each of you was weighed, you will recall, and you that are here—with the exception of Omar Gildig—fulfill the requirement.

Noel asked lightly, ''Why was Gildig included?''

''Is it not clear?'' asked the old man. ''He cannot be the traitor, but he makes an effective sergeant-at-arms.''

''In other words,'' said Conrad dryly, ''the traitor is either Tixon—I mean Captain Pardee, Noel, Jarvis or myself.''

''Exactly,'' said the old man mournfully. ''Our problem is reducing the four to one—and then, reducing the one to nothing. For this purpose we have our zealous sergeant-at-arms here—Omar Gildig.''

''Pleased to oblige,'' said Gildig, now relaxed, almost sleepy.

The old man slid back a panel, drew with chalk on a board.

''We make a chart—and as he spoke he wrote the weight beside each name: ''Captain Pardee: 162; Noel: 155; Conrad: 166; and Jarvis: 163. Next—each of you four were familiar with the Fenn swamp-shrimp, indicating familiarity with the Fenn swamps. So—a check beside each of your names.'' He paused to look around. ''Are you attending, Gildig?''

''At your service.''

''Next,'' said the old man, ''there was blood on the ground, indicating a wound. It was not the blood of the two slain men—nor blood from the treasure. Therefore it must be blood from the traitor; and today I have taken blood from each of the four. I leave this column blank. Next—to the weapons. The men were killed, very neatly, very abruptly—with a Parnassian sliver; Tixon uses a JAR-gun; Noel, dammel-ray; Conrad, a shoot-blade—and Jarvis, a sliver-spit. So—an X beside the name of Jarvis!''

Jarvis began drawing himself up. ''Easy,'' said Gildig, ''I'm watching you, Jarvis.''

Jarvis relaxed, smiling a wolfish grin.

The old man, watching him from the corner of his eye,

said, "This, of course, is hardly conclusive. So, to the blood. In the blood are body-cells. The cells contain nuclei, with genes—and each man's genes are distinctive. So now with the blood—"

Jarvis, still smiling, spoke. "You find it to be mine?"

"Exactly."

"Old man—you lie. I have no wound on my body."

"Wounds heal fast, Jarvis."

"Old man—you fail as Belson's trusted servant."

"Eh? And how?"

"Through stupidity. Perhaps worse."

"Yes? And precisely how?"

"The tracks. . . . In the laboratory you compressed turves of the swamp. You found you needed weight of one hundred and sixty pounds to achieve the effect of the Fenn prints."

"Yes. Exactly."

"Fenn's gravity is six-tenths Earth standard. The compression of one sixty pounds on Fenn is better achieved by a man of two hundred and forty or two-fifty pounds—such as Gildig."

Gildig half-raised. "Do you dare to accuse me?"

"Are you guilty?"

"No."

"You can't prove it."

"I don't need to prove it! Those tracks might be made by a lighter man carrying the treasure. How much was the weight?"

"A light silken treasure," said the old man. "No more than a hundred pounds."

Tixon drew back to a corner. "Jarvis is guilty!"

Noel threw open his gay coat, to disclose an astonishing contrivance: a gun muzzle protruding from his chest, a weapon surprisingly fitted into his body. Now Jarvis knew where Noel carried his dammel-ray.

Noel laughed. "Jarvis—the traitor!"

"No," said Jarvis, "you're wrong. I am the only loyal servant of Belson's in the room. If Belson were near, I would tell him about it."

The old man said quickly, "We've heard enough of his wriggling. Kill him, Gildig."

Gildig stretched his arm; from under his wrist, out his

sleeve shot a tube of metal three feet long, already winging to the pull of Gildig's wrist. Jarvis sprang back, the tube struck him on the bruised hip; he shot the sliver-spit. Gildig's hand was gone—exploded.

"Kill, kill," sang the old man, dodging back.

The door opened; a sedate handsome man came in. "I am Belson."

"The traitor, Belson," cried the old man. "Jarvis, the traitor!"

"No, no," said Jarvis. "I can tell you better."

"Speak Jarvis—your last moment!"

"I was on Fenn, yes! I was the new recruit, yes! It was my blood, yes!. . . . But traitor, no! I was the man left for dead when the traitor went."

"And who is this traitor?"

"Who was on Fenn? Who was quick to raise the cry for Jarvis? Who knew of the treasure?"

"Pah!" said the old man, as Belson's mild glance swung toward him.

"Who just now spoke of the sun rising at the hour of the deed?"

"A mistake!"

"A mistake, indeed!"

"Yes, Finch," said Belson to the old man, "how did you know so closely the hour of the theft?"

"An estimate, a guess, an intelligent deduction."

Belson turned to Gildig, who had been standing stupidly clutching the stump of his arm. "Go, Gildig; get yourself a new hand at the clinic. Give them the name Belisarius."

"Yes, sir." Gildig tottered out.

"You, Noel," said Belson, "Book yourself a passage to Achernar; go to Pasatiempo, await word at the Auberge Bacchanal."

"Yes, Belson," Noel departed.

"Tixon—"

"Captain Pardee is my name, Belson."

"—I have no need for you now, but I will keep your well-known abilities in mind."

"Thank you and good-day." Tixon departed.

"Conrad, I have a parcel to be travelled to the city Sudanapolis on Earth; await me at Suite RS above."

"Very good, Belson," Conrad wheeled, marched out the door.

"Jarvis, I will speak to you further today. Await me in the lobby."

"Very well." Jarvis turned and started from the room. He heard Belson say quietly to the old man, "And now, Finch, as for you—" and then further words and sounds were cut off by the closing of the door.

The Man From Zodiac

I

UPON THE DEATH of Rudolf Zarius, his nephew Edgar Zarius and his granddaughter Lusiane Ludlow each inherited forty-six percent of Zodiac Control, Incorporated.

Milton Hack, Zodiac's field representative, owned the remaining eight percent of the company.

A week after the funeral, Edgar and Lusiane met in the Zodiac offices at Farallon, fifteen miles out in the Pacific from San Francisco. Neither held the other in large esteem. Lusiane was a young woman of striking appearance and extravagant tastes; Edgar, a tall pale man with a long nose and narrowly spaced eyes. Lusiane was self-willed, pampered and vain; Edgar's luxuries were small, fastidious and private. He thought her frivolous; she thought him a bore.

The conference was cautious and constrained. In a careful voice Edgar announced that he was willing to consider the purchase of Lusiane's shares. Lusiane gave a casual assent and named a price which aroused Edgar's amazement. "You must be crazy," he said coldly. "The business hasn't made that much money during its entire existence."

Lusiane glanced around the office, disdainful of the shabby furniture, outmoded irsys (information retrieval system), dusty mementos and testimonials. "Small wonder. This place is a stable. Obviously changes must be made. I suggest first of all that you fire Hack."

"*I* fire him?" Edgar raised his eyebrows. "*You* fire him. You own as much stock as I do."

Lusiane showed her beautiful teeth in a mocking laugh. Milton Hack, with his eight percent interest, represented the balance of power, and neither wished to antagonize him.

"Naturally you tried to buy him out?" said Lusiane.

Edgar gave a curt nod, a sour grin. "No doubt you did the same?"

"I did. What a perverse man!" Lusiane spoke with unusual heat. She had used all her suasions and urgencies upon Hack without visible effect. "Do we need a 'field representative'? His duties are so indefinite. Why don't we put him to selling or supervising or something of the sort?"

Edgar shrugged. "Why not?"

Hack was sent out to solicit new business among the .planets of the Andromeda chain: a task for which he had no great aptitude. Four months later he returned to Farallon with nothing to show for his efforts but expensive vouchers.

Changes had occurred in his absence, going far beyond the perfunctory facelift he had expected. The old offices had been enlarged and redecorated in spectacular style. The lobby was now circular, with black walls leaning in to form a dome at some obscure height. Around the periphery ran a black leather couch; the walls displayed a series of holograms, each the image of one of the settled worlds. Stainless steel strips in the black floor converged upon a circular reception desk of grey fibroid, and here, under a glittering chandelier, sat a rather small girl in a uniform of black and white diaper. Her hair was a smooth dark cap; her face was intelligent, inquiring, devoid of cosmetics, and Hack wondered who had hired her: Edgar or Lusiane.

Hack was forced to admit that the change was for the better, insofar as it affected the corporate image. The alterations of course had cost a great deal of money, eight percent of which derived from himself, and Hack gave a wince of annoyance. He approached the receptionist. "Mr. Zarius, please."

She searched his face, which was square from forehead to cheekbone, thin at the chin, with a precise drooping mouth, a thin crooked nose. Hack was not a large man; relaxing he seemed mild, a trifle pedantic, almost inconsequential. "Yes, sir. You are . . . ?"

"Milton Hack."

"Sorry, Mr. Hack, I didn't recognize you. Will you wait a few minutes? Mr. Zarius is busy with clients."

Hack strolled around the room, inspecting the holograms: perfect windows into space. The worlds depicted hung at perspectives of perhaps ten thousand miles, rotating with ponderous globularity. Hack had visited a number of these worlds: indeed, there was Ethelrinda Cordas, from which he had just returned. Hack went close to the hologram, traced the course of his travels. Wylandia to Heyring to Torre, back to Wylandia; across to the east coast and Colmar, north to Roseland and Seprissa; inland to Parnassus and the palace of Cyril Dibden the Benefactor, then to the island Gentila Mercado, just below the Pirates Peninsula. . . . A planet of paradoxical contrasts, thought Hack: savage and soft, harsh and easy. . . . The orifice into the inner office expanded; three men of Ethelrinda Cordas stepped forth. Hack stared in astonishment. Fantasies? Imaginary constructions? Unfortunately not. They were unmistakable: massive coarse-featured men, indifferent equally to Earth styles and norms of conduct. Their black hair was plaited into twenty-four shoulder-length strands, each caught into a golden fob. They wore varnished black jackets with loose striped breeches, white boots with mother-of-pearl buckles. Despite the flamboyant costumes, they were most notable for their remarkable noses: enormous members inlaid with gems and liver-stone, the patterns splaying out across their cheeks. They stalked past Hack without so much as a glance, ornaments jangling, trailing a reek compounded of many qualities.

The receptionist wrinkled her nose. "What ruffians."

"You should see their wives," said Hack. He went on into

the inner office, which like the lobby seemed calculated more for spectacle than efficiency. Edgar Zarius, tall, morose and saturnine, was an incongruous sight behind the ormolu and black marble desk. "Ah, Hack," said Edgar in a colorless voice. "You're back then. Sit down."

Hack settled into a leather and oak chair of ancient Iberian derivation. "There seem to be changes about the office."

"Miss Ludlow decided the place needed a face-lift," said Edgar in a careful voice which suggested that neither Hack's criticism nor his approval would be considered appropriate. "Ruinously expensive, of course. I hope you had a good trip?"

"Very pleasant, thank you."

"Good. Let's look over your contracts."

"I don't have any."

Edgar raised his eyebrows. "No contracts? No new business?"

"Sorry."

"I'm very much disappointed." Edgar leaned back in his chair. "Disappointed indeed. . . . Hmm." He focused his eyes an inch above Hack's head. "Please don't take what I have to say personally. In essence, all of us must do better! This is the symbolic significance of our new premises: new vigor, new dedication, a new Zodiac!"

Hack made no comment.

"We have been complacent, over-conservative," Edgar went on. "This is a competitive business! We've been losing contracts right and left—to Aetna, to Fidelity, even to Argus!" He glanced sharply at Hack. "In some cases through sheer aimlessness and lassitude!"

"Evaluating a contact," said Hack politely, "is a matter of experience. Aetna and Fidelity concentrate on low-yield, low-risk contracts. We could pick up a dozen if we had the crews. Argus is almost bankrupt. Right now they'll snatch anything in sight."

Edgar spoke in a cold voice. "Argus is an aggressive concern—more so, I fear, than ourselves. I certainly don't counsel recklessness; I do insist however on alertness and enterprise."

Hack had nothing to add to his previous remarks.

After a brief pause, Edgar continued in a voice even more ponderous than before: "To be specific, you have just returned from Ethelrinda Cordas."

"Quite correct."

"What were your activities there?"

Hack reached to the desk, tapped irsys buttons. A Mercator projection of Ethelrinda Cordas appeared on the wall: the single vast continent, two large islands, a spatter of smaller islands. Hack indicated the westernmost of the large islands. "This is Agostino Cordas. Merit Systems has the contract." He pointed to the other. "Juanita Cordas, populated by a few ranchers. Nothing for us here. The big continent is Robal Cordas, mostly wilderness. On the west coast is the Corda Federation: five cities, some towns; an agricultural economy, with some light manufacturing. They have a fifty-year contract with Mutual Benefit, tight as a drum. At Wylandia I chartered an air-car and flew east, across the wilderness." He pointed to the interior of the continent. "Jungle, desert, lava-flows, mountains—uninhabited except for beasts. Here on the east coast—" Hack tapped the complicated shoreline "—the situation is different again. Isolated communities, some of them primitive, some predatory. Colmar, Roseland, Seprissa—I checked them all. Parnassus, with a population of two million, is a potential customer, but Cyril Dibden has his own ideas. The Pirates Peninsula is directly to the east. Cyril Dibden is kept on tenterhooks anticipating raids and forays— the only fly in his ointment. He gave me the run of the place for three days, but wouldn't even discuss a contract."

"Interesting," said Edgar, darting a quick sidewise glance at Hack. "And what else?"

"Not very much. Dibden insisted that I visit Gentila Mercado, a trading depot south of Parnassus. I talked to a group from Sabo on the Pirates Peninsula. They wanted to give us a contract but I turned them down."

Edgar sat up in his seat. "A contract subsequently awarded to Argus Systems."

Here, thought Hack, was the matter toward which Edgar, with his talk of alertness and enterprise, had been bearing.

Edgar asked in his driest voice: "May I inquire your reasons for rejecting this specific contract?"

"It looked like a poor bet. Much grief and no cooperation."

"Their money is good," Edgar pointed out. "So long as we perform our contractual obligations, we don't care whether they cooperate or not."

"They're a bloodthirsty lot," said Hack, "and devious to boot. It makes a poor combination."

"You miss the point," said Edgar, carefully patient, as if explaining a difficult paradox to a child. "Our function is to provide certain services, for which we receive recompense. We are not philosophers or moralists. We make no judgments. We perform the services for anyone who pays for them. Do you feel that the people of Sabo—the Sabols, I believe they call themselves—would refuse to pay our fees?"

"Hard to say. They have money enough. They don't seem niggardly."

"This is my own conclusion," said Edgar. "Did you happen to observe the three persons who left my office just previous to your arrival?"

"I saw them, yes. The receptionist described them as clients."

"They are Phrones from Ethelrinda Cordas. Phronus, I believe, is a community adjacent to Sabo."

"You signed a contract?"

"I did." Edgar struck his fist on the desk. "Compete! compete! compete! We can't let up an instant! Argus snatched the Sabo contract out from under our noses. They made fools of us!" He slid a document across the desk. "The Phronus contract. I wish all were this good. We provide skills and services; they pay costs and salaries plus ten percent. On these terms I'd take a contract on the south end of hell."

Hack examined the contract. It read:

AGREEMENT AND COVENANT BETWEEN
THE STATE OF PHRONUS
AND ZODIAC CONTROL INCORPORATED

Paragraph 1: Statement of purpose and scope of covenant.

All persons be advised that this instrument constitutes a firm and binding covenant between the people of that political entity known as Phronus, situated on the eastern coast of the continent know as Robal Cordas, on the planet known as Ethelrinda Cordas, otherwise described as the sixth planet of that star identified in the Standard Astronomical Almanac as Andromeda 469: these people hereinafter referred to as 'Entity First'; and the Zodiac Control Corporation. situated at Farallon, on the west coast of North America, Earth, hereinafter referred to as 'Entity Second.'

For that consideration defined in Paragraph 3, Entity Second engages to provide Entity First an administrative organization, consisting of expert personnel, with their essential and necessary tools and equipment, and only these, for the purpose of providing Entity First a judicious, efficient, expert and economical management of its public functions, as defined but not limited by Paragraph 2, to the extent and in the degree stipulated by Entity First.

Paragraph: 2 Specific provisions of the contract. The categories of services Entity Second agrees to provide Entity First, to the extent and degree Entity First deems necessary, are as follows:

1. Child and adult education, in all useful and advantageous phases of contemporary knowledge, as further defined in Schedule A of the appendix of this document.

2: Export and import brokerage, including purchasing and delivering to the State of Phronus at the city Grangali or elsewhere, at the option of Entity First, any and all commodities, tools, supplies, or other devices necessary to the implementation of this contract, of high quality, at the lowest prices available to Entity Second; and also including sale of such commodities produced by Entity First at the most advantageous prices, and expeditious delivery of these commodities to the purchaser thereof.

3. Enforcement of such laws and promulgation of such customs deemed proper and desirable by Entity First, in accordance with the so-called 'Traditional Mores and Punitive Methods of Phronus,' including maintenance of public and private order, and protection of public and private property.

4. Protection of territorial integrity, including vigorous prosecution of attack upon and defense against enemies of the State of Phronus, such enemies defined as those who are self-avowed, or those so identified by Entity First, including provision of all necessary equipment and trained personnel.

5. Sanitation, disease prevention, the promulgation of health and longevity, as defined and limited by Schedule B in the appendix to this document.

6. Fire prevention and control, together with the provision of efficacious fire-control equipment and personnel trained in its use, as defined and limited in Schedule C of the appendix of this document.

7. The installation and operation of suitable systems of communication, transportation, water supply, sewage disposal, control of air and water pollution, conservation of scenic beauty, development of natural resources, energy generation and transfer, and any such related amenities or services as Entity First may deem advantageous and useful.

8. All and any other similar and related services which Entity First may require through the duration of this contract.

Paragraph 3: Reimbursements and payments. Entity First will compensate Entity Second for services performed under provisions of paragraphs One and Two in money or such other valuable commodity or medium of exchange satisfactory to both parties, according to the following schedule:

Entity First shall promptly reimburse Entity Second all funds spent on the behalf of Entity First in prosecution of all services desired and authorized by Entity First.

Entity First will make available to Entity Second funds sufficient to pay all salaries and discharge all indebtedness incurred in prosecution of services as is specified in Paragraph 2.

Entity Second shall provide trained personnel of the highest professional quality to implement, conduct and manage the contractual duties of Entity Second as specified in Paragraph 2, but Entity First, at its option, may substitute for any member of such personnel an individual or individuals specified by itself, provided that this individual is competent to perform the duties normal to the position he is required to fill.

In addition to salaries and all costs of materials, supplies, machinery, royalties, drugs, mechanisms, circuitry, printed material, plans, information tabs, and any other expenses incurred by Entity Second in prosecution of the above stated functions, Entity First agrees to pay to Entity Second a further fee of ten percent (10%) of the total expenditures required to implement the programs defined in Paragraph 2 on the final day of each month (Ethelrinda Cordas chronometry).

Paragraph 4: Duration of Contract. The duration of this contract shall be seven years (Ethelrinda Cordas chronometry) after the instant of signing, Entity First retaining option to renew the contract on identical terms for a second period of seven years. It is further agreed that by, and only by, mutual consent of Entities First and Second may this contract be voided before term of completion.

Paragraph 5: Bond of performance. Entity Second guarantees faithful and efficient performance of the terms of this contract and will furnish bond of performance in the sum of one million dollars, deposited to a joint account at that office of Barclay's Bank located at the city Wylandia on the planet Ethelrinda Cordas; or will insure itself to such performance in the same amount with any recognized and reputable bonding agency mutually acceptable to Entities First and Second.

Signatures:
For Entity First: (here an untidy blotch of undecipherable characters).
For Entity Second: Edgar Zarius, President, Zodiac Control.
Witnesses: (further signatures and further blotches).

Hack turned the page, scrutinized the appendix with its set of schedules, then placed the document on the desk. "Who composed the contract?"

"Someone from their side. It seems a reasonable, straightforward contract and guarantees us an excellent profit. Salaries are at our discretion, and there will be no difficulty recruiting an able team."

"You are acquainted with Ethelrinda Cordas, specifically the east coast of Robal Cordas?" inquired Hack delicately.

"No indeed. This is where you enter the picture. As a promotional representative—to be blunt—you have not done as well as could be expected. However, having just returned from Ethelrinda Cordas, you are familiar with local conditions. I have decided to place you in charge of the Phronus project." Edgar scanned Hack's face, but Hack betrayed no emotion.

"You will return to Ethelrinda Cordas, confer with responsible Phrone officials, prepare a phase program, set up a preliminary financial plan. It is of the utmost importance that an operational fund be collected, to avoid using company funds. See to this immediately."

"If feasible," said Hack.

Edgar gave him a blank stare. "Why should it not be feasible?"

"The contract calls for no such prepayment. There is no provision for a reserve fund."

"You must get around the difficulty as best you can, if the difficulty in fact exists."

"I'll do my poor best," said Hack. "Meanwhile I require a drawing account of, say, twenty thousand credits—if only to make sure my own salary and expenses are paid."

Edgar frowned at his fingertips. "This seems a rather unreasonable sum. The reserve fund I mentioned, which you will collect from our clients, should suffice."

"Hopefully. Still, the contract does not specifically define the word 'prompt' in the phrase 'prompt reimbursement.' When my personal interests are concerned, I prefer to be specific."

Edgar was not pleased, but Hack refused to yield. Caustic remarks were exchanged, and Hack wondered aloud whether Lusiane Ludlow might still be interested in buying his holdings, thus increasing her share of the company to fifty-four percent. Edgar hissed between his teeth, threw up his hands and issued the necessary voucher.

He gave Hack his final instructions. "The Phrones are a whole-hearted, whole-souled people, possibly somewhat vehement. You will necessarily enforce public order and compliance with our rules tactfully. In no case do we want dissatisfied or resentful clients; this is the worst advertisement for Zodiac."

"I hope they use the same tact with me," said Hack.

Edgar's response was a dour grunt.

II

Hack took leave of Earth almost as soon as he had arrived, riding the Black Line packet to Alpheratz, thence by Andromeda Line to Mu Andromedae, thence by Algin-Obus Interworld Transport outward in the direction of the Great Nebula to the F6 star Martin Cordas, Andromeda 469 and its seventh planet Lucia Cordas; thence by Cordas transfer to Ethelrinda Cordas and the west coast city Wylandia.

Hack spent three days at Wylandia, a pleasant semi-tropical city built out on piles and stilts into San Remo Bay, with the shoreward section dwarfed under a grove of enormous trees, some of the structures being attached to the trunks and rising behind and above the rest of the city in an irregular terrace. Hack opened a company account at the local branch of Barclay's Bank and another in his own name, into which he paid the sum advanced him by Edgar Zarius. The Marlene Hildenbrand Hotel was an eccentric structure of many wings, balconies and promenades at the end of a twisting pier, overlooking the canals and water avenues of Wylandia on one hand, San Remo Bay on the other. The cuisine and service, if quaint, were more than satisfactory, and Hack, contrasting the cool verandah, the wicker chairs and potted plants, with the east coast of Robal Cordas, was in no hurry to depart; and indeed, he protracted his stay a day longer than was strictly necessary, on the pretext of renewing items of his equipment, repacking his luggage, buying local information tabs for his portable irsys.

Finally, with no further excuse for delay, he chartered an air-car, loaded aboard his luggage, and was flown eastward across the central wilderness.

Now Hack encountered a new annoyance. The charterer, upon reflection, refused to take Hack directly to Grangali, the central city of Phronus. Hack argued, urged, threatened; the charterer only smiled placidly and swinging somewhat to the south, put down at Seprissa, where he discharged Hack with his luggage.

Seprissa, a city of twenty or thirty thousand folk, was the commercial node of a vast hinterland and derived its existence from the growing, packing and export of exotic fruits. Hack learned that the city's only air-cab was in service, hired, so he was informed, by another Earthman for conveyance to Sabo: evidently the representative of Argus Control. In any event, the time was late afternoon, and Hack had no wish to arrive at Grangali after dark. He crossed the central plaza—Seprissa's single concession to a civic identity—and secured lodging at the inn.

His dinner was served under an arbor with three sides open to the plaza. Children, observing his strange clothes, came to stand around him and make quiet comments in their lilting version of Old English. Seprissa was the center of their universe, thought Hack, with Earth the planet remote and bizarre.

He was served fruit, a stew of something like clams in a dark red sauce, garnished with nuts and a sour vegetable, seed-cake, pale yellow beer, all of which he ate without inquiry or speculation. A squeamish man often went hungry on the outworlds.

Dusk came to the plaza. The young folk of Seprissa came out to promenade. Three moons hung in the sky: one tinted a peculiar pale blue, the second large and yellow as an autumn apple, the third a fat golden sequin. Hack sat sipping tea and presently entered into conversation with a man at the next table, the proprietor of a fishing boat. The creatures of all the Cordas seas were inedible, Hack learned, but valuable nonetheless by reason of their by-products, most notably the beautiful liver-stone of the jewel-fish. "Profitable, but a risky business," remarked the fisherman. "I never know when I put out whether I'll be dead or alive by nightfall." He jerked his thumb to the north. "Cutthroats, bandits—they are always to be feared."

"Whom are you speaking of?" inquired Hack.

"The Phrones, the Sabols—who else? When they can't maraud each other they make do with innocent folk elsewhere. See there." He pointed across the plaza to a low flat stone building. "Our armory. We're not warriors, but when they become too bold we give back as good as we get." He presently took his leave, and Hack sat another hour under the three moons.

In the morning he went to the headquarters of the air-cab, but once again was refused transport directly to Grangali. "If I put my cab down, they'd never let it rise," said the pilot. "Yesterday I had a fare for Peraz, in Sabo—an Earthman like yourself, talking about government for the Sabols. Bah. Like shoes for fish. . . . What's your business at Grangali? If you're selling, they'll plunder your samples and fling you into the sea."

"I'm bringing government to the Phrones," said Hack.

"Another?" exclaimed the pilot. "So soon on the other's heels? A pair of hopeful men. I'll do for you what I did for him—drop you off in Parnassus, then you can cross Cyril Dibden's sting-field and take your own chances.''

With this, Hack was forced to be content. Clearly, if he wanted to operate efficiently, he would need an air-car of his own. He loaded his luggage aboard the cab; they rose into the limpid air of Ethelrinda Cordas, so different from Earth's ancient and well-used murk, and flew north across the coastal plains. To the west rose the Hartzac Massif: peaks of granite, frosted with ice, and beyond, twelve thousand miles of wilderness.

The coast retreated sharply, the ocean spread west, thrusting fingers deep into the Hartzacs, receiving a counter-thrust from Pirates Peninsula. Beyond was Parnassus, Cyril Dibden's private Utopia, where two million cosmologists, psychodeles, mathematicians and mentors worked at the creation of a universal metaphysics.

It became necessary to fly across the southwestern limb of Phronus, which extended to the Hartzacs, cutting off Parnassus from the sea. The pilot kept a nervous watch below. ''The Phrones have few weapons, thanks to the Contraband Patrol. Still, they have a gun or two and like nothing better than shooting down aircraft. Dibden, crafty man, so far has held them at bay.''

A few moments later they crossed a great swath cut through the forest. ''That's the boundary; we're over Parnassus now.'' And the pilot, going to his radio, called down for landing clearance. He was answered by Dibden himself, who gave the necessary permission.

Ten minutes later the cab alighted in front of a long low marble mansion, chastely beautiful after some nameless style of the classic past. Hack alighted with his luggage, discharged the air-cab, and turning, found Cyril Dibden himself waiting to receive him.

Dibden was somewhat puzzled. ''Mr. Hack, is it not? I thought that we had settled our affairs quite definitely.''

Hack explained the circumstances occasioning his new visit. '' . . . and since I am somewhat familiar with the region I was assigned to the project.''

Dibden pulled at the tawny beard which lent sagacity to

otherwise undistinguished features. He was a large man, taller and heavier than Hack; he wore a simple white blouse, loose white trousers, sandals of soft leather.

Hack explained further: "The cab pilot refused to take me directly to Grangali. With your help, I will proceed from here."

Dibden nodded thoughtfully. "The situation calls for some reflection. Let us step up to the terrace for a goblet of wine."

He led the way up broad steps flanked by monumental alabaster urns trailing ivy, out upon a terrace tiled with quatrefoils of dull blue glass. They sat upon glass chairs splendidly upholstered in red velvet; three maidens in white gowns brought a platter of fruit, travertine goblets, an urn of mild red wine.

Hack leaned back into the chair, pleasantly aware of the slender figures only partially concealed by the near-transparent gauze of the gowns. The nearer he approached Phronus, the less attractive became the prospect. Parnassus, on the other hand. . . . Hack said, "I am convinced that you and Parnassus alike would benefit from a Zodiac contract. You would avoid the tedious routine of government. Our charges are nominal; we usually save our clients as much or more through efficient methods and optimal import-export management."

Dibden nodded and stroked his beard. "These are the views of the Argus Systems representative who passed by yesterday. My response was then and is now: no. We live a contemplative life; we have neither need nor desire for 'efficiency' or 'economic balance' or 'rational organization.' These ideas are the bane of the universe; give me, rather, splendid inefficiency, noble irrationality!"

"Very well," said Hack. "I can write a contract on those terms."

Cyril Dibden gave his head an obdurate shake. "Your services are needed by the Phrones. Luckily for their neighbors, they direct most of their violence against the Sabols. If they could be tamed, taught peace and meditation, how much better for all concerned. . . . Well, I must see to your transportation." Dibden spoke to one of the maidens, and presently a small air-car dropped upon the meadow. Dibden rose to his feet; Hack, recognizing that the idyllic interlude was at an end, did likewise.

"Naturally I wish you the best of luck," said Dibden. "A final word of advice: the Phrones are violent and headstrong. In order to win their confidence you may be forced to compromise certain normal values. In other words, to steer them, you must lead them."

Hack, wondering what, precisely, Dibden meant, rendered his thanks, climbed aboard the air-car, upon which his luggage had already been loaded. The pilot, a young man with curly auburn hair, a neat beard, a long straight nose, an expression of placid detachment, worked the controls; the car slid off over the countryside. They passed numerous villages, occasionally long low halls which the pilot identified as 'Pansophis temples.'

The landscape became heavily wooded; the pilot took the air-car higher. "The boundary is just ahead," he told Hack. "We maintain a constant lookout, and use the most modern devices to warn us of a raid."

"What happens when the alarms go off?"

"Usually we project a reverbatory field; it heats weapons red-hot." He pointed down at the swath which had been cut through the forest. "The boundary. We are now in Phronus."

They flew up over a range of low mountains, down across the coastal plain, the pilot skimming the tree-tops. At last he settled upon the crest of a hill. "I can take you no closer; these are unpredictable folk, except for their vindictiveness, which is certain." He pointed toward a sprawl of low buildings ten miles distant. "There is Grangali. You may light a signal fire and so attract attention, although a sect of outcasts— the Left-handers—may see the fire before the 'normals' and kill you. Or you may set out along the trail toward Grangali, again at some peril, for you must be on your guard against pitfalls and ambush."

"What of my gear?"

"Best bury it and return when your status is established. Please descend; I am in haste to return for the vespers."

Hack pointed. "What if I walked along the trail yonder?"

The pilot turned to look and Hack, stepping forward, touched a DxDx against the back of his neck. "Sorry, but I don't care to walk. Please take me on down to Grangali."

"If I were not an idealist, you would not have tricked me so easily," grumbled the pilot. "You are as devious as the Phrones."

"I hope so," said Hack. "You need not fear for yourself, or so I hope; they will welcome our arrival."

"Yes, indeed; they will expropriate the air-car."

"If you have such fears, put me down in the center of the city, discharge my luggage and leave before they can come to any such decision."

"Not easy . . . I will swing in as low to the ground as possible, so that they do not shoot at us while we are yet aloft. Be prepared to jump from the car with your luggage."

Grangali, an untidy sprawl of stone and timber, was close ahead. The pilot indicated a plaza paved with cobbles. "Probably the most advantageous spot, where the public torturings take place. Please be quick."

He swooped, landed on the cobbles. Hack leapt to the ground; the pilot tossed out the luggage. From a three-story stone building nearby came a dozen Phrones, roaring commands and brandishing weapons.

"Good-by," said Hack. "Convey my thanks to Mr. Dibden."

The pilot took the air-car aloft amidst a shower of missiles, and by a miracle escaped without damage.

The Phrones cursed, made obscene gestures, then turned to Hack. "And who are you?"

"Milton Hack of Zodiac. I assume that you have been expecting me?"

"We expected more than one man and a few suitcases. Where are the great machines? The weapons? The energetics?"

"All in good time," said Hack. "There is no urgency. I am here to make a study of your needs and set up a program."

"Unnecessary. We know our own needs. We will explain our program."

Hack produced a copy of the contract. "Where are the men who signed this document? Have they returned from Earth?"

"Hoy! A man who can read; anyone at hand?" At last one

came forward to examine the signatures. "Lords Drecke, Festus, Matagan: where are they?"

"Here comes Lord Drecke!" The burly citizens of Phronus stood aside to let another come forward, and Hack recognized one of the men who had issued from Edgar's office. As before he clanked and clashed a dozen assorted swords, cutlasses, daggers, poniards as he walked, and his nose was even more splendidly ornamented than Hack had remembered. Not all the Phrones were so embellished; the enormous noses, inlaid with amethysts, rose quartz, liver-stones, appeared to indicate status or rank.

Lord Drecke halted, looked Hack up and down, examined his luggage, then spat upon the ground. "Is this the total outcome of our journey to Earth? Zarius made grand promises. Someone will suffer!"

"I suggest that we continue our talks in a more orderly style," said Hack. "If we are to make any progress whatever, you must submit to a reasonable social discipline."

A gap-toothed grin split Drecke's face. "We are not a submissive folk. Take us as you find us; you must deal with us, not we with you. This is the function of government!"

Hack wished that by some wonderful mechanism he were able to change places with Edgar Zarius. "If you refuse to cooperate," he told Lord Drecke, "you only cheat yourselves. My salary continues regardless, at your expense, so it is all one to me."

Drecke again showed his grin. "Well then, we might as well make use of you." He jerked his thumb toward a small shack beside a ditch which appeared to serve as latrine and cloacum for the greater part of town. "Lodge yourself yonder."

Hack looked around the plaza, which was littered with disorder, the corpses of dead animals, general filth. The single sound structure appeared to be the three-storied building at his back. "Thank you," said Hack. "I had better stay closer to the government offices, for which I will need the entire third floor of that stone building!"

Drecke stared in outrage. "That is the Nobleman's Lodging Association!"

"I'll make the best of it. What of my luggage?"

"What about it?" growled Drecke with a face like a thundercloud.

"I wish that it should accompany me."

"Bring it along then. Do you expect me to carry it?"

"You or one of your fellows."

Drecke stalked truculently forward. "I must make clear to you that you are not now on Earth. You are surrounded by the men of Phronus, any one of whom is better than your best. Must we then carry your cases?" Drecke's mood changed to fury: his face flushed purple-red, his mouth tensed and twitched. The crowd began an ominous keening sound.

"Let us reason a moment," said Hack. "You have—"

"Are we your slaves?" roared Drecke. With a sinister hunching of the shoulders, he drew a heavy cutlass from one of his dozen sheaths. Hack held up his hand, to display a children's toy: a small whirling disk from which darted colored coruscations, sparks, tongues of green and violet flame. Drecke lurched back in alarm.

"Let us reason the matter out," said Hack. "You have hired Zodiac Control to organize a government for you. For such a government to function, it must command respect. I represent this government. If I carry this luggage, I forfeit respect. The government thereupon fails. You have wasted your time and your money.

"Secondly: a government is essentially a thing of the people it serves. If you insult the government, you insult the people. I represent this government. If you insult me, you insult yourselves. If I carried the luggage, I, the government, would be shaming and insulting you. If you have pride, you will carry the luggage. If you do not do so, you make yourself ridiculous."

Drecke listened, blinking. "I make myself ridiculous if I don't carry your luggage?"

"Certainly. You traveled to Earth to arrange for a government. If you don't cooperate now that I am here, you become a fool and a laughing-stock before all your fellows."

Drecke shook his head fretfully, so that the golden fobs jangled together. "Who says I am a fool?" He glared around the group.

Hack pointed to the luggage. "Take it to government quarters. I will follow."

But Drecke was dubious. "The government can be served by persons of low prestige." He pointed. "You, Gansen! You, Kertz! Bring the governmental luggage! Steal nothing!"

Hack was conducted, gruffly and without affability, to the large stone structure: the Nobleman's Association. Lord Drecke took him to a dark damp chamber underground, uncomfortably close to the dungeons, which were occupied by a dozen or so Sabols and three miserable Seprissans awaiting ransom.

Hack explained that the chamber outraged his dignity, hence the entire Phrone state; after further grumbling he was taken to more commodious quarters on the third level. The boxes and cases were put down; the porters, under Hack's direction, carried out a large proportion of the previous furnishings.

Drecke stood in the arched doorway with legs apart, arms folded, watching as Hack arranged his belongings. Finally he uttered a great guttural sound, half belch, half ejaculation. "Somehow you have tricked me and caused me to lose face; yet I cannot quite define the process. I assure you that I am not a man to be trifled with!"

"This is the least of my intentions," said Hack. "Now to business. As I understand it, Phronus is now controlled by a council of nobles?"

"True," said Drecke. "There are nine members to the Conclave. None of us yields in dignity to any other, and we frequently find ourselves at loggerheads."

"There will be an end to this," said Hack. "I will now make the decisions. The Conclave of Nobles is from this moment dissolved."

Drecke made a series of retching sounds, which Hack perceived to be a laugh. "Best that you break the news to the conclave itself."

"Certainly, if you will be so good as to convene the group."

"All are not in the city. Gafero Magnus is aboard his yawl, pillaging to the south. Sharn Weg has been taken by the Sabols and hangs by his thumbs in the Peraz dungeons.

Detwiler arranges an ambush on Opal Mountain, where Sabols continually trespass.''

Hack, seating himself, assumed a posture of judicious deliberation. "Assemble those who are available. When Gafero Magnus returns from his pillaging, when Sharn Weg has been lowered to the ground and is able to resume his seat, when Detwiler has arranged the ambush to his satisfaction, we will apprise them of our decisions.''

Lord Drecke gave a petulant grunt. "As good as any." He called over his shoulder, the sound echoing down the stone stairs. "Summon the conclave!" Presently he had a crafty second thought and hurried off down the stairs.

Half an hour later, glancing down into the square, Hack saw Drecke conversing with five men, noses bejeweled and swollen as his own. Making signs of mutual accord, they turned and trooped into the Association building.

Hack seated himself at the table, a slab of solid slate, supported by legs of polished timber, where he had already arranged his information bank, his catalogs and analyzers.

The nobles filed into the room. Hack arose, gave them a dignified greeting. The nobles seated themselves along the table, glancing with interest at Hack's informational aids.

Without preamble or formality Hack set forth his program: "You have made a wise decision in hiring a professional management team. Needless to say, Lords Drecke, Festus and Matagan chose wisely: Zodiac Control is the most expert of all such organizations. Our system of operation is simple. We give our clients the government they need, what they have contracted for, and what they are willing to pay for. We realize and we want you to realize that making improvements means making changes. When changes are made, someone is inconvenienced, and you must expect a certain amount of dislocation.

"So now—to specifics. I will make a brief survey of Phronus, to learn the areas of urgency. We can't do everything at once. Automatic fire-prevention system is a luxury in a city of shacks and hovels. We won't lay out horticultural gardens until we install a sewer system.''

"On the other hand," said the oldest of the nobles, a

fox-faced man named Oufia, "there is no point in gilding the lily. Putting sewage underground changes nothing; sewage it is, sewage it remains."

"All in due course," Hack conceded. "Now—as I indicated to Lord Drecke—the Conclave of Nobles, as a policy-making and executive board, has no further basis, and may be considered adjourned. Still, I am anxious to hear suggestions and recommendations. After all, you are the people most intimately acquainted with your own needs."

Lord Drecke cleared his throat, spat on the floor. "Our needs are endless, and, in my opinion, obvious. For instance, the air-car which brought you to the plaza escaped unscathed. We need a radar system and automatic weapon control."

"Our basic problem is Sabo," stated Ofia. "Once we expunge the Sabols, we can maraud Parnassus at our leisure."

"Here is another of our urgent needs," Fetus pointed out. "A device to confound his sting-field."

Hack listened patiently to each in turn. Then he said, "I begin to understand the scope of your requirements. . . . Well then, as to money: I need an initial hundred thousand Universal credits. This sum will be spent to organize a staff, set up schools, a clinic and start a sanitary program. Then we will build a warehouse, a tool-depot and a sewage system."

The noblemen looked blank. "We must be practical," said Matagan. "As Lord Oufia put it, sewage is sewage. And what avail are schools?"

"To teach children the elements of technical weaponry," explained Hack. "They learn to calculate effective weapon ranges, to read scales and gauges. They gain an understanding of warfare and raiding methods of the past, including, as an incidental, universal history."

The noblemen gave nods of dubious approval. "Children are of little use at an ambush or while sacking a village," grunted Drecke. "They only get in the way, and are killed with the other children."

"Matters for the future," said Hack. "The schedules in the contract are there to guide us. Incidentally, which of you gentlemen wrote the contract?"

Lord Drecke performed an unctuous wink. "Let us not embarrass the writer. Let sleeping dogs lie."

Hack was unable to follow Drecke's train of thought. "First I, that is to say, your government needs money. Best that we settle this detail now. A hundred thousand credits—"

Lord Festus made an impatient gesture. "When do the military experts arrive?"

Hack maintained his even demeanor. "If and when the need arises." He considered a moment. "I have warned Cyril Dibden to attempt no aggression. He recognizes that Phronus, under the guidance of Zodiac Control, is a unified and progressive country, and will attempt no mischief."

Lord Prust made an incredulous sound. "Dibden? He poses no threat. We will pillage him and his esthetes at leisure. But the abominable Sabols, aha! We must wipe them out root and stock!"

"First things first," said Hack, "and first is money; then organization, in accordance with the provisions of the contract."

Lord Drecke struck the table with his fist. "Money, money, money! Is that all you think of? How can there be action without the exercising of flexibility?"

"By 'flexibility' you mean what?"

"Your organization must be prepared to allow a certain latitude. In short: assemble your organization, bring in the necessary weapons and vehicles, both air and ground; then prepare a statement and present it to us."

Hack gave a crisp negative. "Zodiac will distribute no largesse. Either provide adequate funds or tear up the contract."

Drecke looked around the circle of nobles as if to gauge their shock and amazement. "We expected no such niggardliness; we are a candid people. . . . Bah! How much do you require?"

"A million Universal credits."

Drecke leaned back aghast. "I thought you said a hundred thousand."

"On reflection, a million will provide greater flexibility."

Wrangling ensued, but finally Drecke wrote out a draft to the sum of one hundred and twelve thousand Universal credits, on the Cordas Bank at Wylandia.

Hack took the draft to his communication box, made contact with the Cordas Bank. The draft, so he was informed, had no validity. Hack turned to Drecke. "There seems to be a mistake."

"Only two counter-signatures and a secret mark," grumbled Drecke. "Turste, Oufia: sign. We are in the presence of a vampire, who wishes to suck our blood."

Again Hack tested the draft at the bank, and this time it was confirmed.

"Thank you," said Hack. "you may now go about your affairs. Zodiac is in control. I will make a brief survey, then set up my staff. Feel free to confer with me at any time. After all, until we are more formally organized, I am your government."

III

Three days passed. Hack insisted on transportation, and from some hidden hoard of loot Drecke brought forth an elaborate air-slider with brocade cushions and a tasseled canopy. In this flying palanquin Hack, with Lord Drecke beside him as a guarantor, inspected the entire territory of Phronus. The land was varied: marshes to the south, home to voracious saurians and large red insects; dark hills to the west along the Parnassus border; a central plain under lackadaisical cultivation. Properly developed, thought Hack, the country would yield a modest prosperity to its inhabitants. There were extensive strands of exotic timber, much in demand on Earth, and a generally metamorphic geology indicative of mineral concentrations. Between Parnassus and the sea was a pleasant countryside with the Hartzac foothills beyond. Hack spoke of the possibility of developing the area as a tourist resort, but Drecke evinced no great interest in the proposal. He pointed northwest, to Parnassus. "Why entice strangers into the country? Far easier to deprecate our neighbor Dibden. But first things first: the Sabols must be destroyed!"

He directed Hack along a line of irregular hills, which slanted up to a great crag. "Notice: Opal Mountain, Phrone ground from the earliest times. Can you believe the turpitude of the Sabols? They claim the mountain as their own! They have hired military specialists from Earth, they are importing great quantities of weapons!" He prodded Hack's chest with his finger. "We must strike before they are ready!"

"Argus Systems has the Sabo contract," said Hack. "By no stretch of the imagination are they military specialists, any more than Zodiac. Furthermore, the import of weapons is impossible; the Contraband Patrol sees to that."

"There are ways, there are ways!" declared Drecke, winking and laying his finger along the cucumber-sized lump of his nose.

"The only way you'll have modern weapons is to build them yourself," said Hack, "starting with schools, a sound economy, hard work."

"It is time we were returning to Grangali," said Drecke in disgust. "You are a man without vision."

Upon their return Hack found that his quarters had been ransacked. Various articles were missing, including the draft for a hundred and twelve thousand dollars.

Hack sent for Lord Drecke who hulked into the chambers and stared coldly this way and that. Hack reported the crime and listed the missing articles. Drecke gave a bark of incredulous laughter. "This is the Nobleman's Association! You imply that there are thieves among us? This is not a charge to be made frivolously!"

"I am not a frivolous man," said Hack. "I especially deplore the loss of the money paid to Zodiac Control."

"We hold your receipt; if the money is missing, the responsibility is yours!"

Drecke started to swagger out of the room.

Hack called after him: "What if the thief can be identified?"

Drecke turned in the doorway. "There is no such thief. Only noblemen have access to the Association; to accuse a nobleman of theft is to court a dreadful revenge!"

"What is the penalty for theft?"

"If the theft be proved—and in this case it is either imaginary or deliberately contrived—the offender must pay the injured party double the value of theft and submit to twenty strokes of the rattan."

"Let us see then." Hack went to a hidden recess and brought forth a camera. He turned back the picture disk, set the camera to project upon a wall. Drecke came reluctantly back into the room.

The image was clear and bright, and depicted Lords Turste, Festus and Anfag, moving without stealth. While Drecke gave snorts of dismay, they pillaged Hack's belongings, gesturing in triumph as they came upon desirable items. When loaded with all they could carry, they left the room.

"Awkward," muttered Drecke. "Awkward indeed. No doubt a prank." The thought cheered him. "Of course! A good-humored prank!"

"Lords Turste, Festus and Anfag are not to be fined and punished?"

Drecke was astounded. "Can you be so sour-souled?"

"Please see that my belongings are returned!"

An hour later Drecke returned with a porter laden with Hack's possessions.

"I must be frank," said Drecke. "Lords Turste, Festus and Anfag are aroused by your accusation. They thought only to amuse themselves, and are angered to find you so surly."

"You maintain them to be humorists?"

"Indeed I do!"

"What if they were shown to be self-confessed thieves?"

"I would strangle them with my own hands! They would have affronted my honor as well as stolen your goods!"

"Well then—once more to the camera. This time we shall listen as well as see."

For a second time Hack and Lord Drecke watched the depredation, and now Hack played back the sound record.

"Aha! Where are the pale devil's valuables?" cried Turste, upon entering the room.

"Here!" called Festus, seizing upon a tabulator. "And I claim this device for my own!"

"Don't be greedy," chided Turste. "There is enough for all."

"The usual system is to cast lots for the more valuable articles," stated Anfag. "This ensures a fair share to each."

"Mind you, the money. This we must find!"

"Hurry then, the fool may return."

"No fear, Drecke has guaranteed to detain him until afternoon."

"No doubt Drecke wants his share!"

"Certainly. Was not this the arrangement?"

Hack turned off the recording. "Well then?"

Drecke's face was swollen and purple. "What scoundrels! Do they hope to implicate me in their bungling attempt at crime?"

"Let's find them," suggested Hack. "I'll watch while you administer justice."

Drecke, tugging at his bejeweled nose, finally heaved a deprecatory sigh. "It amounts to nothing after all. . . . To heed such scurrility would erode my dignity."

Hack decided that nothing could be served by taking the matter further. "Tomorrow I fly west," he told Drecke, "to communicate with the home office. But now I want to make a statement to the people of Phronus."

"Pah!" spat Drecke. "They are nothing, scarcely better than the Left-handers. Only the nobility is of consequence. The others do as they are told."

"Well then," said Hack, "summon whatever nobles are at hand."

"If you wish to make a statement," said Drecke, "speak to the Conclave. We are the single authority in Phronus."

"You forgot," said Hack, "that the Conclave has been dissolved."

Drecke's great ropy mouth twisted in a sneer. "Do you take us for children? The Conclave is as before."

"If that is the case," said Hack patiently, "I will speak to the Conclave."

"As you will."

In due course the nobles sauntered into the chamber, including Lords Turste, Festus and Anfag, who took their places with insouciant ease.

"Since our last meeting," said Hack, "I have inspected the country and am now able to make concrete recommendations.

"First, a staff of twelve men and three women is needed,

these from Earth, to supervise approximately forty local people. Secondly, I recommend a cessation of piracy, raids, looting, and most notably thieving." Here Hack turned brief glances upon Lords Turste, Festus and Anfag, who gave back insolent stares. "Thirdly, I will attempt to negotiate a settlement with Sabo. It is my understanding that they have hired the management control firm of Argus Systems, and we will undoubtedly be able to arrange a compromise of all outstanding difficulties."

Lord Drecke leapt to his feet. "The Sabol vampires must be destroyed!"

"Do not forget the contract!" called Lord Oufia. "You are bound to provide weapons and military technicians! We have been assured of this!"

"By whom were you assured?" asked Hack.

"No matter, it is all one. We even gave you money: a hundred and twelve thousand credits!"

"The money, now that I have recovered it from thieves, must be reserved," said Hack coldly, "for staff salaries, tools, school supplies, and above all, a new sewer."

"Order the weapons additionally," urged Lord Oufia. "You know our requirements. Do not stint. When we have destroyed Sabo, you will be reimbursed."

"Let me make three matters clear," said Hack. "First, Zodiac will provide nothing on speculation."

"This is not speculation; it is investment!" interrupted Lord Matagan. "You can collect your money from the proceeds of the war—even something extra!"

"Secondly, Zodiac will not participate in rapine, murder and pillage; it is bad for our image.

"Thirdly, weapons are contraband. I can't supply weapons under any circumstances."

Lord Drecke began to sputter. "What benefit then is Zodiac Control? It seems that you are nothing but a tiresome nuisance!"

"What of the contract?" demanded Lord Festus. "You are bound to assist us against our enemies!"

"Other matters are more urgent," said Hack. "The city is

a vast slum. You need schools, hospitals, warehouses, a bank, a space-depot, a hotel.''

''And meanwhile the Sabols dig our jewels, cut our throats, saunter back and forth across our property? Have you no shame? Give us at least the means of defense!''

''It may not be necessary, if we can arbitrate the difficulty.''

Drecke again sprang to his feet, but old Lord Oufia pulled him down. ''What do you propose?''

''Argus Systems, as you know, manages Sabo. I will get in touch with the Argus superintendent; we will talk together and try to work out a compromise. We have no prejudices, no preconceptions; you can expect an equitable outcome.''

''We don't want an equitable outcome!'' stormed Lord Festus. ''We want revenge, and Opal Mountain as well.''

Lord Drecke thrust his florid countenance forward. ''Do you think that we would trust our interests to a man so niggling? The idea is preposterous.''

Lord Oufia said, ''Not so fast. There is no harm in trying for an advantage of some kind. But the Conclave must conduct the talks!''

Hack protested that such an arrangement would be cumbersome and tend to intemperate demands. ''The Argus superintendent and I, talking calmly together, can work out a fair settlement of the quarrel. This is the only sensible way to handle the situation.''

Lords Drecke and Festus reacted so vehemently that Lord Oufia threw up his hands in disgust. ''This is how it must be: the arbitration will take place, but only three lords will participate: myself, Lord Drecke, Lord Turste. I believe even this Earth milk-nose will see the folly of trying to deal with the Sabol criminals.''

Hack was forced to be content with this arrangement. The meeting adjourned; the lords swaggered from the chamber, clashing and jangling, and each, passing Hack's chair, turned down a glance of menace, contempt or derision. Hack shrugged. He had won a minor concession: the nobles at least had agreed that the difficulties with Sabo were negotiable. Turning to his communication-box, he sent out a pulse on the Argus band.

There was an instant response, almost as if the Argus representative had been waiting for the call. A voice spoke: "Argus Systems. Sabo Contract, at Peraz, Sabo; Ben Dickerman here."

"This is Milton Hack of Zodiac, at Grangali. We have the Phronus Contract, as you may have heard."

"Ah yes: Hack." Dickerman's face appeared on the screen: a sallow face with harried clamps around the mouth, a fluttering tic of the left eyelid. "We've met before. Weren't you involved at Isbetta Roc?"

"Yes," said Hack, "I was—well, on the scene."

" 'On the scene'?" Dickerman laughed sadly, as if at some tragi-comic recollection. "Still, so I recall, the contract went to Efficiency Associates."

"There was trouble with the Zamindar's mother. A peculiar woman . . . Well, that's all in the past. How is the contract going at Peraz?"

Dickerman's face once more became dismal. "Well enough. I'm preparing a structure analysis, working out organization. . . . A challenging job, really." The attempt at a brave .front collapsed. "Between you and me—" he paused, then burst out in a bitter spat of words: "It's the most miserable situation I've ever been in. The city—if you can call it a city—is unbelievable. The stench, the filth, the monumental sordidness: beyond imagination!"

"Grangali is much the same," said Hack. "Probably worse."

"Not a chance." A spark of animation came to Dickerman's face. He hitched himself forward. "I'll lay a friendly wager—say ten credits—that Peraz is fouler than Grangali. Are you on?"

"I don't think so," said Hack. "Still—you'd have to produce something dramatic to defeat the Grangali sewer."

"No one seems to care," Dickerman complained. "No one wants clean streets and new houses; they want to slaughter Phrones. They want lasers, armored robots, automatic cannons."

"The same way at this end," said Hack. "The bone of contention seems to be Opal Mountain. I've been wondering whether you and I could use our influence to arrange some kind of settlement."

Dickerman gave his head a peevish shake. "I don't have any influence. They can cut each other to ribbons, so long as I get my salary, although this is doubtful unless the peace is preserved."

"I've persuaded the Phrones at least to talk to the Sabols," said Hack. "Why not broach the matter to your side?"

Dickerman made a dubious sound. "They don't want to talk; they want to run berserk. From somewhere they received the impression that we'd bring in shiploads of weapons and help them blast Phronus into the sea. They think I'm dragging my feet; they won't give me my money. They want Argus to finance the war and share in the plunder."

"We've been offered the same proposition," said Hack. "Tell your people the only way to settle the matter is compromise, and to compromise, they've got to talk."

"It wouldn't work," gloomed Dickerman. "They'd be like scorpions in a bottle. We couldn't control the situation."

"We don't have to bring them face to face," said Hack with a trace of asperity. "They can talk by radio. You bring a deputation to your offices. I'll do the same here."

"Useless, useless, useless."

"Try this," said Hack. "Tell them Phronus wants to settle the dispute and is appealing to their generosity."

Dickerman gave a caw of near-hysterical laughter, but finally agreed to make the effort.

IV

At the appointed hour Lords Oufia, Drecke and Turste hulked into Hack's chambers, reeking with a dire thick-blooded ferocity. Their plaits were newly varnished, silver cheek-plates framed and accented the bejeweled bulbs of their noses.

"Well then," grated Lord Drecke, "turn on your radio; we will hear what they have to say."

The conference began, by radio only; Hack's theory being that the transfer of images would serve only as incitement.

Hack and Dickerman performed the introductions, which were acknowledged on both sides with sardonic restraint.

Hack said, "Our purpose is to reconcile the differences which have alienated your two great states. I think our first step should be to recognize that all of us are basically men of good will—"

He was interrupted by Drecke's muttered remark: "How can Left-handers be considered men?"

Hack and Dickerman both frantically spoke: Hack chiding Lord Drecke; Dickerman trying to suppress the furious retorts of his group. But the situation did not mend itself. There were claims and counter-claims, invective and threats. Hack and Dickerman pled fruitlessly for moderation.

"I personally will hurl your defiled corpses into the sea!" bellowed Drecke.

"Step forward and meet me face to face!" challenged the Sabol Duke Gomaz. "Craven that you are, taking refuge in distance! Your right-handed cowardice stinks from here!"

Hack surreptitiously turned off the radio. For some minutes Lords Drecke, Festus and Turste raged furiously at the instrument, not realizing that it was offering no response. Finally they stamped from the room, cursing and belching and congratulating each other.

Hack sat limp. The contract was a farce. He brought out the draft given him by Drecke. He should have cashed it at once; unlikely that it was still negotiable. Stung by the thought, Hack jumped to his feet. He packed a case with the most valuable of his belongings, went to the roof where he found the flying palanquin. He threw his case aboard, took off. Certain of the noblemen came out into the plaza to look up and shake their fists; one or two desultory shots were fired: casual insults rather than serious efforts to inflict injury.

Hack pushed the palanquin to its top speed, a stately fifty miles an hour, and in due course reached Seprissa. He rode by air-cab south to Colmar, terminus of the weekly cross-continent air-service and was lucky enough to make an almost immediate connection.

A day later he walked the streets of Wylandia. Great trees rose above him, home to thousands of fluttering white creatures: jerboas with moth-wings. Along the sidewalks were booths, offering cool drinks, fruit and skewered morsels of meat with tantalizing odors. The streets were clean, the inhabitants polite, the moth-winged jerboas made pleasant chirping sounds. . . . Hack felt as if he had emerged from a hallucination. He came to the Cordas Bank, a long low structure with a facade of woven glass. He entered, took the Phrone draft to a wicket. The draft was honored, the funds paid into the Zodiac account. Hack was surprised and disappointed. Had the draft not cleared he could reasonably have washed his hands of the entire contract. . . . He crossed the street to the communications center, put through an inquiry to the Cordas System Post Office at Spaceport on Lucia Cordas.

The response returned affirmative. An automatic printer ejected the message, stamped with Hack's name and the transmission charges.

Hack paid the fee, unsealed the letter, which had been sent by Edgar Zarius, apparently no later than two days before, if Hack's quick calculations were accurate.

The information contained in the message was unsettling:

Milton Hack, Zodiac Control
Poste Restante, Wylandia
Ethelrinda Cordas

To date no report has been received from you in regard to the Phronus contract. Presumably all is going well. I hope this reaches you before your operative plans solidify. In order to maximize efficiency and minimize cost, I have purchased the Sabo contract from Argus Systems, Incorporated.

You will therefore amalgamate operations to the fullest extent and administer both programs through a central agency.

You will notify Mr. Ben Dickerman, Argus representative at Peraz, Sabol, of the altered circumstances, and instruct him to return to Earth.

You will take control of all money paid into the Argus account by Sabol authorities, and pay this money into the Zodiac account, for the funding of the joint Phronus-Sabo contract.

Please prepare and file a preliminary report at your soonest convenience, so that we may get this project rolling.

> Edgar Zarius, President
> Zodiac Control, Incorporated
> Farallon, North America
> Earth

Hack sank slowly upon a stone bench to re-read the letter. He folded it, tucked it into his shirt, sat staring blankly off across the motley Old Town, standing on stilts above San Remo Bay. For a time Hack's mind moved sluggishly. Only by degrees did the issues take shape. He began to recognize possible courses of action.

First of all, he could return to the east coast and implement Edgar Zarius' instructions. . . . Or he could urge Edgar to sell, or give, both contracts to Argus. Or he could resign his connection with Zodiac, take a suite at the Marlene Hildenbrand Hotel and settle himself upon the verandah for a month. . . . His decision was preordained, and derived from a perverse quirk in his mentality. At his deepest, most essential level, Hack knew himself for an insipid mediocrity, of no intellectual distinction and no particular competence in any direction. This was an insight so shocking that Hack never allowed it past the threshold of consciousness, and he conducted himself as if the reverse were true. So, while his innermost elements winced and grimaced, Hack, outwardly easy and composed, made plans to cope with the new situation.

He returned to the communications depot, despatched a message:

> Edgar Zarius, President
> Zodiac Control, Incorporated
> Farallon, North America
> Earth

Your message received. The situation at Phronus is confused. There are many cross-purposes. I have not yet been able to set up a primary organization. I will follow your instructions in regard to Sabo as best I can. As soon as I am able to make definite recommendations, I will notify you.

Milton Hack, Zodiac Control
Poste Restante. Wylandia
Ethelrinda Cordas

An absolute necessity was an air-car. At Wylandia there was a single agency which sold the Stranflite line at inflated prices. For fifteen thousand credits he bought a deluxe blue Merlin four-seater, loaded with options: macroscope, automatic controls with ever-visible charting, platform ride, a three-year energy cell, commode, beverage dispenser, sunscreen which allowed the entry of light but gave the sun the semblance of a black disk: in short, an environment far more comfortable than his quarters in the dank Nobleman's Association at Grangali.

Hack was in no hurry to leave Wylandia. He explored the Old Town, sauntering along the rickety walkways like a tourist, occasionally buying some oddment which caught his fancy. He dined in a restaurant hanging five hundred feet above ground in the branches of a tree, riding up in a birdcage-like contrivance dangling on a rope, and from the vantage of the terrace watched sunset fall over the city and the ocean beyond. Phronus and Sabo seemed remote indeed.

Descending in the bird cage, he walked out the dog-leg pier to the hotel and passed the night. In the morning he could find no reason, rational or irrational, to delay. He climbed, somewhat heavy-footed, into the Stranflite Merlin and flew east.

For thirty miles the land was inhabited and the soil cultivated, up to the very base of the Inland Barrier, a scarp rising a sheer mile. Beyond stretched the primeval interior of Robal Cordas. Hack set the controls to automatic; the Merlin flew quietly east.

Something after midnight local time he passed above Cyril Dibden's palace. A ball or festival was in progress; Hack glimpsed soft white lights, color and movement, then he was over and beyond, with the gloomy mountains ahead, and presently these too were behind him. In the east spread the ocean, with two of the four moons, thin as scimitars, casting light trails.

Hack veered north, over Opal Mountain, and into Sabo. Peraz was dark, with the exception of two or three flickering orange lights.

Hack set the Merlin to sweeping wide slow circles at an altitude of five thousand feet, stretched himself out and went to sleep. He awoke at dawn, took stock of himself and his surroundings.

The new moons were fading; the sky was a bowl of violet and electric blue; the landscape was a black crumple without detail. Hack flicked on the radio, called the Argus frequency. The response bulb presently glowed. "Dickerman speaking."

"Hack here."

"Where in thunder have you been?" Dickerman's voice was petulant. "I've called you twenty times!"

"What's the trouble?"

"More than trouble. The whole shebang has gone up in our faces. Your confounded Phrones are invading. They've pushed ten miles across Opal Mountain. The people here can't be controlled."

For an undisciplined instant Hack thought to flick off the radio and return full speed to Wylandia. He finally regained use of his voice. "I'm afraid I have more bad news for you," he said dolefully.

Dickerman's voice went almost falsetto with apprehension. " 'Bad news'? How so?"

"You're out of a job. Zodiac has bought the Sabo contract from Argus. The powers that be figured they could run two jobs cheaper than one."

Dickerman's voice quivered. "You're not pulling my leg?"

"Absolutely not. I'll show you my orders, or you can call your home office."

"No, no!" exclaimed Dickerman. "I accept your word. Oh my, yes. How soon will you take over?"

"I'm right above you. Where do I land?"

"On the Charterhouse, near the waterfront. What are you flying?"

"A Stranflite Merlin, blue with white underhull. Make sure your people don't shoot me as I come in."

"I'll do my best."

Hack traced the outline of the shore and finally located Peraz. He dropped vertically down upon the largest structure visible: a menacing stone block on a spit of rock overlooking the harbor. He landed on the flat roof without hostile demonstration of any sort: not so much as a shot or a hurled stone.

Dickerman stood waiting, his face alight, almost twitching with hope.

Hack asked why his arrival had aroused such small attention. "There's no one of fighting age in town!" explained Dickerman. "They've all gone south to fight the Phrones." He conducted Hack down the stone stairs to his office, where he set all lamps aglow and prepared a pot of tea. Hack brought out the letter from Edgar Zarius, but Dickerman waved it aside. "Your word is enough for me. . . . I don't have much to turn over to you: mainly the contract." He tossed the document on the table. Hack read, at first with interest, then perplexity. Here, provision for provision, was a duplicate of the Phronus contract.

Dickerman became apprehensive. "Something wrong?"

"No. Nothing in particular."

"It's a droll contract," said Dickerman. "Argus doesn't have too many jobs going, or I don't think they'd have taken it. In fact. . . ." Tactfully he cut himself short.

Hack made no comment, still puzzled by the peculiar identity of the contracts. A stock form, obtainable at Colmar or Wylandia? The work of an itinerant negotiator? Had there been consultation between Phronus and Sabo?

Dickerman interrupted Hack's cogitations. "Your first concern is the war. "Candidly, I don't quite understand how you'll be able to merge operations." Here Dickerman hastily held up his hand. "Not to discourage you, of course."

Hack laughed. "No fear. Everything's under control, merely a matter of organization. I'll arrange a truce, work out some kind of compromise. These people aren't totally irrational."

"Of course not. Perhaps you can take me into Seprissa."

"Certainly. But first I'll want you to introduce me to the Sabo authorities."

Dickerman gave a wry wince. "I suppose it's only appropriate. They're all out under Opal Mountain."

Dickerman gathered his gear; they went up to the roof, boarded the Merlin, rose into the sky. The sun was now high: big yellow Martin Cordas, the light slanting across the rolling, oddly beautiful countryside. Ahead loomed Opal Mountain and the turmoil.

"According to my information," said Dickerman, "the Phrones came down east of the mountain; they plundered Slagnas Lodge, marauded through Broken Bone Valley. . . ." He used the macroscope to search the landscape and presently pointed. "There's the Sabol camp. We'd better land somewhat out of weapon range. . . ."

Hack landed the Merlin in a field two hundred yards below the camp, which was surrounded by tall black and white battle trucks, evidently of local manufacture, the rude and irregular wheels powered by indestructible torque-cells.

Hack and Dickerman alighted, waited by the air-car as the Sabol war-leaders came forward: men massive and heavy-featured like the Phrones, their noses similarly inlaid and encrusted with jewels. The fobs had been detached from the coarse black plaited hair, which now was coiled under war-bonnets. In scabbards at each side of the waist harness they carried a dozen or more daggers, cutlasses and swords, while strapped under their arms were pellet guns, rocket launchers, lasers of antique design and, Hack suspected, of small efficacy.

Dickerman gingerly performed introductions: "Duke Gassman, Duke Holox. . . ." And finally, "I present to you my successor, Mr. Milton Hack of Zodiac Control. He is an expert military strategist, as well as an economic authority; with your cooperation, he will solve the various problems of Sabo."

"We have only a single problem," grunted Duke Gassman. "How best to destroy the repulsive Phrones, which is difficult when they refuse to face us in combat."

"Strange," said Hack. "I understood them to be resolute fighters."

"By no means. Only this morning we sent them hopping and skipping. We are bringing down reinforcements from a skirmish to the north; then we intend to strike deep into Phronus. We will need weapons: you must provide them!"

"Weapons are contraband merchandise," said Hack. "Smuggled weapons are expensive. How much can you afford to pay?"

Duke Gassman made a peremptory gesture. "Furnish the weapons; later we will talk of pay!"

At the moment, thought Hack, there was small hope of presenting his point of view convincingly. "I will survey the terrain. In the meantime, instruct your men under no circumstances to fire on my air-car."

Duke Gassman, making an incomprehensible sound in his throat, swung away.

Hack flew Dickerman to Seprissa; Dickerman nimbly jumped from the Merlin, as if he feared that Hack might decide to take him north again. Hack returned to the air and flew north to Grangali, landing in the plaza before the Nobleman's Association. Like Peraz, Grangali seemed deserted, Hack, making inquiry, learned that all able-bodied warriors had taken the field against Sabo.

Once again Hack took the Merlin aloft. He flew high, and hovering above Opal Mountain, studied the ground below.

To the east of the mountain was the Sabol camp which he had visited during the morning; to the west, on a plateau overlooking the Sabol plain, he discovered another encampment, apparently that of the Phrone war party. Hack landed the Merlin somewhat to the north of the camp, and awaited the arrival of the Phrone leaders.

Lord Drecke marched in the van, daggers and swords clashing with each step. In addition to his usual costume Drecke wore enormous epaulettes fashioned from the carapace of a sea-beetle, with decorations fashioned from human jaw-bones and teeth. He halted directly in front of Hack, who moved back a step to avoid the organic reek characteristic of Phrone and Sabol alike.

Drecke, obviously in a villainous mood, scowled down at Hack. "Well then, your news?" he barked. "The weapons are on order? What is the precise date of delivery?"

"All in good time," said Hack. He indicated the camp. "Why are you here, instead of back at Grangali, repairing the sewer or doing something useful?"

Drecke half-drew a cutlass. "Do I hear right?"

"You hear the voice of your government, in which you have invested one hundred and twelve thousand credits."

"Bah," sneered Drecke. "The Sabols thought to catch us unawares. They attacked down Opal Mountain; we charged, sent them screaming back like the left-handed popinjays they are. We now await a reconnaissance squad which fought a skirmish somewhat to the west; then we invade Sabo."

Hack gave his head a disapproving shake. "A rash act."

"Quite the reverse," maintained Drecke. "It is a precautionary war. A great corporation of Earth has allied itself with the Sabols. They are receiving high-quality weapons by the shipload."

"Nothing of the sort," said Hack. "Earth corporations supply nothing unless they are paid in advance."

"This is not the language of our contract," called Lord Anfag over Drecke's shoulder. "Zodiac Control must supply goods, stores, munitions and weapons at demand."

"Whereupon you must pay for them promptly," Hack reminded him. "Which is to say, within three seconds."

"I doubt if you have our interests truly at heart," complained Drecke. "Are we not your clients?"

"You are indeed, and Zodiac expects your cooperation. Otherwise you waste your money."

"Once we expunge the Sabols, matters will be different," declared Lord Drecke. "It is to your best interests to provide us the weapons we need: lasers, automatic killers, eye-guided rockets, dazzle flares." A shout attracted his attention. "The reconnaissance squad returns." And Lord Drecke marched away to greet the leader of the platoon, which was mounted on a troop of hammerheaded yellow ponies. They conferred a moment or two, then with a sweeping gesture Drecke roused the entire company into motion.

Hack stepped into the Merlin and took it aloft before Lord Drecke thought to commandeer his services.

V

Hack hovered above Opal Mountain, watching as the armed bands came together for what both had vowed would be a climactic battle, a massacre of the opposing force.

With great care the Phrones and Sabols maneuvered for advantage, each trying to win the high ground, but each being repelled by darting sorties of the other's cavalry.

Little by little the encounter worked itself down to the plain, as if impelled by the force of gravity. Hack drifted overhead in the Merlin, marveled at the complicated maneuvers. There were feints, lunges, massing and shifting of forces, but very little fighting, and wherever such fighting occurred, unless either side could bring an overwhelming force to bear, it was quickly broken off.

The Phrones and Sabols were not necessarily cowards, thought Hack; they merely did not wish to be killed.

The battle continued most of the afternoon, and began to subside, both armies drooping with fatigue, an hour before sundown. Considering the number of men involved, the skirmishing and maneuvers, the charges and retreats, there had been few casualties indeed.

With the coming of sunset both armies drew back. Baggage wagons, which had remained untended during the battle, were trundled up; bonfires were built, cauldrons hung on tripods, and the armies settled down for their evening meal. Hogsheads of wine were broached; the Phrones and Sabols drank, and becoming elevated, danced hornpipes and jigs to the music of tambourines, rattles and horns. Others swaggered out to the edge of the firelight to peer across at the opposing camp; here they postured indecent antics, bawled insults and bluster, then, after some final grossness, returned to the applause of their fellows.

The sky became dark; two moons rose full in the east; half the pale blue moon hung overhead. The bonfires burnt low;

grumbling and complaining, the warriors wrapped themselves in robes and hulked down in untidy bundles to sleep.

Hack landed the Merlin on a nearby ridge. It seemed that both parties to the conflict were too arrogant, too torpid, too lazy to worry about a night raid. Twenty deft men could slit every throat in both camps. No question as to Phrone blood-thirstiness or Sabol courage. Still, neither cared for undue risk or inconvenience. Hence, reflected Hack, the emphasis on weapons of longrange destruction; which suggested a crafty subterfuge.

He took the Merlin aloft, returned to his quarters at Grangali, where he elaborated on his plot.

On the following day, the armies awoke, quarrelled among themselves, fed, loaded the wagons, donned their war costumes, and about mid-morning resumed the battle. The participants were now becoming bored with the sport and maneuvered with less zest and daring than that which had marked the action of the day before.

During the heat of mid-afternoon, both armies drew back to refresh themselves with wine, to bind such wounds as they had incurred, to enlarge upon their exploits and jeer at the enemy warriors, little more than two hundred yards distant. It was discovered that the baggage trucks were empty of provisions. After a final exchange of taunts and obscenities, both armies flung their weapons and gear into the wagons and set off toward their respective cities.

The following day Hack requested a meeting of the Conclave. In due course the group came swaggering and sneering into the chambers.

"How went the battle?" asked Hack.

"Well enough, well enough," responded Lord Drecke. "We sent the vermin scuttling; they will not stand to fight. Why do you not provide us weapons so that we can give them what they deserve?"

"I have gone over this ground before," said Hack. "Weapons are illegal contraband; Zodiac Control will supply nothing that you are unwilling to pay for."

"Bring us weapons!" stated Lord Oufia. "We will pay!"

"As you know, I am an expert military strategist," said

Hack. "I have evolved a scheme which I believe will satisfy everyone. It is a subtle plan and somewhat long-range, and it will require a large outlay of money, but—"

Lord Drecke interrupted roughly, "What is the plan?"

"How would you like to press a button," asked Hack, bringing to his normally expressionless face what he hoped to be a leer, "and instantly blow all Peraz sky-high?"

Lords Drecke, Oufia, Anfag, Turste and the others sat back in their chairs. "But you claim you can buy no weapons!"

"I can buy mining machinery. Do you realize that a power mole can tunnel the distance to Peraz in perhaps thirty days? I can buy explosives. No problem there."

Drecke spat on the floor. "Why did we not think of this ourselves? We need not have performed that old epicene's elaborate rigamarole."

"What old epicene?" asked Hack. "What elaborate rigamarole?"

"No matter, no matter. What will all this cost?"

Hack went to his information box, ran his fingers over the buttons. "There are eight or ten varieties of mole. Some with mechanical jaws, others with rotary cutters. This particular device—" he paused at a holograph "—melts the rock ahead and rams it aside to form a cylindrical tube walled with dense glass." He brought another picture to the screen. "This model melts the rock, shapes it into building blocks and loads a conveyor with the blocks. It is cheaper, and for our purposes preferable, since it is noiseless."

"And the cost?" demanded Anfag.

"This particular model, which melts a tube eight feet in diameter, sells for three hundred thousand credits. I can arrange a discount of five percent for cash. Explosives? Another twenty or thirty thousand credits. We want to do a thorough job. A trained crew is a necessity: a surveyor, three operators, three mechanics, an energetics technician, an explosion engineer, a tramline engineer, three tramline operators, an accountant, a payroll clerk, a cybernetician. We will bring in temporary housing, and there will be no need to vacate this building. You will supply whatever unskilled labor is required."

"The total?" inquired Anfag.

"In the neighborhood of half a million credits, which will include ten percent to Zodiac."

The Phrone nobles rolled their eyes upward. "A large sum," intoned old Oufia.

Hack shrugged. "What do you think weapons cost, even if you were able to buy them?"

Drecke said briskly, "Our comrade has produced a sound scheme! Which of us is so penurious that he would not welcome the opportunity to blow Peraz to smithereens once and for all?"

"At really a trifling cost," mused Anfag.

"So be it," declared Oufia. "We will declare a special tax, and it will cost none of us a great deal."

"Give me a draft upon the Cordas Bank at Wylandia," suggested Hack, "and I will set affairs into motion at once."

Hack flew the Merlin to Peraz where he called the Dukes to the Charterhouse for an important conference.

"I observed the recent battle," said Hack. "While I was much impressed by Sabol tactics, I can see that they will never defeat the Phrones."

"Agreed," said Duke Gassman. "And why? Because they refuse to fight! They are dodgers, dancers, they run this way and that, they hide among the rocks. It is pointless trying to come to grips with them!"

"Weapons!" rumbled Duke Bodo. "We insist that you perform according to the terms of the contract!"

Hack once again explained that his company was unable to deal in weapons, owing to the rigid weapon-licensing laws of Earth. "However, there is no law which prevents us from importing mining machinery."

"What avail is mining machinery?" Duke Wegnes demanded. "Do you take us for troglodytes?"

"Quiet!" commanded Duke Gassman. "The man has something at the back of his mind. Speak on, Earthman."

"What would be your reaction to a scheme for blowing Grangali into the sea?" asked Hack.

Duke Gassman made a fretful movement. "Waste no more of our time with idle questions. Is the project feasible or is it not?"

"It is feasible," said Hack. "It will cost a considerable amount of money, but far less than an equally effective arsenal of weapons."

"Money is of no account," declared Duke Bodo. "We will spend any amount on a worthwhile purpose. What then is your plan?"

"We will need a tunneling machine. Please give your attention to the catalogue. . . ."

VI

Edgar Zarius, looking over Hack's requisition, frowned in perplexity, then nodded slowly. He reflected a moment, then put through a call to Lusiane Ludlow who eventually was traced to the lounge of the St. Francis Yacht Club, at the foot of the Marina in San Francisco.

Her face appeared on the screen. "Yes?"

"Nothing urgent," said Edgar. "I thought you might like to hear the news from Ethelrinda Cordas."

Lusiane's face for a moment was blank. "Oh, of course. I thought, for a moment—but never mind. That's the planet where—excuse me, Edgar." She looked aside to speak to someone beyond Edgar's range of vision, and returned smiling to the screen. "Ethelrinda Cordas, out in the Cordas System where we have two ridiculous contracts. I suppose they've blown up in our faces, as I predicted?"

"Not so ridiculous," said Edgar stiffly. "Hack has set things straight as I knew he would. I've got a requisition here for mining machinery, supplies, technicians—a fairly large crew, somewhat unbalanced, I suppose. . . ."

Lusiane's eyebrows became straight lines over her beautiful blue eyes. She hated to be proved wrong. "Requisition— what about payment?"

"Oh, the money's here too. Hack usually does things right, for all his peculiarities."

"Between you and the insufferable Hack," snapped Lusiane, "I don't know whom to feel the most thankful to." She broke off the connection, leaving red concentric rings on Edgar's screen.

Edgar smiled faintly. A certain degree of gloating, after all, was in order. His vision, his acumen, had been vindicated. He had been proved right. Hack had rejected the Sabol contract, disapproved of the Phronus contract, Lusiane had ridiculed both, and now both contracts had been demonstrated sound conservative ventures.

Edgar, well pleased with himself, signed the requisition and tucked it into the out-slot.

The moles arrived at Wylandia in a single crate, as did the auxiliary items. Hack ordered a separation and repacking of the equipment into two similar parcels, and arranged for trans-shipment to Peraz and to Grangali.

The two crews arrived a few days later, and for a time Hack was extremely busy. He started the sub-Grangali tunnel from a point near the border but concealed from Phrone observation by a dense grove of dicallyptic sapodillas.

The sub-Peraz tunnel had its origin no great distance away on the Phronus side of the border, in an eroded mountain of limestone, slate and an odd blue stone which Hack tentatively identified as dumortierite.

The tunnels proceeded at an average rate of a mile a day, at a mean depth of a hundred feet below the surface. Each mole jetted forward a cone of irresistible heat; the rock, whatever its composition, melted to magma, which when tamped and molded yielded vitreous bricks, which were then automatically loaded on cars, trundled to the mouth of the tunnel and stacked under the trees.

Hack spent half of the time in Phronus, half in Sabo, conferring with the grandees of the two cities. Both groups were much impressed by the efficiency of the Zodiac management, and Hack was held in great esteem.

Thirty-five days after the first ground-breaking, the surveyor in charge of the sub-Peraz tunnel announced that Hack's requirements had been met. The tunnel described a circle under the city, extended in a pair of spurs under outlying districts.

The mole was withdrawn; the explosive engineer loaded the tram with crates, electronic gear, charts and detonation schedules.

Something under three days later, the same sequence of events occurred in Sabo, in connection with the sub-Grangali tunnel.

VII

The Phrone nobles were jovial, almost boisterous, as they filed into Hack's quarters on the third level of the Nobleman's Association and took their accustomed seats. Stewards poured beakers of smoky brown wine, set out small tubs of "tongue-stabber," the stimulating black paste used by Phrone and Sabols alike.

The group composed itself. Lord Drecke turned to Hack. "What is the outlook for the next few days?" And he turned a wink of elephantine humor down the table.

"The project, as of now," said Hack, "is in the 'Ready' condition. Directly below Peraz is a precisely calculated pattern of charges which will obliterate that vile pig-sty of a city."

Drecke blinked. "I had never thought of Peraz in quite those terms. It is a city not unlike Grangali. . . ."

"No place for sentiment!" called Lord Oufia. "It is home to the Sabols! It must be destroyed!"

"I will take it upon myself to touch the activating button!" proffered Lord Anfag.

"Best leave that responsibility to me," said Hack. "Detonation time will be mid-morning, the day after tomorrow, in case anyone wishes to station himself where he can witness the event, perhaps from the shore of the Merrydew estuary, or on Kicking Horse Ridge."

Somewhat later the same day Hack addressed the Council of Grandees in the Charterhouse at Peraz. "I am pleased to report that the tunnel is complete. Demolition charges have been arranged below Grangali. I have scheduled detonation for the day after tomorrow, sometime during the morning, if such an hour suits the convenience of all." Hack looked questioningly from face to face, but no one put difficulties in the way.

"Very well," said Hack. "Mid-morning of the day after tomorrow."

VIII

On the following day Hack transported the tunnel crews and office personnel to Seprissa; the Phrones and Sabols were an unpredictable people, especially when excited.

That night passed: a balmy summer night disturbed only by revelry at both Peraz and Grangali. Hack elected to sleep aboard the Merlin, which he set down on a western crag of Opal Mountain.

The sun Martin Cordas rose; Hack awoke, stepped out of the air-car to stretch his legs. He had nothing to do now but wait. He sat on a rock, looked over the valley. To the left, barely visible across the broad Merrydew, was the gray and black sprawl of Peraz. To the right, somewhat closer, was Grangali.

The sun swung up in the sky. Hack took the Merlin aloft. He slid out over Grangali. In the macroscope he inspected the wasteland immediately south of the city. He saw no one; the area was empty. Hack selected the small black box "Grangali," arranged it on the console. With his forefinger he touched the button on its face.

The wasteland disappeared beneath a vast eruption of dirt, garbage and stones. Hack gave a satisfied nod: excellent. Precisely accurate.

A half-minute later came another explosion, a hundred yards north of the first, then another, and another, each an ominous hundred yards closer to the outskirts of Grangali. The dismal shacks at the city's edge poured forth their occupants who stood gaping at the advancing front of destruction. They retreated to the north, to avoid falling debris. There were further explosions, shattering the south slums, herding the residents north. Throughout all of Grangali was confusion and presently a pell-mell flight north.

Hack swung the Merlin out across Sabo. He hovered above the mud flats east of the city, where a single glance assured him that the area was untenanted. Again and with the same nicety of motion, he arranged the signal box marked "Peraz" on the console, touched the button. The mud flats exploded.

The nobles of Phronus, awaiting the destruction of Peraz on the shores of the Merrydew River, were startled by the rumble of continuing explosions from the direction of Grangali. Certain of the group wanted to ride for home as swiftly as possible, but even as the argument was in progress, Peraz began to disintegrate. Blast after blast marched across the landscape.

The Phrones watched with mixed feelings. "Too many Sabols are escaping!" cried Anfag in irritation. "The explosions were poorly conducted!"

Lord Drecke gave a grunt of disgust. "Not satisfactory. I will have a word with that blundering Earthman."

"Look!" Lord Oufia pointed: "There: he lands in his sky-car. Let us hear what excuses he offers. If they are unsatisfactory. I suggest that we kill him outright; he impresses me unfavorably."

They watched Hack approach, eyes narrow, hands resting on the hilts of their swords.

Drecke pointed to the destroyed city of the Sabols. "The project is a fiasco! After so much time and money, the population has escaped!"

"Such seems to be the case," said Hack. "Well, at least we have removed an outrage to civilized sensibilities from the landscape."

"Ridiculous!" thundered Oufia. "We are not impressed by such petti-foggery. The city means nothing; it was little worse than Grangali."

"In this connection, I am in a position to bring you some news," said Hack.

"The Sabol ruling clique, with motivations apparently similar to your own, required their control organization to tunnel under Grangali, and blow it out of existence, exactly as we just now destroyed Peraz. Did you by any chance hear the explosions?"

"Explosions! You mean that Grangali is. . . ."

"The site is marked now by a shallow crater."

The Phrone nobles raised their arms in the air, turned contorted faces toward Sabo, and rivaled each other in execrations.

"How many escaped?" groaned Lord Drecke at last. "Do any of our folk remain?"

"Yes," said Hack. "The explosions were planned and executed so as to warn the entire population, to allow everyone time to evacuate his unhealthy sub-standard hovel. In this respect, the demolition of the city is not an unmitigated cataclysm. An enormous number of obsidian blocks were formed during the mining operation, from which Zodiac Corporation can build a model community, perhaps close to where we now stand."

"But what of our memorials, our fetishes, our regalia? Is it gone—all gone?"

"All gone," said Hack. "However—if I may interpose an outsider's point of view—it was largely obsolete. In the new city, which Zodiac Control will help you build, these would be considered little more than barbaric survivals, mementoes of a rather grotesque period in your development."

Drecke heaved a great sigh. "You are very cheerful, but it was not your city which was blown up. Who is to pay for this new city you speak of? Zodiac Control?"

"Why not the Sabols?" suggested Hack. "After all, they destroyed the old one!"

For once the lords could not be aroused. Drecke gave his head a rueful shake. "This is grasping after one of the moons: totally unrealistic."

"Not altogether," said Hack. "If you recall, we drove a tunnel under Sabol territory, where my technicians discovered high grade mineral deposits. In due course these should yield a great deal of money."

"But they are on Sabol territory!"

Hack nodded. "This fact suggests a means to trick the Sabols, to force them to pay for the rebuilding of Grangali."

"How is this?" demanded Lord Oufia.

"I will place myself in communication with Sabol authorities," said Hack. "I will point out that with both cities devastated, the time is ripe to forget old animosities, to join together and pool all resources, to jointly reconstruct Grangali and Peraz, or even better, a single commercial and administrative center. We will thereupon announce the discovery of the ore deposits on Sabol territory, and thus finance the new construction."

The faces of the lords reflected mixed emotions. Drecke said grudgingly, "It is a sly scheme, and I must say offers some practical advantages. Is it feasible?"

"We won't know till we try," said Hack. "All I require is your assurance that you will put aside the old rivalry and form the association I mentioned."

The lords screwed up their faces in disgust. "Left-handers, everyone!"

Hack said, "It is a means by which to plunder the Sabols, in essence."

Lord Drecke said reluctantly, "Under the circumstances I suppose we have no great choice. . . . It is either this or penury. . . . One or two matters puzzle me. It seems strange that the explosions should occur so closely—almost at the same time."

"Not so strange," said Hack. "When Zodiac Control acquired the Argus contract, I was put in charge of both projects, and naturally tended to make similar recommendations to similar problems." Hack started back toward the Merlin, leaving the Phrones staring after him. Hack called back, "I suggest then that you return to the neighborhood of Grangali and wait there till you hear from me. If I can sell the Sabols on this idea, things will be happening—fast."

"I can understand your indignation," Hack told the Sabol Grandees whom he had intercepted en route back to Peraz, just as they had glimpsed the small irregular bay which once had been the site of their city. "The Phrones are unquestionably a depraved people of unspeakable duplicity. I believe I have arrived at a scheme to pay them back in their own coin."

"How is that?" demanded Duke Gassman. "We have already destroyed Grangali; how can we do more?"

Hack worked his face into the sly leer which was fast becoming a habitual and chronic grimace. "When we drove the tunnel under Phrone territory, I noticed many valuable ore deposits. Here is how to victimize the Phrones. Request a merger, an amalgamation of your two countries, to form a single political entity—managed naturally by Zodiac. Then when wealth pours from the Phrone mines, half the money must be used to Sabol profit. Essentially the Phrones will build you a new, modern and sanitary city to replace Peraz!"

"Ha, ha!" croaked Duke Bodo. "There is justice, at any rate! But will the Phrones agree to such a plan?"

Hack shrugged. "There is no harm in making the proposal. I will do so at once."

IX

A week later Hack crowded Drecke, Oufia, Gassman and Bodo into the Merlin, and swinging the power dial far over, sent the air-car lurching west. Over the Opal Mountain they flew, where the nobles, pointing here and there, reminisced over old campaigns. Presently they crossed the swath in the forest which marked the Parnassian border. Hack took the Merlin down at a long slant, and landed on a meadow near the palace of Cyril Dibden.

A maiden in a gauzy white gown came forth to inquire their purpose in landing, and Hack requested an audience with Cyril Dibden. The maiden bowed with a graceful spreading out of her hands and led the group into a cool garden, where other maidens served fragrant cakes and a soft sweet wine. The nobles of Phronus and Sabo, Hack noted, after grunts of disgust for "effete delicacy" and "moony estheticism" enjoyed the comfort of the chairs, cakes and wine no less than the attendance of the beautiful maidens. Hack nudged Drecke. "This is how we will do it in the new city!"

Drecke hawked, cleared his nose and throat. "Sometimes old ways are better." He spat under the table. "Sometimes not."

Cyril Dibden appeared, smiling with pained disapproval at the sight of his guests. "To what do I owe the honor of this visit?"

Hack introduced his associates. "You will be interested to

know that Phronus and Sabo are no longer separate states. The ruling cliques, in order to pursue a more effective foreign policy, have formed a political union.''

''Well, well, well!'' exclaimed Cyril Dibden. ''Congratulations and well wishes are certainly in order!'' He called for more wine.

''We have come to study your methods,'' said Hack. ''We hope to do something similar when we rebuild.''

''I suppose I should be flattered,'' said Dibden.

''During the next year you'll see a great deal of us all,'' Hack went on. ''My clients have been bad neighbors and want to make amends.''

''Hmm, indeed. . . . Very nice, of course. Still, we live a quiet life at Parnassus, and receive few visitors. . . .''

An hour passed. The nobles became jovial. Drecke tried to capture one of the maidens, in spite of Dibden's alarm. When the maiden had escaped and the four nobles were once more seated, Hack took Dibden for a solitary walk along the banks of the little pond which graced the garden.

Dibden immediately poured forth his resentment for what he considered Hack's discourtesy. ''At great expense I built a border control to isolate myself from these cutthroats. Now you fly them over the boundary and bring them into my palace with not so much as a by-your-leave!''

''Not so loud,'' warned Hack. ''They're on their good behavior; don't antagonize them. They'll tunnel under the border with their new mining equipment and break up into your very bedroom.''

Dibden gave Hack a sharp look. ''Quite frankly, I don't understand and I don't like your attitude. It appears to me that you are attempting intimidation.''

''No more than you deserve,'' said Hack, perhaps a trifle primly. ''You inveigled the Phrones and Sabols—separately of course—into soliciting management contracts, going so far as to write the contracts for them—'' Hack held up his hand as Dibden sputtered an angry protest. ''You convinced them the management corporations would provide weapons, so that they could more expeditiously destroy each other.''

''Ridiculous,'' snorted Dibden.

"Your motives? I assume that you want to extend Parnassus to the sea. I assume that you resent the necessity of guarding your border."

"Assume as well that I resent the very existence of these animals! These callous murderers, these gross and odorous lack-wits!"

"They are Zodiac clients," said Hack, "and they would never tunnel under the border of another Zodiac client."

Cyril Dibden swung about. "Do you hint, do you suggest, that I award your company a contract to manage Parnassus?"

"I do."

"This is pure extortion."

Hack shrugged. "When you run with the wolves, don't complain of sore feet. You plotted to victimize me with the Sabol contract, which was hardly philanthropy. On the other hand, a Zodiac contract can be of benefit to you. We will save you money, discourage marauding and tunneling and in general relieve you of drudgery."

In a strangled voice Dibden started to blurt out a rejection of Hack's proposal. He stopped short, tugged at his beard, then walked rapidly back and forth, head down, hands behind his back. He halted in front of Hack. "Very well. I'll give it a try. Perhaps it might even work out for the best. I will insist on a stringent contract, with absolutely select personnel. . . ."

"Well done, Hack," said Edgar Zarius in measured tones. "The arrangements are just about what I originally had in mind. I couldn't have done better myself. Good work!"

Hack started to speak, but Lusiane made a quick fluttering gesture. "Oh come now, Edgar, don't go all maudlin. Hack is paid to do his job. If he didn't, we'd fire him."

"I suppose that's true," said Edgar with a small twitch of a smile. "After all, Hack, I did have to jack you up a bit, eh?"

Hack seemed at a loss for a reply. Lusiane rose to her feet, turned an ineffable glance down at Hack, swung her cape over her shoulders. "I have an engagement and I must be on my way. I suppose I can fly you ashore, Hack, if you are finished with Edgar."

Edgar looked up sharply. "I had been planning to talk over

Hack's new assignment. A very peculiar situation has arisen.''

Hack interrupted him. ''If it's all the same with both of you, I'll leave by myself.''

''Just as you like,'' said Edgar.

Lusiane sauntered off and Edgar shook his head soberly. ''I'm afraid that there's something about you, Hack, that rubs Miss Ludlow the wrong way.''

''I'm sorry to hear that,'' said Hack.

''You'll probably be well advised to keep out of her way as much as possible. She's a capricious young woman and— well, there's no point in causing her vexation or whatever it is you do.''

''Naturally not,'' said Hack. ''Good afternoon, Mr. Zarius.''

Golden Girl

THE *DES MOINES POST* scooped the world on the greatest single story in history, and Bill Baxter became a hero.

An hour after the edition hit the streets, every road leading to Kelly's Hill was choked by caravans of the curious—the amateur public and the professionals: reporters, photographers, and correspondents to the news-services, domestic and foreign.

The FBI and Army Intelligence had arrived first. Roadblocks turned back a thousand cars, cordons through the fields intercepted walkers, fighter planes chased off airplanes which wafted toward Kelly's Hill like moths to a light.

The survivor of the crash lay through the night at Dr. Blackney's small hospital where Bill Baxter had taken her. She awakened early in the morning, lay staring at Dr. Blackney, clenching the sheets with golden fingers.

A pair of federal agents stood by the door to her room; dozens of others guarded the hospital and turned back the crowds of those who came to stare and marvel and murmur among themselves.

An Army doctor and a spare aseptic individual reputedly connected with the Secret Service confirmed Blackney's diagnosis of a cracked collarbone and attendant shock, approved his treatment. The woman submitted with an air of helpless distaste.

The secrecy stimulated rather than deterred the Press. Imagination was encouraged to run wild. The crash was a wind from exotic islands, an intimation of tremendous new fields of truth. The rest of the world dwindled into a locality; the lustiest news seemed stale and trivial. Thousands of columns were filled with speculation, tons of newsprint lavished on rumor, acres of photographs, charts, star-maps, imaginative drawings were published. Someone had even located a picture of Bill Baxter—the reporter who, thinking to investigate a spectacular meteorite, had found a wrecked spaceship and pulled out the limp young woman with the golden skin. To add the final touch to this magnificent bubble of sensation— the final compelling overtones—it was now rumored that the golden woman was beautiful—young and fantastically beautiful.

From the first, Bill Baxter refused to be separated from the woman. Every minute possible he spent in the armchair across the room, covertly studying the fragile sleeping form. The golden woman was something intimate and intricate, a wonderful jewel he had found in the night. She fascinated him; she aroused his fiercest protective instincts, as if by lifting her from the burning hull he had taken upon himself the responsibility for her survival.

His assumption of sponsorship met grudging acceptance, as if even the government recognized some primitive law of possessive right—or at least admitted that Baxter had as much right to act as her agent as anyone else. Dr. Blackney accepted his presence as natural and desirable; the federal agents watched him closely, making quiet sarcastic remarks to each other, but made no attempts to limit his contact.

She ate little, mostly broth and fruit juice, occasionally a piece of toast, rejecting eggs, milk, meat with faint repugnance. For the most part, during the first days, she lay limp and passive, as if stunned by the catastrophe which had beset her.

On the third day, she raised to her elbow, stared around the room, looked through the window a minute or two, then slowly lay back. She gave no heed to Baxter and Dr. Blackney, who were watching her from across the room.

Blackney, a grizzled country doctor with no pretensions to omniscience, clicked his tongue thoughtfully. "It's not right for her to be so limp . . . she's perfectly healthy, perfectly sound. Her temperature's a degree up, but that might be normal to her race. After all, we know little about her."

"Normal." Baxter seized on the word. "Is she a—*normal* human woman, Doctor?"

Blackney smiled faintly. "The scans X-rays show a— humanoid skeleton, and apparently human organs. Her features, conformation—well, you can see for yourself. The only distinguishing feature is the metallic hue to her skin."

"She seems only half-conscious," muttered Baxter. "She takes no interest in anything. . . ."

"Shock," said Blackney. "Her brain is readjusting slowly. . . . That's why she's not being moved."

"Moved?" cried Baxter. "Where? By whose orders?"

"Orders from Washington," said Blackney. "But there's no hurry. She's weak, confused. She should have time to recover. She's just as well off here as anywhere else."

Baxter agreed emphatically. In Washington, among so many official people, he might be shouldered aside. He rubbed his chin, compressed his lips. "Doctor, what would you estimate her age to be?"

"Oh—if she's aged according to our rates, perhaps nineteen or twenty."

"If so, she's a minor in the eyes of the law. . . . Do you think I could get appointed her legal guardian?"

Blackney shook his head. "Not a chance in a thousand years, Bill. Don't forget this girl is not an ordinary waif."

"Somebody's got to look after her," said Baxter stubbornly.

Blackney smiled faintly. "I imagine she'll be made a ward of the government."

Baxter frowned, clenched his hands in his pocket. "That remains to be seen."

On the afternoon of the fourth day, Baxter was astonished

to see her throw off the coverlets and leave the bed with no evidence of weakness. She went to the window, where she stood gazing out across Blackney's garden.

Baxter fidgeted behind her like a nervous hen, worried lest she weaken herself, yet reluctant to thwart her in any way. At last she turned, and in the long white nightgown she seemed absurdly young and inoffensive. For the first time she appeared to notice Baxter—surveying him from shoes to hair with a scrutiny most casual and cool.

Baxter employed the technique recommended by a thousand precedents. He took a step forward, touched his chest, and said, "Bill."

She raised her eyebrows as if surprised that he commanded an intelligible thought, and repeated "Bill" in a soft voice.

Baxter nodded eagerly, pointed to her. "You?"

She touched herself and spoke a word full of slurred consonants and throaty vowels. The closest Baxter could approximate was a sound like *Lurr'lu*, or *Lurulu*.

Earnestly he began to teach her the language, and though unenthusiastic, she grasped ideas instantly and never forgot a word once spoken.

Her story, as Baxter gathered it bit by bit, was simple enough. Her home was a world "very far past the stream of blue stars"—so she expressed it, and she called it *Ghh'lekthwa*. Baxter, unable to master the beginning guttural, pronounced it merely *Lekthwa*, which appeared to amuse the girl.

The spaceship was a pleasure-craft, she told him, on the order of an Earthly yacht; they had chanced on Earth with no particular end in view. A careless repair had weakened one of the drive engines, which—failing at a critical time—had plunged the ship to destruction against Kelly's Hill.

On the seventh day Blackney pronounced the girl in good health, and Baxter sent a nurse out for clothes. When he returned to the room—although she exhibited no trace of personal modesty—he found her examining herself in a mirror.

"Were any of my personal garments found in the wreck? These—" she pulled at the cashmere skirt "—they are picturesque, but they chafe, they feel strange against my skin."

Baxter, who thought her magnificent, stammered a reply. "Everything was destroyed in the fire . . . But if you'd tell me what you want, I could have something made for you."

She shrugged. "I will wear these."

Baxter asked a question which had long been burning inside him. "Do you—expect to be able to return to your home? Can you communicate with your own people? Do you know spaceflight mechanics?"

She stared off across the garden. "No, just the barest principles. . . . *Lekthwa* is many stars distant. I would hardly know how to begin."

Baxter looked at her sharply. Her voice had been cool, very soft, like a dark, quiet pool in the forest. With an anxious tightness in his throat, he reached for one of the books he had brought. Joining her at the window, he showed her a map.

"This is where we are," and he indicated their position. She bent her head, and Baxter studied her profile. This was the closest he had been to her since the night he had carried her in from the flaming wreck, and a strange fluttering pulse awoke in him.

She glanced up, and Baxter stared deep into the amber eyes. He saw the pupils change, and she moved slightly away. She turned her eyes back to the map. "Tell me more about your world."

Baxter gave her a thumbnail history of civilization, indicating the Nile, Mesopotamia, the Indus Valley. He showed her Greece, described Hellenic thought and its effect upon European culture, sketched the Industrial Revolution, and brought her to date.

"So today there are still sections of the world that rival and are hostile to each other?"

"That is unfortunately true," Baxter admitted.

"Several hundred thousand years ago." mused Lurulu, "we had a period called 'The Era of Insanity'; this was when the white-haired people of the south and the golden-haired people of the north purposely killed each other." She paused, then said vaguely, "They had a culture roughly equivalent to yours."

Baxter examined her. "Your hair is a very light golden."

"The white-haired and the golden-haired peoples are well-mingled now. In the barbarous ages, there was great prejudice against the golden-haired people, who were somehow considered less admirable. It seems so peculiar and cruel now."

She put down the book, went to the window. "I would like to be in the sunlight. Yours is a sun much like ours." An airplane passed across the sky. "And there is air flight on Earth?" she asked in mild surprise.

Baxter assured her that air travel was commonplace, and had been so for many years. She nodded abstractedly.

"I see. Well—let us go for a walk outside."

"As you wish," said Baxter.

The government agents in the hall followed, slightly to the rear.

Lurulu motioned to the guards. "What is their function, and what is yours? Am I a prisoner?"

Baxter hurriedly reassured her. "They are merely to guard you from annoyance by eccentrics. As for me—I am your friend." And he added stiffly, "I will not intrude upon you, if you do not wish it!"

Lurulu did not answer, but walked out on the sidewalk, looked up and down the street. The police had erected barriers across the ends of the block, and at either end stood a small crowd, hoping for a glimpse of the out-world woman. The guards ran out ahead, waved them back.

Lurulu ignored the onlookers, completely indifferent to the staring eyes and excited babble. Baxter, uncomfortable and vaguely resentful, followed at her elbow as she turned up the street. She seemed to enjoy the sunlight, and held her hand outstretched, as if feeling the texture of the light. Her skin glowed like rich satin. She breathed deeply, glanced in at the houses which lined the street. Blackney's small clinic was in a pleasant suburb, shaded with great elms, and the houses sat well back among gardens.

Suddenly she turned to Baxter. "Your people all live on the ground, then?"

"Well—we have apartment houses," replied Baxter. "Some

go thousands of feet up into the air. . . . How do you live on *Lekthwa*?''

''We have pleasant palaces floating in the sky—sometimes out in the clear sunny air, sometimes among the clouds. There is no sound but the wind. We enjoy the aloneness and the splendid vistas.''

Baxter stared, half in disbelief. ''No one lives on the ground? Are there no houses?''

''Oh—'' she made a vague gesture ''—occasionally by some beautiful lake or forest there is a cottage or a camp. The face of *Lekthwa* is for the most part wild—except for the Industrial Segment.''

''And who works in the industries?''

''Young people mostly—children. The work is part of their education. Sometimes they improve the machinery or develop new bio-types—is that a word? No?—No matter. After a period of machine tending, those who wish become designers or engineers or advanced technicians.''

''And those who prefer otherwise?''

''Oh—some are idle, some become explorers, some artists, musicians, some do a little of everything.''

For a few seconds Baxter marched in glum silence. ''Sounds stagnant to me. . . . Sounds as if you'd be bored.''

Lurulu laughed aloud, but made no answer or argument, which annoyed Baxter even further.

''And are there any criminals?'' he asked presently.

She glanced at him, still smiling slightly. ''On *Lekthwa* everyone likes living, enjoys his own individuality. Only rarely do offenses exist, and these are treated by a form of psychotherapy.''

Baxter grunted.

''Crime occurs when the social structure is in itself inattentive and unwieldy,'' she added offhandedly, ''when the culture provides no scope for fulfillment.''

Baxter asked with a slight edge of sarcasm in his voice: ''How can you discuss social problems so authoritatively when you don't have any on *Lekthwa*?''

She shrugged. ''We know of several worlds where social

problems exist. We have installed missions on these worlds, and are gradually bringing about reform.''

Baxter asked in perplexity, ''Do men—human beings—live on these other worlds too? I consider it very strange that our two worlds have produced identical species. . . .''

She smiled wryly at the word. ''I suppose our physical structure is more or less the same. But we are hardly 'identical.' ''

She stopped to examine a bed of flowering red geraniums. Baxter wondered what her reaction would be if he put his arm around her waist. His arm twitched—but the guards sauntered close behind, and eyes watched from all sides.

They reached the corner and halted. Lurulu looked into the corner grocery store, observed the meat market. She turned to Baxter wide-eyed. ''Are those carcasses?''

''Well—yes,'' admitted Baxter.

''You eat dead animals?''

It began to irritate Baxter to be constantly on the defensive. ''They're not poison,'' he growled, ''and they're a healthful source of proteins.''

''You haven't fed me any of that—that animal flesh?''

''So far, very little. You seem to prefer fruits or greens.''

Lurulu turned, walked quickly past the store.

''After all,'' said Baxter, ''it's only carbon, oxygen, hydrogen. . . . You're displaying a rather peculiar prejudice.''

Her voice had become cool and vague once more. ''There are psychological reasons for not putting death in our mouths. . . .''

The next morning a black car of an unmistakably official nature pulled up in front of the clinic; a man in an Army uniform and two others in civilian clothing alighted.

The FBI guards stiffened slightly. There was a muttered interchange and the three swung up the steps. In the front office they were met by Dr. Blackney.

''I am Major-General Devering,'' said the one in uniform. ''From the CIA. This is Dr. Rheim, of the Institute of Advanced Research, and this is Professor Anderson of Ledyard University.''

Dr. Blackney shook hands with each in turn—Major-General Devering, a thick-set man with a pink lumpy nose and shining, slightly protruding eyes; Dr. Rheim, long, thin, solemn; Professor Anderson, short, fat, equally solemn.

"I suppose," suggested Dr. Blackney, "that you've come in connection with my guest?"

"That's right," said Devering. "I suppose she's well enough to be questioned? My men tell me she took a walk yesterday and appeared to be conversing freely with Mr. Baxter."

Blackney squinted thoughtfully, pursed his lips. "Yes, she's sound enough physically. Perfectly well, as far as I can see."

"Perhaps then," suggested Dr. Rheim, "it would be possible to move her to a place more readily accessible to us?" He raised his eyebrows questioningly.

Blackney frowningly rubbed his chin. "Accessible for what purpose?"

"Why—for study, various types of examination. . . ."

"She's physically able to go anywhere," said Blackney. "But so far her legal position has not been established. I really see no need to move her—unless she herself wants to go."

Major-General Devering narrowed his eyes. "Aside from that aspect, Doctor, this young woman may have information of great value to the country. Don't you think it's important that we check into it? In any event, you have no authority in the matter."

Blackney drew his chin back, twice opened his mouth to speak, twice snapped it shut. Then he said: "I have authority over who enters this office. However, you may speak to the young woman."

Devering stepped forward. "Please show us to her room."

"Down this hall, please."

Bill Baxter sat beside Lurulu, reading to her from a thick book. He looked up, in surprise and annoyance.

Blackney introduced the visitors. "These men," he said to Lurulu, "wish to ask you about your life on *Lekthwa*. Do you object?"

She glanced at the three with little interest. "No."

Major-General Devering moved forward. "We have a rather extensive program, and would like you to accompany us to new quarters—which will be more convenient for everyone concerned."

Baxter jumped up. "Absolutely not!" he shouted. "God, you've got your nerve! One thing that's *not* going to happen is an 'extensive program,' third degree, whatever you want to call it!"

Devering eyed him stonily. "I'd like to remind you, Mr. Baxter, that you have no official standing in regard to the young lady; and that she is the ward of the government, and subject to national security statutes."

"Have you got a warrant?" inquired Baxter. "If not, you're in a worse position officially than I am. As far as questioning goes, I appreciate that there's much that you want to know, and I'd like to help you—but you can do your questioning here, an hour or so a day. You can fit your questioning to the young lady's convenience, rather than she to yours."

Devering's mouth opened slightly, showing white teeth, and his chin protruded. "We'll damn well do what we see fit, with no interference from some damn, small-town reporter."

Dr. Blackney interposed. "May I suggest, gentlemen, that you leave the decision to the lady? After all, she is the one person most directly involved."

Lurulu had been watching with a slightly wrinkled forehead. "I do not care to go with these men. But I will answer their questions."

A nurse entered, whispered into Blackney's ear. Blackney raised his eyebrows, quickly rose. "Excuse me, it's the President calling."

"Let me talk to him," said Baxter wildly. "I'll tell him a thing or two."

Blackney ignored him, left the room. A sullen silence fell, Devering and Baxter glowering at each other, the scientists eyeing the Lekthwan woman, and she, oblivious, watching a hummingbird outside the window.

Blackney returned, breathing rather hard. "The President,"

he told Lurulu, "has invited you to spend a week at the White House."

Lurulu looked involuntarily at Bill Baxter. Grudgingly he said, "I suppose it would be the best thing for her, under the circumstances. When does the visit start?"

Blackney reflected. "I suppose right away. I didn't think to ask."

Baxter turned. "We might as well leave at once."

Devering wheeled toward the door, departed without a word, and the two scientists, after bows to the Lekthwan woman, followed.

Washington reacted to the Lekthwan woman with unprecedented fervor.

In the first place, she was no celebrity of the usual sort. She had built no empires, destroyed none, had been elected to no office, performed no antics on stage or screen, was not associated with any vice or depravity. She was a visitor from another star. Further it was reported that she possessed a wonderful beauty. The total effect was dramatic and tumultuous.

Lurulu seemed indifferent. She went to several parties, attended the opera, and received numerous gifts from publicity-hungry manufacturers—four new automobiles, clothes of every description, perfumes, baskets of fruit. One contractor offered to build her a house to any specifications she cared to submit.

She was taken on a lavish sight-seeing tour to New York. Mrs. Bliss, hostess of the expedition, inquired if such monumental edifices existed on her own planet. No, replied Lurulu, she doubted if on all *Lekthwa* there was a structure even three stories in height, or a bridge longer than a few feet of tree trunk spanning a brook.

"We have no need for these great masses," she told Mrs. Bliss. "People are never assembled in groups large enough to need large buildings, and as for rivers and seas, they are merely part of the planet's surface above which we spend much of our lives."

Baxter was her constant companion, an association which she now encouraged. Baxter was aware of her likes and dislikes, and protected her from most of the hostesses and agents. And as she came to find him useful, so did he come to feel necessary to her, and nothing in his life had meaning other than Lurulu.

A lewd rumor reached his ear, and in a troubled spirit he confided it to Lurulu. She looked up in surprise. "Really?" Then she took no further interest in the subject. Baxter departed in anger.

He arranged short daily interviews with scientists—biologists, physicists, linguists, historians, anthropologists, astronomers, engineers, military tacticians, chemists, bacteriologists, psychologists and others. These found her general knowledge vast and exciting, but vague in detail—helpful mainly in that she was able to indicate boundaries of scientific regions yet to be explored.

After one of these sessions, Baxter found her in the apartment he had rented for her, alone on a settee. The time was early evening and she sat looking across the park, into the luminous blue-gray sky.

He sat down beside her. "Are you tired?"

"Yes—very tired. Of curious people . . . ponderous questions . . . talk . . . nonsense. . . ."

He said nothing, sat staring out into the darkening twilight. She sensed the quality of his silence.

"Excuse me, Bill. I never mind talking to you."

His mood instantly changed; he felt closer, more intimate with her than at any time of their association.

"You've never mentioned your personal life," he began diffidently. "Were you . . . married?"

She answered quietly. "No."

Baxter waited.

"I was an artist—of a sort unknown to you here on Earth." She spoke softly, her eyes still out on the evening sky. "We conceive in the brain—color, motion, sound, space, sensation, mood; all moving, shifting, evolving. When the conceiver is prepared, he imagines the whole sequence of his creation, as vividly as possible—and this is picked up by a psychic recorder and preserved.

"To enjoy or experience the creation, a person inserts a

record into an apparatus, and this plants the same images into his mind. Thus he sees the motion, the color pattern, the flows and fluxes of space, the fantasies in the artist's mind, together with the sights, the sounds, and most important, the varying moods of the piece. . . . It is a difficult medium to master, for it requires tremendous concentration. I am merely a novice, but certain of my imageries have won praise.''

"That's very interesting," said Baxter heavily. Then after an interval: "Lurulu."

"Yes?"

"Do you have any plans for the future?"

She sighed. "No. Nothing. My life is blank." She stared into the sky where now the stars were showing. "Up there is my home and everything I love."

Baxter leaned forward. "Lurulu—will you marry me?"

She turned, looked at him. "Marry you? No, Bill."

"I love you very much," he said, looking out into the sky. "You've become everything in the world to me. I worship you—anything you do—or say—or touch. . . . I don't know whether you care anything for me—I suspect not—but you need me, and I'd do anything in the world to make you happy."

She smiled faintly, abstractedly. "On *Lekthwa* we mate when we find someone in rapport with us psychically. To you we may seem cold-blooded."

"Perhaps you and I are psychically right," suggested Bill Baxter.

She shuddered almost imperceptibly. "No, Bill. It's— unthinkable."

He arose. "Good-night." At the door he paused, looked back to where she sat in the dark, still staring up at the night sky, the far white stars.

Returning to his own apartment, he found Dr. Blackney awaiting him, sitting comfortably in an armchair with a newspaper.

Bill greeted him with subdued warmth. Blackney watched intently while Bill mixed a couple of stiff highballs.

"I thought I'd see how my ex-patient was adjusting herself to life on Earth."

Bill said nothing.

"What's your opinion?" Blackney asked.

Bill shrugged. "She's getting along all right. Tired of seeing so many people. . . . I just now asked her to marry me."

Blackney leaned back with his highball. "And she said no—"

"That's about it."

Blackney put down his glass, picked up a book beside him on the couch. "I just happened to chance on this, rummaging through some old stuff. . . . It's rather a long chapter. I won't read it. But the gist of it—" he opened the book to a page covered with fine print, looked quickly up at Bill. "The title, incidentally, is *Strange Tales of the Seven Seas*. Published in 1839, and this chapter is called 'Shipwrecked Off Guinea, a Personal Diary.'

"It's about a wreck—in 1835, when a British ship went down in a gale off Equatorial Africa. In the confusion Miss Nancy Marron, a girl of gentle upbringing, found herself alone in one of the ship's lifeboats. The boat weathered the storm, presently drifted near a small island, then uncharted, but now known as Matemba. The continent of Africa lay about thirty miles past the horizon, but this proximity was unknown to Nancy Marron.

"In any event, she was able to drag herself ashore and up on the beach, where a native found her and took her to his village." He turned the page. "She was received with great reverence. The natives had never seen a white man or woman, and thought her a divinity.

"They built her a grand new thatched hut; they brought her food, much of which, so she noted in her diary, she found inedible—slugs, entrails, and the like. In addition, they were cannibals, eating the bodies of any of their tribe who died."

Blackney looked up. "Her diary tells all this rather objectively. She was a good reporter and, in the main, keeps her homesickness out of the text.

"She learned the native tongue, found that she was the first white person ever seen on Matemba, and that vessels never approached the island. This discovery ended her last trace of hope. The last entry reads: 'I can stand it no longer here among these savages, friendly as they seem to be. I am sick at heart, I long for England, the faces of my family, the sound of my own blessed tongue, the smells and sounds of the pleasant countryside. I know I shall never see or hear them again in this world. I cannot bear this hideous loneliness any longer. I have a knife, and it will be very easy for me to use it. May God understand and forgive.' "

Blackney looked up. ''There the diary ends.''

Baxter sat like a statue.

After a moment he jumped to his feet.

He ran up the stairs, two at a time, turned down the hall, stopped by a white door. He rang the bell, waited . . . waited.

He threw himself against the panel; the lock splintered and Baxter staggered into the dark room.

He switched on the lights, stood staring at the figure on the floor, the golden figure lying in a pool of bright red blood. . . .

The Planet Machine

I

THE BARTENDER was the biggest man at the Hub. He had a red slab-sided face, a chest and belly like a barrel of meat and bone. He bounced his drunks by butting them out the door with this belly; thrusting like an uncouth and elephantine cooch-dancer. Reliable information compared the belly-blow to the kick of a mule. Marvin Allixter, nervously lean and on his way to forty, thought the bartender a blackguard, a double-dealing pinch-penny, but cautiously restrained his tongue.

The bartender inspected Allixter's merchandise. He twisted the bubble back and forth, inspecting the enclosed little creature from all sides. It glowed and glinted like a prism—sun yellow, emerald, melting mauve, bright pink—the purest of colors. "Twenty franks," he said without enthusiasm.

"Twenty franks?" Allixter dramatically beat both fists against the bar. "Now *you're* joking."

"No joke," rumbled the bartender.

Allixter leaned forward earnestly. "Now, Buck, look here. The bubble is pure rock crystal, maybe a million years old. The Kickerjees dig a year and grind and polish and twist and turn and then one slip—*smash!*—the bubble breaks, the mite oozes out and dies.''

The bartender turned away to pour straight shots for a pair of grinning warehousemen. ''Too fragile. If I bought it and one of these drunks busted it I'd be out of twenty franks.''

''Twenty franks?'' Allixter asked in astonishment. ''That's no figure to mention in the same breath with this little jewel. Why, I'd sell my ear for twenty franks first.''

''Suits me.'' Buck the bartender jocularly flourished a knife.

Allixter now thought to arouse the man's cupidity. ''This item cost me five hundred franks at the source.''

The bartender laughed in his face. ''You guys on the tube gang all sing the same song. You pick up a trinket somewhere off in the stations, you smuggle it back through the tube, you spin a fancy yarn about how much it cost you and hustle the item to the first sucker who listens to you.'' He drew himself a small glass of water, drank it with a wink to the nearby warehousemen.

''Sure, I got stuck once. I bought a little varmint from Hank Evans, said it could dance, said it knew all the native dances of Kalong, and the thing looked like it could dance up a storm. I put down forty-two franks for the animal. Come to find out it had sore feet in the new gravity and was just hopping from one to the other to ease the pain. That was the dancing.''

Allixter shifted uneasily, glanced over his shoulder to the door. Sam Schmitz, the dispatcher, had been buzzing him for an hour and Sam was an impatient man. He lounged back against the bar, attempting an air of nonchalance. ''Look at the colors the little rascal goes through—*there!* That red! Ever see anything so bright? Think how that would look hung around some lady's ivory-white throat!''

Kitty, the sumptuous blonde hostess, said in a breathless contralto, ''I think it's lovely. I'd be proud to wear it myself.''

The bartender took up the bubble once more. ''I don't know no ladies.'' He inspected it doubtfully. ''It's a pretty little trinket. Well, maybe I'll spring twenty franks.''

The screen at his back buzzed. The bartender turned on the video without waiting for the caller's identification, then took his bulk to the side. Allixter had no time to duck. Sam Schmitz was staring at him eye to eye.

"Allixter!" barked Schmitz. "You've got five minutes to report. After that, don't bother!" The screen went blank.

Now Allixter stared under thoughtful dark eyebrows at the bartender, who regarded him placidly. "Since you're in a hurry," said Buck, "I'll make it twenty-five franks. It's a cute little bobbet."

Allixter rose to his feet, still staring at the bartender. He juggled the bubble from hand to hand. Buck reached out in alarm. "Easy—the thing might break." He dived into the till. "Here's your twenty-five franks."

Allixter said, "Five hundred."

"Can't do it," said the barkeep.

"Make it four hundred."

Buck shook his head, watching Allixter from craftily narrowed eyes. Allixter turned, wordlessly walked from the bar. The bartender waited like a statue. Allixter's long dark face returned through the door. "Three hundred."

"Twenty-five franks."

Allixter screwed his face into an expression of agony and departed.

In the street he paused. The depot, a big cube of a building, rose like a cliff in the wintry sunlight, dominating the rather disreputable purlieu of the Hub. At its base spread warehouses, glittering aluminum banks, each a quarter mile long. Trucks and trailers nuzzled at side-bays like red-and-blue leeches.

The flat warehouse roofs served as cargo decks where flexible loaders crammed airship holds with produce from a hundred worlds. Allixter watched the activity a moment, conscious that, for all the activity, nine-tenths of the traffic passed unseen along the tubes—to continental Earth stations, to stations among the planets, out among the outworlds and far systems.

"Rats!" said Allixter. He walked without haste to the corner transit, considering the little bubble. Perhaps he should

have sold—twenty-five franks was twenty-four franks profit.
He rejected the idea. A man was able to carry only so much
along the tubes and expected a decent profit from his enterprise.

The bubble actually was a kind of sea-creature washed up
on the pink beaches of—Allixter couldn't remember the name
of the planet—9-3-2 was the code to the station. He tucked it
away in his pouch, climbed into the shell at the transit,
swerved, rose, popped out into light. Soon after, stepped out
upon the depot administration deck.

A few feet distant was the glass-enclosed cubicle where
Sam Schmitz, the Service Foreman and Dispatcher, sat perched
on a high stool. Allixter slid back a pace, said, "Hello,
Sam," in a friendly voice. Schmitz had a round pudgy face,
fierce and red, with the undershot chin and expression of a
bulldog.

"Allixter," said Schmitz, "This may surprise you. We're
tightening up around here. You guys on the repair crew have
picked up the idea that you're a bunch of aristocrats, responsible only to God. This is a mistake. You were due on
standby three hours ago. For two hours the Chief's been
chewing my rear end for a mechanic. And I find you in
Buck's bar. I want to be good to you guys, but you've got to
help out once in a while."

Allixter listened without concentration, nodding at the right
places. Where next to peddle the bubble? Maybe wait till he
got a week's leave, take it down to Edmonton or Chicago. Or
better yet, stash it away till he had accumulated a few other
items and then make Paris or Mexico City, where the big
money was. Schmitz paused for breath.

"Anything on the docket, Sam?" Allixter asked.

The response startled him. Sam's chin quivered in rage.
"Blast it! What do you think I've been talking about the last
five minutes?"

Allixter desperately sent his mind back, recalled a phrase
here, a sentence there. He rubbed his thin cheek and jaw, and
said, "I didn't quite catch all of it, Sam. Maybe if you'd go
over it again. . . . Just what's the complaint?"

Sam flung up his arms in disgust. "Go see the Chief. He'll
give you the picture. I'm done talking."

Allixter crossed the deck, turned down a hall, stopped at a tall green door with bronze letters which read: SERVICE AND MAINTENANCE DIRECTOR. ENTER.

He pushed the button. The door slotted and he entered the outer office. The secretary glanced up. Allixter said, "The Chief's expecting me."

"That's no secret." Then she said into the intercom, "Scotty Allixter's here." She listened to her earplug, nodded at Allixter, keyed back the lock on the inner door. He slid it aside, stepped into the office. The air, as always, had a harsh medicinal odor which irritated Allixter's nose.

The Chief was a small man, built to an angular design. His skin was wrinkled and yellow, parched like an old lemon. His eyes were small black balls that seemed to snap with some kind of inner electricity. A few wisps of kinky hair rose from his head, some white, some black, without apparent design. His neck was corrugated like an alligator's and the right side was marred all the way to his knobby chin by a heavy welt of scar tissue. Allixter had never seen the Chief laugh, had never heard him speak other than in a dry monotonous twang.

The Chief said without preliminaries, "Schmitz probably gave you the picture on this job."

Allixter took a seat. "To be frank, Chief, I didn't quite get it."

The Chief spoke as if he were explaining table manners to an idiot—softly, with careful enunciations. "You've been through to Rhetus Station?"

"Code six minus four minus nine. Sure thing. They've got a new Mammoth installation."

"Well, six minus four minus nine is coming in out of phase."

Allixter's thick straight eyebrows rose in an arch. "So soon? Why, we just—"

The Chief said drily, "Here's the story. The tube came in, just barely scraping over the edge of the tuner. I computed thirty one-hundredths-of-a-percent slack in the phase."

Allixter scratched his chin. "Sounds as if there's a leak in the selector unit."

"Possibly," agreed the Chief.

"Or maybe they've got a new dispatcher playing with the adjustments."

The Chief said, "To make sure we hit the unit dead center, I'm sending you out on six minus four minus nine, slacked down the same percentage that it came in."

Allixter winced. "That sounds dangerous. If the code doesn't home in on the contacts, I'll come out scattered all over Rhetus."

The Chief pushed himself back in his chair. "Job for a service man. You're on standby. So it's yours."

Allixter frowningly looked through the window, across the misty reaches of the Great Slave Lake. "There's something strange here. That's a new Mammoth and they work well within our system-tolerance."

"True."

Allixter shot a narrow glance at the Chief. "Sure it was Rhetus?"

"I didn't say that. I said the code was six minus four minus nine."

"Got a reading on that code?"

The Chief wordlessly tossed him an oscillograph pattern.

Allixter said, "Amplitude six, frequencies four and nine." He frowned. "Almost six, almost four and nine. Not quite. Close enough to lock into the contacts."

"Correct. Well, get your gear, climb through the tub, service that installation."

Allixter anxiously pulled at his wedge-shaped Gaelic chin. "Maybe. . . ." He paused.

"Maybe what?"

"Do you know what I think?"

"No."

"Looks like it might be an amateur station or a hijacking outfit. The Rhetus tube runs valuable cargo. Now if some outfit could divert the tube to their own station. . . ."

"If you think so, you can take a gun with you."

Allixter rubbed his hands together nervously. "Sounds like a police job to me, Chief."

The Chief raked him with his snapping black eyes. "It sounds to me as if the code is thirty one-hundredths-of-a-percent slack. Maybe some idiot is punching wrong buttons on that Mammoth. I want you to go straighten it out. What do you think you're drawing a thousand franks a month for?''

Allixter muttered something about the infinite value of human life. The Chief said, "If you don't like it, I know better mechanics than you who will."

"I like it," said Allixter.

"Wear Type X."

Allixter's thick black eyebrows became question marks. "Rhetus has a good atmosphere. Type X is antihalogen—"

"Wear Type X. We're not taking unnecessary chances. Suppose it is a hijack installation? Take along the Conceptualizer, too, in case you need the local language. And a gun—a Jar, if you've got one."

"I see we're of the same mind," said Allixter.

"Don't forget spare power. And check your breather. Evans reported a leaky tube on the last requisition. I had it condemned but maybe they're all that way."

II

The mechanics' locker room was deserted. In glum silence, Allixter pulled on the Type X—first a thick neck-to-toe coverall webbed with heating elements, then a thin sheath of inert film to seal him from an inhospitable atmosphere, then high boots of woven metal and silicone impervious to heat, cold, dampness and ordinary stress. A belt strapped around his waist and over his shoulder supported his tool kit, a breather and humidity-control unit, two fresh power packs, a sheath knife, a "Jar"—a disrupter handgun—and a small laser unit.

In the corridor he met Sam Schmitz. "Carr's at the controls. He's checking you out on the adjusted transmission code. . . ."

A door labelled DANGER, KEEP OUT slid aside for them and they entered the central depot, a long hall filled with sound, activity, dust and, most notably, a thousand odd odors, whiffs of spicy reeks, balms and fetors from the thousand off-planet commodities coming in on the near conveyor.

The luminous ceiling gave off a cold white glare which bleached out every shadow. There was no concealment in this light—every item on the belts minutely displayed itself to the eyes of the checkers. The walls were painted in ceiling-to-floor blocks of various colors, the better to designate the bays, where various shipments, temporarily stacked, awaited routing.

A narrow glass-fenced platform cut the depot in two. Back and forth from platform to the belts jumped the clerks in blue and white smocks, checking the merchandise incoming on the near side, outgoing on the far—crates, sacks, boxes, bales, bags, racks and cases.

Machinery, metal parts in ingots and machined shapes, consignments of Earth fruit and vegetables going out to the colonies, the homesteads, the mines. Other consignments of off-world exotics incoming to entice and stimulate the sophisticates of Paris, London, Benares, Sahara City. Tanks of water, oaken casks of whiskey, green bottles of wine.

Prefabricated houses, flyers, automobiles, speedboats for the lakes of the Tanagra Highlands. Beautiful woods, richly mottled and marked from the hardwood swamps of a jungle planet. Ores, rocks, minerals, crystals, glasses, sands—all riding the conveyors, either approaching or leaving the twin curtains of dark flickering amber at the far end of the hall.

At the curtain end of the out-belt a large blond man sat in an elevated box, viciously chewing gum. Allixter and Schmitz ducked across the in-belt, stepped over the clerks' platform, rode the out-belt to the operator's box.

Carr moved his arm and the conveyor eased to a stop. "All ready to go?"

"Yep, all set," said Schmitz cheerfully. He hopped up into the box while Allixter stood glumly eyeing the curtain. "How's the wife, Carr?" asked Schmitz. "Heard she got a dose of dermatitis from something you carried home on your clothes."

"She's okay," said Carr. "It was some dust from Deneb Kaitos. Now let's see—I've got to set up this phony code. Hey, Scotty," he called down to Allixter, "made out your will yet? This is like jumping out of an airplane and hoping you'll hit water."

Allixter made a nonchalant gesture. "Just routine, Carr, my boy. Set those dials—I want to be back sometime tonight."

Carr shook his head in rueful admiration. "They pay you a thousand franks for it—brother, it's all yours. I've seen some of the stuff that's come out of the tubes when the settings were a little out of phase. Wood panels come through looking like cheesecloth handkerchiefs—one time a turbine agitator turned into a gallon of funny-looking rust."

Allixter's mouth tightened over his teeth and he cracked his knuckles.

"There she is," said Carr. A light on the panel flared red, flickered, wavered through smoky orange, glared white. "She's through."

Schmitz leaned down over the box. "Okay, Allixter, all yours."

Allixter pulled the hood over his head, sealed it, inflated the suit. Carr chuckled into Schmitz' ear, "Scotty's sweating blood over this one."

Schmitz grinned. "He's afraid he's walking into some hijacker's warehouse."

Carr turned him a blankly curious side-look. "Is he?"

Schmitz spat. "Hell no! He's going to Rhetus, to make adjustments on the coder. That's how I figure it." He spat again. "Of course, I might be wrong."

Allixter lifted up his hood, yelled to Schmitz, "You better get me down a Conceptualizer."

Schmitz asked with a grin, "Can't you talk English? That's all you'll hear on Rhetus."

"The Chief says take the Conceptualizer. So roll her out."

A buzzer sounded on Carr's panel. Carr grunted. "Get him his analyzer.

I can't tie up the belt all day. Old Hannegan's hollerin' to get his grapes off to Centauri."

Schmitz snapped a few words into a mesh and moments later a runner from the shop appeared, rolling the Conceptualizer ahead of him, a black case slung between two wheels.

"Be careful of that job," said Schmitz. "It's expensive and it's the only decent outfit we got left since Olson burnt out his equipment. Don't leave it on Rhetus."

"You worry too damn much about that Conceptualizer," muttered Allixter, "and not enough for old Scotty Allixter."

He sealed the hood over his head and, trundling the Conceptualizer ahead of him, stepped through the curtain.

Allixter stood on a bone-white platform, open to the heavens. He felt a stir of morose triumph. "I'm still alive. I'm not a cheesecloth handkerchief or a gallon of rust. I guess the Chief figured okay—got to give the old buzzard some credit. But. . . ."

Allixter stared around the landscape, a gray and black plain without horizon. At precise intervals, massive concrete rotundas rose from the ground, most of which had been shattered as if by great explosions. Some odd-looking creatures stood nearby.

"This isn't Rhetus—nowhere near Rhetus. And those aren't men and they aren't Rhets. . . ." He turned an anxious look to the tube installation—it was of a type strange to his eyes—a portal of dark gold-brown fog which seemed to be swirling slowly around a vortex.

Where in creation was he? He looked at the sky—a hazy violet, spangled by a myriad distant suns, random gouts of colored fire. Was it day or was it night? He searched the landscape with anxious eyes, sweating inside his air-film. Perspectives were strange, the lighting was strange, the shadows were strange. Everywhere he looked was suffused with the unhuman wildness of the remote out-worlds.

"I'm lost," thought Allixter.

It was a dreary landscape, a dingy plain studded with tremendous gray wrecks. Where the shattered walls had once stood, fallen machinery could be seen—wheels, shafts, banks of complex gear and circuits, squat housings and cases. All were broken, silent, corroded.

Allixter turned his attention back to the amber portal. This was the incurtain, but where was the installation to send him back? Usually the two were combined. The creatures who stood along the outer edge of the white platform approached, apparently with indecision and puzzlement. Allixter made no move for his Jar. He thought that if it were possible to crossbreed a seal with a man and plant a palmetto thatch of red-green quills on the scalp of the issue—here would be the result.

As they approached, watching him from big dull-surfaced eyes, they made sounds of communication—squeaks, windy whistling tones, hisses; forming these noises by trapping a pocket of air under their arm-pits, squeezing it past a flap of skin.

Allixter said, "How do you do, my friends. I'm the representative of Tube Maintenance and it looks like I've crossed over into an entirely different mesh, a million light-years from Earth. I'm entirely divorced from my own set of stations and you don't look like you can tell me how to find my way home."

The natives ceased their noise as he spoke, then commenced once more. Allixter chewed his lip in amusement. He dropped a pair of legs to steady the Conceptualizer, swung the shutter away from the screen. "Come on over, Joe," he said, motioning to a creature who stood slightly in the lead. "Let's see if we can get along."

He set the controls for Cycle A. The screen glowed white. Geometric figures appeared—a circle, a square, a triangle, a line and a point.

As the others crowded around his back, Allixter pointed to the circle and said, "Circle," to the square—"Square," and likewise for other shapes. Then, motioning to "Joe," he pressed the record key and pointed to the circle.

Joe was silent.

Allixter released the key, went through the priming sequence again. Again he set the banks to record, pointed to the circle. Joe squeezed a skirl of a sound from under his armpit. Allixter pointed to the other figures and Joe made other sounds.

Encouraged, Allixter proceeded to Step Two—Enumeration. The screen depicted symbols representing the agglomerative numerals—a series of lines, one dot in the first line, two dots in the second line, three in the third, four in the fourth, in such fashion up to twenty. Joe, alive to his task, made sounds for each of the numbers in turn. Then the screen displayed a random multitude of dots and Joe created another sound.

Now Allixter tried colors. Joe stared at the screen impassively. Red—no response. Green—no response. Violet—no response. Allixter shrugged. "We'll never get together here. You must see by infrared or ultraviolet."

The cycle passed on to more complicated situations. A dot moved swiftly across the screen, followed by another, moving slowly. The sequence was repeated and Allixter pointed to the first dot. Joe created a sound. Allixter indicated the slow dot and Joe made another sound.

From the bottom of the screen a line rose nearly to the top. Another line lifted about an inch. Joe made sounds which Allixter hoped were "tall" and "short" or "high" or "low."

A circle swelled almost past the outer verge of the screen and beside it appeared a minute dot. Joe's sounds for "large" and "small" entered the memory banks.

Presently the comparative sequences were exhausted and the screen depicted noun objects—mountains, an ocean, a tree, a house, fire, water. Then came more complicated objects—turbine in a plastic housing to convey the idea of machinery—a conventionalized drawing of a dynamo with an exterior circuit first coiled around a bar, from which a magnetic field radiated, then continuing to a point where the circuit was broken and lightning-like flashes jumped the gap. Allixter pointed to these flashes and the Conceptualizer recorded Joe's sound for electricity.

Two hundred basic nouns were so recorded. Then the cycle turned to interpersonal relationships. The machine had been designed for use by men—the stock situations depicted men. Allixter hoped confusion would not arise.

First, a man was shown attacking another man, striking him with a club. The victim fell with a crushed skull. Allixter pointed; the analyzer filed the words for dead, or corpse. Then the murderer turned a savage face out of the screen, rushed forward with club upraised to strike. Joe jumped back, squeaking. Allixter, grinning, ran the sequence again, and the analyzer noted the word for enemy or assailant.

An hour passed—a score of situations were pictured and analyzed. It seemed to Allixter that the natives showed signs of nervousness. They cast restive glances in all directions, gestured with agitated flutters of their hand-members.

Allixter searched the landscape but no menace was evident in the perimeter of his vision. However, by a kind of empathy, he found his own nerves growing taut, found it difficult to concentrate on the Conceptualizer.

Cycle A was completed—all the words and situations of the basic vocabulary had been recorded, although more useful and near-essential abstractions, such as interrogatives and pronouns, were still absent from the file.

Allixter switched the machine from Cycle A to Converse. He spoke into the auditory receiver, careful to use only words of the basic vocabulary. "Desire return through machine. Lead to out-machine."

The Conceptualizer absorbed the words, found their counterparts in the recorded squeaks, hissings, trumpetings and voiced them from the speaker.

Joe listened with attention—then he looked blankly at Allixter. His shoulders quivered. Air creaked and sputtered past the skin at his armpits.

The Conceptualizer searched the files, voiced the words: "Call to machine . . . Desire . . . Machine man . . . Broken machine . . . Man come through machine . . . Bad. . . ."

There had obviously been more words spoken. The Conceptualizer translated only the sounds it could match against its recorded patterns.

Allixter said, "Use words given to machine."

Joe stared with great dull eyes. His tall thatch of red and green plumes drooped noticeably. He made a further effort. "Man call for distant machine builder. Man come. Desire friend to repair machine."

Allixter looked in frustration around the drab horizon, looked up into the spangled violet sky where there would never be night or day. He considered running Cycle B on the Conceptualizer—a process which would tax the patience of both himself and Joe but which might eventually enable him to locate the installation to send him back to Earth.

He tried once more. "Desire return through machine. Lead to out-machine." He gestured to the amber portal. "See in-machine. Desire out-machine."

Something was wrong. The natives' nervousness became marked and increased. They crouched on the bone-white platform in smooth balls, crests folded around them like partly closed umbrellas. Allixter looked for Joe. Joe was at his feet, as huddled and compact as his companions.

In sudden anxiety, Allixter closed up the Conceptualizer screen, snapped the lid down over the controls. A nearby building caught his eye. The machinery within was moving—grinding, pounding, snapping. Electricity or some other flow of energy arched across old contacts.

Corroded shafts shuddered and twisted and strained. Wheels moaned and whined around dry bearings. Without warning the building exploded. Chunks of concrete and metal flew up in a crazy tangle, fell clattering in all directions. Smaller debris was blown and scattered across the platform, and the natives trumpeted in terror.

Some small fragments struck Allixter, bounded off his resilient air-film. It occurred to him that he knew nothing of the atmosphere, that if the film were punctured he might be poisoned.

From his pouch he brought a spectrometer and let air into its vacuum chamber. He pressed the radiation button and read the dark lines on the ground glass against a standard scale. He gazed speculatively at the structures. Fluorine, chlorine, bromine, hydrogen fluoride, carbon dioxide, water vapor, argon, xenon, krypton—not exactly a salubrious environment for the likes of him, he thought.

He looked back to the exploded building, now in utter ruin. It suddenly glowed white hot and the heat seemed not to dissipate but to increase. The wreckage melted into a pool of seething slag. The ground in the immediate vicinity steamed, scorched, slumped into the widening pool of lava.

Allixter thought—That's hard energy and dangerously radioactive—deadly even through my suit.

He pushed the Conceptualizer ahead of him to the edge of the platform, prepared to jump down to the gray-black ground.

Behind him the natives still huddled, balls of seal-soft flesh, neatly covered by their thatch.

Joe stirred, looked up, saw Allixter. He scampered forward on flexible short legs, making urgent sounds. Allixter quickly reactivated the Conceptualizer.

"Danger, danger, bad, deep, death," translated the Conceptualizer, the intonations calm and matter-of-fact.

Allixter jerked back from the edge. Joe stopped alongside, tossed a fragment of rock to the ground. It cast up a puff of feathery dust, sank quickly out of sight. Allixter blinked.

There but for the grace of God went Scotty Allixter, he thought. It was an ocean of ashes out there—soft deep fluff. With new eyes he gazed across the flat gray plain, where the blasted buildings rose like islands. He shrugged. It was beyond his understanding. He knew of Earthmen who had lost their minds trying to comprehend the paradoxes and peculiarities of the outer stations.

A sudden intuition struck him. He glanced around the circumference of the bone-white platform. It was like a raft on the gray sea, with the slow-whirling portal at the center. How then had the natives made their way here? Could it possibly be that they had arrived through the portal from an out-world, just as he had done?

Joe's soft fingers fumbled at his arm. He squeaked, pumping his shoulders loosely, expertly, and the Conceptualizer translated, "Off. Come. Lead toward large machine."

Allixter said hopefully, "Desire out-machine. Desire return. Lead to out-machine."

Joe squeezed out further sounds. "Come—follow. Friend to large machine corpse. Large machine wreck friend. Large machine desire friend. Come—follow. Repair large machine."

Allixter thought that whatever it was, it could be no worse than standing on this platform.

Joe fumbled with a grating, pulled it aside, descended a steep flight of steps. Trundling the Conceptualizer ahead of him, Allixter followed.

The corridor became dark. Allixter flicked on his suit light. Ahead he saw a pair of brown-gold curtains, the 'in' distinguished from the 'out' by a subtle difference in their golden flicker.

Joe stepped through the out-portal, disappeared. As Allixter hesitated, he bobbed through the in-portal, beckoned with a certain querulous insistence, once more popped back out.

Allixter sighed. Pushing the Conceptualizer ahead of him, he stepped through.

III

Allixter stood in a wide corridor tiled with vitreous white squares. Ahead of him, Joe slid through a tall vaguely Romanesque archway. He followed and came out on a pavilion open to the sky. The floor was of the same vitreous tile, squares six feet on a side. It was lacking in furnishings or fittings. Around the edge of the floor pipe-stem columns supported a disproportionately heavy pediment and Allixter paused in trepidation, half expecting the whole construction to buckle and fall crashing at his feet.

He walked cautiously out into the center of the pavilion, noting a trembling underfoot as from heavy machinery. In renewed apprehension, he estimated the stability of the columns and was not reassured to find them quivering and swaying. Joe seemed oblivious to the danger. Allixter gingerly approached the edge of the pavilion.

The view was different from the outlook across the drab sea of ash, and he took some time to study it. Here the panorama, if strange and unearthly, had a certain haunting charm. A long low valley lay cradled between two rows of hills. Two or three miles distant, at the bottom of the valley, lay a glass-calm lake and the mirror of its surface reflected all the varied hues of this world's several suns.

Along the hills, purple shrubs grew; in the valley, black-green paddies lay in rectangular blocks to the limit of his vision. He noticed what appeared to be a village about half-way to the lake—a row of neat sheds open at front and rear under a line of spindle-shaped, lime-green trees.

There was a sharp sound, a terrific crack which reverberated across the valley. Joe screeched, ducked back, huddled trembling in the middle of the pavilion.

The hill to his right had opened in a vast split at least a mile long and perhaps a hundred yards wide. A sheet of white flame issued from this seam and blasted up at a slant clear across the valley. Heat seared Allixter's face and he dodged behind one of the slender columns, which shuddered and swayed before his face.

Joe came cringing up beside him like a frightened dog in search of comfort. Allixter grinned in spite of himself. "I can see why these boys act like they're scared to death. No telling where the next outburst takes place."

He studied Joe with a new concentration. Round dull-eyed face under a ludicrous head-dress, face without expression, only coincidentally human. Round arms fringed with black hair, round sinuous legs joining the torso like pipes to a boiler.

Allixter speculated as to Joe's ultimate motives. Whatever they might be, whatever thoughts passed through the creature's organ for thinking, they were certainly indescribable in Earth terms. "We've got something in common, Joe," said Allixter. "Neither one of us wants to be blown to atoms."

There was one vestige of hope to be derived from the situation, thought Allixter—Joe's mental patterns apparently were not those of an evolutionized predator. By Gram's Theorem the carnivore that evolved to civilization retained the ferocity and callousness of his prototype. The herbivore tended to placidity, discipline and convention—while the omnivores were erratic, prone to nervous disorders and unpredictable emotion.

Joe tugged at Allixter's arm. Allixter held back a minute, then relaxed and followed. "There's no point in arguing with you; I'll never get home. Maybe now you're taking me to the out-tube—and that reminds me, I've got to watch for any small trinkets to take back, just in case. A man can't get rich on a thousand franks a month."

He swept the spangled sky with curious eyes. "I must be in the heart of a cluster—maybe past the Milky Way. I'm a long way from home. It's avarice which has brought me out here, the old fault. Oh well, let's see what good old Joe wants.''

Joe led him around the side of the pavilion along a walkway built of thin stone slats. Allixter felt them vibrate and throb under his feet as if to the impulse of powerful machinery nearby. Behind the pavilion rose a hill. A stone building thrust forward, its after end under the slope.

The walls were great rusty gray-yellow masses of masonry, studded and strapped with metal bars like a fortress. The walkway of stone strips came to an end. They walked now on the bare ground and it throbbed beneath them with an ever heavier pulse. Joe stopped at a heavy door which, slightly ajar, vibrated to his touch.

Joe squeaked suddenly; Allixter turned on the Conceptualizer.

''Large machine bad. Repair good. Danger. Large machine wreck friend one. Friend two,'' here he tapped Allixter's chest. ''Friend two. Repairman come through hole. Go see large machine. Danger. Wreck friend. Large danger. Large machine enemy. Make large wreck.''

Allixter gingerly approached the door. ''You don't make this project sound too inviting.'' He squinted through the slit into a large bare hall. The floor was flagged with great squares of polished red stone, eight feet on a side. The walls were faced from floor to ceiling with rectangular panels, evidently removable. Where one of the panels had been swung aside, Allixter glimpsed masses of exquisitely complicated and delicate machinery.

A track appeared to make a circuit of the hall; at the range of Allixter's vision a trolley supported a high black casing. From the controls and dial settings at one side, this mobile case appeared to be another massive mechanism.

Such were the inorganic aspects of the hall and Allixter noted them with a single glance. Then he gave his attention to another object, more immediate and with chilling implications regarding his own future. It was a corpse on the floor—a roughly humanoid figure with a crushed skull.

The face of the dead man was gaunt and greenish-yellow. His body was thin, his skin stretched taut over sharp bones.

The effect was that of an exotic bird stripped of its feathers, murdered and flung in a heap.

The body had apparently lain in its present state for several days and Allixter was glad that, self-contained in his airfilm, he was not forced to breathe directly the air of the hall.

Unconsciously breathing shallowly, he scrutinized the corpse. No pressure suit was in evidence. Somehow, the man had been able to breathe the halogens which poisoned the atmosphere for humans. Odd, reflected Allixter. Joe pushed him forward. "Go. Large machine wreck. Danger."

Allixter held back. "Desire life. Avoid danger. Fear."

Joe said, "See." He opened the door, slid inside with a sidewise motion. As he loped around the hall, he pumped his shoulders furiously, squeezing forth a steady flow of shrill sound.

"Joe," said Allixter admiringly, "if we were back on Earth, I'd take you to Scotland and list you with the Queen's Own, where you'd play lead without the bagpipes."

Joe never halted his trumpeting till once more he joined Allixter outside the door.

"Go," said Joe. "Talk, danger absent. Silence, danger." He tapped Allixter's chest. "Large machine repairman come through hole, repair large machine."

The first glimmerings of enlightenment came to Allixter. "I think I see it. There's some kind of machine in there you want me to fix. It's dangerous if it's not fixed and it's dangerous while I'm in there unless I keep making noise." He uttered a sharp bark of laughter.

"Schmitz should see me now. He calls me the Silent Scot." He sighed. "A thousand franks a month—so long as I survive my job. Oh well, at least I'll never starve. . . ."

He looked into the hall once again, chewing his lip in frustrated silence and wishing he had established interrogatives in the native language.

"I may be the world's best mechanic," said Allixter, "but coming coldturkey on an off-planet machine, not knowing what's wrong with it, not even knowing what it's supposed to do in the first place—this is what sent old Willy Johnson to an early grave."

Joe prodded him anxiously. Far in the distance he heard a great thud, a blast as of an enormous explosion. Joe quivered, squeaked in agitation, fanned the quills of his headdress in all directions.

"A man dies but once," reflected Allixter, "and if this is my time at least the Chief and Schmitz won't have the satisfaction of sifting the remains."

He pushed the door wide and was about to step into the room when Joe pointed over his head, squeaked, "Danger."

Allixter looked up. Overhead a great hammer, swinging from a ball and socket joint in the center of the ceiling, hung cocked back against the wall—apparently the agency by which the corpse on the floor had been crushed.

"Danger," said Joe. "Talk many."

Allixter entered the hall, pushing the Conceptualizer before him. "I wish I was home," he said in a loud voice. "I wish I knew where the tube came out. So near and yet so far and here I am depending on my voice for my life and piping like a canary."

The Conceptualizer, picking up translatable words, squeaked and groaned. The hall rang with mingled sounds.

Allixter thought, "Why should I have to talk when there's a perfectly good mechanical talker right here under my hand?" He pushed the Conceptualizer to the middle of the hall, set the index so that Cycle A was repeated, together with Joe's recorded interpolations. Now, he thought, there should be sufficient sound to distract anyone and anything.

Warily eyeing the poised hammer, Allixter scrutinized the hall. Beyond doubt repairs to the machinery had been underway when death had stopped the hand of the mechanic. Panels had been removed from the wall and the face of the mobile unit had been demounted. Various cams, gears, shafts, assemblies of indescribable nature mounted in small cases, lay neatly in a tray beside a rack of tools. Apparently the mechanic had barely started when—Allixter turned an anxious glance at the poised hammer.

No, he thought, too precarious—too chancy.

Deftly, weighing each placement, he climbed up the side of

the mobile unit. Perching on the top, he took from his belt the laser which served both as weapon and tool. Stretching across the gap he played the laser on the shaft. Fire spattered, the metal melted in a shower of sparks, the hammer dropped with a clatter, missed the Conceptualizer by inches. Allixter jammed the torch back in his belt.

A voice cried out in the native language, screaming, hissing, groaning. Allixter hurriedly descended to the floor, stood searching for the source. Sweat running off his back made small rivulets down his spine.

He was alone in the room.

The voice continued, and after a moment he located its source—a metal diaphragm at the far end of the hall. Directly above, a many-faceted lens about six inches in diameter was mounted so that it projected slightly into the room.

He wheeled the Conceptualizer close, said, "Friend, friend. Come out, see." It must be a fellow to the corpse, thought Allixter—perhaps one who watched by remote through the faceted lens.

The speaker said in English, "Build across many words. Build words through machine."

Evidently the watcher was intelligent, thought Allixter. Very well, Cycle B. He started the sequence but the voice made no attempt to supply words for the automaton. "Man talk. Man talk," it repeated insistantly.

Allixter settled to the task and supplied English words for the depicted sequences and relationships.

Cycle B, with the pronouns, was complete. He started Cycle C. The voice said, "More words, faster. All comes understood and remembered."

"Hmm," muttered Allixter, "I've got a ruddy genius on my hands. A mind like a sponge. Very well, I'll give him as much as he can take." And he described the screen situations in great detail, supplementing the prime concepts with additional nominal and verbal materials.

In two hours he had completed Cycles C, D, E and F— normally the work of a month.

As he flicked the switch he said, "Now, my friend, wherever you are, you should be able to talk to me, and maybe you'll answer a few of my questions.''

Allixter stared in surprise. His own voice returned from the spcaker. ''Ask—the files will return information. That is their function.''

''First. . . .'' Allixter paused. What was first? As he considered he heard a grind, a swish. Overhead the stump of rod swung toward him. If the hammer were still attached and had descended, Allixter would have been one more corpse on the floor.

Allixter crouched in alarm. ''Who's trying to kill me? Why? All I want is to get back to my home world.''

The speaker said with disarming calmness. ''The protective instruments try to kill you because the inhibitor circuit is disorganized.''

Allixter gave a worried glance at the corpse. ''How am I supposed to survive?''

''A constant impulse from the attention units drains ergs from the B-sub C monitor and holds the relay open. As long as you supply material that occupies the perceptors, the auto-.matic protective devices will not function.''

''I'll try as hard as I can,'' said Allixter. ''Is conversation safe?''

''As long as attention is occupied. Three seconds is the critical lapse. This is the time required to leak the charge past the condensers.''

''Who are you? Who's speaking?''

''This voice is the courtesy unit of the Planet Machine.''

''Will you repeat that last sequence?'' asked Allixter in puzzlement.

The message was repeated. Allixter stared in bewilderment and awe. ''Then, you're a kind of—computer?''

''Yes.''

Three seconds passed swiftly. Hurriedly Allixter asked, ''What's your function? What do you do?''

''When operational, machine directs worldwide installations which collect energy from the suns, apply this energy to the designated uses.''

''Which are?''

"Machine mines, smelts, refines ore, alloys and shapes metal parts, manages photosynthetic tanks producing fluoro-silicon and fluoro-carbon compounds, combines and fabricates items in Classification Zo, Schedules Ba-Nineteen through Pec-Twenty-five. When complete, products are delivered to the master planet Plagigonstok through the transfer."

Allixter found a hint of enlightenment in the explanation. "I understand then that this planet is a colony of another world? And the natives, where do they fit in?"

"The natives supply what unskilled and flexible labor may be necessary. They are paid in commodities."

Allixter glanced at the corpse. "Where are all the—what do you call them?"

"Question is inexact."

"What kind of creature is that dead person on the floor—what race?"

"He is a Plag, a Lord of the Universe."

Allixter snorted. "Are there any others nearby?"

"There are twelve, similar in condition to this one."

A chill ran along Allixter's neck. "What do you mean—similar condition?"

"Bodily functions disrupted by disorganization of mental centers."

"Dead?"

"Disfunctional."

"You killed them?"

"Protective instruments killed them."

"Why?"

"Inhibitor circuit is not functioning. Machine is fundamentally ordered not to kill Plags. This order is occluded. Now machine kills Plags freely without inhibition and destroys Plag installations at random."

"Then why don't you kill the natives?"

"Inhibitors concerning autochtones are still in place. Machine protects autochtones. Machine kills alien lifeforms who enter this room, the processing center of the machine. You survive only by accident—attention units, draining from B-sub C monitor, shunt out exterminators."

Allixter grimaced. "There's a serious oversight somewhere."

The machine was silent. Allixter waited for a reply. One second—two seconds—he realized with a prickle of urgency that the machine responded only to questions, that the circuits were not set up to exchange small-talk with casual passers-by.

He blurted, "Yes. No. I've seen computers and robotic mechanisms but I've never seen anything like you. You're a pretty big piece of machinery—er, aren't you?"

"Yes."

One second—two seconds. Allixter's mind was blank.

"Ah—the Plags built all this machinery?"

"The Plags organized the nucleus, consisting of planning, engineering, mechanical, energy and operating segments, delineated the ultimate ends desired. Subsidiary elements were conceived by the planning segment, designed by the engineering segment, constructed in the central factory. The entire planet is now noded with various agencies which the planning segment considers useful."

"Why all the blasting? The exploding buildings, the hillsides spitting out fire?"

"Installations benefiting Plags are being destroyed. Destructive agencies exist. Inhibitors formerly restrained them. Now destructive agencies go into effect at random."

Allixter grinned. "The Plags won't like this—will they?"

"Accurate information unavailable."

"How will the Plags fix the machine?"

"No information. As soon as Plags arrive, they are killed."

"How come the natives were waiting for me at the portal?"

"Precise information unavailable. Possibility exists that they dispatched message to Plagigonstok requesting service crew, and were awaiting reply."

"Ah!" Allixter nodded sagely. "How long has the machine been out of order? And why did not the Plag service man repair it at once before it went out completely?"

"When machine is in disrepair, the maintenance unit moves along tracks to the rupture and makes the necessary renewals. The service mechanic never repairs the machine. It is too complex. In this case, the maintenance unit was out of order and the mechanic was occupied in repairing it. The inhibitor circuit fused. The fundamental orders went into effect and the exterminators killed the Plag.''

Allixter sighed. Then, remembering that sighs occupied time, he said, "How can I extend this three-second time limit? I can't stand here forever asking you questions."

"You can supply problems to occupy the perceptors or you can repair either the inhibitor circuit or the maintenance units."

"And while I'm working, you kill me?"

"Yes."

"Why does a chicken cross a road?"

"Presumably the motivations and restraints in reference to the prospective action settle into an equilibrium which prompts the motion rather than the stasis."

"When do two and two make three?"

The voice said, "Perceptors will be occupied with the problem for six minutes. This is the time necessary to explore all possible conditions in all the various regimens of mathematics built into my nucleus."

Allixter glanced at his watch. "Good. I'll have time to think up some corkers in the meantime."

He relaxed, dented his air-film to rub his forehead. Six minutes—would he ever sleep again? And the old life back on Earth! With longing and nostalgia he thought of Buck's Bar at the Hub, the familiar faces around the walnut oval, the glass steins foaming over the top. . . .

He brought himself back to the present. Apparently his future would be occupied in entertaining this planetary computer in puzzles, riddles and mathematical recreations. At least, thought Allixter with a sour grin, he knew how to tie it up for more than three seconds. The thing to do was to get to the source, repair the machine. What the devil was wrong with it? The inhibitor circuit? The maintenance unit? Both out—a sorry situation. The repair system exists to keep the machinery operating but no provision had been made to repair the repair system.

He sauntered across the floor, examined the interior where the side panel had been removed. Complexity upon complexity, unfamiliar shapes, conductors and leads, rank on rank.

There'd be a month's work merely tracing down a corner of the mechanism.

He picked up one of the instruments. My God, thought Allixter, there's some fine equipment here. It's worth a fortune—if I could reproduce this little pocket winch, I could buy Buck's bar.

But this conductor appliance . . . we've got the same thing on Earth. Same design, identical—strange. One of those odd coincidences, when you run back and forth world to world. . . . My God, the time! He looked at his watch. Five seconds.

But he was in no immediate danger; the computer had much to report. "Filed under solubility indices, there exists a number of situations where two units of one substance and two units of another substance, mixed, result in three units of an end substance. These are not rigorous cases and may be dismissed. However in the case of. . . ." The voice droned into mathematical terminology which meant nothing to Allixter.

He listened several minutes but the flow of symbology showed no signs of coming to an end. Attending with half an ear he paced back and forth, examining the hall. The red tiles of the floor were of a rubbery plastic substance, laid with microscopic precision.

Allixter hacked out a sliver with his knife, stuffed it into his pouch. There'd be a fortune in it, back on Earth—plastic to resist fluorine. His fingers hit a hard round object, a familiar shape. He drew it out.

Ah, the little sea-crystal which shone with such intriguing shafts of radiance. Only twenty-four hours before he had picked this little ball off the beach of—what was that planet? —and now. . . . Allixter grinned sourly. A thousand franks a month to nurse a lunatic computer to sanity, to wander a strange gray planet, looking for the doorway back to Earth.

He noticed the door. It hung a trifle ajar. He walked forward to open it. If things got rough he could retreat. The door moved. *Click!*

Allixter cursed. Deceitful little devils! There was silence in the hall. The voice of the Planet Machine had ceased. In its place sounded a sharp hissing.

He twisted anxiously. "What's going on?"

His own voice from the speaker said, "Protective system has been engaged. You are being exterminated by an infusion of pure nitrogen."

"I see," said Allixter. He gingerly felt the surface of his air-film. "I don't care to be killed. Maybe we had better concentrate on—"

An explosion shook the machinery, jarred him from head to foot. Outside he heard the anguished squeaks of the indigenes. "Good God, what's that?"

"The scavenging and rural simplification program, uninhibited by safety precautions, is leveling useless relics of past operations. A great number of fabricating and—" the voice whirred and gurgled. "No word on file for concept. Plag industrial plants are being destroyed. There is no order on file to contravene demolition—"

Allixter said hastily. "For God's sake, don't wreck the transfer. That's my only way home!"

"Orders placed in appropriate file," said the dry voice.

"We'd better get your inhibiting circuit back in order before—" A staccato burst of explosions cut him off short. Allixter continued shakily, "I was going to say, before you do any real harm."

IV

Allixter asked, "What's the fastest way that circuit can be put back in working condition?"

The computer said, "The maintenance unit is designed to adjust, tune, lubricate and replace the worn parts of the circuit in four-point-three-six minutes. A Plag technician can perform the same routine in twenty-six hours."

Allixter scowled at the mobile repair unit. "What's the best way to activate repair machine?"

"No data on extent of damage."

Allixter said sarcastically, "You're a fine computer—don't even know what's going on in front of your nose."

"Machine's optical system cannot penetrate opaque panel." Was there a trace of tartness in the reply?

"Where on the track can you see?"

"Radian two-point-six-seven, as indicated in white characters, is optimum."

Allixter sniffed. "I can't read those characters. They're in Plag graphics."

"Information filed appropriately," came the toneless acknowledgment.

Allixter said, "I'll move the unit—tell me when you register it. In the meantime," he said thoughtfully, "you can compile a list of prime numbers ending in the digits seven-nine-seven."

The speaker made a short bleating sound which once more seemed to carry near-human overtones. Allixter set his shoulder to the mobile unit.

It moved slowly around the track. At last the speaker said, "Optimum." Then, "The list of the first hundred prime numbers is as follows—"

"File them," said Allixter, "Give your attention to this machine. And don't try to kill me while I'm busy. Do you agree to that?"

The toneless voice said, "Protective mechanism acts independently."

"Okay," said Allixter. "You seem to be interested in mathematics. Suppose you make a list of prime numbers which when multiplied by the prime numbers immediately before and after, and the product taken to the sixth power, divided by seven and the remainder dropped, yield a prime number ending in the digits one-one-one."

The speaker stuttered, rumbled briefly, to heavy silence.

"These calculations will be performed," said Allixter, "when your attention is not given to the repair job. Now, what's first?"

"Remove panels from both sides."

Allixter obeyed.

The machine was well-engineered. After a half-hour's work Allixter discovered the cause of the breakdown—a small fused switch.

"Spring back double spirals with tool in corner of tray.

Grip shaft with clamp, turn ninety degrees—prongs will separate, releasing ruptured part."

Allixter did as he was bid and the offending part came loose.

"Module is standardized," said the machine. "Spare switch will be found in third locker at opposite end of hall."

"Keep busy on that little list of numbers while I'm getting the bearing," said Allixter.

"Memory bank is .513 of capacity, now," announced the computer.

"When the unit is full, discharge it and start over."

"Instructions filed."

Allixter crossed the floor, passed the crumpled body of the Plag. In sudden curiosity, he turned it over with his foot, looked down the front. It was definitely human in all the primary characteristics, though the nose and chin were long and gnarled, the skin a peculiar plucked-chicken yellow, the hair like steel-wool. The creature wore a garment of dark green velvet, lustrous and rich.

"That's odd," said Allixter to himself, reaching down, tugging at a small metal loop. "A zipper. First one I've seen on an off-Earth garment. Now if he was only equipped with something *better . . .*"

He stared at the dead Plag, scrutinized the face, the zipper, and then, gingerly searched the body.

There was nothing in the pocket save a pair of small metal objects like keys and what looked like a fiber-bound notebook inscribed with green-black ink. In the pouch were a few small hand-tools.

Allixter, whistling softly, found the switch, returned to the repair unit. "Machine."

"Attending."

"This inhibitory circuit—was it rendered totally inoperative?"

"No."

Allixter waited but the computer, having answered the question, found no reason to expatiate. "I didn't think so. You would need almost as many positive inhibitors as there are possibilities for action. Right?"

"Correct."

"For instance, the inhibitor against killing the native population holds. So does the inhibitor against burning out your own circuits. And it seems that if you really had incentive enough you would find little difficulty killing me. In other words, the mere excition of your perceptor units would not disturb a deep-seated impulse to kill a presumably hostile alien."

The computer asked, "How many times do you wish the memory banks filed with prime numbers ending in one-one-one and discharged?"

"Are you getting bored with the problem?"

"Concept incomprehensible."

"Well—just for the sake of novelty consider each square foot of the planet in sequence, compute the chances of a ten-pound meteor plus or minus six ounces striking each of these square feet in the next ten minutes."

The speaker was silent except for a faint buzzing. Allixter continued with the suspicion which was gradually forming in his mind. It was of such great scope and implication that he found it incredible—at first.

Allixter went back to the corpse, looked in the frozen face once more. He turned toward the speaker. "What sections of the inhibitor are burnt out?"

"Shreds R eight-sixty-six-ninety-two through R Nine-eleven-ninety-one."

"And these refer to the Plags?"

"Yes."

"To such an extent that in the place of the inhibitor preventing you from harming a Plag or a Plag construction you are now more than likely to destroy everything Plag on the planet?"

"Yes."

Allixter mused a moment. "Where is the transfer portal?"

"On the north side of this building, a door of yellow metal opens into a large hall. At the rear of the hall is the terminal."

"What is the setting for Plagi—Plagi—" Allixter shook his head. "The Plag planet?"

"Phase ten, frequencies nine and three."

"In what kind of units?"

"In Plag units."

"Translate these into equivalent Earth units."

"Phase eight-point-four-two, frequencies seven-point-five-eight and two-point-five-three."

"*Ha*," thought Allixter. There'd soon be some surprises in high places. But there was still another aspect to be considered. "What are the dial settings for the Earth station? In English," he added.

"Dial one on top—set at the symbol resembling a B on its flat side. Dial two—set at the symbol resembling N inside oval. Dial three—set at symbol consisting of two concentric triangles."

Allixter jotted co-ordinates onto the Plag notebook, if such it was, and tucked it back into his pouch.

"Now," said Allixter, "I want to excise certain particular inhibitions from your main memory curcuits. What is the easiest method?"

"Beside the panel is a series of symbols and a plunger. Set the keyboard correctly, press the plunger. This act erases significance from the shreds."

"Fine," said Allixter. "Then when the circuits are repaired, they'll be blank but capable of accepting new programs. Correct?"

"Correct."

"Excellent." Allixter went to the dials. "Now show me how to reprogram and issue new instructions."

The computer proscribed the symbols, Allixter repeated the process; time passed in absolute silence.

"Now," he asked, "are those inhibitions permanently erased?"

"Yes."

"And you'll destroy every Plag who sets foot on the planet?"

"Machine has no instructions to the contrary. Plags will be obliterated."

"Can you now self-program from voiced instructions?"

"Yes."

"It is forbidden to kill me."

"Command conflicts with basic order. Command has been held up by monitor circuit."

Allixter gritted his teeth in vexation. "How the devil can I get home then? As soon as I leave you alone you will take steps to kill me."

"Problem contains variables without predictability."

"Thanks for nothing," said Allixter. "In other words, I figure it out for myself. Okay—let's see. You're still working that problem I gave you?"

"Yes."

"How near completion are you?"

"Approximately half finished. Computaton of such material is largely automatic. It is scanning that takes time."

"Hmm." Allixter rubbed his chin through the airfilm. "All right. Acknowledge readiness for new instructions."

"Acknowledged."

"Do not destroy any installation which will harm the natives or interfere with their livelihood."

"Instructions noted."

Now, will I be able to set the transfer to automatic and leave the planet before some other violent action occurs?"

"Problem contains unpredictable variables."

Allixter paced in a circle, thinking. "If I fix the machine's attention, I'll get away. If not, I'm executed as an undesirable alien. Computers should have hobbies, something to keep them occupied, out of mischief. Now maybe. . . ." He hesitated.

He pulled the quartz sphere from his pocket and the little crystalline creature inside glowed, glanced, sparkled in changing colors—hyacinth, rose, sea-green. Allixter set the sphere on the top of a console. "Can you see this little sphere?"

"Yes."

"Do you see its colors?"

"Yes."

"Observe this sphere and its changing colors. This is to be a hobby for you, to amuse you through the lonely hours. You're to observe the patterns of change and then predict the color next to appear. When you err, review your computations, re-observe and predict once more."

"Instructions noted." said the computer.

Allixter touched the smooth quartz ball. "Now, my little jewel, be as erratic as you like. I'll bet on any free-will tippet of life to confuse a machine, no matter how complex and how wise. So shine all your pretty colors and shine 'em as wild and clever as you know how."

The door was still locked. Allixter burnt it open with his laser, stepped out onto the path of stone slats overlooking the hazy gray valley. Overhead blazed the myriad suns—colored balls of various flames, near and far in the violet sky. He stood still for a moment.

"North is up here," said Allixter. "There's the warehouse and there's the golden door. . . ."

V

The depot back at the Hub was quiet when Allixter emerged through the transfer tube. The belts carried only lugs of green-white grapes, and a quantity oxygen—bound for a mining station on an ore-rich asteroid.

Allixter ducked past the dispatcher's office but Schmitz spotted him, slid back the panel. "Hey, Scotty," he bellowed. "Come back here and turn in your report. You think this is Liberty Hall? Can't you read the rules?"

Allixter paused, then turned back.

"Here," said Schmitz, tossing over a yellow form. "Fill this out—and do it without me riding herd on you. I got my job to handle, too. You guys run me ragged, ducking in, ducking out. Then when they come and ask me who's been where and who's done which—"

"Look here, Sam," said Allixter, "I want to use your phone."

Schmitz looked up in surprise. "Go ahead, use it. I don't care. Just so long as you file the right papers. Use my phone, anything . . . My God, man! Where's the Conceptualizer? The Chief will kill us if—"

"I left it in the depot." Allixter thumbed through the

directory. He looked up. Schmitz was watching him intently, bright blue eyes gleaming in the round red face.

Allixter closed the book. "No, I think I'll wait. Good day to you, Sam Schmitz."

"*Hey!*" roared Schmitz. "The report!"

"I'll be back shortly."

"When's shortly? Don't forget, I'm responsible for all this. It's me who gets reamed when you guys goof off. . . ."

Allixter said in a voice like silk, "Give me fifteen minutes, Sammy dear. I'll write you a report you'll wish you could take home and frame." He walked quickly past.

Forty minutes passed. Schmitz fidgeted, growled out loud, looked through his assignment sheet. "That damn Allixter, he's the worst. . . . Hey now, I believe he's back."

The four men with Allixter wore gray uniforms and looked curiously alike. All were tall, spare of form, controlled of motion. Their faces were uniformly blunt, their eyes sharp and probing, their mouths tight.

"Good God!" barked Schmitz. "It's World Security Intelligence. Now what's Allixter gone and done?" Automatically he reached for the intercom to the Chief's phone.

"*Hold it,* Schmitz!" yelled Allixter. "Leave that phone alone!"

One of the WSI men opened the door into Schmitz's cubicle, motioned. "I think you'd better come with us."

Protesting volubly. Schmitz followed, hopping and bounding on his short legs to keep pace. The WSI men stood, two on each side of the big green door with the bronze letters. Allixter pushed the button, the door slid back, he entered. The secretary looked up. Allixter said, "Tell the Chief I'm back."

She hesitantly pushed the button. "Scotty Allixter reporting."

There was a pause. "Send him in."

She keyed back the lock. Allixter stepped to the inner door. The WSI men entered the office behind him. One strode to the desk where the secretary had made a swift movement for the speaker controls, caught her arm.

Allixter slid back the door. The room's air, smelling like a laboratory, wafted in his face. He entered with the WSI platoon at his back.

The Chief, sitting at his desk, his back to the light, stirred a trifle, then sat quiet. "What does this mean?" he asked tonelessly.

The WSI lieutenant said, "You're under arrest."

"On what grounds?"

"Grand theft and espionage, to begin with. There may be further charges when a complete investigation is made."

"Do you have a warrant?"

"In my hand."

"Let's see it," said the Chief in a flat voice.

The lieutenant stepped forward with a blue-bound folder. The Chief glanced at the printed page, his mouth curled sardonically. Allixter thought—all the years I've come into this office, talked with the man, been intimidated by him, and only now I see him as he is, a creature of an outer world with yellow goose-flesh skin and a breath of poisonous vapor.

Allixter suddenly noted that the atmosphere, characteristically sharp and medicinal, had acquired a new harsh bite. He yelled, "Gas! Clear out, the devil's poisoning us!"

The Chief moved swiftly now, jumped to his feet.

The Lieutenant came forward. "Stop, or I'll shoot you."

Allixter flung the door wide and saved his life. From the edge of the alien's desk a plane of smoky yellow fire slashed out, burnt four men in half. Allixter stumbled back from the crackling ions which, deflected by the metal wall, seared past inches from his waist.

Allixter was weaponless. He ran to the secretary's phone. She pressed back against the wall, numb with shock. Allixter pushed the emergency button, bellowed, "Murder, the tube terminal maintenance office—" He heard stealthy motion inside the Chief's office, looked desperately toward the outer door. To escape, he would have to cross the line of fire from the inner office.

Slow footsteps from inside were approaching cautiously. The Chief was edging close to the far wall on the opposite side of the doorcase. Allixter pushed the button, the door slid shut. As he dashed for the outer door, a Jar spat behind him and the wall beyond the corridor shattered.

Allixter ran across the corridor into the quiet depot. He ducked between fifty gallon drums of acetone, sprang across the clerks' platform, jumped up into the operator's box.

Breathless, fighting to make himself speak slowly and distinctly, he said, "This is a WSI emergency . . . Open the in-contacts, set this code—phase eight-point-four-two, frequencies seven-point-five-eight and two-point-five-three."

The operator stared at him. "What the hell kind of code is that? I never heard—"

"Shut *up!*" yelled Allixter. "Set the code! And route whatever you get into depot delivery."

The operator shrugged, set the coordinates. "Eight-point-four-two—what was those other readings?"

"Seven-five-eight! Two-five-three!"

The operator pushed the activation switch. Allixter jumped down to the shimmering amber curtain, at the point where the belt rolled up out of the floor.

Ten seconds . . . fifteen seconds. He stared into the flickering light, until—motion. The Chief appeared, looking over his shoulder. He turned his head, his mouth fell open.

Allixter jumped, caught him from behind, flung him to the belt. The Chiefs gun thudded free. Allixter seized it, rose to his feet.

"Chief," Allixter whispered, "I'm going to introduce you to something called the Planet Machine."

VI

Allixter was the center of a respectful audience in Buck's Bar. Beer flowed freely, the finest imports from Germany and the Netherlands.

The story had been told several times but among the audience were those to whom some feature of the episode was not completely clear. Of these, Sam Schmitz was the most insistent.

"Allixter, look here," he said plaintively, "how could you be so sure it was the Chief? I don't see how you figured it."

"Look at it this way, Sam." Allixter refreshed his throat with a half-pint of Hochstein Lager. "I was sent out on a phony call. For awhile after I landed on that planet, I thought it was an honest mistake. But a lot of little peculiarities kept nagging at me. The Chief insisted I take the Conceptualizer. Why would I need one on Rhetus? The answer was the Chief knew I'd be running into natives who spoke from under their arms.

"Then why did he make sure my airfilm was Type X, halogen-proof? Because he knew the atmosphere where I'd be going was full of fluorine. And when I saw the dead Plag on the floor, I was bothered by a few things. He was dressed in clothes with an Earth-style zipper. Not only *like* Earth-style, but a zipper identical in every respect."

"Might have been coincidence," said Buck, the red-faced bartender.

Allixter nodded. "Might have been. But how about the pen the guy wrote with? When I saw all these items lying around, I thought to myself, there's been some kind of contact with Earth. And it's been one-way because I knew I'd never seen any long-nosed yellow Plags on Earth.

"And then I thought of the Chief. He looked a lot like the corpse. I remembered other peculiarities. Then when the computer told me that it killed Plags automatically, I figured everything out."

"So?" asked Schmitz.

"The Plags wanted to keep the transfer station open to the planet—I don't know what their name for the place is. I wouldn't be surprised if they operated a number of these subsidiary worlds, equipped with master computers, milking each planet and shipping the produce to . . . Plagigonstok.

"Well, the computer was programmed to kill Plags as soon as they appeared. So it was necessary to get a mechanic of another race in to fix the computer. I was the lad."

"Sounds like a case of last resort," growled Buck.

Allixter spread his hands. "What could they lose? Either I'd fix their computer or I'd be killed. So they made contact with the Chief, told him to send his best mechanic."

Schmitz thoughtfully lifted his glass to drink, found it

empty. "How come you knew the code the Chief would try to escape on?"

Allixter cocked his thick black eyebrows knowingly. "I asked the computer what the code was. He gave it to me and I knew it wasn't on our list—wasn't even in our units. The Plags evidently had discovered the transfer system independently and set up a network of their own. Somehow they discovered our set-up and smuggled in a representative, who became the Chief. Maybe there's more of them around."

"How did the Chief breathe?" said Bernard. "This kind of air should have smothered him."

Allixter drained his stein before replying. Buck slid it back brimming with foam. Allixter asked, "Did you ever notice the scar on the Chief's neck?"

"Sure. Nasty thing."

"That was no scar. That was a breather tube, running under his skin into his throat. It supplied him with fluorine, carried hydrofluoric acid gas back to a filter for absorption. Not that our air would hurt him, but it wouldn't do him any good."

Barnard struck the bar with his fist. "I always claimed the Chief's office smelled like a hospital!"

Schmitz said dolefully, "I wonder what's going to happen now?"

"Well," said Allixter, "they've been robbing us blind, those Plags. Our ideas, tools, techniques—all going out. That's not so bad in itself but we were getting none of their stuff in return.

"That was the Chief's function. Send out merchandise—from the transfer depot when no one else was around, or out the private hatch in his office—pay for it in platinum or uranium the Plags mined cheaply on some mechanical planet. Or maybe with counterfeit money. The WSI says they found a case of brand new hundredfrank notes in the Chief's office."

"So that's who's been flooding my till!" roared Buck. "I've lost a thousand franks in those bills!" The enormity of the Chief's crimes now seemed to dawn upon him.

"Tough," said Allixter in a faraway voice. "He cost me five hundred franks too, when I had to leave that valuable little jewel behind. But I happened to pick up this rare and lovely scarab. Prime yellow fluorspar, a beautiful piece, and it's the sacred seal of the indigenes. There's only one like it. The Curator of the Out-world Museum offered me eight hundred franks for it, but I'd have to wait a month for his purchase order. Buck, I'll let you have it for six hundred, today."

Buck picked up the octahedron. "Sacred seal? Looks like a lot of chicken-scratches. I'll give you five franks for it; maybe I can unload it on a drunk for ten."

Allixter rescued the fluorspar with an expression of hurt indignation. "Five franks? I'd sell you my right ear first!"

Crusade to Maxus

I

THE FORTIFIED STATION hung ten miles above Maxus—a heavy white ring a mile in diameter, beaded with observation windows. Across the thin air every detail was sharp, clear, distinct.

There was no immediate challenge to Travec's ship. He waited, half-crouched over the controls, glancing out to the station, back to the transcom, out to the station. A minute—two minutes. . . .

He swore silently, flipped the switch on the communicator, spoke for the second time into the mesh. "Visitor's permit eleven-A-five hundred and six. . . . I want to pass down. . . . Send me instructions—a signal, an acknowledgment."

A voice rattled back. "Permit is being checked. Await our orders."

Travec sank back into the seat, then stood up and looked down at the city of Alambar. Out to the horizon and beyond, the metropolis spread, a figured rug of somber colors—tarnished greens and blacks, dark russets and ochers, gray of smoke and concrete and brick.

Directly below him, three leaden rivers merged and puddled into a lake of quicksilver, which was surrounded, overshadowed by the great administration buildings, the palaces and townhouses of the Overmen. Elevated roads straddled the city like exposed veins; everywhere there was a ceaseless twinkling of motion.

Travec stared indecisively across space to the inspection port. He might pull the ship down, ram through the shield, plow across the city. Line up the Lords of Maxus, rip their faces, gut their bellies. . . .

"Eleven-A-five hundred and six," said the speaker, "approach Stage Six, prepare to receive an inspection team."

Travec leapt for the seat, sent the ship forward. A series of flat bays edged the inner periphery of the station. Travec settled to the stained concrete of the bay marked 6. Three men in suits appeared, rapped at the outer port. Travec admitted them—hard-faced men, black-haired, gaunt, pale, wearing black uniforms and pointed leather caps.

The corporal stepped up on the control deck—a man with a long narrow face, hollow cheeks, hooked nose. "Let's look at your permit."

Travec gave him the paper. The corporal curled his lip as he read, "Planet of origin—Exar. Bond posted—ten thousand sil. Intended duration of visit—one week. Motive for visit—" His eyebrows rose. "Oh, well," he said indulgently, "good luck."

Travec said nothing.

"You'll be chasing Arman's load."

"Yes."

"Should have made it here sooner," said the corporal. He tossed the permit to the chart table. "Everything's in order." He looked down at his two men, who were returning from the after section. "How's it look?"

"Clean."

The corporal nodded. The two men left the ship.

The corporal leaned across the table. "A man on your kind of errand carries money. And he's in a hurry. I'd like to help you but there's a field keeper who's asleep and won't be waked without a growl—unless I bring him something. And naturally, if he doesn't open the field, you don't get down."

Travec pressed his lips together. "How much?"

"Oh—two hundred sil."

Travec turned his back, pulled certificates from a billfold. "Here's two hundred."

"Five minutes and you'll be down," said the corporal. "Go to the landing port just beyond the park. Who is it, your wife?"

"My mother, two sisters, a brother."

The corporal whistled between his teeth. "You must be a millionaire." He hesitated, glanced down at Travec's pocket.

"I'm not," snapped Travec. "And I'm in a hurry."

"You're probably too late, if it's Arman's load. Now watch that globe. When the light goes on drop down through, descend vertically to an altitude of thirty thousand, then you're on your own. Don't veer off any higher, or the field will burn you."

Travec forced the ship to a grinding halt. He opened the port, leapt out into air that smelled of smoldering stone and smoke. He ran to a portal of black brick that opened on a narrow street, passed through, stiffened, leapt back to avoid a whirring vehicle. He hesitated a few seconds, cautiously scanning the barren street.

Passers-by—tall hatchet-faced people, dark and saturnine— stared at him with bright curiosity. He heard a child in a maroon jacket pipe, "Look at the Orth. He's got no mark!"

And Travec heard a subdued hiss, "Shh!—no one's bought him yet."

He approached an old man in a close-fitting black jumper. "Where is the Slave Distribute, please? How do I get there?"

The man eyed him a long moment, then said in a flat voice, "Take the strip, follow the red-and-green band. When you pass the second tunnel you'll find a brown concrete building to your right."

"Thank you." Travec turned, crossed the street, stepped aboard the strip. Varicolored stripes of light lay on the surface. He found the red-and-green band, walked forward as swiftly as traffic would permit.

The red-and-green band edged to the side. Travec followed. The strip split, his band entered a narrow tunnel that smelled of ammonia and coal-gas. There was a period of echoing darkness, then he was out once more into daylight.

Tall steep-gabled residences lined the strip, complex structures fronted by columns of polished stone—carnelian, jasper, onyx. A mile; two miles—then the strip swung away from the townhouses, circled a hill of decaying shale, led up a slope lined with food markets. The air smelled sharply of dried fish, vinegar, fruit.

Travec lengthened his stride, broke into a trot. The strip led up to a steep-faced embankment, plunged into another tunnel. Time seemed interminable. Travec extended his trot to a run. He collided with a tall figure in the dark, ignored the harsh curses, ran on.

A faint patch of light appeared. He was out under the hazy sky of Maxus. To his right rose a huge brown block of concrete, windowless, blank-faced. As Travec approached, a shuttered airship left the roof, floated off on its shimmering field of force.

Travec watched it lift off, in an agony of frustration. He saw the street-level door before him and approached, panting and out of breath. A guard in a black leather uniform stepped out, barred his way.

"Your pass."

"I don't have a pass. I just arrived on the planet."

"No matter. No one gets in here without a pass signed by the High Commissioner."

Travec leaned forward, half-lowered his head. The guard leaned against the wall, laughed quietly, slapped a hand on the weapon against his black-clad leg.

"The gate is locked. Tear it down with your fingernails if you care to."

Travec said hoarsely, "Where is the High Commissioner?"

The guard said, "His headquarters are in the Guchman Arch." He motioned to the strip. "Go back the way you came, change at Bosfor Strall to the orange and brown. If you hurry you might still be able to make an appointment." His mouth twisted in a cadaverous grin.

"Now if I were you, I'd give myself away—to a man like me. The High Commissioner's got an agile mind. He might think up some real unpleasantness. But I'd sell you to a high-class lord for kitchen duty. You have my word."

Travec's temples throbbed. He eyed the guard's face, then turned, walked back to the strip.

The High Commissioner sat half-reclining in a crimson-furred seat, twisting a milk-blue goblet between his fingers. He was needle-thin with black hair pasted in a pointed lock down his forehead. His eyelids hung in a supercilious droop, his nose cut his face like a sickle, his skin was the color and texure of eggshell. He wore a robe of grass-green silk and a huge ruby dangled on a golden chain from one ear.

After a slow scrutiny of Travec, he indicated a seat. Travec sat down.

"What is your business?" asked the High Commissioner courteously.

"I want a pass into the Slave Distribute. I'm in a hurry, I've got to return at once to be in time."

The High Commissioner nodded. "Of course. Relatives? Wife?"

Travec said, "My mother, my two sisters, my brother."

"A blow, a blow indeed," said the High Commissioner, sipping from the goblet. "I can appreciate your desire for haste. Especially if they were in the load brought in by—let's see, his name is. . . ."

"Arman."

"Arman. Correct. A new dealer, very successful." He leaned back in his seat. "I fear you are too late."

"I'm sure to be," muttered Travec, "unless I get back."

The High Commissioner smiled faintly, scribbled on a card, tossed it to him. "There you are. After your visit, please stop by again, I would like to speak with you further."

Night seeped down like murky water, and the lights of Alambar glowed white and yellow. A chilling wind cut into Travec's cheek as for the second time he approached the Slave Distribute.

The guard raised his black eyebrows at the sight of the pass, turned it over between his fingers.

"Hurry, man!" yelled Travec.

The guard shrugged, spoke into a cell at his back.

The door opened. Travec was in a small room without apparent exit. He sensed an inspection—rays searching for weapons, explosives, drugs. The end of the room snapped aside. He stepped out into a bright corridor, asked a woman at a desk, "Where is the buyers' chamber?"

"At the end of the corridor. The inspection chambers are to your right as you pass through."

Travec ran down the corridor. He passed through an opaque air curtain and found himself in a large room. An old man in a glistening apricot surcoat surveyed him. "Pass, please."

Travec showed it to him. "Has the load Arman brought from Exar gone yet?"

The old man shrugged, wheezed, "They come, they go. I believe we processed such a listing this morning."

Travec leaned forward, his face livid. "I've got to find out!" He reached to seize the old man's shoulder, remembered his precarious standing as a permit visitor, stood back. "Where can I make sure?"

The old man, who had started to rise, waved his hand. "Over there is the listing bill, with descriptions. The material yet unsold is confined in the inspection chambers."

Travec crossed the room. To his left was a line of couches upholstered with soft leather. Here a number of the Overmen sat at ease, consulting lists, drinking from heavy goblets, talking. The arena before them was vacant at the moment.

Travec found the postings, ran his fingers down the lists for the day. Near the bottom, heavily marked with different colors, he found what he sought:

NEW SHIPMENT FROM EXAR

Prime material, handsome and healthy, from the salubrious Principian Peninsula.

No.	Name	Sex	Age	Remarks	Minimum Bid
1	Vitaly Galwane	F	4	Cheerful, attentive	M 600
2	Donal Carrius	M	4	Intelligent	400
3	Rabald Retts	M	5	Quick to learn	200
4	Glee Kerlo	F	8	Will grow to beauty	1000
5	Temmi Helva	M	9	A lovely well-shaped lad	2800
6	Jonalisma Stanisius	F	9	Obedient, sweet tempered	1000

Most of the names had heavy checks in blue crayon before them; these had been sold, Travec assumed. He ran his finger down the list:

| 29 | Lenni Travec | F | 14 | Fresh as a flower | 5000 |

A heavy blue check preceded her name. Breath rasped in his throat. Pale, staring-eyed, he continued.

| 64 | Thalla Travec | F | 18 | Exquisite | 5000 |

No check—blankness. He read on.

| 115 | Gray Travec | M | 21 | Metallurgical engineer | 3000 |

A blue check. Travec licked his dry lips. Now far down the list:

| 427 | Iardeth Travec | F | 58 | Pleasant, charming | 300 |

The name had been untidily scratched out—Travec had almost missed it. After the name, the word *Dead* was scribbled.

Travec stared, head swimming. There was a noise behind him, voices, a shuffle of feet, a crackle of laughter.

"Six thousand five hundred," said a voice, "and I hear sixty-six—sixty six—sixty-six—sixty-seven. . . . My lords, my lords, a delicate bit of flesh. Speak, sirs, speak! Sixty-eight—sixty-nine—sixty-nine—ah, seven thousand from Lord Erulite. Seven thousand—seven thousand—is that all, my lords? You there, my Lord Spangle? No? *Sold,* to Lord Erulite for seven thousand sil. Sold, I say.''

Travec swung around, saw his sister naked on the floor. Her purchaser, a tall stout man of early middle age with a fleshy nose, a head half-bald, a complexion of purplish-pink, was circling her, evidently pleased with his possession.

Travec yelled, *"Thalla!"*

Lord Erulite looked up; the auctioneer turned a startled glance across the floor as Travec ran forward.

"Dyle! Did they get you too?"

Travec thrust himself past the glowering Erulite, put his arms around the girl. She was trembling, panting.

Travec said, "I came as fast as I could, to get you both."

Thalla said, "Dyle, mother died this morning." She cried silently on his shoulder.

Travec turned to Lord Erulite, who stood scowling nearby. "Sir, this is my sister. Will you kindly permit me to pay the auction price and take her home?"

Lord Erulite grew red in the face. Finally he said, "She is now my property. I do not care to part with her. I acquired her legitimately. . . ."

Travec said, "Sir, I beg you not to take this poor girl away from me. I came eighteen light years to find her and the others of my family."

A voice from behind said, "Don't let the Orth wheedle you, Erulite. You've bought and paid for her."

Lord Erulite flung out his chest. "Stand aside stranger. Be discreet."

The same voice from the crowd called, "Orth, you're here on visitor's permit. If you so much as violate a traffic law, you can be seized and sold."

Thalla said in a small voice, dead and bloodless, "Dyle, it's no use."

"Lord Erulite," said Travec, "I'll pay you ten thousand sil for my sister."

Erulite stepped to the side, the better to examine his purchase.

"Not on your life," he said in a complacent voice. "Not for fifteen thousand. I doubt if I'd sell for twenty thousand."

Travec said, "I'll give you fourteen thousand cash and my bond for seven thousand."

Erulite scowled in sudden fury. "Away with you and your propositions!"

Thalla pressed close to Travec. She was cold, tense, quivering. He felt her tears on his neck. "I'm sorry, Thalla!" he muttered bleakly.

Thalla stirred, drew in a deep sobbing breath. "Dyle, you can't help me now. Be careful."

He laughed hollowly.

"Dyle, don't," she whispered. "Your life's ahead of you and maybe . . . you can help someone else." She swallowed hard. "There's another girl—they've been saving for last. She took care of mother. She gave me all her food. Dyle, if you could help her. . . ."

"I'll try, Thalla. Where is mother?"

Thalla closed her eyes tight. "They carried her out. They put her in a room they call the Abattoir. It's for dead people— and for killing too, I guess. . . ."

Travec's eyes felt like balls of fire. He could not speak.

II

Erulite took hold of Thalla's shoulder, pulled her away. "Enough, enough, this scene is most affecting. It can't go on any longer."

Thalla shuddered under his grasp, pulled away. He looked at her sharply. "None of that, young woman, you're my property now. You'll find I'm a kind master if you make my will your own. Now go to the waiting room while I finish here."

He turned away. Travec stood still. Someone in the crowd spoke harshly to Erulite, who declared loudly, "Well, then, I'll take her myself." He bellowed to the auctioneer, "When do you bring forth this flower you praise so highly?"

"In a short time, my lord—twenty minutes."

He said to Thalla, "Come, we go to the registrar." He walked through a portal. Thalla followed him, looking wretchedly back at Travec. He took a short step after her, stopped, then followed.

The corridor passed the inspection chambers; Thalla paused by a window. "There she is, Dyle—the girl in the corner. Her name is Mardien."

Travec saw a girl in a light blue smock, leaning against the wall. She was looking at her hands, touching one with the other, and her expression was rapt, almost blank. As they watched, she moved her head and a lock of pale hair slipped along her cheek.

"Come!" called Erulite from down the hall. "I have little leisure."

They continued slowly.

At an iron door in the wall, Thalla stopped. "Here is the room they call the Abattoir—and in there is our mother."

Travec's hand went out as if impelled by a force past his will. He pushed. The door swung in. Icy air gushed out around their knees. Thalla gave a deep sigh, swayed into the room like a somnambulist. Travec followed stiffly.

The room was walled with dark brown brick, the ceiling was arched and buttressed. To the right was a square cockpit filled with a sump. It was freshly washed down but water had not rinsed stains from the brick. At the other end was a casual stack of corpses.

Thalla sat grotesquely down on the brick, buried her head on her knees. Travec stood unable to move. Somewhere in the stack of dead flesh lay something he had loved. Best now to leave it stay—best to turn away, turn his gaze toward the man who had brought them here—Arman.

A rough impatient voice said, "Come, come, come—at *once*!"

Snarling, Travec sprang forward. He threw a terrible blow at the purple-pink face. Erulite jumped back, mouth in a loose fleshy circle. Travec's fist struck his shoulder, glanced to his neck.

Erulite croaked in anger, "Damned Orth, now I'll kill you!" He clapped his hand to the back of his belt, hitched loose a gun. Travec stepped close, swung a heavy fist into

Erulite's side as he fired. Energy scorched here and there around the room. Corpses quivered, jerked.

Travec closed in, flailed aside Erulite's arm, grappled his throat. The white beam bit the floor, spat along the ceiling.

The gun fell from Lord Erulite's flexing fingers, his body squirmed and jerked. Eventually, it lost mobility, relaxed. Travec released his grip, rose panting to his feet. "Thalla—"

Thalla was dead. A deep black stripe ran diagonally down her face where the gun had struck.

Travec stood stiffly, arms held away from his sides. He looked up at the ceiling, around the walls. Slowly, laboriously, like an old man, he reached down, picked up Erulite's gun, pocketed it. . . . A thud of footsteps sounded, loud voices in the hall. Travec looked up, head thrust out in a feral pose, wild as a wolf.

The sounds passed the door, which had swung shut on Erulite's entry, died in the distance.

"Why not?" Travec inquired, of the dank room and the corpses. "It will be a good life. Killing monsters. . . ."

He turned, picked up the body of his young sister, laid it gently beside the others.

Now Erulite. The embroidered jacket, flame-red, was conspicuous. Travec ripped it off the meaty back. He felt a hard object in a pocket, pulled it out: Erulite's money-case. Inside was a neat sheaf of thousand-sil notes. Travec pocketed the money, tossed the case into a hopper. Erulite's clothes followed, then Travec dragged his corpse to the stack.

He slid out into the corridor, returned to the auction room. No one noticed his entrance. All eyes were on the arena, on the girl being sold by the auctioneer.

". . .you gentlemen are too cautious!" said the auctioneer, "These bids are ridiculously conservative; you will hurt this exquisite creature's feelings. Seven thousand, says my Lord Spangle. Now—ah, Lord Jonas, seven thousand five hundred. . . . Is there other money? Lord Hennex, seven thousand six hundred. Come, come, sires, who'll say eight thousand?"

"Seven thousand seven hundred," said the hoarse voice. Travec placed it as the property of Lord Spangle, a thin stooped man with sparse black hair, a loose jowl, an enormous beak of a nose.

Travec came slowly up close. The girl Mardien looked at him. She is indeed beautiful, thought Travec, and intelligent.

Mardien wore a set expression, neither frightened nor angry. She seemed a bystander, rather than an object on sale.

"Seven thousand eight hundred," said Lord Jonas.

"Eight thousand," said Lord Spangle.

The auctioneer relaxed, became bland. The pattern was clear. Low bids at first, the customers feigning disinterest. Small chance of the merchandise going cheaply.

"Eight thousand one hundred," piped a voice from the end of the room.

"Eight thousand two hundred," returned Lord Jonas.

"Gentlemen, my lords," begged the auctioneer, "let us proceed faster. Nine thousand, do I hear nine thousand?"

"Nine thousand," piped the voice.

"Nine thousand one hundred," said Lord Spangle.

"Who'll say nine thousand five hundred? Nine thousand five hundred? Nine thousand five hundred?"

"Ten thousand," said Travec in a flat voice.

"Ah—good there, sir. Ten thousand, ten thousand, ten thousand—"

The girl had turned her head at Travec's voice. He met her eyes, sensed the flavor of her personality—fruit, wine, perfume, rain. She looked away.

Spangle said in his hoarse voice, "It's the Orth. Damned outrage, letting them in here to bid!"

"Should be on the block himself," muttered Lord Jonas. "I'd buy him if it cost my last ana, the savage. I'd work him in the sulfur banks till he was yellow as Ollifans' coat."

"Ten thousand—ten thousand—ten thousand," yelped the auctioneer.

"Ten thousand five hundred," said Lord Spangle.

"Good, my Lord," cried the auctioneer. "Now there's ten thousand five hundred. And who'll pay what this blossom is worth in sheer joy alone? Who'll say eleven thousand?"

"Eleven thousand," said Travec.

"Eleven thousand five hundred," said Spangle. "Curse it, I should have had her for eight."

"Eleven thousand six hundred," said Travec.

Jonas nudged Spangle. "He's weakening, he's short. Eleven thousand seven hundred will take her."

"Eleven thousand seven hundred," said Spangle.

"Twelve thousand," said Travec.

"Twelve thousand," cried the auctioneer happily. "Twelve thousand, I hear!"

"Thirteen thousand," came the piping voice from the end of the hall.

Travec's mind raced. He had sold the family's holdings on Exar, he had slaughtered the herds, sold what jewels and artifacts he possessed—and had made up a total of forty one thousand sil. Eleven thousand had bought his ship, there had been a bond of ten thousand sil, many other expenses. He estimated his cash at fifteen thousand. He said, "Thirteen thousand one hundred."

Spangle growled, "The Orth is inflating values. Such is the case when we permit them to buy back their kin. I'll say thirteen thousand two hundred if I have to pawn my crest."

"Fourteen thousand," came the high-pitched voice.

"Fourteen thousand one hundred," roared Spangle desperately.

"Fifteen thousand," said Travec.

"Fifteen thousand—fifteen thousand—fifteen thousand!" cried the auctioneer. "Do I hear sixteen?"

Spangle sat heavily down on the seat.

"Fifteen thousand one hundred," he muttered.

Travec found it hard to think. Forty one thousand. One thousand for a visitor's permit, the five hundred bribe, two thousand for fuel, one thousand for charts and stores, the two hundred sil squeeze to the corporal in the fort—fourteen thousand sil he still owned.

Failure again—he turned his head away from the questioning glance of the auctioneer. An outlander bidding past his means was no doubt guilty of a misdemeanor, might be seized and sold. And the bidding was already too high for him.

He could sell his space-boat—but that would hardly help him now. He noticed the glances stealing in his direction. Triumph, malice, distaste—feeling for his money-case, his hand came in contact with an unfamiliar bulk: Erulite's money.

"Fifteen thousand five hundred," he said.

There was silence. Then the auctioneer said, "Fifteen thousand five hundred has been bid. . . ."

Spangle cursed, softly, thickly.

"Fifteen thousand five hundred—who'll say sixteen thousand? You sir? *You*, Lord Jonas? Lord Hennex? Lord Spangle? Sixteen thousand? No? . . . Sold then, sold, she's yours, sir, this precious yellow-haired jewel."

Travec spoke no word to the girl. He paid the money to Ollifans, the old man in the apricot surcoat, received a pink certificate of ownership.

Ollifans thumbed through a file. "Her penal frequency is twenty-six and seven hundred thirty-three thousandths megacycles. I'll write it on the certificate."

"Penal frequency? What's that?"

Ollifans chuckled. "I forgot. You're an Orth. Unsophisticated. A circuit is blasted into the skin of her pretty back—a web of conductive dust that resonates at frequency.

"If she's lost and you would find her, send out a signal at the right frequency, and it'll bounce back her whereabouts to you. If she's insolent and lazy and won't stand still for a beating, tune up the signal strength and the mesh will heat and then she'll know where authority lies."

Ollifans shoved his fingers through loops on his apricot-golden jacket, leaned back, nodded pompously. Travec opened his mouth to speak—closed it, said finally, "Tell me, who bought these two persons?" He indicated numbers twenty-nine and one hundred fifteen on the bill—his brother and sister.

Ollifans wrinkled his brow, pursed his mouth. "That is forbidden information."

"How much?" Travec asked, grinning like a mask of carved wood.

Ollifans hesitated. Travec placed five hundred sil on the desk.

"A thousand," said Ollifans.

Travec laid down another five hundred.

"What's going on here?" demanded a hoarse voice. Lord Spangle appeared, his eyes darting from the money to Travec and Ollifans. "Do I detect the bribing of a Distribute servant? If so—"

"No, no, my lord," protested Ollifans, drawing the money to the pouch at his belt. "A gratuity, my lord, only a gratuity. As you are aware, I am incorruptible."

Lord Spangle turned to Travec. "Be off with you then, you money-dripping Orth."

Travec slowly turned toward the door.

"Now, Jonas," said Spangle in a grumbling tone, "if that lax fellow Erulite would return as he promised, we'd be away."

As they passed out the door Mardien said hesitantly, "He called you an Orth. Are you an outlander then?"

Travec said, "Do I resemble one of these Overmen?"

"No—very little."

"I came from the Great Farees Island on Exar," said Travec. "To buy my mother, my two sisters and my brother. I failed. My mother and one sister are dead. My brother and my younger sister are sold—as good as dead. The sister that is dead, Thalla—"

Mardien shot him a puzzled glance. "Thalla—*dead*?"

"Yes," said Travec. "She asked me to buy you and return you home. I will do that if I can."

She turned away. "Oh!"

Travec looked at her sharply. The tone in her voice was not exultation. Was it sadness at Thalla's death—or disappointment?

She said slowly, "I thought you bought me because—you needed a slave."

"No," said Travec. "I need no slaves. As soon as we leave the planet—and we're leaving tonight." He glanced behind. There was no excitement. Erulite's body still lay in the Abattoir—"I'll tear up this certificate. Until then—I might need to show proof of possession."

They came to the woman at the desk. She glanced at the certification, punched a button. The partition snapped aside.

They passed out into the cold damp night of Maxus. Travec breathed deeply. Out here he could at least run.

Three of the five moons had risen and the stern buildings of Alambar were hoary and frosted in the white light.

Mardien shivered. Her light smock was hardly warm. Travec unclipped his cape, threw it around her shoulders.

Mardien said in a withdrawn tone, "I don't want to leave Maxus."

"*What!*"

"I have a mission here."

Travec felt a sudden heady anger.

"What mission is this?"

She said in the same abstract voice, "A private matter."

Travec turned away. "Private or not, you're coming away."

She gave him a long cool glance that seemed to say, "You failed to help your own family—so I must be dragged away to soothe your ego."

Travec said sharply, "Where is your home?"

"It's not on Exar."

"Where then?"

Her constrained manner nearly slipped away. For an instant her expression revealed an inner world of fire and feeling of gorgeous color masked. Then she turned away.

"I won't tell you that."

III

This was just fine, thought Travec. Ingratitude, perversity—how did the quotation go?—woman is thy world-shape. Devil take her then! He'd drop her at the first civilized planet and consider his duty done.

Then—his life was still before him. How easy and broad it seemed now! No ambiguities, no vacillations, the future was fixed. First—and Travec smiled a wide smile that showed his teeth—first Arman. *Arman!*

He knitted his brow. But who was this monster? Mardien might know. As the strip bore them through the tunnel, now dim-lit in blue, he asked, "You must have seen Arman, the slaver?"

She stiffened. "Yes."

"What is he like?"

Her voice at first was guarded. "He is a magnificent man. As young as you, taller, a head—oh, marvellous! Like Penthe's dream. His voice is clear and beautiful. He stands on the deck of his ship like a god."

Travec's mouth twisted askew. "You sound like you admire him."

She was silent a moment. Then, "You don't know him?"

"I intend to know him," said Travec. "Very well indeed. And he will know me, too. Mine will be the last face he looks on."

She withdrew into herself. Travec hardly noticed her disdainful toss of head. How to find Arman? How to look through the north end of the galaxy with its half billion stars.

One man on Maxus would know Arman's whereabouts— the High Commissioner. And the High Commissioner had suggested a second interview.

Travec's mind churned. They swept out of the tunnel, down the slope lined with the food markets, now shuttered for the night. A great black cat scuttled ahead of them down the strip. Through trees to their left came the metallic glint of the three moons on one of Alambar's rivers.

Travec tried to arrange the elements of the situation into a pattern. Erulite's body would soon be discovered. Then the hunt would begin. And if he were caught they would not waste him at an execution. He would be assigned to a gang in the lead mines under the Sraban Ice-cap. He would never see the sky again. Therefore—leave Maxus while there was still time.

Still, Arman must be located. The High Commissioner might know where to look, but would he talk? A successful slaver was an asset to the Overmen of Maxus.

Then there was Mardien. He glanced at her sidelong, saw the glint of her eyes flashing away. She had been watching him. He felt the tingle of her nearness—disturbing, distracting. Her beauty was more than conformation of bone and flesh. It was a witchery of the mind. She was a nymph-thing, a creature of silk and dreams and the pale night-lotus.

Could he take her on his ship and not fall prey to her charms? And if he forgot his mission, forgot his promise to Thalla. . . . Mardien was technically his slave. What if she resisted him?

With an effort, he wrenched his mind away. Damned woman! What did she want on Maxus? Arman had brought her. She had been selected for a purpose; obviously her beauty had played a part.

But beautiful spies were useless on Maxus. When a slave passed through the Distribute, she was lost to the rest of the Universe. Damn the woman. Why so many secrets?

He stood up and stretched. There were other problems. He could probably allow himself one night before the alarm would go out. Indeed, if slaves disposed of the bodies, Erulite's presence among the corpses might go unreported.

Everything considered, it seemed safe to visit the High Commissioner once more. But Mardien—what to do with her? It was uncomfortable having her so close to him, but if she really wanted to stay on Maxus, he could not let her out of his sight. She might easily slip away. He decided suddenly but definitely that he did not wish that to happen.

"Come," he said brusquely. "This is the Bosfor Strall. We change here. We're going to visit the High Commissioner."

His Excellency, the High Commissioner, wore a glossy cinnamon-colored sheath with a rather foppish collar of watered green silk. He was standing at the far end of a library carpeted in bright green, walled with panels of white marble between squat black brick piers. In his hand he held a large limp libram of pale brown leather. This he laid down as Travec entered, Mardien a pace behind him.

Travec motioned his erstwhile slave to a chair. "Sit there."

The High Commissioner waved an elegant hand. "Well, Sir Travec, what luck in your quest?"

"Very little," said Travec.

The High Commissioner seated himself on a metal bench, motioned Travec to do likewise. "No doubt you feel a measure of resentment against the folk of Maxus?'' His black eyes watched Travec intently.

Travec said, "I cannot deny it."

The High Commissioner laughed ruefully. "It is the measure of the misunderstanding from which we suffer. Do you know, Sir Travec, how many Overmen live on Maxus?"

Travec shrugged. "I have never heard a reliable figure."

"There are something over forty million of us. Think of that, Travec! A mere forty million! We design and manufacture for half the galaxy. Our industries produce the complicated mechanisms that allow you of the outer planets to subdue your environments. Forty million men own and manage the greatest industrial complex of all time!"

Travec, not wishing to become embroiled in sociological argument, said nothing.

"Overmen supply the brains," the High Commissioner continued. "We organize and superintend. And then *we* are exploited throughout the galaxy. We trade everywhere. Your garments are spun on Maxus looms. Your ship was built at Pardis Junction.

"But"—the High Commissioner leaned forward—"the forty million brains are needed at the top. We cannot waste our strength. So we use whatever labor we find expedient and—I repeat—the whole galaxy benefits."

Travec said evenly, "You present an aspect of life on Maxus I had not considered."

The High Commissioner rose and paced the bright green carpet. The tight bronze sheath emphasized his eel-like figure. A ridiculous fop, thought Travec, with his careful lock of black hair, his ruffled collar. And yet—as he met the High Commissioner's brilliant eyes—a man with quickness and intelligence.

"Now," continued the High Commissioner, "forty million Overmen manage a labor force of—I say—a large number of workers. And here is the seed of a precarious situation." He laughed at the expression on Travec's face. "You are thinking of revolt or insurrection? Bloody-handed slaves singing in the streets? Nonsense, the possibility does not exist.

"We have a central control system which positively, theo-

retically and finally makes such an occurrence impossible."
He licked his lips, cocked his eyebrows quizzically at Travec.
"I speak of our industrial techniques. They are our fundamental treasure. For instance, give me a few ounces of iron, a
sheet of mica, a trifle of polonium for a catalyst, and I will
build a cell which, when exposed to the air, will generate
several thousand amperes steadily for years on end.

"Look." He put a finger under a corner of the table.
"Foamed silicon. As light as air, and stronger than any
wood. Our brick—the black bricks we use to build houses:
strong, cheap, and excellent insulators. They are simply slag,
reformed from our mine retorts, twenty million at a time.

"The force units which we sell by the billion, the automatic air-conditioner which cools a room by expelling neutrinos through the walls, and warms it by absorbing neutrinos
from the atmosphere, converting the energy to heat: these and
other secrets are our very life!

"We grow no food, our seas are poisonous, our soil is wet
ash. So you see—once a worker has been committed to a
factory, once he learns the techniques of the Maxus industries, we can never permit him to leave."

He resumed his seat, looked at Travec expectantly. as if
waiting for applause. Travec said, "Your caution is under-
standable."

The High Commissioner made an offhand gesture. "Of
course, if a person like yourself arrives on Maxus and is able
to recover a friend or relative before he is assigned, then we
are glad to oblige. In the first place"—he laughed openly—
"the outlander will pay top prices at the Distribute. More
than the person he seeks is worth as a worker. And then—we
are not without humanity."

"I am glad to hear these sentiments," said Travec dryly.
"My brother and my younger sister were sold before my
arrival. The clerk refused my bribe—or rather, he took the
bribe, but refused me any information—when he realized one
of your Lords was watching him."

"Too bad," said the High Commissioner. He nodded
toward Mardien. "This, I presume, is your other sister."

Travec remained silent.

"And your mother?"

"Dead."

The High Commissioner fluttered his fingers. "My regrets."

Travec said abruptly, "Will you locate my brother and sister for me? I will gladly pay."

The High Commissioner shook his head. "I am sorry; it is impossible. This would set an awkward precedent. Our Patriarch, for all the remarkable scope of his vision"—he winked with pursed mouth at Travec, a sly, sarcastic gesture—"is adamant in this respect. He would demand an accounting and I would be at a disadvantage."

"Why, then," demanded Travec, "did you wish to see me again?"

"It was in connection with this fellow Arman," said the High Commissioner, buffing his fingernails on his sleeve. "My spies have now identified him."

"Indeed?" Travec leaned forward.

"He is no ordinary slaver."

"I gather that."

"He was the son of a Maxus Lord and a female slave from the planet Fell. Usually such children become guards but the father, in this case, took a fancy to the child, gave him an education and sponsored his status as a member of the military caste." The High Commissioner shook his head.

"The result of such largesse was disastrous. He became an acrobat, a gymnast jackanapes. Soon tiring of that livelihood, he established a religious cult among our elderly women. This new religion flourished, until one day Arman was accused of strangling some of his benefactors for their jewels."

There was a small sound from Mardien. The High Commissioner glanced at her curiously, then continued. "So you see, he has varied interests. First, a wastrel, then an acrobat in purple tights, and finally a murderer of old women.

"Thus we Lords of Maxus became aware of him. It was necessary for him to leave quickly or be sentenced to slavery. He accomplished the impossible—he escaped. What do you think of that?"

"I'm interested."

"He commandeered the Patriarch's private yacht." The

High Commissioner smiled faintly as at a joke. "The Patriarch's Chief Consort ordered it up for him, a magnificent conveyance—bathrooms carved from solid ivory, carpets of angelesine floss, chambers upholstered in violet silk crumple.

"The Patriarch naturally was aroused. He will be more so when he finds that Arman, under the immunity of a visitor's permit, has just sold us a large cargo of slaves. He will also be curious as to why I have not arranged that Arman be suitably punished for his crimes. The Patriarch has a memory for insult like the mythical land-leviathan."

Travec smiled bitterly. "Why don't you send out one of your firebrand lords to kill him? Lord Spangle, for instance, who seems to be the soul of valor."

The High Commissioner shook his head. "The Overmen never leave Maxus except in a warship. A single man might be captured, tortured free of all our secrets. At the very least he would be killed, since outside peoples make no amicable pretense with us. All our agents are Orths—or, I should say, outlanders."

"So?"

"So," said the High Commissioner, "the news of Arman's death would be a great comfort to me and to the Patriarch. Arman delivered alive would be a cause for rejoicing. I select you for these confidences, you understand, because you presumably have inclinations of your own for Arman's discomfort."

Travec stirred. "What do you offer?"

"You spoke of a brother and a sister?"

Travec looked irresolutely at the floor. To kill Arman—his dearest wish. But not to become a paid assassin, a cutthroat. And yet, Lenni and Gray. His jaw hardened. Had he hesitated even an instant? "Yes. A brother and a sister," he said.

"When Arman's death by your hand is verified they will be at your disposal."

"Unharmed? My sister. . . ."

"Untouched. Your sister will be placed in the service of a dowager."

"I accept your terms."

"Now," said the High Commissioner, "as to money. Do

you require further funds, or was Lord Erulite's wallet ample for your needs?''

Travec squinted, for the moment speechless.

''A lazy, ne'er-do-well, was Erulite,'' observed the High Commissioner. ''But you have not responded to my offer.''

''I can always use money,'' said Travec, stifling his distaste.

''Excellent. Your answer reassures me. Here.'' The High Commissioner tossed him a packet. ''Thirty thousand sil. Your ship has been serviced, refueled. You will leave at once.''

''Bound for . . . ?''

The High Commissioner poured a trickle of crimson liquid into a goblet, offered it to Travec, who declined. He then tasted it himself, puckered his lips, made a sucking, smacking noise with his tongue.

''I cannot say definitely. But we have a technique for discovering these things and I will confide it to you. We carefully note the purchases made on Maxus by members of the ship's crew. For instance, we know that Arman's steward has stocked fresh fruit for two weeks. Highly significant—too scant for an extended voyage.

''Arman, however, loaded fuel to the ship's capacity. And his steward put aboard a large supply—several months stock—of glyd. Which, as you may be aware, is a fermented pulp consumed almost exclusively by races of Hyarnimmic extraction, such as we Overmen, the Clas of Jena, the Luchistains.''

He eased himself into a chair, stroked his face. ''All very significant. Again, the medic stocked his locker with parabamin-67 for use in oxygen-rich atmospheres and several million units of pink-lip serum, as well as the usual deallergizers and cell-toners.

''And then Arman's cargo—very suggestive. No small robomatics but cases of light-samplers and power-meters. No force units—but tri-dimensional duplicators and ingots of crystallized lead.'' He eyed Travec with polite curiosity. ''Now what would you make of all this?''

Travec said, ''I imagine that first you laid out a sphere at a two-week radius from Maxus and listed the inhabited planets on that sphere.''

"Correct. There are forty-six."

"An oxygen-rich atmosphere implies a world heavily vegetated. Pink-lip suggests humidity. A planet with extensive swamps and jungles."

"Continue."

"A planet with fresh fruit but no glyd. Therefore a planet inhabited not by Hyarnimmics but by Savars, Gallicretins or Pardus. A people without extensive research centers—with small factories producing for local consumption rather than designing or originating."

The High Commissioner made an airy motion. "Only one world of the forty-six meets all these conditions. And that is Fell—the third planet of Ramus."

"Fell," said Travec thoughtfully.

The High Commissioner said, "On Fell live a curious people, set apart from the rest of the population by local superstition—the Oros. Arman's mother was an Oro. They are said to be uniformly insane."

IV

The strip eased them through the darkness. It was long after midnight, the streets were bare. A chilly wind, smelling of industrial waste and drainage, bit at their backs. Buildings hulked up dull and lifeless on either side. They showed no lights to the street and rime glistened on the black brick where the infrequent street lights shone. It was hard to imagine humanity within those heavy complex masses.

They were alone on the strip. The streets were bare as far as they could see ahead. The dingy alleys opening at intervals were untenanted, damp, dead. A fine rain began to fall and the wind whipped ghostly veils at the streetlights.

Finally the portico to the central field loomed out of the rain. Two cressets, memorializing an event of the past, flared wildly on each side of the arch, hissing in the drip of the rain. They left the strip, passed through the arch out onto the field. The rain stopped suddenly. The three moons broke through the ragged silver clouds but the light spent itself on the intricate roof silhouettes and they could not see the fused earth which crunched and crackled under their feet.

He found his ship among the dozen other craft on the field. Travec climbed aboard and Mardien followed. He looked around the cabin, where he had spent so many frantic days and nights, and sighed with gloom and frustration.

Wasted energy, wasted time, wasted emotions, how could he hope to overcome the force and inertia of Maxus? He sighed a second time, went to the controls, turned power to the generator, arranged the controls for take-off.

He turned his head. Mardien was standing in the middle of the cabin, as strange and out of place there as a flowering tree. Her face was drawn and forlorn. Her pale yellow hair was damp and hung in clammy strings. Travec said in a voice as friendly as he could manage, "I'll take you to any port you like in the quadrant I'm heading for."

Mardien made no direct reply. Looking up and down the cabin, she asked, "Where are my quarters?"

Travec laughed wearily. "Quarters? You'll be lucky to have a locker for your clothes. I'll run a curtain across that corner and there will be your quarters."

He watched as she carried her small belongings across the cabin. With an effort he wrenched his eyes from her supple back and slender legs. A sadness—sweet but remote and impersonal—came over him. He could not permit himself distracting thoughts. No soft things, no possession he could not jettison. He must be flexible and free.

Mardien said in a soft voice, "Why do you look at me like that?"

Travec blinked, "Like what?"

"Have I done something wrong?"

"Nothing I know of. In any event, your life is your own."

"You bought me. I am your property by the laws of Maxus."

The signal light flashed. Travec pressed down the sealing-ring. He reached in his pocket, handed her a slip of paper. "In ten minutes we will be past the Portal Fort, out into clear space. Then you will hear the only command I will ever give you."

He slid into the pilot's seat, moved the controls. The ship rose from the ground, up into the light of the three moons. Alambar fell below, became a panorama in a thousand tones of black and gray.

The inspection at the satellite was brief. Then they were beyond, and out in space. "What is your wish, Travec?" Mardien asked.

"Tear up the certificate of ownership."

She obeyed him, then turned away. "Thank you."

"I want no thanks," said Travec. "Thank the memory of my sister. Thank your own kindness, for which she must have loved you. Have you decided where you want to land?"

"Yes," said Mardien. "At Huamalpai, on the planet Fell."

A pair of human beings in a glass-and-metal hull, fleeting through space like dreams through a sleeping mind: two personalities thrust one against the other, forced into a confining closeness.

But the circumstances were unique. Travec's rapt concentration seemed to subvert his more overt virility. He recognized the possibilities at hand—his eyes lingered on the curve of the girl's hip and the line of her thigh—but he felt no compulsion.

After awhile Mardien, who had previously prepared herself for physical abuse as an inevitable corollary to slavery, found his disinterest puzzling. It was even subtly troubling. Did he find her unpleasant? Was Travec unnaturally inclined? Eyeing his regular features, his short dark thatch of rough hair, his compressed controlled gestures, she didn't think so.

Perhaps he was bound to another woman.

"Travec?"

He turned his head. "Yes?"

"You have no more family on Exar?"

"No."

She settled beside him. "What was your business before you left Exar?"

"Architecture—industrial design." He eyed her with a glint of curiosity. "And you?"

"Oh—I instructed small children in social responses."

"And where is your home?"

She hesitated, then said, "It is on Fell—on the Alam Highlands above Huamalpai. You are taking me home."

Travec stared at her an instant, glanced across the room to the *Directory of Inhabited Worlds*.

"But that is where the Oros live. Are you Oro?"

"Yes."

Travec studied her a moment. "You're not perceptibly abnormal. But the Directory describes the Oros as a race of lunatics and—well, read it for yourself." He rose, found the reference, handed her the book. She read passively as he watched, wondering. She put the book down.

"Well? True or not?"

She shrugged. "Do I appear supernatural or superhuman?"

He smiled briefly. "No. *Are* you?"

Mardien shook her head. "Of course not! We're normal human beings. Our children are no different from Exar children. But we've been trained in ways that give us some advantages."

"What kind of advantages?"

She paused. "It is not a matter we care to talk about."

"All right. Keep your secrets to yourself."

She turned a troubled glance on him. "I don't mean to be mysterious. But our people—well, it's a custom." She hesitated, then said impulsively, "You have been very good to me and if you wish I'll make you one of us. Then you'll know more than I could tell you."

Travec grinned. "Would I then become a lunatic?"

"If you accept our beliefs, you will probably become as we are."

"No," said Travec. "Religions, cults, rituals—forms of insanity—don't interest me."

"As you wish," she said coldly. "But I must point out that a person with a closed mind learns nothing."

Travec said, "If your knowledge or system—whatever you call it—is useful, why haven't you extended it across the galaxy?"

"There are reasons. In the first place, we are wary of the lowlanders and other . . . predatory men."

Travec said with a brittle overtone in his voice, "You don't fear Arman?"

She looked at him quickly. "Arman is a hero—an Evangel."

Travec sneered, "The High Commissioner thought otherwise. First an acrobat, then a religious cultist and a murderer of old women, then a slaver. Now you say he is a hero."

"Sometimes," said Mardien slowly, "a man's motives are misrepresented, sometimes his actions are distorted by others."

Travec said, "I saw warm corpses in Farees Village. I saw Arman's ship rise from the island with six hundred of my people in the hold. There is no way this action could be distorted to any further discredit."

"Sometimes," said Mardien, stammering, "a few must suffer that many shall gain. . . ."

"Indeed," said Travec, "and sometimes many must suffer that one shall gain."

Mardien asked fervently, "Have you ever seen him, Travec? Have you ever spoken to him? Have you ever looked into his eyes?"

Travec replied sourly, "No. But you seem to have done all these things."

She said coolly, "I have. I worship him."

Travec said, "Then you must be crazy like the other Oros."

The friendship had soured. There was a chill in the cabin, the alienation of withdrawn minds. Time passed, and then one day the generators wound down a thousand unheard octaves and the ship rippled across the shift to normal space.

Ahead hung a giant red star, Ramus, and glowing like a coal, the planet Fell.

It ballooned before their gaze. Travec traced out the continents and conformations listed in the Directory. A peach-tan belt was the North Polar Desert, a magenta-green-brown expanse was the jungle surrounding the continent Kalhua. On the western rim was the chief city, Huamalpai, and directly behind rose the plateau of the Alam Highlands.

Travec set the ship down without delay. The landing field was in the flat country on the swampward side of Huamalpai—a dry plain dancing in the rosy light of Ramus. Huamalpai itself lay ten miles distant among low hills, which gave some slight protection against the raids of slavers.

Mardien packed her few belongings with eager hands, glancing out the port toward the great palisade of rock that marked the edge of her homeland. Travec saw her in a sudden new light: a girl very enthusiastic, very idealistic—and very young. He turned away with a faint flush of guilt and busied himself with his dose of parabamin-67, which adjusted him to the highly oxygenated atmosphere.

There was a rap at the outer port. Travec identified himself to the representatives of King Daurobanan, short flat-featured men with straight black hair worn in twin pigtails. Their uniforms were loose, shimmering blue breeches with a peculiar shoulder-ornament like great dragon-fly wings, serving no clear function. They were silent, quick, non-committal. Travec paid the small port fee and the officials departed.

He threw a cape over his shoulder, clipped his pouch to his chest strap and was ready to leave. Mardien jumped to the ground, turned, waited while Travec locked the ship.

The wind, raising dust-whirls on the field, stirred Mardien's yellow hair. Over her shoulder, across the field, Travec saw a black ship with a bulldog bow and a big barrel of a cargo hold. The same ship that had lurched up from Great Farees, her belly full of slaves—Arman's ship.

Mardien saw a quiver, sensed his muscles tighten. She saw the expression on his face, followed his gaze.

She turned away slowly. "Good-by, Travec. You've been very good to me."

"Thank my dead sister," said Travec.

Mardien moved slowly across the field to a ramshackle waiting room. Travec saw her step into an aircar. It rose and took her through the pale, pink sky toward Huamalpai.

V

Travec stood on the ground, looking out toward the horizon with a sensation of physical release. Distance on all sides of him and overhead the vast dome of the sky. After weeks in the cramped cabin he felt free, full of pent energy.

He walked past the air-cabs, through an open-air waiting pavilion and set out on foot.

The road led off across a barren plain pebbled with hard gray-green button fungus. Little puffs of dust, whirling wind-devils, spun in from the distance—stained pink, rose, red—wandered down the perspectives out of sight. Ahead, a dark finger of swamp.

When Travec drew abreast of it, he found the ground marshy and sour-smelling. Reeds in rusty clumps lined the road. Streaming spider-web beards blown in from the deep jungle floated past. Presently the swamp retreated. The road turned, paralleled a plantation of mealie-grass.

Travec walked on, whistling between his teeth with the feathery tufts swaying and bobbing above him. Arman and the Oros—why? It was a problem which intrigued him. Of course Arman was half-Oro.

He considered hints in the Directory: ". . . for all their personal eccentricities they cooperate magnificently in any crisis, such as the expulsion of King Vauha's army from North Alam Forest. Lowlanders impute supernatural abilities to the Oros—immortality, second sight and the like—and many strange stories are told about this peculiar race. . . ."

In a sense, the association fitted what he knew of Arman; a mystic with a conviction of destiny. Apparently Arman hoped to reinforce the dogma of his cult with established Oro ritual. Immortality? Second sight? All religions grew from human dread of death, reflected Travec—the brassier the claims for afterlife, the more popular the creed. Travec smiled faintly as he walked. Was this Arman's dream—a net of minds across the galaxy?

His smile faded. There were practical difficulties which even an irresponsible blackguard like Arman could not over-look. In the first place, the powerful Overmen would never tolerate such an organization. They had the means to detect it: a net of spies and secret police. And they had power to crush it: embargo, mass assassination and as a last resort formal military force.

Travec stopped. Arman no doubt had seen the circle of contradiction. To organize a power bloc it was necessary to defeat the wealth, immense power and industrial mass of Maxus. And to defeat Maxus, an equally vast industrial complex, a planetary organization was necessary.

He gazed with unseeing eyes down the dusty road. There was a syllogism hidden somewhere, a grouping of ideas which would clarify the issue. He shook his head. Too many factors were unknown, and those few he knew were variable.

Travec raised his eyes to the Alam Highlands. Mardien would be home now, among her family, her friends. Would she seek out Arman? He kicked and scuffed the dust. Such thoughts were unsettling. They interfered with the impetus of his life.

First, kill Arman or bring him alive to Maxus. Second, seek out and kill other slavers. Some men hunted wolves, Travec would hunt slavers. He would assemble a gallery of their heads for display.

A clanking sounded behind him. He jumped to the side of the road, turned around. A truck loaded with fat gray animals drew abreast. Travec held up his hand. The truck wheezed, halted. The animals grunted and squealed.

The driver peered down from the high cab. "Where do you go?"

"Huamalpai," said Travec.

"Climb aboard."

Travec swung up the ladder, settled on the thin padding of the seat. The truck, an antiquated charcoal burner of local manufacture, gasped clouds of smoke and steam. The big drive wheels groaned into motion.

The driver was a slight man about his own age, with black hair worn in pigtails, a flat face. Travec listened tolerantly to the flow of talk.

". . . fifteen hectares next solstice we'll put in paddy. That's been required in Huamalpai, the meat-butts thrive on it. It's said spiders keep their distance too, since there's a rancid oil the leaf gives off, but I've never seen the spider yet that was discouraged by a bad smell."

"Spiders?" asked Travec.

The driver nodded emphatically. "They're monstrous—some of them. They come in from the swamps for the meat-butts. Others, of course, are no larger than my pet mishkin. And then there's one kind of beast with eight legs and yellow-green on the belly. He can take a meat-butt under each of his two front legs and stroll back in to the jungle like there's nothing to it. . . ."

As they drove, the country became more settled, the dry plains were left behind. Vines and irrigated paddies lined the road. Little wooden huts appeared, with roofs of shiny blue thatch. In the distance rose a group of hills, along which the wooden walls of Huamalpai spread, clung and dripped like frosting on a dark cake. Behind Huamalpai the Alam Palisade reared up, two miles of black rock against the pink sky.

Noting the direction of Travec's gaze the driver said, "That's the Alam Highlands." He paused, turning expectant bright eyes on Travec.

Travec said, "Isn't that where the Oros live?"

"Correct."

"I hear they're a strange sort of people."

The driver paused a moment. "Crazy as sack-beetles. One man wears a red cape with blue half-moons on it, then another comes along in a cape with similar patterns. And what happens? They both tear off their cloaks and burn them and stay home till their wives can make new ones. Or one man may be singing, or just talking to friends. Another fellow will walk up and shout 'Shut up!' . . . Then. . . ."

"They fight?"

"No indeed. They shake hands. There's great laughter and merriment."

"What do they fight about?"

The driver shrugged. "For one thing, they won't take orders. And it's an insult to enter another man's house."

"I wonder why."

"Oh—just plain craziness."

"How do they treat strangers?" asked Travec.

"Ignore 'em for a day or so, then chase 'em away. They revel in their isolation." The driver shook his head. "We

lowlanders don't go up there much. What we don't understand, we don't like. And it's gotten worse, lately.''

"How so?"

The driver's flat forehead creased.

"It's hard to say." He hesitated.

Travec said, "I've heard some talk."

The driver snorted. "Probably true—whatever was said.
They're a strange people and I wouldn't want anything to do
with them—even if they acted normal. It's said they have no
souls."

Travec made appropriate sounds of amazement.

"Now you hear there's a prophet dropped down from space,"
said the driver. "He's preaching miracles and they come from
all over the Highlands to listen and sigh like swamp-ghosts.
Of course," he added modestly, "that's just gossip, but I get
into town often and I'm not easily fooled."

Travec asked, "How can a common man see this with his
own eyes?"

The driver considered. "There's any number of ways. He
can walk the Fortitude Trail, straight up out of Huamalpai, or
he can drive forty miles under the rim of the Palisade to
Nuathiole Notch. There's a road that's passable to a car, only
once up on the Highlands it's very poor, so I'm told—"

Travec squinted up at the cliff. "Why not fly?"

The driver said, "That's the third method. There's a
hangar in Huamalpai that rents out copter-cars—slave-built on
Maxus, I must tell you. If you can pay the rent you can whisk
up like a bird."

When the truck finally pulled into Huamalpai, Ramus hung
low and red and the sky verged on magenta. Travec alighted
from the high cab, took leave of the driver.

He stood silent a moment, rubbing his chin, his eyes fixed
on the rim of Alam Palisade.

Arman was so close. Why wait? He looked around him.

Up at the head of the street rose King Daurobanan's palace,
a tremendous clutter of cupolas, panoplies, pilasters, balconies and rococo scroll-work. Nearer were the shops and markets, various places of business—all with square fronts of

carved pale brown wood. Travec stopped a passerby, learned the whereabouts of the rental hangar.

He turned along the bank of a blood-colored river, passed an untidy line of piers and wharves poking helter-skelter out of the mud. By the time he found the hangar and rented an air-car night had come. The sky showed a lavender afterglow that cast a dull sheen on the nearby water.

The flier controls were Maxus standard. Travec lifted the car straight up through the warm air. Huamalpai dropped below, an untidy straggle of houses followed the hills.

Up, up, to the Alam Highlands. He passed the escarpment, peered curiously through the murk. The face of the country-side was blurred by darkness but he sensed a vast table land rolling out to the horizon.

Spatters of colored lights shone here and there—twinkling reds, greens, blues, yellows, purples, as if every village held a carnival.

Somewhere below was Arman. Where? Travec scowled at the colored display. Arman would conduct his affairs as quietly as possible, he would certainly be aware of the long reach of Maxus vengeance. Among the Oros, any inquiry from an outlander, no matter how casual, would excite suspicion.

Mardien would know where Arman kept himself. She might even be at his side. How to find Mardien? Drop down and ask? No—

Travec thought of a way. He bent over the controls. The flier swooped, slanted back toward Huamalpai.

Travec once more hung above the Alam Highlands. On the seat beside him wobbled the clumsy bulk of a native-built transmitter.

Find Mardien, find Arman. He flipped the switch, dialed to 26.733 megacycles. The resonance of her penal circuit, at its lowest intensity, would guide him to Mardien. He meant to locate, not punish, not even disturb. He swiveled the antenna around the black rim of the horizon, listened.

Silence.

He adjusted the controls; the car took him up—high into the air. He tuned the transmitter again, listened, heard a faint *pip—pip—pip*. He increased the power and the sound strengthened. He lined the antenna against the compass—north and west—turned the flier, followed the direction of the signal.

The signal grew louder as he flew and Travec turned down the power lest a tingling should alarm his quarry. Ten, twenty, thirty miles passed. Travec looked off ahead; the Highlands were only fifty miles wide.

Another ten miles and the antenna pointed down. He hovered, peered over the cheek of the dome. Darkness lay below, relieved by no sprinkle of many-colored lights such as marked towns elsewhere over the plateau. Nothing but the darkness of uninhabited country. He examined the transmitter skeptically. The dial was set correctly but was it calibrated to any exact standard?

The only way to find out was to land. And he looked without pleasure at the dark blur below. He thought of the night-scope, but like many of the Overmen's instruments it was not for outland use.

Travec squinted at the altimeter. It read two thousand feet above surface. The tactigraph needle flickered between 6 and 7—the density and texture of forest foliage.

He dropped the car on a steep slant. A thousand feet—five hundred—four hundred—three hundred—he stopped short. Directly below loomed an amorphous mass which seemed to boil and seethe—the crest of a giant tree.

Travec moved uneasily in the seat. The flier's engine made little noise—a rotary whirr—but the blades created a swish which might or might not be lost in the sounds of the forest.

He descended cautiously. Darkness now lay on all sides, a trifle less dense to his right. He slanted to the right, swung through soft air and settled unhindered to solid ground.

Travec jumped out. He stood tensely beside the car—silent, looking into the darkness. The air was quiet, damp, smelled of an unfamiliar balsam—enough to remind him that he walked on a strange world.

His eyes adjusted to the darkness and he found that it was not quite complete. Rotting timber generated a phosphorescent blue glow along the ground.

Travec hesitated. If he left the flier he would never find it

again. Once out of his range of vision—a hundred feet in the
darkness—he might wander for hours through the forest.

He climbed back in the cabin, sent out the feeblest of
pulses and the *pip—pip—pip* returned strong and sharp. He
lined the antenna exactly, sat considering. His eye fell on the
flier's compass, a cheap magnetic device and consequently
useful for his purpose. He wrenched the compass loose, lined
it along the axis of the antenna. Northwest by north. . . .

He set out swiftly, walking with long strides over the
spongy turf. His footprints glared suddenly blue behind him.

He was not sure how far he walked. The dim blue light
showed black boles on all sides, rising cleanly, without
branches. The wood was hard and cold as metal. His feet
crunched through brittle fungus, sank into humus. He stepped
on heavy tendrils that gave beneath his foot like a human
arm.

A pinkish-yellow glow waxed in front of him, rising from
the ground. Travec advanced slowly as the light spread outward and illumined fronds of foliage sixty feet above.

The forest ended, the ground fell away. Travec looked over
a lip of rock into a sandy amphitheater. A tent of dull red
cloth closed off the light. Rows of benches curved around a
platform built of rough black planks beside a carved railing.
The benches were three-quarters full of men and women.

Travec studied them. They were tall, well-formed, with
straight regular features. The Oros of the Alam Highlands—
were they really crazy? From what he saw, Travec found it
hard to assume differently. The clothes of each man and
woman were completely unique in style and color.

VI

The gathering was like a masqued ball, like the carnival
suggested by the colored lights of their towns. One man wore
a jerkin of pale green leather, bronze satin trousers—another
white pantaloons and a voluminous purple blouse. Here a woman
was cinctured in gold ribbons—there one wore a pleated robe

of blue silk—another a gray coverall with black epaulets and yellow gores down the legs.

Their headdresses were equally distinctive—arrangements of bronze bristles, balls of red puff, feathers, helmets of metal and transparent sheets. In bewilderment Trevec looked from face to face. Perhaps the occasion was one of festivity. No, the expressions were uniformly serious.

Trevec searched among the faces. There was nothing to hint at insanity, nothing to indicate supernatural power. In spite of the fantastic dress, he found a serenity, a relaxation and calm that smoothed their features and gave them a youthful cast.

Was Mardien somewhere in the audience? He scanned the circumference of the arena. There were no ushers, no guards, no gatemen. Newcomers to the audience aroused no attention. A strange costume should evoke no notice here, thought Trevec. His gray coverall would be conspicuous only by its lack of color. He stepped out into the pink-yellow glow, walked down an aisle, took a seat. No one heeded him. A half dozen middle-aged women sat in front of him. He was amused to hear their speech.

". . . so gracious, Teresha said. He actually held her hand! She said his touch made her shiver."

"Teresha exaggerates, you know."

"I've a mind to invite him to our nocturne. . . ."

They giggled. "I doubt if he'd come. He keeps so busy and studies all the time. He reads eight ancient languages. . . ."

The benches filled quickly. The amphitheater was soon crowded. An old woman in a lime-yellow martingale, wearing a sheaf of roses in her hair, sat on one side of Trevec. A youth of fifteen in a green coat sat on the other. Neither gave him a second glance.

A pink-white spotlight played on the platform and Arman appeared. A half-heard hiss came from the crowd.

Trevec's breath became shallow with the rigidity of his attention. He saw a man of magnificent stature and beauty, radiating certainty and intelligence. His face was the composite of a thousand champions, all the heroes on all the medallions.

Arman addressed the crowd. His voice was somber, rich,

melodious, giving urgency to the most ordinary sentence. He enhanced this effect by speaking with his head down, meeting the eyes of his audience. Observing him, Travec could understand Mardien's reluctance to think evil of him. Arman was a dynamic, charismatic being, radiant with *virtue*.

"Men and women of the future," said Arman, "tomorrow our great adventure begins. Tomorrow we leave the Highlands." He paused, swung his eyes around the amphitheater; Travec felt a momentary impact. Arman continued in a slow voice.

"I have not much to tell you. Even here in the forest, having summoned you by personal call, I fear the eyes and ears of Maxus. So I must restrain much of what is in the mind of the God."

Travec stirred in his seat? God? What God?

Arman spoke with great eloquent phrases, like an inspired artist laying color on a canvas. His theme was less political than spiritual and Travec himself felt troubled as he listened. Such enthusiasm and fire would be hard to counterfeit. If Arman believed in his own preachings. . . .

Man had lost hope, said Arman, had lost faith in the destiny which once had sent him to the reaches of the galaxy. A new focus was needed, a new flame to fire men's hearts, a new crusade.

"A crusade must be launched by true believers," said Arman softly, "and it is you who will go with me tomorrow. The centrality, the focus is here within. Call it God—Fate— Destiny—Purpose—it is here." He touched his chest. "It gives me tongue. It makes me what I am, what you see before you. This God, this Destiny, looks from my eyes. When I speak, this God speaks. Cast off the rags of your old life, wear the golden clothes of the new universe!

"Humanity sinks in the mire. Maxus wallows in wine and orgy, eats the fat of its victims. Maxus is a great leech which feeds upon humanity.

"The old frontiers are falling back. Plague takes one world. On another, civilization grows feeble, dwindles and dies. And so mankind's pitiful ruins are scattered among the stars."

Arman magnified his voice and the skin prickled on Travec's neck. The figure on the stage seemed to grow.

"We must set our hearts to resolution! Together we shall purge the universe. The slaves shall be masters and the masters shall be slaves! They shall sweat, toil and die as their own slaves have died! We shall build a new society and serve a new God! Our bricks will be human minds, our mortar the Oro way. The mansion we build together will be a new universe!"

Arman stood back, breathing heavily. As one, the crowd sighed—a high-pitched gust from the diaphragm. Travec shifted fretfully, annoyed by the rasp between his mind and his emotions. First Mardien, now Arman himself, conspired to blur the clarity of his intentions.

Arman said in a firm low voice. "Tomorrow we embark on our great adventure. You who come shall see a strange world. You shall see the dark rot of a culture based on evil.

"Together we shall accomplish great events! It is history we are living this night on the Alam Highlands. We who meet here in the forest are the seed and spark of a glorious future."

VII

Travec sat numbly, in a kind of trance. He saw the light flicker away from Arman, heard the crowd arise, leave. Action of some kind was imminent. A crusade, against Maxus, against the great slave state itself—by an amphitheater-full of queerly dressed men and women? Ridiculous. Arman was as crazy as his kin.

But was he? Maybe Mardien had told the truth. Maybe Arman's motives had been misrepresented. Maybe to Arman six hundred lives were nothing. Maybe he *was* the God, the Destiny—whatever he called himself.

Indecision was worse than torture! In the core of his mind a message struggled to reach his consciousness. Travec stirred; the daze dissipated. What was it? The key to his dilemma. He bent forward, sat a moment rubbing his temples, then rose to his feet, stared at the platform. The crowd had left the arena.

Arman was gone. He became aware of another presence, of a suspicious scrutiny. He glanced at the teenage boy who sat beside him. They were almost alone in the fading light.

The boy said, "You're no Oro." It was a flat statement.

Travec said with a forced calm, "How do you know?"

The boy said, "I see it in your face, the troubled lines of the death-men. I can sense it in your mind, which has a surface like the Granite Desert. You are no Oro."

"So?"

"If you are a Maxus spy, you will be killed."

"If I were a Maxus spy how would I have found my way here?"

The boy shook his head, backed away. Travec saw that he was ready to shout for help. The arena was empty but men would not be far distant.

Travec said, "Well, we'll see whether I'm a spy or not. We'll go to Arman."

The boy hesitated. "You wish to see Arman? Are you leaving tomorrow?"

"Possibly," said Travec. "I haven't decided yet."

The boy stood watching Travec from the corners of his eyes.

"Let's go find Arman," said Travec. "You are more familiar with the forest. You lead the way."

The boy stared at Travec, who did not fit his mental picture of a spy. Spies were small, shifty-eyed, full of false smiles. Travec was large, lean, sinewy like a sand cat. . . .

"I'll tell you where to find Arman," he said indecisively. "But I won't take you there."

The arrangement suited Travec very well. "As you wish."

The boy changed his mind. "No, I'll take you myself. Then I'll *know* everything's all right. I'm a Junior Engineer," he added self-consciously.

"Excellent," said Travec. "And what is your role in the great adventure?"

"Oh!" The boy chose his words carefully. "I will translate ideas into accurate drawings. That is my specialty."

Travec nodded. "I see, I see. And now, we'll go see Arman."

The boy hesitated. "Perhaps I'd better take you to my father and let him decide."

Travec stood as if deliberating. "No," he said at last, "I have little time. It would be better to go to Arman directly."

The boy wavered. He had never been in Arman's presence, had never exchanged words with the great man. Perhaps this would be his chance. "Follow me," he said.

They left the arena, threaded a path across a paved road and plunged back into the woods. They walked five minutes. The forest lost its density. They came out into an open area. In the east a bright planet shone like a monstrous rosy pearl. Travec saw that they were on a rolling heath. A damp wind blew into his face, smelling strongly of the swamp. Ahead glowed the lights of a small cottage.

The youth came to a sudden indecisive halt. Would he be thanked for bringing a stranger to disturb the hero? What if this grim, black-haired man were an enemy, a Maxus spy? His legs began to shake.

"We've come the wrong way," said the boy huskily. "We'd better go back, into the forest. I'll take you to my father."

Travec reached almost casually, caught the nape of the boy's neck in one hand, felt between the muscles, squeezed. The youth froze, arms dangling woodenly, legs barely supporting him. Travec groped in his pouch, withdrew a palm-injector—a small sac of drug with a sting-needle. His hold relaxed. The boy's arm flew up in a reflex motion. He cried out hoarsely.

Travec clamped his teeth, tightened the grip. He forced the limp youth to the ground, slapped the injector on his neck. The boy stiffened. Travec released his hold and the boy lay still.

Travec stood waiting in the dark. The noise had evidently not been heard. He moved carefully toward the cottage—a farmhouse with a marvelously high gable, oval windows and a door in the shape of three discs.

The windows seeped cracks and points of golden light but gave no vision within. Travec circled the house, passed hutches, sheds, outbuildings, found a rear entrance.

He pulled at the latch, but the door was barred. He dipped into his pouch for a torch and, choking in the quick smoke, burnt a hole above the latch. Reaching through the glowing splinters, he slid back the bar, put his shoulder to the door, eased it open.

The room was dark and smelled of spoiled fruit. A frame of light revealed another door opposite. Travec beamed a light around, crossed the room swiftly, stealthily.

No sound from within, no voices, no rustle of movement. He adjusted his torch and amplified its range. Holding it ready, he swung open the door.

Arman sat on a bench by the fireplace, brooding into the flames. He was alone. Travec stepped quietly forward. Arman sensed his presence, glanced up.

"Silence," said Travec, showing his weapon. Arman rose to his feet, stood quietly watching, a handsome man with fair features. His presence was tremendous, disconcerting. Travec hesitated—should he kill the man here? It would be easy. But Arman brought alive to Maxus would be more valuable than Arman dead on Fell. There were not only Travec's brother and sister but many others whom Arman might ransom.

"Turn around," said Travec. Arman obeyed, watching over his shoulder with great luminous eyes. He did not speak.

Travec approached carefully. Arman, a powerfully built man, looked dangerous. Travec reached out, flicked Arman's neck with the injector.

From behind came a thin wail of fear. Travec stepped away from the stiffening Arman. A young woman stood in the doorway, wearing black slacks, an open green and white blouse. She was blond as Exar sunlight and as beautiful: Mardien.

Arman crumpled. Travec said to Mardien, "Come in quickly or I'll kill you right there."

She came forward, her eyes filmed with a peculiar glaze. "Kill me?" Her voice was puzzled rather than frightened. "Why?"

Travec glared, suddenly at a loss. The answer to her question was related to the pang he felt on seeing her, here in

Arman's cottage. Mardien looked at the prone figure and one hand went to her throat.

She asked, "Have you killed him—so soon?"

"No, he is not dead."

"Then what are you planning?"

"Take him to Maxus, trade him for my brother, my sister, as many of my friends as possible."

"But they will torture him!" She looked back at Travec and the glaze was leaving her eyes.

Travec shrugged, glanced down at the silent body on the floor. "He should have thought of that before he became a slaver."

Mardien came toward him. "Travec—*Dyle*! You don't understand! You can't do this. Please!"

Travec made a grim sound, half chuckle, half snort. "Maybe you're blind. Maybe you've been duped."

She said, white-faced, wide-eyed, "There's nothing behind what you say but emotion."

Travec said sardonically, "The same words apply to you."

"But I know! I *know*!" she said between clenched teeth.

Travec shrugged. "He spoke of leaving tomorrow. Why? And where?"

The answer angrily burst through her lips. "To Maxus with six hundred of my people. That's how much we believe in Arman! Six hundred have volunteered themselves."

"Volunteered? For what?"

"Volunteered their bodies for slavery."

Travec stood rigid, eyes probing hers. "Why?"

She looked away. "I have said too much."

Travec said slowly. "Do I understand that six hundred Oros are allowing themselves—voluntarily—to be sold as slaves? And Arman collects their value?"

"Yes!"

"Now I know you're crazy—all of you."

"You're a fool!" snapped Mardien. "The money buys technical equipment—for factories, power plants, tools."

"Who will work these factories?"

"We Oros."

"And who will protect your industries from Maxus?"

"We will have a field like the screen around Maxus."

"That," said Travec, "is one of the best-kept secrets on all Maxus—how to shield a planet."

Mardien smiled. "Once the Oros are slaves on Maxus, there will be no more secrets. Those who go are technically trained."

Travec stood frowning. "I don't understand you."

"Naturally. You are not an Oro."

"No," said Travec. "I'm not. How will you get these secrets off the planet?"

"That is one of *our* secrets. We will seek out every formula, every structural design, every circuit, every phase of knowledge on Maxus. And here in the Alam Highlands we will recreate their technology.

"We will shield Fell from the Maxus warships till we have warships of our own. Then we will take our techniques to the other planets. Maxus will fall back before us."

"Very imaginative," said Travec drily. He leaned back against the wall. "But why exchange the occasional predations of Maxus for the tyranny of this slaver," he nudged Arman with his foot, "this murderer?"

"There will be no tyranny under Arman!"

Travec shook his head slowly. "You are trusting and innocent! When he says 'the masters shall be slaves,' you still believe him."

" 'The masters shall be slaves,' " she repeated slowly. "You were at the meeting."

"Yes."

"What do you mean, then?"

"I mean that you conceivably might create an industrial capitalist system, but you'll need many more millions of men to work it than there are on Fell. Are you aware how complicated a warship is? How many man-years of labor go into building even a cruiser?"

"No," she said faintly.

"And how many man-years of labor go into merely building the machinery, the equipment, necessary just to get started?"

"We'll start out on a small scale."

"There's no such thing as a small scale. It's either big or it doesn't exist at all. It takes forty million Overmen to merely superintend the Maxus industries. And there are only a few million of you. Where will all this additional man-power come from? Arman gave you the answer in his speech. It leaps to his mind since he's a slaver by profession. Slaves!

"Another thing—while your industrial system is expanding, do you think the Overmen will go to sleep? They're realists. They'll expand with you, faster than you. They'll enslave more planets, build more factories—and they've got a two-thousand-year head-start.

"If your plot succeeds, you don't win—nobody wins. Everybody loses. There won't be just Maxus ravaging the planets—there'll also be slavers from Fell. Two industrial systems, competing for galactic markets to buy enough food to feed their slaves."

"No, no, *no*!" cried Mardien. "That's not our plan at all!"

"Of course not," Travec said mildly. "You're an idealist. The idealists are always the revolutionaries, the cat's-paws. Then the realists consolidate, compromise and liquidate the opposition."

They stood looking at each other across the room, and between them lay Mardien's prone idol. She said in a subdued voice, "What do you propose then? You try to destroy my faith but you offer me nothing."

Travec said quietly, "I'm sorry. I can't offer any pleasant solutions—except to make slaving so dangerous that monsters like this"—he nudged Arman with his foot—"will stick to acrobatics. I think that will be my life. And I'll start with the slaver that robbed me of my family—Arman.

"After I give him to the High Commissioner at Alambar there will be no more quarter." His voice took on a harsh brilliance. "I'll kill them as I find them."

There was a strange pallor on Mardien's face, Travec noticed the direction of her gaze, fixed in fascination on the floor.

Too late, he stepped away from movement at his feet. A swift supple massiveness struck him at the waist, hurled him thudding down. The torch clattered to the planks of the floor. Mardien gasped, ran toward it.

Travec kicked outward, caught Arman in the abdomen. Arman staggered. At the same moment, Travec caught sight of Mardien holding the torch, her face twisted in doubt. Her eyes were wide and glazed.

Travec twisted aside as a needle of red light charred the floor beside him.

He jumped to his feet, dodged behind the gasping figure of Arman, caught up a stool, flung it at Mardien. It caught her head and shoulder. She fell. Then Arman leapt at him with a blazing face, a roaring mouth.

VIII

It was massive weight and fanatical fury against wary craft and cunning strength. Travec was a mountaineer of Exar and had fought many times. But Arman's own endurance seemed inexhaustable. It seemed to flood from a superhuman reservoir. They wrestled violently, sprang back, crashed together again. Gradually, Travec's vision began to dull and blur, while Arman still seemed eager and fresh.

He lunged across the room—Travec staggered away. Arman swung an arm like a club, missed. Travec moved in, caught the arm, jerked, applied leverage—and Arman slammed prone to the floor. In that moment Travec stepped forward, kicked his head. Arman howled and rolled away. He hit the wall, groaned, clawed the floor in agony, slumped down, was still.

Mardien was crawling toward the torch; Travec threw himself forward, recovered it, backed away.

He stood panting, eyes swimming, heart pounding, knees like loose hinges, bruised in a dozen places, blood dripping from cheek and mouth and chin. Mardien sat glaring on the floor and Travec caught a glimpse of a wild, primordial beast. It was the swiftest of visions and he thought what marvelous disguises were beauty and civilization.

"You're as bad as he is," he panted. "You're his lover, mistress to a slaver."

"And you're jealous—that's why you hate him," she whispered. "That's why you hate me." Then she looked away from him. "If I were, if I am, it's nothing I am ashamed of."

He had no answer. Silence held the group, Arman lying with great arms sprawled, Mardien sitting tautly, Travec leaned against the wall, panting. His eye fell on the palm-injector— why hadn't it immobilized Arman?

He picked it up, examined it. The needle was broken, the sac was empty. He stood stiffly a moment, considering. Events were moving too fast for him, jostling and crowding past his control. Where was the boy? Had he fled for help?

Arman groaned again, shook his head painfully and slowly forced himself up on his arms.

"Sit still," said Travec and Arman looked up at him. "Hold your arms behind you."

Arman obeyed. Travec pocketed the torch, drew his knife, limped over and bent forward with a roll of adhesive tape. A bony thing sprang on his back, tangled his arms. The boy.

Travec dropped the tape and struggled to draw the torch from his pocket. It clattered to the floor.

Arman sprang forward, seized the weapon. The boy stood back now, babbling explanation.

" . . . knew he was no good the minute I saw him. So I kept an eye on him—anything to help you, Lord Arman. . . ."

There was a bright gleam in Arman's eyes as he watched Travec, who stood with arms down, waiting for death. Mardien sat feeling the bruises where the stool had struck her, watching without expression.

"Drop that knife!" said Arman. Travec slowly lowered his head, slumped into a crouch. "*Quick!*" barked Arman, "or I'll burn you where you stand."

Travec dropped the knife.

"I know about you," said Arman. "You hoped to take me to Maxus—alive."

Travec said nothing.

"A man like you will sell for two thousand sil at Alambar." He raised his voice and spoke into a mesh, "*Krosk!*"

Soon there was a scrape of feet along the hallway. A squat man in white overalls shoved his face into the room. He had a brown face seamed with wrinkles, eyes like prunes. "What'll you have?"

"Spray this man."

The squat man, without change of expression, applied a hypospray to Travec's neck. There was a sharp hiss.

Arman said, "You'll awake in Alambar. The price of your body will be useful. Every sil is useful."

Travec felt a slow dizzy tide rising over his head. His knees buckled, his arms hung loosely. He saw the faintly smiling Arman gesture to the simian little man, who came forward to catch him. Mist flooded his vision.

IX

There was a feel of fingers on his face, a buzzing at his ears, a vibration at his scalp.

He opened his eyes. An old man was trimming his hair. Travec jerked to a sitting position. He was in a large white-tiled room, on a cold slab of gray slate. He was naked.

A damp sensation and the sight of a hose on the floor informed him that he had been washed. On other slabs lay about fifty men and women, all naked, glistening damply. Two other attendants were working with shears on the still bodies.

There was constraint at his wrist. He looked down. He was handcuffed. The attendant come forward with a key, removed the cuffs. "Sometimes newcomers are nervous—wild, you know—when they wake up," he said, almost apologetically.

Travec relaxed back on the slab. "I suppose I'm in Alambar?"

"Correct," said the attendant.

"At the Distribute."

"Correct."

Travec looked woodenly around the room. "And those others were in the same load with me?"

The attendant nodded. "Six hundred at a crack. Arman's load."

"How long have I been here?"

"You were discharged this morning."

Travec rose to his feet, staggered a trifle. His arms and legs were pale. His tissues seemed flabby. The attendant said, "A day or two of solid food will fill you out as good as new."

Travec muttered angrily, "Where are my clothes?"

The attendant sniffed. "Be quiet, man, quiet. Loud talk never helps. You're stamped with a penal circuit now and they'll singe your hide for any excuse the first few weeks. They like you to struggle and roar. It's the only fun they have."

Travec muttered, "I want to see the High Commissioner."

"Tell one of the Overmen. I'm just a slave like yourself."

Travec sank back to the slab. Time passed. A few of the others moved fitfully, sat up. Travec looked from face to face. But they maintained perfect order and gravity.

They were past the first glow of youth. The men were neither muscular nor heavy; the women were not shapely or beautiful. These might well be trained for technical occupations.

A bell sounded, a door opened, a guard in a black uniform entered the room. He carried a light limber whisk, which he swung jauntily. Travec, meeting his eyes, felt anger.

The guard said, "Titus, this is a well-behaved crew. Not a yell from the lot. Those of you who are alive, jump up now! Form a line and follow me. As you pass the commissary take one suit of underwear, one smock, one pair of sandals—no more, no less. Quickly now, let's start off right." He cut the air with his whisk.

They were herded past a counter where they received clothes, past a desk where a badge was hung around their necks. The men were diverted through one door, the women through another.

Travec found himself in a long well-lighted hall, faced with thick glass. It was familiar—like the room in which he had first seen Mardien. About fifty other men occupied the hall, some walking with heads bent, others staring blankly at the glass. A few talked in somber undertones. A boy was sniffing mournfully.

At the end of the hall stood a hulking red-haired slave in a black and green harness—an orderly who evidently enjoyed his position. Travec walked up to him, met an eye as cold and blank as a frog's.

Travec said, "How do I make a call?"

"You don't. For you, those days are over."

"I want to call the High Commissioner—a friend of mine."

The orderly enjoyed the remark. "And I'm the Patriarch's uncle."

Travec said in a measured voice, "If there's any delay, the responsibility is yours."

The guard blinked. Stranger things had happened. "Just a minute."

He took Travec to a central office, Travec told his tale to a lieutenant in a tight black-and-gold uniform. The lieutenant hesitated. After a moment he gestured to a screen. "There it is. Use it."

A seven-pointed star appeared, a voice said, "Connection."

"The High Commissioner," said Travec.

A scowling visage appeared, a face with heavy black eyebrows, a coarse mop of hair, a hooked beak of a nose. "Well?"

Travec said, "I want to speak to the High Commissioner."

His eyes raked Travec's face and costume. "You're a slave."

"If you value your life, tell him Dyle Travec is here."

The man turned away, spoke softly for a time. His face vanished. Travec found himself looking into the narrow face of the High Commissioner.

"Ah, Travec," said the High Commissioner—and laughed a thin merry delicate laugh. Travec stood grimly silent. The High Commissioner said at last, "This is ridiculous and sad. I send you out to bring me Arman and instead he sells you to the Distribute for a slave. Is that not humorous?"

"Humorous indeed," agreed Travec. "However, if you'll get me loose from this pen, I'll be delighted."

The High Commissioner shook his head. "My dear fellow, I'm afraid I am powerless. You are out of my hands now. The Patriarch would be indignant if I meddled with the labor supply. I could treat with you when you held a visitor's permit. Then you had protection.

"I had hoped you would bring me Arman. Instead he brings me you. I bear you no ill will but you are more valuable to Maxus as a millhand than as a kidnaper. Serve well and behave and let me hear no more from you."

The screen faded.

Travec stared, his mouth still full of words. Behind him the lieutenant said in a practical voice, "Return him to the hall."

X

Gradually Travec became accustomed to constant appraisal from the hall. Narrow-eyed personnel foremen estimated his resistance, strength, flexibility. Lords seeking lackeys considered his poise and carriage. The ladies of the great colonnaded townhouses, in search of footmen and attendants, studied his physique and features.

A bony-nosed thin-lipped face caught his eye. It frowned in puzzlement, then turned excitedly toward a companion, pointed. Recognition came to Travec: Lord Spangle.

The auction began the same afternoon. One by one the occupants of the hall were ordered out into the arena. Travec's turn came at once. He gazed stonily over the crowd.

The auctioneer whispered, "Look pleasant, lad, there's ladies here. If you don't get one, it's the mines or heavy metals and that's the end. Look pleasant and smile and maybe you'll win yourself a soft bed."

He raised his voice, "A full-muscled and handsome man from Exar. Notice the fine chest, observe the straight neck, the strong legs. A valuable man in any capacity, so, ladies and gentlemen, let me hear your bids."

"Eight hundred sil."

"Eight hundred and fifty" . . . "nine hundred and fifty. . . ." These were emotionless careful voices of men from the industrial plants.

"One thousand sil," said a hoarse voice with a gleeful overtone. Travec remembered it—Lord Spangle's. Against his will, Travec looked around the room. Spangle was whispering behind his hand into the ear of a man in a gorgeous yellow-and-green doublet: Lord Jonas.

A woman said doubtfully. "One thousand one hundred."

"One thousand one hundred and fifty," said one of the foremen. The others were silent, relaxing back in their seats.

"One thousand two hundred," said Spangle, easily.

The auctioneer said, "Ladies and gentlemen, more action. Speak up, speak up! This is a valuable man. He is intelligent, educated on Exar, a qualified engineer, astute and reliable. Now speak up, who'll say one thousand five?"

One of the foremen stirred but a big bony woman raised a finger. "One thousand three hundred."

Spangle said silkily, "One thousand four hundred."

The woman said, "One thousand four hundred and fifty," in a determined voice.

Jonas laughed at one of Spangle's comments and said, "One thousand five hundred."

"One thousand six hundred," said Spangle, looking reproachfully at Jonas.

The bony woman sniffed, looked away.

"One thousand six hundred? One thousand six hundred?" barked the auctioneer. "Do I hear one thousand seven hundred?"

"One thousand seven hundred," said a sharp voice to the side.

"One thousand eight hundred," said a woman from the rear.

"One thousand nine hundred," said Spangle sourly,

"Two thousand," said the woman.

Spangle shrugged. "Two thousand one hundred."

"Two thousand two hundred," from the woman.

"Two thousand two hundred bid," cried the auctioneer. "A fine valuable man. Two thousand three? Where's two thousand three hundred?"

Silence. Spangle half opened his mouth to speak, closed it again, eyeing Travec with a reptilian vindictiveness.

"Sold, then!" cried the auctioneer. "Sold to the lady for two thousand two hundred sils." He turned to Travec. "Step down, go over to the registration desk."

Travec moved wordlessly across the floor. He looked at the woman by the table. "Mardien."

She smiled. He saw that her eyes were moist.

"It was the least I could do."

XI

Mardien and Travec walked out under the gray skies of late afternoon, past the dark and grim black-brick warehouses. They traversed a tunnel, fog swept damply across their cheeks. They passed the elegant townhouses and out into the busy heart of Alambar.

Travec said stiffly, "I suppose I must thank you." He paused uncomfortably.

She turned her head. "Well?"

He laughed. "Thanks. Although I don't understand why you rescued me. A couple weeks ago you were glad to have me killed."

"That was two—or rather, three weeks ago. And I think, in those three weeks, I've left a lot behind."

Travec said, "There's a tavern. Let's sit down."

It was a flat-faced building of glazed brick, with a square wooden door painted rusty-red. Inside it was warm and quiet. Light seeped through windows of stained glass, fell pleasantly over the tables.

Flat bread and salted fish were set before them and presently a bottle of warm wine, which shone at once watery-green and pink in their mugs. Looking across the table at Mardien, Travec gave himself to relaxation. She reached, took his hand in both of hers.

Travec said, "You must have reached a decision, or you would not have come for me."

She chewed her lip doubtfully. "I don't know. There are so many things involved."

"I think you've decided, and your certainty is making itself known to you."

She asked with a rueful half-smile, "How can you be sure?"

"Because you're here with me. Instead of with Arman."

His tone was so evidently bitter that she drew her hand back. Then she said, "Dyle, I accused you of jealousy once but I didn't believe it. Are you—really?"

He didn't answer.

"Dyle, this isn't easy to say. I never wanted to be anything to Arman except a follower, an Armanite. If you overlook perfectly normal enthusiasm and hero worship." She looked away, blushed a trifle. "He might even have—had me if he'd been less devious. Now I've found out. Arman is weak."

Travec drank wine, feeling oddly comforted. "He needs killing."

Mardien said abstractedly, as if in reply, "He compels respect and he's quick to use it. He's crafty with his tongue but he has no compassion."

"Where is he now?"

She looked at him soberly. "Dyle, when I helped you I made no conditions. I'd like to make one now."

"What is it?"

"That you do nothing without talking it over with me."

He said in a low voice, "I'll never rest while there are slaves and slavers, now."

She leaned back in her seat. "I thought that Arman promised an end to those things. But Arman is misguided."

Travec snorted. "Misguided. That's a weak word for a murderer, slaver, and witch doctor."

She shuddered. "I know, Dyle. I hate even to think that six hundred of my people have been led from their homes and sold into slavery."

"But *why*?" cried Travec. "I see no logic in it. Are you Oros truly cazy?"

"Not in the way you think. Our clothes, houses, mannerisms, they're just a reflection of our inner selves, and that is the secret of our race."

Travec wordlessly drank wine.

"Our victory over death."

Travec watched her quietly.

She said, "Dyle, I love you. I link my life to yours. Once

before I offered to make you one of us. I loved you then but I could not admit it.''

"I can't become an Oro without help?''

"Oh, no. In the beginning there was only one—Sagel Domino. The difference was his brain: he was strongly telepathic. He could read minds easily.

"He made contact with his best friend, established a rapport. And they found the rapport had stimulated the friend's brain. He was not so strongly telepathic but he *could* create a rapport. He converted some of his friends and so did Sagel Domino.

"And now we are several millions. We are not truly telepathic, but none of us fears death. When we are in danger, or dying, we establish rapport with someone we love and it's like stepping from a sinking boat onto solid ground.''

Travec grimaced. "There can't be much privacy among you.''

She shook her head vehemently. Her silky blond hair flew. "But there *is*! There is no conflict of wills. The old consciousness is given continual awareness without a break. The old memories fade and there is only the sense of continuity.

"For the dying it's like putting down one interesting book and taking up another. And for the living, remember, we only make rapport with those we love.''

He looked at her curiously. "And how many people are in you?''

She winced. "Dyle—you do not understand! I am I. I am *me*! Even if forty people had moved into me I would still be myself. Indeed, we overcompensate in singularity. We need the reassurance of individualism, we carry it to an extreme.

"Other races achieve a melancholy peace by making themselves as similar as possible, *outwardly*. Our identification is *inner*. The outer symbols of persistence are unnecessary. There are no tombs on the Alam Highlands, no hoarding of wealth.

"My mother loved her garden. She had many flowers. She died and now lives within me. I have no yearning whatever for flowers or plants. I worry about people and the future and social evils. So you see the link is one of awareness.''

"What did you feel when your mother's soul came into you?"

"Only a great joy," said Mardien earnestly. "As if I had saved her from drowning. I felt her presence for a few weeks, as if she were in the room. Then gradually she melted completely into me."

"And Arman," asked Travec, "is he an Oro? Will he live after his death?"

She nodded shamefacedly. "His mother was one of the few Oros the Overmen have ever enslaved. Usually we escape through death."

"But who is Arman in rapport with? *You*?"

She blushed even pinker. "No more. I blocked him out on the ship."

"Tell me," said Travec, "why did six hundred Oros come to Maxus as slaves?"

Mardien was silent a moment. Then she said, "If nothing else, Arman has aroused us to a sense of responsibility. For centuries we have been selfish, insular, jealous of our secret." She met Travec's eyes. "Among the six hundred are our most highly developed telepaths. They are our spies. They will edge themselves into the critical industries, and transmit the guarded techniques back to Fell."

"And then?"

Mardien nodded with a sad smile. "And then—we'll have two slave states. I see that now. Others will also. But—can we stop now? The crusade is in motion. Six hundred of us are here on Maxus."

Travec said woodenly, "Your emphasis is misplaced."

"How do you mean?" she asked, startled.

"You worry about six hundred Oros. Think of the hundreds of millions of slaves who are already on Maxus."

Her gaze wavered, turned down at the table. "I have no influence. Arman is leader. As soon as his ship takes on cargo he's going back for another load."

Travec leaned forward. "But there must be some center of authority among the Oros."

"Oh yes—the Elders, the township councils. But they have

no particular mandate. Arman has organized a private crusade. The Armanites are the active element.''

Travec drummed the table with his fingers. ''There's something missing. I wonder if your people realize how long they'll have to remain on Maxus, how well the Overmen guard their secrets, how many of them will be killed.''

''That means very little to us,'' Mardien said quietly.

''If all the slaves were Oros,'' said Travec at last, ''if none of the slaves feared death—there would no longer be a slave state.'' He looked at Mardien. ''If your six hundred Oros indoctrinated the other slaves there would no longer be any discipline. The system would collapse.''

Mardien said with growing excitement, ''If only twenty percent of the new Oros were telepathic. . . . We've got to get back to Fell—to the telepaths who can connect to the six hundred.''

''Two considerations,'' said Travec. ''First Arman. He's an obstacle. He's got to be removed. And then. . . . my brother and sister.''

XII

The great black hulk of the ship towered silently on the field, surrounded by activity. From the long black warehouse at one side of the field an endless transport carried a slow-moving line of boxes to a hatch in the side of the ship. Drays loaded with heavier crates pulled up on a floating platform under the bay and the crates were winched aboard.

A ragged cloud-wrack hung over Alambar and a cold wind blew litter along the field. Arman's cloak flapped at his legs as he approached the ship. Inside it was warm and quiet. He passed down the corridor, climbed the stairwell to the control dome, stood looking across the field toward the olive-green roof of the Patriarch's palace, which rose in the distance.

He reached up his hands, felt the swelling muscles of his chest, breathed deeply. Peace, relaxation—no worries, no decisions to make. The slaves were safely out of his hands, the cargo was loading. Three uneventful weeks now lay ahead.

He thought of Mardien. With nothing serious on his mind it was time to consider his pleasures. He was Arman. She should be proud to receive him. If she had put him off, she had put him off long enough.

He looked toward the door to her cabin. Sounds of movement came from within. Blood pounding in his ears, he strode to the door, knocked.

"Yes?" came the answer from within. Her voice was breathless, nervous. Ah, she knew his intentions. He tried the door. It was locked.

"Mardien," said Arman huskily. "Open the door."

"No, Arman."

"Open! Your god desires you, Mardien." He heard her rise to her feet. He rattled the door handle. "Let me in or I'll burn open the door."

"Very well," said Mardien in a strange voice.

The door opened. Arman walked into the room. A man stood there with his back to the light.

Furiously Arman turned to Mardien. "What is this?" He peered at the man who advanced a step. Arman blinked, his shoulders sagged. His hand dropped to the pouch at his belt. Travec fired first.

"Murder," said the policeman, looking up from the corpse to Travec.

"Self-defense," said Mardien. "I saw it."

Travec said, "This dead man is Arman."

"I realize that," said the patroller. "What is your status?"

"Slave," said Travec dryly.

The patroller sprang to his feet. "This is a terrible crime!"

"Let us visit the High Commissioner," suggested Travec, "and discover his opinion."

The High Commissioner was pacing the floor when they finally gained admittance to his chamber. He wore a long cloak of watered black silk with a blue sheen and it rustled rhythmically to his steps. His face was flushed, excited. He seemed absorbed with some inner problem and took small notice of his visitors.

Mardien and Travec stood close together with the patroller a pace distant in a subtle attitude of accusation.

The High Commissioner stopped short, faced the three. His eyebrows shot up at the sight of Travec. He murmured, "Travec? I am astonished."

"He's recently committed murder, your Lordship," said the patroller.

"Murder now? That's very serious. Who? Where?"

"The slaver Arman, sir. Just an hour or so ago."

"Hah!" The High Commissioner snapped his fingers. "Now that's interesting. Murder, you say?"

"Yes, sir. In Arman's own ship."

"Sordid, sordid!" The High Commissioner shook his head, then waved his hand. "You can go. Make arrangements for the body."

The patroller departed; the High Commissioner flung himself back into a seat. "My dear Travec, I fear your zeal has brought you into trouble."

"I don't understand you."

The High Commissioner said with hands expressively turned outward, "It's surely clear! Murder is a serious crime here on Maxus. Especially murder of an Overman by a slave. You are a slave, are you not?"

"Regardless of my status, Arman was not an Overman."

"He visited Maxus on special permit. Thus he is accorded Overman privileges. It has to be so. We can make no exceptions."

Mardien said, "It was clearly self-defense, your Lordship."

"No excuse," declared the High Commissioner. "No excuse whatever. A slave may not value his own life so highly. You may think me legalistic but these are definitions on which we base our civilization."

"But," Travec pointed out indignantly, "you employed me to kill Arman in the first place."

"The circumstances were different. An event which takes place on the planet Fell is one I can applaud or disapprove on a personal basis. Here on Maxus I must enforce the law."

Mardien grew desperate. "You don't know the circumstances, Lord! I bought Travec from the Distribute. He was in my cabin. Arman demanded to be let in, he threatened to burn the door in. He—he planned to force himself on me. I opened the door and when he saw Dyle, he flew into a rage and tried to shoot us both. Dyle acted in my defense and his own. He was there as my guard, as my protector."

The High Commissioner stroked his chin doubtfully. "You would submit to hypnotic examination on that testimony?"

"Yes indeed."

The High Commissioner sighed. "Very well. On such a questionable imbroglio we won't press the charges. There were no other witnesses, I presume?"

"No."

"Very well then." He drew himself up to his desk. "But the Patriarch insists on stern enforcements. If he hears about this—this killing, I fear the worst. If I were you I would leave the planet as soon as possible."

Travec looked at him through suddenly narrow eyes. The accusations, the strict reading of the law—were these side-issues to evade other commitments? It would, he thought, be dangerous to press too hard. The High Commissioner clearly was in a restive mood.

"My Lord," said Travec gently, "in any event, regardless of the method, motive, time and place, I fulfilled my—our objective. I eliminated Arman. Now will you return my brother and sister, as you promised?"

The High Commissioner looked up slowly. "My dear Travec—do I hear you rightly? Just now, on the unsupported word of this girl, I take the responsibility of releasing you—and you make demands of me! You are amazingly bold!"

Mardien tugged Travec's arm. "Come, Dyle."

"Do I understand then," asked Travec, "that you will not return my brother and sister?"

The High Commissioner's brow dropped into a straight line. "Naturally not. They are integrated happily into their new lives. Your brother operates a power tool. Your sister occupies—an interesting position elsewhere. You are presumptuous. The Patriarch would have my head. Now leave before I reconsider my generosity!''

''Come on, Dyle,'' whispered Mardien.

Reluctantly Travec turned away. The High Commissioner spoke quietly behind him. ''You understand, Arman's ship is impounded, together with its cargo. In the presumable absence of heirs and recognizing Arman's debt to the patriarch, whose private yacht he stole, the state will undoubtedly take title to the ship. It will be wise to remove your personal effects immediately.''

Mardien and Travec stood in the street, the Guchman Arch looming overhead.

''Failure again,'' said Travec, clenching and unclenching his fists. ''Played for fools and turned away.'' Mardien pulled his arm, urged him to walk, hoping that as long as Travec was moving he would do nothing rash.

''Failure! My poor little sister—so trusting and innocent. . . .''

''Dyle, don't brood. It won't help. We're both lucky to be alive.''

Travec stopped dead in his tracks, turned, looked back towards the High Commissioner's suite.

''There's the man I should have killed. If he and his kind did not exist—there would be no Armans.''

''Nonsense,'' said Mardien. ''There have always been evil men, there always will be. Now come on, Dyle, dear—before you get in more trouble. We'll buy ourselves passage back to Fell on one of the cargo ships.''

Travec muttered, ''It's not over yet.''

XIII

The Reverend Patriarch of Maxus and his High Commissioner were both insect-thin. From pale foreheads, their noses cut down past hollow eyesockets like blades of bone. The Patriarch was taller by a head and his hair was gray. The High Commissioner's hair, shiny black, was looped, swirled, pasted according to the Alambar mode.

The Patriarch's expression was mercurial, wide-eyed, suspicious. The High Commissioner affected a heavy-lidded stare. The Patriarch was the more hard-handed and unresponsive, the High Commissioner the more subtle. By a coincidence today they both wore heavy scarlet robes.

The Patriarch paced the cerise rug. The High Commissioner sat quietly in a soft chair upholstered in strips of human skin dyed yellow and black. The Patriarch rubbed his hands together, fingers flashing at his pale wrists.

"Harmless or not—religious cult or not—it represents organization. Organization among slaves we cannot permit."

The High Commissioner made a careless grimace. "It affords a sop, an opiate. It fulfills a need."

"Need?"

"Certainly. Consider the rapidity with which this movement has permeated the slaves—here, there, everywhere. If it did not satisfy a longing it would not have met such rapid acceptance."

"It represents organization," stated the Patriarch obstinately.

"I cannot agree. It is amorphous, there is no centrality. It is a mere fad, a popular cult. I say, let them revel in it, let them exhaust their nervous energies in ritual. We will have fewer disciplinary problems and consequently higher productivity. Already I notice a more widespread docility, especially among the least amenable ratings."

"*Pah*! Slaves are docile only when there is power in the penal circuits." He swooped to a seat, drank from his cup of hot brew. "And how do you know what codes and secret symbols are present in these rituals?"

The High Commissioner fingered the ruby dangling from his ear. "I have spies and informers who tell me—"

"So," the Patriarch burst out triumphantly, "you feel concern you do not admit! Beware, Underman, do not attempt subterfuge!"

"Of course not, Magnificat. I merely demonstrate my determination to overlook no conceivable source of disquiet, no minor node of unrest."

"See that you continue to do so." The Patriarch resumed his pacing. "There is yet a question of—"

A servant in a red-white-and-gray tunic entered the room, coughed timidly. The High Commissioner spoke angrily. "Can't you see we are in discussion?"

The servant bent his head. "Excuse me, Lord, there is a man who insists on an immediate audience."

"Immediate audience! At this time of the morning? Who is it?"

"His name is Dyle Travec. He has just arrived from Fell and he insists on the urgency of his business. I warned him that you were in consultation but he impressed me with the importance of his business. He seemed confident that you would see him."

The Patriarch said petulantly, "Who is this man Travec?"

The High Commissioner stood a moment without reply, staring at the door.

"Who is he, I say?"

"Remember the slaver Arman?" the High Commissioner asked in an absent tone of voice.

"Don't mention that name."

"Travec killed him. A rather sordid murder in Arman's ship. He was released on evidence of self-defense."

"What does he want now?"

"I have no idea. But he's here from Fell and it's the Oros, if you'll remember, who seem to have promulgated this new cult."

The Patriarch nodded to the servant. "Search him for weapons, then show him in. Double the guards at the door."

Travec entered. He nodded to the High Commissioner, casually saluted the Patriarch. He wore a handsome cloak of dark blue cloth embroidered with a pattern of vines and leaves. He carried himself with an assurance that irritated the High Commissioner.

"Well, Travec? I thought I had seen the last of you."

"Your time has come."

The two men in the scarlet robes stared at him. "What do you mean?"

"There are four hundred million slaves on this planet. You Overmen number forty million. Your slaves surround you like water around fish."

The Patriarch opened and closed his mouth wordlessly. The High Commissioner advanced slowly, until he stared eye to eye with Travec. He said, "You hardly present us with a novel discovery."

"What does he want?" croaked the Patriarch. "Is this man an assassin?"

Travec turned his eyes to the Patriarch, smiled faintly. "You live in an aura of fear. Would you not prefer a happy world, without the words master and slave, without the penal circuits, without the lash, without the degradation? Would you not prefer a world of people on equal terms, cooperating to the benefit of all?"

The High Commissioner said, "It is hardly a matter of preference. Such is the society we live in. Only a cataclysm could change it."

"Then there will be such a cataclysm."

The High Commissioner said, narrow-eyed, "Are you threatening us?"

"Yes," said Travec. "I am."

There was a pause.

"And when will this cataclysm occur?"

"At this very moment."

The Patriarch had sidled back to the mustard-colored wall-hanging, his hand behind him. "Wait!" called Travec. "It is to your advantage to wait."

The guard, summoned by the Patriarch's signal, entered. "Take him out," the Patriarch gasped throatily. "Kill him."

The High Commissioner held up a hand. "Wait, Magnificat, if you will. Perhaps this man has something to tell us."

Travec seemed to be listening to the air. He turned his head suddenly, said, "I have, indeed. I will inform you that about a million Overmen died in the last thirty seconds."

"*What*?"

"Is there a window overlooking the street?"

The High Commissioner turned, darted a calculating glance at the Patriarch, who stood rigid, eyes staring dark and large from his pale face. The High Commissioner said decisively, "This way."

He went with swift strides through the door, into the dark

barrel-vaulted hall. He swept aside the coverings at a high window, peered out and down, saw swarming confusion, tangles of broken vehicles and scattered bodies.

The High Commissioner's shoulders hunched forward. His hands gripped at the drapes. The Patriarch said hoarsely, "What is it?" He pushed to the window, bent his head, gasped.

Travec said, "We would have preferred a less bloody demonstration—but here is a spectacle the Overmen will understand. In Alambar, in Crevecoar, in Beloat, in Murabas—in every city on Maxus—every mechanism carrying Overmen and guided by a slave has been destroyed. The streets are filled with wrecks."

The High Commissioner turned his head and his eyes blazed. "There will be terrible retribution for this crime. There will be a great flowing of blood, a laying bare of white Orth bones."

Travec shook his head. "You don't understand our power. We encompass you like a fist around a handful of grapes. Now the fist has nerves, discipline. When the order comes to squeeze, a million Overmen are dead."

The High Commissioner raised his hands to his hair but stopped short of disturbing the pasted locks. He put his hands down.

Travec said, "There must be an understanding—now, before the hour is out. If not, there will be no Overmen left on the planet. The cataclysm has come. Now what is your word?"

The High Commissioner looked to the Patriarch. The Patriarch said in a husky whisper, "He is a madman."

Travec laughed.

"Then listen—but no, you cannot hear." He tilted his head as if he were hearing a faint but significant sound. He looked up.

"The Glauris Dyke has been breached. It is night on Glauris Bottom. The Overmen are sleeping in the pleasure-cabins, in the great inns, on the barges along the Yellowpetal. It is the night of the summer solstice, evening of the Lords' Convocation." He paused.

"The Pheresan Sea is now flowing a hundred feet deep

over Glauris Bottom and another million Overmen are dead, including twenty thousand lords.''

The High Commissioner went to the wall, spoke into a communicator. ''Get me the Rolite Nauton Hotel. . . . What? Then get the Glauris Maintenance Station—quick! . . . Yes, yes, now listen, look over the Bottom. What do you see? . . . Don't *scream*!'' His voice was itself a scream. ''*Water*?''

He turned to the Patriarch. ''We are being bled to death, Magnificat.''

''And there will be more death.''

They stared at Travec. He seemed tall and stern, his face commanding. And they were shrunken, dry, weak as mummies in their scarlet robes.

''What do you plan to do?'' asked the Patriarch.

''We can make rubble of this palace and all Alambar for miles around. All life will be crushed. You will die, Commissioner, and you will die, Patriarch.''

''And *you* will die,'' the High Commissioner pointed out. There was no more arrogance or anger in his voice. Now he was bargaining again, pushing for advantage. ''And what of your brother and your sister?''

Travec smiled. ''My brother and sister are safe, and I have no fear of dying. A hundred thousand slaves have just died killing Overmen. Death is nothing to Oros, it is immaterial.''

''You see, you *see*,'' bawled the Patriarch. ''It should have been stopped.''

''What is it you want from us?'' inquired the High Commissioner.

''The Patriarch will order all uniformed guards, militia and patrollers to their barracks. They must leave their weapons at the door. The Penal Control must be vacated. Then he will make a planetary broadcast, a declaration announcing that there are no longer slaves and Overmen on Maxus, that we all are free men, that a representative government will be formed.''

The Patriarch groaned, his knees wobbled, he supported himself on the wall hangings. The High Commissioner turned to him, with new authority. ''They win. Our day is over. Obey him.''

The shadow of old habits struggled visibly across the Patriarch's face. His hands clawed at the drapes and he pulled his long shape erect.

"Do what he asks!" said the High Commissioner harshly.

"No," cried the Patriarch. "I cannot—I will not. It is unthinkable."

The High Commissioner brought out his small gun, fired. The Patriarch's bony body slumped to the floor.

"I will make the announcement," said the High Commissioner. He went to the screen on the wall.

"Citizens of Maxus, as of today, there are no more slaves on Maxus," he began.

Three-Legged Joe

It might be well to make, in passing, a reference to the old time prospectors whose experience was gained through vast hardship and peril. No cause for wonder that as a group they are secretive and solitary. Their friendship is hard to win; they are understandably contemptuous of academic training. Much of their lore may soon die with them and this is a pity, since locked in their minds is knowledge that might well save a thousand lives.—*Excerpt from Appendix II, Hade's Manual of Practical Space Exploration and Mineral Survey.*

JOHN MILKE AND OLIVER PASKELL sauntered along Bangout Row in Merlinville. Recent graduates of Highland Technical Institute, they walked with an assured and casual stride, to convey an impression of hard-boiled competence. Oldtimers on porches along the way stared and muttered to each other.

John Milke was rubicund, energetic, positive; when he walked, his cheeks and tidy little paunch jiggled. Oliver Paskell, who was dark, spare and slight, affected old-style spectacles and an underslung pipe. Paskell was noticeably less brisk than Milke. Where Milke swaggered, Paskell slouched; where Milke inspected the quiet gray men on the porches with a lordly air, Paskell watched from the corner of his eye.

Milke pointed. "Number 432, right there." He opened the gate and approached the porch with Paskell two steps behind.

A tall bony man sat watching them with eyes pale and hard as marbles.

Milke asked, "You're Abel Cooley?"

"That's me."

"I understand that you're one of the best outside men on the planet. We're going out on a prospect trip; we need a good all-around hand, and we'd like to hire you. You'd have to take care of chow, service pressure suits, load samples, things like that."

Abel Cooley studied Milke briefly, then turned his pale eyes upon Paskell. Paskell looked away, out over the swells of naked granite that rolled six hundred miles west and south of Merlinville.

Cooley said in a mild voice, "Where you lads thinking to prospect?"

Milke blinked and frowned. It was his understanding that such questions were more or less taboo, though of course a man had a right to know where his job would take him. "In strict confidence," said Milke, "We're going out to Odfars."

"Odfars, eh?" Cooley's expression changed not at all. "What do you expect to find out there?"

"Well—Pillson's Almanac indicates a very high density. Which, as you may know, means heavy metal. Then the Deed Office shows neither claims nor workings on Odfars, so we thought we'd survey the territory before someone beat us to it."

Cooley nodded slowly. "So you're going out to Odfars . . . well, I tell you what to do. Get Three-legged Joe to wait on you. He'll make you a good hand."

"Three-legged Joe?" asked Milke in puzzlement. "Where do we find him?"

"He's out on Odfars now."

Paskell came closer. "How do we locate him on Odfars?"

Cooley smiled crookedly. "Don't worry about that. Leave it to Joe. He'll find you."

From the house came a dark-skinned man five feet tall and four feet wide. Cooley said, "James, these boys are going prospecting out on Odfars; they're looking for a flunky. Maybe you're interested?"

"Not just now, Abel."

"Maybe Three-legged Joe is the man to see."

"Can't beat Three-legged Joe."

Paskell drew Milke out to the street. "They're joking."

Milke said darkly. "No use trying to get work out of those old bums. They get by on their pensions; they don't want an honest job."

Paskell said thoughtfully, "It might be less trouble, in the long run, to go out by ourselves. These old-timers don't understand modern methods. Even if we found a man that satisfied us, we'd have to break him in on the Pinsley generator and the Hurd."

Milke nodded. "There'll be more work for us, but I think you're right."

Paskell pointed. "There's the other place—Tom Hand's Chandlery."

Milke consulted a list. "I hope this doesn't turn out to be another wild goose chase; we need those extra filters."

Tom Hand's Chandlery occupied a large dirty building raised off the ground on four-foot stilts. Milke and Paskell climbed up on the loading platform. A scrawny near-bald man approached from out of the shadows. "What's the trouble, boys?"

Milke frowned at his list while Paskell stood aside puffing owlishly on his pipe. "If you'll take us to your technical superintendent," said Milke, "I think I can explain what we need."

The old man reached out two dirty fingers. "Lemme see what you want."

Milke fastidiously moved the list out of reach. "I think I'd better see someone in the technical department."

The old man said impatiently, "Son, out here we don't

have departments technical or otherwise. Lemme see what you want. If we got it, I'll know; if we don't, I'll know.''

Milke handed over the list. The old man hissed through his teeth. "You want an ungodly amount of them filters."

"They keep burning out on us," said Milke. "I've diagnosed the trouble—an extra load on the circuit."

"Mmph, those things never burn out. You've probably been plugging them in backwise. This side here fits against the black thing-a-ma-jig; this side connects to your circuits. Is that how you had 'em?"

Milke cleared his throat. "Well—"

Paskell took the pipe out of his mouth. "No, as a matter of fact we had them in the other way."

The old man nodded. "I'll give you three. That's all you'll use in a lifetime. Now for this other stuff, we got to go around to the front."

He led them down a dark aisle, past racks crammed with nameless oddments, into a room split by a scarred wooden counter.

At a table near the door three men sat playing cards; nearby stood the dark thick man called James.

James called in a jocular baritone, "Give 'em a jug of acid for Three-legged Joe, Tom. These boys is going out to prospect Odfars."

"Odfars, eh?" Tom scrutinized Milke and Paskell with impersonal interest, "Don't know as I'd try it, boys. Three-legged Joe—"

Milke asked brusquely, "What do we owe you?"

Tom Hand scribbled out a bill, took Milke's money.

Paskell asked tentatively, "Who is this Three-legged Joe? . . . A joke? Or is there actually someone out there?"

Tom Hand bent over his cash box. The men at the table snapped cards along the green felt. James had his back turned.

Paskell put the pipe back in his mouth, sucked noisily.

On the way back, Milke said bitterly, "It's always the same; when these old-timers have a laugh on strangers, they play it for all it's worth. . . ."

"But who or what is Three-legged Joe?"

"Well," said Milke, "sooner or later, I suppose we'll find out."

Odfars ranked fourteenth in a scatter of dead worlds around Sigma Sculptoris, drifting in an orbit so wide that the sun showed like a medium-distant street lamp.

Paskell gingerly handled the controls, while Milke scanned the face of the planet with radar peaked to highest sensitivity. Milke pointed to a mirror-smooth surface winding like a fjord between axe-headed crags. "Look there, an ideal landing site—perfect!"

Paskell said doubtfully, "It looks like a chain of lakes."

"That's what it is—lakes of quicksilver." Milke turned Paskell a chiding glance. "It's absolute zero down there; it can't help but be solid, if that's what's on your mind."

"True," said Paskell. "But it has a peculiar soft look to it."

"If it's liquid," scoffed Milke, "I'll eat my hat."

"If it's liquid," said Paskell, "neither one of us will eat—ever again. Well—here goes."

The impact of landing substantiated Milke's position. He ran to the port, looked out. "Hmmph, can't see anything in this dark without my Intensifier. In any event, we'll have a good level floor for our tent."

Paskell saw in his mind's eye a page from Hade's Manual: *"The assay tent is customarily a balloon of plastic film maintained by air pressure. Its use eliminates noxious, acrid or poisonous fumes inside the ship, formerly a source of great annoyance. Certain authorities advise a field survey before bringing out the tent; others maintain that erecting the tent first will facilitate examination of samples taken on the survey, and I generally favor the latter practice."*

Milke said off-handedly. "Some of the boys like to wait before they put up their bubble; others set it out first thing to give them a place to drop off their samples. I generally like to get it up and out of the way."

"Yes, yes," said Paskell. "Let's get it up."

In pressure suits, with Intensifiers on their helmets, they left the ship. Paskell looked across the quicksilver lake, up

into the jutting rock—icy bright and black through their glasses.
The lake gleamed like a buffed nickel, terminating nearby in
a long finger pointing up a defile. In the direction opposite it
dropped off around the curve of the horizon.

Paskell said in a tone of dubious humor, "I don't see
Three-legged Joe anywhere."

Milke's snort sounded loud in the earphones.

"He's supposed to know we're here."

Milke said crisply, "Let's get to work."

From an exterior locker they took the assay tent, carried it
fifty feet across the quicksilver to the length of the air hose.
Milke adjusted the valve; the tent swelled into a half-sphere
fifteen feet in diameter.

Milke tested the lock with a deftness attained on lunar field
trips. He squeezed the lock compartment against the tent,
forcing the enclosed air into the tent through a flap valve;
then entering the lock, he sealed the outside entry, opened the
inside valve, let the compartment fill with air and entered the
tent.

"Works fine," he told Paskell confidently. "Let's get the
equipment."

From the locker they brought the knock-down bench, carried it inside through the lock. Milke brought out a rack of
reagents and the pulverizer. Paskell carried out the furnace,
then went into the ship for the spectroscope.

"That should be good for a while," said Milke. He shot a
glance up at distant Sigma Sculptoris. "It's a six hour day
here—about two hours of light left. Feel like taking a quick
look around?"

"Might be a good idea." Paskell fingered the empty loop
at his belt. "I think I'll get my gun."

Milke chuckled. "There's nothing alive here; it's a vacuum, absolute zero. You've let that talk of Three-legged Joe
get you down."

"Quite right," said Paskell. "In any event, I'll feel better
armed."

Milke followed him into the ship. "Might as well get in the
habit of wearing the thing." He fastened his own weapon.

They set out across the lake, past the tent, up the narrow

finger of quicksilver, into the defile. "Strange stuff," said Paskell chipping a fragment from the cliff.

"Can't be chalk," said Milke. "Chalk is sedimentary."

"Whatever it is," said Paskell, "it's still strange stuff, and it still looks like chalk."

The fissure widened, the cliffs fell away almost at once; another quicksilver lake spread before them. "Makes for easy walking," observed Milke. "Better than scrambling through the rocks."

Paskell eyed the mirror-like surface, which wound like a glacier past alternating bluffs and into a perceptible curve out over the horizon. "It might easily be connected all the way around."

Milke motioned to him. "See that pink stone? Rhodocrosite. And look down at the end—somehow it's been fused and reduced, leaving the pure metal."

"Very encouraging," said Paskell.

"Encouraging?" boomed Milke. "Why it's downright wonderful! If we found nothing else but this one vein, we're made . . . it might even be economical to mine the quicksilver. . . ."

Paskell glanced at the sun, "There's not much daylight left; perhaps—"

"Oh, just around the next bend," said Milke. "It's easy walking." He pointed ahead to a massive knob of shiny black material projecting from the crag. "Look at that knob of galena—interesting."

Paskell felt a throb and hum at his side. He looked down to the dial, stopped short, walked to the left, turned, walked back to the right. He looked up toward the knob of shiny black rock. "That's not galena, that's pitchblende."

"By Jove," breathed Milke reverently, "you're right! As big as the Margan-Annis strike. . . . Oliver, my boy, we're made."

Paskell said with a puckered brow, "I can't understand why the planet hasn't been developed. . . ." He glanced nervously up into the deep shadows, perceptibly lengthening. "I wonder—"

"Three-legged Joe?" Milke laughed.

"Fairy-tale stuff." He looked at Paskell. "What's the matter?"

Paskell said in a husky whisper, "Feel the ground."

Milke stood stock still.

Thud-bump. Thud-bump. Thud-bump.

The sun dropped behind a crag; even the boosters found no light in the sudden shade. "Come on," said Paskell. He turned, paced hurriedly back up the lake.

"Wait for me," said Milke breathlessly.

At the ridge of chalky rock which divided the two lakes, they paused, looked back. The ground felt solid, immobile under their feet.

"Strange," said Milke.

"Very strange," said Paskell.

They crossed the ridge; the hulk of their ship caught the last flat rays from Sigma Sculptoris.

Paskell came to a sudden halt. Milke stared at him, then followed his gaze. "Our assay tent!"

They ran forward to where the fabric lay in a crumped heap. "There's been a hole cut in it," muttered Paskell.

"Three-legged Joe?" inquired Milke sarcastically. "More likely there's a leak."

Paskell kicked at the material, now stiff as sheet metal with the cold. "We'll have a devil of a time finding it."

"Oh, not so bad. We'll pump in warm air—"

"And then?"

"Well, there's a leak. As soon as the air hits the vacuum the water vapor condenses. So we look for a little jet of steam."

Paskell said in a precise voice, "There's no leak."

"No? Then why—"

"We never turned on the heat. The air inside liquefied."

Milke turned away to look out over the lake. Paskell quietly plugged in the cord; power circulated through elements meshed into the tent fabric.

Milke turned back, slapping his gloves together. "That's about all we can do until the air thaws out. . . ." He looked at Paskell, who again was standing as if listening. Irritably he asked, "What's the matter now?"

Paskell made a furtive motion toward the ground. Milke looked intently down.

Thud-bump. Thud-bump. Thud-bump. Thud-bump.

"Three-legged Joe," whispered Paskell.

Milke looked hurriedly in all directions. "There can't be anything out there." He turned. Paskell had disappeared.

"Oliver! Where are you?"

"I'm in the ship," came a calm voice.

Milke backed slowly toward the port. Night had come to Odfars; starlight shone on the quicksilver lake, intensified by their lenses to near the illumination of moonlight. Was that a black shadow standing in the defile? Milke hurriedly backed against the port.

It was locked. He pounded against the metal. "Hey, Oliver, open up!"

He looked over his shoulder. The black shape seemed to have moved forward.

Paskell came to the port, looked carefully out past Milke, threw back the bolts. Milke burst through the air-lock, on into the ship. He took off his helmet. "What's the idea locking me out? Suppose that damn whatever-it-is was hot on my trail?"

Paskell said in a practical voice, "Well, we'd hardly want him inside the ship, would we?"

Milke roared, "If he got me first, I wouldn't care whether he got into the ship or not." He jumped up into the central dome, played the searchlight around the lake. Paskell watched from the sideport. "See anything?"

"No," grumbled Milke. "I still don't believe there's anything out there. Let's eat dinner and get some sleep."

"Perhaps we should keep watch."

"What do we watch for? What good would it do if we saw something?"

Paskell shrugged. "We might be able to deal with it, if we knew what it was."

Milke said, "If there *is* anything out there—" he slapped the weapon-clip at his belt, "I'll know how to deal with it. . . .

A couple of bursts into its hide and we'll have to sift-screen for its pieces.''

The ship vibrated; from the tail came a harsh sound. The floor jarred under their feet. Milke looked askance at Paskell, who puffed rather desperately at his pipe. Mike ran back to the searchlight. But the central dome interrupted the backward path of the beam and the tail was left in darkness.

''I can't see a thing,'' fretted Milke. He jumped down to the deck, looked indecisively at the after port.

The vibrations ceased. Milke squared his shoulders, pulled the helmet back over his head. Slowly Paskell followed suit.

''You bring a flashlight,'' said Milke. ''I'll have my gun ready. . . .''

They stepped into the air lock. Paskell gingerly thrust his arm out, aimed the light toward the tent. ''Nothing there,'' grumbled Milke. He pushed past Paskell, stepped down to the ground. Paskell followed, played the light in a circle.

''Whatever it was, it's gone,'' grunted Milke. ''It heard us coming—''

''Look,'' whispered Paskell.

It was no more than a zigzag of shadows, a moving mass.

Milke held out his arm; his gun spat pale blue sparks. Explosion—a great splash of orange light. ''Got him!'' cried Milke exultantly. ''Dead center!''

Their eyes adjusted to the pallid illumination of the flashlight. Nothing but the glistening sheen of the quicksilver and—a rumpled, tumbled mess where the assay tent had stood.

Milke said in an outrage too deep for vehemence, ''He's ruined our gear—our tent!''

''Look out!'' screamed Paskell. The flashlight took lunatic sweeps over the lake. Milke sent shot after shot at a tall shape; the explosions rained debris back over their suits; the orange glare blinded their eyes.

Thud-bump . . . *Thud-bump* . . . ''Inside!'' gasped Milke. ''Inside, we can't hold him off. . . .''

The outer port slammed. A breathless moment later the hull was jarred and scraped raggedly along the frozen quicksilver. Milke and Paskell stood haunted and pale in the center of the deck.

Metal creaked at the stern under pressure or torsion. Milke's voice came high-pitched. "We're not built to take that kind of stuff—"

The ship lurched to the side. Paskell put his pipe in his pocket, grabbed a stanchion. Milke jumped up to the controls. "We'd better get out of here."

Paskell cleared his throat. "Wait, I think it's stopped."

The boat was quiet. Milke thought of the searchlight, flicked the switch. "Hah!"

"What is it?"

Milke stared out the port. He said slowly, "I really don't know. Something like a one-legged man on crutches . . . that's how it walks."

"Is he big?"

"Yes," said Milke. "Rather big. . . . I think he's gone, through that fissure." He came down to the deck, split open his space suit, climbed in nervously. "That was Three-legged Joe."

Paskell took a sudden seat on the bunk, reached for his pipe. "Quite an impressive fellow."

Milke laughed shortly. "I can certainly understand how he scared the bejabbers out of those old bindlestiffs."

"Yes," Paskell nodded earnestly. "I can too." He lit his pipe, puffed reflectively. "He can't be invulnerable. . . ."

Milke dropped leadenly upon his own bunk. "We'll get him—somehow or other."

Paskell craned his neck out the port. "There'll be light in a few hours. . . . I suppose we might as well sleep."

"Yes," said Milke. "If Three-legged Joe comes back, I imagine he'll let us know about it."

Sigma Sculptoris washed the quicksilver lake with the palest of lights. Milke and Paskell glumly examined the wreckage of their tent.

Milke's indignation brimmed over the restraints he had set upon himself. He clenched his fists inside the gloves, glared toward the defile. "I'd like to lay my hands on that three-legged devil. . . ."

Paskell busied himself among the tatters of the tent. "Nothing but ribbons."

Milke said gloomily, "No use to think about mending it. . . ." He watched Paskell curiously. "What are you looking for?"

"I wonder what possessed him to break into the tent."

"Sheer destructiveness."

Paskell said thoughtfully, "I notice one thing—" he paused.

"What?"

"All our reagents are gone."

Milke bent over the wreckage. "All of them?"

"All the acids. All the bases. He left distilled water, the salts. . . ."

"Hm," said Milke. "What do you make of that?"

Paskell shrugged inside his suit. "It's suggestive."

"Of what, if I may ask?"

"I'm not sure." Paskell wandered out over the quicksilver, searching the surface. "He was about here when you shot at him?"

"Just about."

Paskell bent. "Look here." He held up a rough brownish-gray object the size of his thumb. "Here's a piece of Three-legged Joe."

Milke examined the fragment. "If this is all our weapons did to him—he's tough. This stuff is flexible!"

Paskell took back the fragment. "Let's take it in and run it through the analyzer."

They returned into the ship. Paskell clamped the specimen in a vise and after exasperating difficulty, succeeded in slicing free a brittle shaving. He forced it flat between a slide and a cover glass, examined it under the microscope. "Remarkable."

"Let's see." Milke applied his eye. "Mm . . . it's like a carpet—woven in three dimensions."

"Right. No matter which way you cut or tear, fibers mat up against you . . . now let's see what he's made of."

"You're the technician," said Milke.

Paskell looked up from the work bench an hour later. "It's a very complex silicon compound. The spectroscope shows silicon, lithium, fluorine, oxygen, iron, sulfur, selenium, but I can't begin to put a name to the stuff.''

"Call it Joe-hide," Milke suggested.

Paskell blew into his pipe, looked solemnly down at the workbench. "I have a tentative theory about Joe's inner workings. . . ."

"Well?"

"Obviously he needs energy to exist. His hide shows no radioactivity, so he must use chemical energy. At least I can't think of any other form of energy that he could be using."

Milke frowned. "Chemical energy? At absolute zero?"

"He's insulated. No telling how high his internal temperature gets."

"What kind of chemical energy? There's no free oxygen, no fluorine, nothing. . . ."

"Presumably he uses whatever he can get—anything that reacts, to produce energy."

Milke pounded his fist. "We could bait him into a trap, with, say, a chunk of solid oxygen!"

"I should certainly think so. But what kind of trap?"

Milke scowled. "A dead-fall."

"Here on Odfars gravity is not too strong . . . we'd have to stack ten thousand cubic yards of rock to make an impression."

Milke paced up and down the room. "I've got it!"

"Well?" said Paskell mildly.

"Perhaps you could make a detonator that we could set off from the ship."

"Yes, that could be done."

"Then here's what we'll do. We'll set out about twenty pounds of myradyne, with the detonator in the center. Joe will come past, tuck this bundle into whatever kind of stomach he's got. We wait till he gets a few hundred yards from the ship, then set it off."

Paskell pursed his lips. "If events proceeded exactly along those lines, everything would be fine."

"Well, why shouldn't they? You claim that Joe eats—"

"Not 'claim'—'theorize.' ''

"—anything that produces energy. Well, the myradyne

should look to him like ice cream and candy and cake all mixed together. It's nothing else *but* energy.''

"It's a different kind of energy—the energy of instability. Perhaps he only digests energy of combination.''

"You're quibbling," said Milke with disgust. "I say the idea's worth trying.''

Paskell shrugged. "Get out your myradyne.''

"How long will it take you to fix up a detonator?''

"Twenty minutes. I'll hook up a battery and a spare head set to the cartridge. . . .''

While Milke gingerly carried the packet of explosive across the lake, Paskell stood by the port watching. Milke surveyed the landscape with fine calculation, setting down the packet, moving it a few yards to the right, another few yards toward the defile. Finally satisfied, he looked back to Paskell for approval. Paskell signaled casually, and his hand fell against the detonation switch. He looked out toward Milke, hastily jumped into his suit, let himself through the port, ran across the lake.

Milke asked, "What's the trouble?''

Paskell said, "That remote detonator doesn't work. I'd better take a look at it.''

Milke stared at him truculently. "How do you know it doesn't work?''

Paskell made a vague gesture, knelt beside the packet, unfolded the wrapping.

"You couldn't have just sensed it," Milke insisted.

"Well, as a matter of fact, my hand accidentally hit the switch, and it didn't go off—so I thought I'd better run out and see what was wrong.''

Milke seemed to sink inside his suit. For a moment there was silence. "Ah," said Paskell. "Nothing very serious; I neglected to clip down the battery leads. . . .now it's ready to go—''

"I'm going back to the ship," said Milke thickly.

Paskell glanced up toward Sigma Sculptoris. "Yes, there's only a few moments of daylight left. . . .''

Inside the ship was dark; night apparently had already settled on quicksilver lake.

Milke roused himself from his bunk where he had been quietly sitting, went up into the control blister. "Nothing in sight."

Paskell said mildly. "Maybe Joe won't be back."

Milke, with his back to Paskell, said nothing.

"Maybe he's been watching us all day," Paskell remarked.

Milke leaned forward. "There's something moving in the gulch. . . . there goes the daylight. Blast it! Now I can't see anything . . . and the dome's in the way of the searchlight again."

In sudden inspiration Paskell said, "Use the radar!"

Milke ran to the screen, set the key on short range. Paskell swung around the transmission dish. "Hold it!" said Milke. "Right there!"

Paskell and Milke bent close to the screen. The plane of the lake, the bulk of the mountains, the gap were all clear. Three-legged Joe, much closer, was a blur. "Can't you adjust it finer?" demanded Paskell.

Milke ran to the locker, came back with a power wrench, set the adjustment to its limit. "How's that?"

"Turn off the lights. I feel like I'm in a peep-show."

Milke came back to the screen. Three-legged Joe was a barrel surmounted by a keg. The legs were a blur; flickering wisps of light to either side of the trunk seemed to indicate arm-members.

"Look," sighed Milke. "He's stopping by the package."

The great trunk seemed to waver, collapse.

"He's reaching for it."

The shape once more reached its full height.

"He's stopped," said Paskell.

"He's eating the myradyne. . . ."

Three-legged Joe came forward, and presently blurred out past the resolving power of the set.

The ship jerked tentatively. Milke and Paskell braced themselves. Nothing more. Silence. The radar screen was empty. Paskell swivelled the receptor. Nothing.

"He's gone," said Milke. "Where's the detonator switch?"

"Wait!" Paskell whispered. He turned on the lights. "Look!"

Milke jerked back. Pressed close to the port beside his face was a rough silvery brown-gray substance.

The port suddenly showed black. A flicker of movement passed the stern port.

"Off with the lights," hissed Milke. "Back to the radar."

A blur of golden light resolved into an ambling barrel and keg.

"Now," said Milke, "press the button! Quick! Before he gets out of range."

"Just a moment," said Paskell. "Suppose he's smarter than we think?"

"No time for theorizing now," cried Milke. "Where's the button?"

Paskell pushed him away stubbornly. "First, we'd better take a look around." He climbed into his space suit while Milke fumed and ranted.

Taking no heed, Paskell left the ship. Out the port Milke could see the glimmer of his suit light.

The outside port sighed open, thudded shut. Paskell came back into the ship. Milke had his finger on the switch. Paskell, unable to talk through the helmet, banged his glove against the wall. In his other hand he held up a brown packet.

Milke's fingers fell nervously away.

Paskell split himself out of the suit. "I didn't think he'd like myradyne," he said in modest triumph. "The wrong kind of chemical energy. He left it beside the ship."

"God!" said Milke hastily. "Twice on the same day I'm blown to smithereens. . . ."

Paskell carefully removed the detonator. "Every day we're learning more about Three-legged Joe."

Milke's voice was warm with emotion. "Every day we come closer to killing ourselves."

"Tomorrow," said Paskell, "we'll try again."

Over a cup of hot coffee Milke asked, "How do you mean, try again? So far as I can see, we're licked. Our guns are no good, he refuses to eat our explosives. Certainly nothing in the world could poison him.''

"True.'' Paskell tamped black shag into his pipe. "The methods for killing human beings don't apply to Three-legged Joe.''

"No wonder those old goats at Merlinville gave us the laugh.''

Paskell puffed thoughtfully. "If we could concentrate enough heat on Joe, for a long enough time—''

"Nuts!" said Milke. "If we had an ocean we couldn't even drown him.''

Paskell said through the cloud of smoke. "If we melted a puddle in the quicksilver and he fell in, and the quicksilver froze around him—''

"Impossible. Quicksilver at absolute zero is superconductive. We'd have to heat half the planet.''

"Superconductive. . . . Right. So it is." Paskell stared dreamily into the haze. "I wonder how far the quicksilver extends around the planet?''

"What difference does that make?''

"Maybe we'll electrocute Joe.''

"Hah!" spat Milke. "With what? Our two thousand-watt generator?''

Paskell said, "First we'll have to check on the quicksilver.''

"On foot? With Joe pounding along behind us, breathing down our necks?''

Paskell said carelessly, "I imagine we can move as fast as Joe.''

"I'm not sure. Maybe he runs like a greyhound.''

"We'll have our guns.''

"Fat lot of good they'll do.''

"Well—I suppose we could take up our ship and cruise around the planet. In fact it might be better. . . .''

The ship began descending from a low orbit. Absorbed in his theorizing, Milke called out in alarm, "You're almost setting down in that defile!''

"Good," said Paskell. "We want to have the ship as near to the gap as possible.''

"I don't see why," Milke said petulantly. "In fact I don't understand what you're up to."

"We're planning to electrocute Three-legged Joe," said Paskell patiently. "We've been around the planet; we've established that the quicksilver is interconnected everywhere except at this fifty-foot saddle of gray chalk. We've got enough lead and copper aboard to bridge the gap with a fairly heavy cable—which we will do. We can melt a good connection into the quicksilver with thermite."

"So then?"

"While you're installing the cable, I'll be rigging up some kind of fancy induction coil to take power from our generator and build up watts in the round-planet circuit."

Milke stared incredulously at Paskell. "What good will that do?"

"You'll arrange the cable so that when Joe comes along the defile, he'll have to take hold of the cable to break it. As soon as he does, he'll get everything that we've been feeding into the circuit."

Milke shook his head. "It won't work."

Paskell puffed at his pipe. "And why not, pray?"

"Think of the hysteresis in all those miles of quicksilver—the inlets and bays and channels. There'll be a billion little whorls and eddies. . . ."

"There's no energy lost," said Paskell. "There's no resistance, so there can't be any production of heat."

"There'll be field conflicts," insisted Milke.

"Only for a few hundredths of a second. After that the fields will necessarily enforce a flow pattern that minimizes the impedance."

Milke shook his head. "I hope you know what you're talking about. . . . But—" he raised a finger "—we've got another problem."

"What's that?"

"The planet's natural magnetism. If we start current flowing around the planet, we're setting up artificial north and south poles. We'll be fighting the natural field."

Paskell blinked owlishly. "There is no natural field to this planet. I checked for it earlier."

Milke threw up his hands. "Go to it, Oliver. It's your party."

Milke and Paskell stood contemplating the defile, across which, at the height of their eyes, dangled a rude cable. Near the lake, the cable passed through a long box, from which came leads running to the generator inside the ship.

Paskell said solemnly, "There's a trillion amps running through the cable."

"A few more," said Milke, "it'll swell like a poisoned pup."

"There is a practical limit," admitted Paskell. "At absolute zero the resistance of super-conductive metals is infinitesimal, but still is greater than nothing. When the cable carries a load that generates heat faster than the heat radiates off, the temperature in the cable rises until it reaches the lower limit of super-conductivity."

"And then?"

Paskell flung up his arms. "No more cable."

Milke regarded his handiwork anxiously. "Perhaps we'd better check."

"How? We don't have a thermocouple aboard that sensitive."

Milke shrugged. "All we can do then is hope."

"Right. Hope that Joe comes down that pass before the cable goes." He looked up at the sun. "Still an hour or two of light."

Milke said doubtfully, "The set-up doesn't look very lethal. Suppose Joe grabs the cable and breaks it, and nothing happens—what then?"

"Something's got to happen. We're feeding a constant two thousand watts into that circuit. When Joe breaks the cable those watts have to go somewhere—they just don't evaporate. They keep on going—through Joe. And if Joe doesn't feel it, I'll personally go after him with a pocketknife."

Milke turned Paskell a surprised glance: strong talk from modest Oliver Paskell.

Paskell was restlessly beating his hands together. "We're forgetting something."

Milke turned, looked toward the ship.

"Ah, yes," said Paskell.

Milke made a strange noise. His arm jerked up.

"The bait," said Paskell. "We want to set out some acid."

"Never mind the bait," rasped Milke. "We're the bait . . . Joe's behind us. . . ."

Paskell sprang around. Three-legged Joe stood in front of the ship, looking at them.

"Run," said Milke. "Up under the cable . . . and if it doesn't work—God help us. . . ."

Three-legged Joe came lurching forward.

Paskell stood frozen. "Run!" screamed Milke. He darted back, seized Paskell's arm.

Paskell broke into a shambling run.

"Faster," panted Milke. "He's gaining on us."

Paskell ran to the mountainside, tried to claw his way up the sheer rock.

"No, no!" yelled Milke. "Through the defile!"

Paskell turned, ducked under one of Joe's enormous arms, scuttled toward the defile.

Milke tackled him. "Under the cable—not through! *Under!* He grabbed Paskell's legs, drew him under the cable. Three-legged Joe ambled casually after them.

Paskell rose to his feet, looked wildly around. "Easy," said Milke. "Easy. . . ."

Cautiously they backed up the defile. Milke panted, "No use running now. If your contraption doesn't work, we might as well reconcile ourselves to death."

Paskell asked suddenly, "Did you turn on the generator?"

Milke froze. "The generator? Inside the ship? You mean the power out to the circuit? I don't remember!"

Paskell said despairingly, "You'll know in a minute. Here comes Joe—"

Three-legged Joe paused by the cable, then walked forward. The cable touched his chest. He lifted up his arms. "Close your eyes," cried Paskell.

The sudden glare spattered darts of light through their eyelids.

"The generator!" said Milke.

Three-legged Joe lay forty feet distant, twitching feebly.

"He's not dead," muttered Paskell.

Milke stood looking down at the silver-gray hulk. "We can't cut him up. We can't tie him. We can't. . . ."

Paskell ran to the ship. "Get out the grapples."

Returning from the Merlinville Deed Office, Milke and Paskell stepped into Tom Hand's Chandlery for a new tent and a replacement set of reagents.

Lounging at the table were Abel Cooley and his friend James. "Ah, here's the prospectors back from Odfars," said Cooley.

Tom Hand limped forward. His eyes were red, there was alcohol on his breath, and a series of black and blue bruises showed on one side of his face. "Well, young fellow," he said to Milke in a thick voice, "what'll it be?"

"First, we need a new assay tent."

From the table by the window came a chuckle. James called out in his jocular baritone, "Three-legged Joe maybe tried to bunk in with you?"

Milke made a noncommittal gesture; Paskell sucked at his pipe.

Tom Hand said, "Pick up your tent out on the loading platform. What else?"

"A set of assay reagents." Milke handed over a list.

Tom Hand looked at them from under his eyebrows. "You boys still going out prospecting?"

"Certainly. Why not?"

"I should think maybe you had a bellyful."

Milke shrugged. "Odfars wasn't too bad. We never expected an easy life from prospecting. Joe gave us a pretty hard time, but we took care of him."

Hand leaned forward, red eyes blinking. "What's that?"

"We don't mind letting it out. We've got everything in sight sewed up and officially recorded."

Abel Cooley said, "You took care of Joe, did you? Talk him to death maybe?"

"No. He's still alive. We've got him where he can't get away. A research team from the Institute is coming out to look him over."

James stepped forward. "You've got him where he can't get away? I've seen Joe break out of a net of two inch cable like it was string. We blasted a mountain down on top of his cave. Twenty minutes later he pushed his way out. . . .Now you tell me you've got him where he can't get away."

"Right," murmured Paskell. "Exactly right."

Milke turned to Tom Hand. "Give us about a hundred gallons of hydrogen peroxide, two hundred gallons of alcohol."

"We've got to keep Joe alive," Paskell explained casually.

Abel Cooley snorted. "Hogwash."

Tom Hand shrugged, turned away into the recesses of his shop.

James said, in an oil-smooth voice, "Suppose you break down and tell us just what you did to poor old Three-legged Joe."

"Why not?" said Paskell. "But I'm warning you—stay away from him."

"Never mind the jokes . . . I'm still listening."

"Well, first we electrocuted Joe. It stunned him."

"Yeah?"

"We couldn't kill him or tie him—so while he was still twitching, we threw grapples around his leg, hoisted him twenty miles out into space and put him in orbit around Odfars. That's where he is now—alive and well and feeling rather foolish, I imagine."

James pulled at his chin. He looked at Abel Cooley. "What do you think, Abel?" he asked.

Abel Cooley snorted, looked out the window.

James sat down by the table. "Yeah," he said heavily, "I expect Joe *is* feeling rather foolish."

"About like the rest of you birds," came Tom Hand's voice from behind the shelves.

Sjambak

HOWARD FRAYBERG, Production Director of *Know Your Universe!* was a man of sudden unpredictable moods; and Sam Catlin, the show's Continuity Editor, had learned to expect the worst.

"Sam," said Frayberg, "regarding the show last night. . . ." He paused to seek the proper words, and Catlin relaxed. Frayberg's frame of mind was merely critical. "Sam, we're in a rut. What's worse, the show's dull!"

Sam Catlin shrugged, not committing himself.

"*Seaweed Processors of Alphard IX—* who cares about seaweed?"

"It's factual stuff," said Sam, defensive but not wanting to go too far out on a limb. "We bring 'em everything—color, fact, romance, sight, sound, smell. . . . Next week, it's the Ball Expedition to the Mixtup Mountains on Gropus."

Frayberg leaned forward. "Sam, we're working the wrong angle on this stuff. . . . We've got to loosen up, shift our perspective! Give 'em the old human angle—glamor, mystery, thrills!"

Sam Catlin curled his lips. "I got just what you want."

"Yeah? Show me."

Catlin reached deep into his waste basket. "I filed this just ten minutes ago. . . ." He smoothed out the pages. " 'Sequence idea, by Wilbur Murphy. Investigate "Horseman of Space," the man who rides up to meet incoming spaceships.' "

Frayberg tilted his head to the side. "Rides up on a *horse?*"

"That's what Wilbur Murphy says."

"How far up?"

"Does it make any difference?"

"No—I guess not."

"Well, for your information, it's up ten thousand, twenty thousand miles. He waves to the pilot, takes off his hat to the passengers, then rides back down."

"And where does all this take place?"

"On—on—" Catlin frowned. "I can write it, but I can't pronounce it." He printed on his screen: CIRGAMESÇ.

"Sirgamesk," read Frayberg.

Catlin shook his head. "That's what it looks like—but those consonants are all aspirated gutturals. It's more like "Hrrghameshgrrh.' "

"Where did Murphy get this tip?"

"I didn't bother to ask."

"Well," mused Frayberg, "we could always do a show on strange superstitions. Is Murphy around?"

"He's explaining his expense account to Shifkin."

"Get him in here; let's talk to him."

Wilbur Murphy had a blond crew cut, a broad freckled nose, and a serious sidelong squint. He looked from his crumpled sequence idea to Catlin and Frayberg. "Didn't like it, huh?"

"We thought the emphasis should be a little different," explained Catlin. "Instead of 'The Space Horseman,' we'd give it the working title, 'Odd Superstitions of Hrrghameshgrrh.' "

"Oh, hell!" said Frayberg. "Call it Sirgamesk."

"Anyway," said Catlin, "that's the angle."

"But it's not superstition," said Murphy.

"Oh, come, Wilbur. . . ."

"I got this for sheer sober-sided fact. A man rides a horse up to meet the incoming ships!"

"Where did you get this wild fable?"

"My brother-in-law is purser on the *Celestial Traveller*. At Riker's Planet they make connection with the feeder line out of Cirgamesç."

"Wait a minute," said Catlin. "How did you pronounce that?"

"Cirgamesç. The steward on the shuttle-ship gave out this story, and my brother-in-law passed it along to me."

"Somebody's pulling somebody's leg."

"My brother-in-law wasn't, and the steward was cold sober."

"They've been drinking *bhang*. Sirgamesk is a Javanese planet, isn't it?"

"Javanese, Arab, Malay."

"Then they took a *bhang* supply with them, and some *hash*, and other sociable herbs."

"Well, this horseman isn't any drug dream."

"No? What is it?"

"So far as I know, it's a man on a horse."

"Ten thousand miles up? In a vacuum?"

"Exactly."

"No space-suit?"

"That's the story."

Catlin and Frayberg looked at each other.

"Well, Wilbur," Catlin began.

Frayberg interrupted. "What we can use, Wilbur, is a sequence on Sirgamesk superstition. Emphasis on voodoo or witchcraft—naked girls dancing—stuff with roots in Earth, but now typically Sirgamesk. Lots of color. Secret rite, sacrifices. . . ."

"Not much room on Cirgamesç for secret rites."

"It's a big planet, isn't it?"

"Not quite as big as Mars. There's no atmosphere. The settlers live in mountain valleys, with airtight lids over 'em."

Catlin flipped the pages of *Thumbnail Sketches of the Inhabited Worlds*. "Says here there's ancient ruins millions of years old. When the atmosphere went, the population went with it."

Frayberg became animated. "There's lots of material out there! Go get it, Wilbur! Life! Sex! Excitement! Mystery!"

"Okay," said Wilbur Murphy.

"But lay off this horseman-in-space angle. There *is* a limit to public credulity, and don't you let anyone tell you different."

Cirgamesç hung outside the port, twenty thousand miles ahead. The steward leaned over Wilbur Murphy's shoulder and pointed a long brown finger. "It was right out there, sir. He came riding up—"

"What kind of a man was it? Strange looking?"

"No. He was Cirgameski."

"Oh. You saw him with your own eyes, eh?"

The steward bowed, and his loose white mantle fell forward. "Exactly, sir."

"No helmet, no space-suit?"

"He wore a short Singhalût vest and pantaloons and a yellow Hadrasi hat. No more."

"And the horse?"

"Ah, the horse! There's a different matter."

"Different how?"

"I can't describe the horse. I was intent on the man."

"Did you recognize him?"

"By the brow of Lord Allah, it's well not to look too closely when such matters occur."

"Then—you *did* recognize him!"

"I must be at my task, sir."

Murphy frowned in vexation at the steward's retreating back, then bent over his camera to check the tape-feed. If anything appeared now, and his eyes could see it, the two-hundred million audience of *Know Your Universe!* could see it with him.

When he looked up, Murphy made a frantic grab for the stanchion, then relaxed. Cirgamesç had taken the Great Twitch. It was an illusion, a psychological quirk. One instant the planet lay ahead; then a man winked or turned away, and when he looked back, "ahead" had become "below"; the planet had swung an astonishing ninety degrees across the sky, and they were *falling!*

Murphy leaned against the stanchion. " 'The Great Twitch'," he muttered to himself, "I'd like to get *that* on two hundred million screens!"

Several hours passed. Cirgamesç grew. The Sampan Range rose up like a dark scab; the valley sultanates of Singhalût, Hadra, New Batavia, and Boeng-Bohôt showed like glistening chicken-tracks; the Great Rift Colony of Sundeman stretched down through the foothills like the trail of a slug.

An amplified voice rattled the ship. "Attention, passengers for Singhalût and other points on Cirgamesç! Kindly prepare your luggage for disembarkation. Customs at Singhalût are extremely thorough. Passengers are warned to take no weapons, drugs or explosives ashore. This is imperative!"

The warning turned out to be an understatement. Murphy was plied with questions. He suffered search of an intimate nature. He was three-dimensionally X-rayed with a range of frequencies calculated to excite fluorescence in whatever object he might have secreted in his stomach, in his abdomen, in a hollow bone, or under a layer of flesh.

His luggage was explored with similar minute attention, and Murphy rescued his cameras with difficulty. "What're you so damn anxious about? I don't have drugs; I don't have contraband. . . ."

"It's guns, your Excellency. Guns, weapons, explosives. . . ."

"I don't have any guns."

"But these objects here?"

"They're cameras. They record pictures and sounds and smells."

The inspector seized the cases with a glittering smile of triumph. "They resemble no cameras of my experience; I fear I shall have to impound. . . ."

A young man in loose white pantaloons, a pink vest, pale green cravat and a complex black turban strolled up. The inspector made a swift obeisance, with arms spread wide. "Excellency."

The young man raised two fingers. "You may find it possible to spare Mr. Murphy any unnecessary formality."

"As your Excellency recommends. . . ." The inspector nimbly repacked Murphy's belongings, while the young man looked on benignly.

Murphy covertly inspected his face. The skin was smooth,

the color of the rising moon; the eyes were narrow, dark, superficially placid. The effect was of silken punctilio with hot ruby blood close beneath.

Satisfied with the inspector's zeal, he turned to Murphy. "Allow me to introduce myself, Tuan Murphy. I am Ali-Tomás, of the House of Singhalût, and my father the Sultan begs you to accept our poor hospitality."

"Why, thank you," said Murphy. "This is a very pleasant surprise."

"If you will allow me to conduct you. . . ." He turned to the inspector. "Mr. Murphy's luggage to the palace."

Murphy accompanied Ali-Tomás into the outside light, fitting his own quick step to the prince's feline saunter. This is coming in pretty soft, he said to himself. I'll have a magnificent suite, with bowls of fruit and gin pahits, not to mention silken girls with skin like rich cream bringing me towels in the shower. . . . Well, well, well, it's not so bad working for *Know Your Universe!* after all! I suppose I ought to unlimber my camera. . . .

Prince Ali-Tomás watched him with interest. "And what is the audience of *Know Your Universe!*?"

"We call 'em 'participants.' "

"Expressive. And how many participants do you serve?"

"Oh, the Bowdler Index rises and falls. We've got about two hundred million screens, with five hundred million participants."

"Fascinating! And tell me—how do you record scents?"

Murphy displayed the specialized recorder on the side of the camera, with its gelatinous track which fixed molecular designs.

"And the odors recreated—they are like the originals?"

"Pretty close. Never exact, but none of the participants knows the difference. Sometimes the synthetic odor is an improvement."

"Astounding!" murmured the prince.

"And sometimes. . . . Well, Carson Tenlake went out to get the myrrh-blossoms on Venus. It was a hot day—as days always are on Venus—and a long climb. When the show was run, there was more smells of Carson than of flowers."

Prince Ali-Tomás laughed politely. "We turn through here."

They came out into a compound paved with red, green and white tiles. Beneath the valley roof was a sinuous trough, full of haze and warmth and golden light. As far in either direction as the eye could reach, the hillsides were terraced, barred in various shades of green. Spattering the valley floor were tall canvas pavilions, tents, booths, shelters.

"Naturally," said Prince Ali-Tomás, "we hope that you and your participants will enjoy Singhalût. It is a truism that, in order to import, we must export; we wish to encourage a pleasurable response to the 'Made in Singhalût' tag on our *batiks,* carvings, lacquers."

They rolled quietly across the square in a surface-car displaying the House emblem. Murphy rested against deep, cool cushions. "Your inspectors are pretty careful about weapons."

Ali-Tomás smiled complacently. "Our existence is ordered and peaceful. You may be familiar with the concept of *adak*?"

"I don't think so."

"A word, an idea from old Earth. Every living act is ordered by ritual. But our heritage is passionate—and when unyielding *adak* stands in the way of an irresistible emotion, there is turbulence, sometimes even bloodshed."

"An *amok*."

"Exactly. It is as well that the *amok* has no weapons other than his knife. Otherwise he would kill twenty where now he kills one."

The car rolled along a narrow avenue, scattering pedestrians to either side like the bow of a boat spreading foam. The village men wore loose white pantaloons and a short open vest; the women wore only the pantaloons.

"Handsome set of people," remarked Murphy.

Ali-Tomás again smiled complacently. "I'm sure Singhalût will present an inspiring and beautiful spectacle for your program."

Murphy remembered the keynote to Howard Frayberg's instructions: *"Excitement! Sex! Mystery!"* Frayberg cared little for inspiration or beauty. "I imagine," he said casually, "that you celebrate a number of interesting festivals? Colorful dancing? Unique customs?"

Ali-Tomás shook his head. "To the contrary. We left our superstitions and ancestor-worship back on Earth. We are quiet Mohammedans and indulge in very little festivity. Perhaps here is the reason for *amoks* and sjambaks."

"Sjambaks?"

"We are not proud of them. You will hear sly rumor, and it is better that I arm you beforehand with unvarnished truth."

"What is a sjambak?"

"They are bandits, flouters of authority. I will show you one presently."

"I heard," said Murphy, "of a man riding a horse up to meet the spaceships. What would account for a story like that?"

"It can have no possible basis," said Prince Ali-Tomás. "We have no horses on Cirgamesç. None whatever."

"But. . . ."

"The basest idle talk. Such nonsense will have no interest for your most intelligent participants."

The car rolled into a square a hundred yards on a side, lined with luxuriant banana palms. Opposite was an enormous pavilion of gold and violet silk, with a dozen peaked gables casting various changing sheens. In the center of the square a twenty-foot pole supported a cage about two feet wide, three feet long, and four feet high.

Inside this cage crouched a naked man.

The car rolled past. Prince Ali-Tomás waved an idle hand. The caged man glared down from bloodshot eyes. "That," said Ali-Tomás, "is a sjambak. As you see," a faint note of apology entered his voice, "we attempt to discourage them."

"What's that metal object on his chest?"

"The mark of his trade. By that you may know all sjambak. In these unsettled times only we of the House may cover our chests—all others must show themselves and declare themselves true Singhalûsi."

Murphy said tentatively, "I must come back here and photograph that cage."

Ali-Tomás smilingly shook his head. "I will show you our farms, our vines and orchards. Your participants will enjoy these; they have no interest in the color of an ignoble sjambak."

"Well," said Murphy, "our aim is a well-rounded production. We want to show the farmers at work, the members of the great House at their responsibilities, as well as the deserved fate of wrongdoers."

"Exactly. For every sjambak there are ten thousand industrious Singhalûsi. It follows then that only one ten-thousandth part of your film should be devoted to this infamous minority."

"About three-tenths of a second, eh?"

"No more than they deserve."

"You don't know my Production Director. His name is Howard Frayberg, and. . . ."

Howard Frayberg was deep in conference with Sam Catlin and was showing signs of what Catlin called his philosophic phase, which, of all things, Catlin feared most.

"Sam," said Frayberg, "do you know the danger of this business?"

"Ulcers," Catlin replied promptly.

Frayberg shook his head. "We've got an occupational disease to fight—progressive mental myopia."

"Speak for yourself," said Catlin.

"Consider. We sit in this office. We think we know what kind of show will work. We send out our staff to get it. We're signing the checks, so back it comes the way we asked for it. We look at it, hear it, smell it—and pretty soon we believe it: our version of the universe, full-blown from our brains like Minerva stepped out of Zeus. You see what I mean?"

"I understand the words."

"We've got our own picture of what's going on. We ask for it, we get it. It builds up and up—and finally we're like mice in a trap built of our own ideas. We cannibalize our own brains."

"Nobody'll ever accuse you of being stingy with metaphors."

"Sam, let's have the truth. How many times have you been off Earth?"

"I went to Mars once. And I spent a couple of weeks at Aristillus Resort on the Moon."

Frayberg leaned back in his chair as if shocked. "And

we're supposed to be a couple of learned planetologists!''

Catlin made grumbling noise in his throat. ''I haven't been around the zodiac, so what? You sneezed a few minutes ago and I said *gesundheit,* but I don't have a medical degree.''

''There comes a time in a man's life,'' said Frayberg, ''when he wants to take stock, get some new perspective.''

''Relax, Howard, relax.''

''In our case it means taking out our preconceived ideas, examining them, checking our illusions against reality.''

''Are you serious about this?''

''Another thing,'' said Frayberg, ''I want to check up a little. Shifkin says the expense accounts are frightful. But he can't fight it. When Keeler says he paid ten munits for a loaf of bread on Nekkar IV, who's going to call him on it?''

''Hell, let him eat bread! That's cheaper than making a safari around the cluster, spot-checking the local markets.''

Frayberg paid no heed. He touched a button; a three-foot sphere full of glistening motes appeared. Earth was at the center, with thin red lines, the scheduled spaceship routes, radiating out in all directions.

''Let's see what kind of circle we can make,'' said Frayberg. ''Gower's here at Canopus, Keeler's over here at Blue Moon, Wilbur Murphy's at Sirgamesk. . . .''

''Don't forget,'' muttered Catlin, ''we got a show to put on.''

''We've got material for a year,'' scoffed Frayberg. ''Get hold of Space-Lines. We'll start with Sirgamesk, and see what Wilbur Murphy's up to.''

Wilbur Murphy was being presented to the Sultan of Singhalût by the Prince Ali-Tomás. The Sultan, a small mild man of seventy, sat crosslegged on an enormous pink and green air-cushion. ''Be at your ease, Mr. Murphy. We dispense with as much protocol here as practicable.'' The Sultan had a dry clipped voice and the air of a rather harassed corporation executive. ''I understand you represent Earth-Central Home Screen Network?''

"I'm a staff photographer for the *Know Your Universe!* show."

"We export a great deal to Earth," mused the Sultan, "but not as much as we'd like. We're very pleased with your interest in us and naturally we want to help you in every way possible. Tomorrow the Keeper of the Archives will present a series of charts analyzing our economy. Ali-Tomás shall personally conduct you through the fish-hatcheries. We want you to know we're doing a great job out here on Singhalût."

"I'm sure you are," said Murphy uncomfortably. "However, that isn't quite the stuff I want."

"No? Just where do your desires lie?"

Ali-Tomás said delicately. "Mr. Murphy took a rather profound interest in the sjambak displayed in the square."

"Oh. And you explained that these renegades could hold no interest for serious students of our planet?"

Murphy started to explain that clustered around two hundred million screens tuned to *Know Your Universe!* were four or five hundred million participants, the greater part of them neither serious nor students. The Sultan cut in decisively. "I will now impart something truly interesting. We Singhalûsi are making preparations to reclaim four more valleys, with an added area of six hundred thousand acres! I shall put my physiographic models at your disposal; you may use them to the fullest extent!"

"I'll be pleased for the opportunity," declared Murphy. "But tomorrow I'd like to prowl around the valley, meet your people, observe their customs, religious rites, courtships, funerals. . . ."

The Sultan pulled a sour face. "We are ditch-water dull. Festivals are celebrated quietly in the home; there is small religious fervor; courtships are consummated by family contract. I fear you will find little sensational material here in Singhalût."

"You have no temple dances?" asked Murphy. "No firewalkers, snake-charmers or voodoo?"

The Sultan smiled patronizingly. "We came out here to Cirgamesç to escape the ancient superstitions. Our lives are calm, orderly. Even the *amoks* have practically disappeared."

"But the sjambaks—"

"Negligible."

"Well," said Murphy, "I'd like to visit some of these ancient cities."

"I'd advise against it," declared the Sultan. "They are shards, weathered stone. There are no inscriptions, no art. There is no stimulation in dead stone. Now. Tomorrow I will hear a report on hybrid soybean plantings in the Upper Kam District. You will want to be present."

Murphy's suite matched or even excelled his expectation. He had four rooms and a private garden enclosed by a thicket of bamboo. His bathroom walls were slabs of glossy actinolite, inlaid with cinnabar, jade, galena, pyrite and blue malachite, in representations of fantastic birds. His bedroom was a tent thirty feet high. Two walls were dark green fabric; a third was golden rust; the fourth opened upon the private garden.

Murphy's bed was a pink and yellow creation ten feet square, soft as cobweb, smelling of rose sandalwood. Carved black lacquer tubs held fruit; two dozen wines, liquors, syrups, essences flowed at a touch from as many ebony spigots.

The garden centered on a pool of cool water, very pleasant in the dripping humidity of Singhalût. The single shortcoming was the lack of the lovely young servitors Murphy had envisioned. He took it upon himself to repair this lack, and in a shady wine-house behind the palace he made the acquaintance of a girl-musician named Soek Panjoebang. He found her enticing tones of quavering sweetness from the *gamelan*, an instrument named after an ancient percussion orchestra in Old Bali. Soek Panjoebang had the delicate features and transparent skin of Sumatra, the supple long limbs of Arabia and in a pair of wide and golden eyes a heritage from somewhere in Celtic Europe. Murphy bought her a goblet of frozen shavings, each a different perfume, while he himself drank white rice-beer. Soek Panjoebang displayed an intense interest in the ways of Earth, and Murphy found it hard to guide the conversation. "Weelbrrr," she said. "Such a funny name, Weelbrrr. Do you think I could play the *gamelan* in the great palaces of Earth?"

"Sure. There's no law against *gamelans*."

"You talk so funny. Weelbrrr. I like to hear you talk."

"I suppose you get rather bored here in Singhalût?"

She shrugged, "Life is pleasant, but it concerns with little things. We have no great adventures. We grow flowers, we play the *gamelan*." She eyed him archly sidelong. "We love . . . We sleep. . . ."

Murphy grinned. "You run *amok*."

"No, no, no. That is no more."

"Not since the sjambaks, eh?"

"The sjambaks are bad. But better than *amok*. When a man feels the knot forming around his chest, he no longer takes his kris and runs down the street—he becomes sjambak."

This was getting interesting. "Where does he go? What does he do?"

"He robs."

"Who does he rob? What does he do with the loot?"

She leaned toward him. "It is not well to talk of them."

"Why not?"

"The Sultan does not wish it. Everywhere are listeners. When one talks sjambak, the Sultan's ears rise, like the points on a cat."

"Suppose they do—what's the difference? I've got a legitimate interest. I saw one of them caged in the village. That's torture, pure and simple. I want to know about it."

"He is very bad. He opened the monorail car and the air rushed out. Forty-two Singhalûsi and Hadrasi bloated and blew up."

"And what happened to the sjambak?"

"He took all the gold and money and jewels and ran away."

"Ran where?"

"Out across Great Pharasang Plain. But he was a fool. He came back to Singhalût for his wife; he was caught and set up for the people to look at, so they might tell each other, 'thus it is for sjambaks.' "

"Where do the sjambaks hide out?"

"Oh," she looked vaguely around the room, "out on the plains. In the mountains."

"They must have some shelter—an air-dome."

"No. The Sultan would send out his patrol-boat and destroy them. They roam quietly. They hide among the rocks and tend their oxygen stills. Sometimes they visit the old cities."

"I wonder," said Murphy, staring into his beer, "could it be sjambaks who ride horses up to meet the spaceship?"

Soek Panjoebang knit her black eyebrows, as if preoccupied.

"That's what brought me out here," Murphy went on. "This story of a man riding a horse out in space."

"Ridiculous; we have no horses in Cirgamesç."

"All right, the steward won't swear to the horse. Suppose the man was up there on foot or riding a bicycle. But the steward recognized the man."

"Who was this man, pray?"

"The steward clammed up. . . . The name would have been just noise to me, anyway."

"*I* might recognize the name. . . ."

"Ask him yourself. The ship's still out at the field."

She shook her head slowly, holding her golden eyes on his face. "I do not care to attract the attention of either steward, sjambak—or Sultan."

Murphy said impatiently. "In any event, it's not who—but *how*. How does the man breathe? Vacuum sucks a man's lungs up out of his mouth, bursts his stomach, his ears. . . ."

"We have excellent doctors," said Soek Panjoebang shuddering, "but alas! I am not one of them."

Murphy looked at her sharply. Her voice held the plangent sweetness of her instrument, with additional overtones of mockery. "There must be some kind of invisible dome around him, holding in air," said Murphy.

"And what if there is?"

"It's something new, and if it is, I want to find out about it."

Soek smiled languidly. "You are so typical an old-lander—worried, frowning, dynamic. You should relax, cultivate *napaû*, enjoy life as we do here in Singhalût."

"What's *napaû*?"

"It's our philosophy, where we find meaning and life and beauty in every aspect of the world."

"That sjambak in the cage could do with a little less *napaû* right now."

"No doubt he is unhappy," she agreed.

"Unhappy! He's being tortured!"

"He broke the Sultan's law. His life is no longer his own. It belongs to Singhalût. If the Sultan wishes to use it to warn other wrongdoers, the fact that the man suffers is of small interest."

"If they all wear that metal ornament, how can they hope to pass unnoticed?" He glanced at her own bare bosom.

"They appear by night—slip through the streets like ghosts. . . ." She looked in turn at Murphy's loose shirt. "You will notice persons brushing up against you, feeling you," she laid her hand along his breast, "and when this happens you will know they are agents of the Sultan, because only strangers and the House may wear shirts. But now, let me sing to you—a song from the Old Land, old Java. You will not understand the tongue, but no other words so join the voice of the *gamelan*."

"This is the life," said Murphy the next morning. "Instead of a garden suite with a private pool, I usually sleep in a bubble-tent, with nothing to eat but condensed food."

Soek Panjoebang flung the water out of her sleek black hair. "Perhaps, Weelbrrr, you will regret leaving Cirgamesç?"

"Well," he looked up to the transparent roof, barely visible where the sunlight collected and refracted, "I don't particularly like being shut up like a bird in an aviary . . . Mildly claustrophobic, I guess."

After breakfast, drinking thick coffee from tiny silver cups, Murphy looked long and reflectively at Soek Panjoebang.

"What are you thinking, Weelbrrr?"

Murphy drained his coffee. "I'm thinking that I'd better be getting to work."

"And what do you do?"

"First I'm going to shoot the palace, and you sitting here in the garden playing your *gamelan*."

"But Weelbrrr—not *me*!"

"You're a part of the universe, rather an interesting part. Then I'll take the square. . . ."

"And the sjambak?"

A quiet voice spoke from behind. "A visitor, Tuan Murphy."

Murphy turned his head. "Bring him in." He looked back to Soek Panjoebang. She was on her feet.

"It is necessary that I go."

"When will I see you?"

"Tonight—at the Barangipan."

The quiet voice said, "Mr. Rube Trimmer, Tuan."

Trimmer was small and middle-aged, with thin shoulders and a paunch, but he carried himself with a swagger. His skin had the waxy look of lost floridity, his tuft of white hair was coarse and thin, his eyelids hung in an off-side droop that amateur physiognomists like to associate with guile.

"I'm Resident Director of the Import-Export Bank," said Trimmer. "Heard you were here and thought I'd pay my respects."

"I suppose you don't see many strangers."

"Not too many—there's nothing much to bring 'em. Cirgamesç isn't a comfortable tourist planet. Too confined, shut in. A man with a sensitive psyche goes nuts pretty easy here."

"Yeah," said Murphy. "I was thinking the same thing this morning. That dome begins to give a man the willies. How do the natives stand it? Or do they?"

Trimmer pulled out a cigar case. Murphy refused the offer.

"Local tobacco," said Trimmer. "Very good." He lit up thoughtfully. "Well, you might say that the Cirgameski are schizophrenic. They've got the docile Javanese blood, plus the Arabian elán. The Javanese part is on top, but every once in a while you see a flash of arrogance. . . . You never know. I've been out here nine years and I'm still a stranger." He puffed on his cigar, studied Murphy with his careful eyes. "You work for *Know Your Universe!*, I hear."

"Yeah. I'm one of the advance men."

"Must be a great job."

"A man sees a lot of the galaxy, and he runs into queer tales, like this sjambak stuff."

Trimmer nodded without surprise. "My advice to you, Murphy, is lay off the sjambaks. They're not a healthy subject around here."

Murphy was startled by the bluntness. "What's the big mystery about these sjambaks?"

Trimmer looked around the room. "This place is bugged."

"I found two pick-ups and plugged 'em," said Murphy.

Trimmer laughed. "Those were just plants. They hide 'em where a man might just barely spot 'em. You can't catch the real ones. They're woven into the cloth—pressure-sensitive wires."

Murphy looked critically at the cloth walls.

"Don't let it worry you," said Trimmer. "They listen more out of habit than anything else. If you're fussy, we'll go for a walk."

The road led past the palace into the country. Murphy and Trimmer sauntered along a placid river, overgrown with lily pads, swarming with large white ducks.

"This sjambak business," said Murphy. "Everybody talks around it. You can't pin anybody down."

"Including me," said Trimmer. "I'm more or less privileged around here. The Sultan finances his reclamation through the bank, on the basis of my reports. But there's more to Singhalût than the Sultan."

"Namely?"

Trimmer waved his cigar waggishly. "Now we're getting in where I don't like to talk. I'll give you a hint. Prince Ali thinks roofing-in more valleys is a waste of money, when there's Hadras and New Batavia and Sundaman so close."

"You mean—armed conquest?"

Trimmer laughed. "You said it, not me."

"They can't carry on much of a war—unless the soldiers commute by monorail."

"Maybe Prince Ali thinks he's got the answers."

"Sjambaks?"

"I didn't say it," said Trimmer blandly.

Murphy grinned. After a moment he said, "I picked up

with a girl named Soek Panjoebang who plays the *gamelan*. I suppose she's working for either the Sultan or Prince Ali. Do you know which?''

Trimmer's eyes sparkled. He shook his head. ''Might be either one. There's only one way to find out.''

''Yeah?''

''Get her off where you're sure there's no spy-cells. Tell her two things—one for Ali, the other for the Sultan. Whichever one reacts you know you've got her.''

''For instance?''

''Well, for instance, she learns that you can rig up a hypnotic ray from a flashlight battery, a piece of bamboo, and a few lengths of wire. That'll get Ali in an awful sweat. He can't get weapons. None at all. And for the Sultan,'' Trimmer was warming up to his intrigue, chewing on his cigar with gusto, ''tell her you're onto a catalyst that turns clay into aluminum and oxygen in the presence of sunlight. The Sultan would sell his right leg for something like that. He tries hard for Singhalût and Cirgamesç.''

''And Ali?''

Trimmer hesitated. ''I never said what I'm about to say. Don't forget—I never said it.''

''Okay, you never said it.''

''Ever heard of a *jehad*?''

''Mohammedan holy wars.''

''Believe it or not, Ali wants a *jehad*.''

''Sounds kinda fantastic.''

''Sure it's fantastic. Don't forget, I never said anything about it. But suppose someone—strictly unofficial, of course— let the idea percolate around the Peace Office back home.''

''Ah,'' said Murphy. ''That's why you came to see me.''

Trimmer turned a look of injured innocence. ''Now, Murphy, you're a little unfair. I'm a friendly guy. Of course I don't like to see the bank lose what we've got tied up in the Sultan.''

''Why don't you send in a report yourself?''

''I have! But when they hear the same thing from you, a *Know Your Universe!* man, they might make a move.''

Murphy nodded.

"Well, we understand each other," said Trimmer heartily, "and everything's clear."

"Not entirely. How's Ali going to launch a *jehad* when he doesn't have any weapons, no warships, no supplies?"

"Now," said Trimmer, "we're getting into the realm of supposition." He paused, looked behind him. A farmer pushing a rotary tiller bowed politely, trundled ahead. Behind was a young man in a black turban, gold earrings, a black and red vest, white pantaloons, black curl-toed slippers. He bowed, started past. Trimmer held up his hand. "Don't waste your time up there; we're going back in a few minutes."

"Thank you, Tuan."

"Who are you reporting to? The Sultan or Prince Ali?"

"The Tuan is sure to pierce the veil of my evasions. I shall not dissemble. I am the Sultan's man."

Trimmer nodded. "Now, if you'll kindly remove to about a hundred yards, where your whisper pick-up won't work."

"By your leave, I go." He retreated without haste.

"He's almost certainly working for Ali," said Trimmer.

"Not a very subtle lie."

"Oh yes—third level. He figured I'd take it second level."

"How's that again?"

"Naturally, I wouldn't believe him. He knew I knew that he knew it. So when he said 'Sultan,' I'd think he wouldn't lie simply, but that he'd lie double—that he actually was working for the Sultan."

Murphy laughed. "Suppose he told you a fourth level lie?"

"It starts to be a toss-up pretty soon," Trimmer admitted. "I don't think he gives me credit for that much subtlety. . . . What are you doing the rest of the day?"

"Recording preliminaries. Do you know where I can find some picturesque rites? Mystical dances, human sacrifice? I've got to work up some glamor and exotic lore."

"There's this sjambak in the cage. That's about as close to the medieval as you'll find anywhere in Earth Commonwealth."

"Speaking of sjambaks. . . ."

"No time," said Trimmer. "Got to get back. Drop in at my office—right down the square from the palace."

Murphy returned to his suite. The shadowy figure of his

room servant said, "His Highness the Sultan desires the Tuan's attendance in the Cascade Garden."

"Thank you," said Murphy. "As soon as I reload my camera."

The Cascade Room was an open patio in front of an artfully constructed waterfall. The Sultan was pacing back and forth, wearing dusty khaki puttees, brown plastic boots, a yellow polo shirt. He carried a twig which he used as a riding crop, slapping his boots as he walked. He turned his head as Murphy appeared, pointed his twig at a wicker bench.

"I pray you sit down, Mr. Murphy." He paced once up and back. "How is your suite? You find it to your liking?"

"Very much so."

"Excellent," said the Sultan. "You do me honor with your presence."

Murphy waited patiently.

"I understand that you had a visitor this morning," said the Sultan.

"Yes. Mr. Trimmer."

"May I inquire the nature of the conversation?"

"It was of a personal nature," said Murphy, rather more shortly than he'd intended.

The Sultan nodded wistfully. "A Singhalûsi would have wasted an hour telling me half-truths—distorted enough to confuse, but not sufficiently inaccurate to anger me if I had a spy-cell on him all the time."

Murphy grinned. "A Singhalûsi has to live here the rest of his life."

A servant wheeled a frosted cabinet before them, placed goblets under two spigots, withdrew. The Sultan cleared his throat. "Trimmer is an excellent fellow, but unbelievably loquacious."

Murphy drew himself two inches of a chilled rosy-pale liquor. The Sultan slapped his boots with the twig. "Undoubtedly he confided all my private business to you, or at least as much as I have allowed him to learn."

"Well—he spoke of your hope to increase the compass of Singhalût."

"That, my friend, is no hope; it's absolute necessity. Our

population density is fifteen hundred to the square mile. We must expand or smother. There'll be too little food to eat, too little oxygen to breathe.''

Murphy suddenly came to life. "I could make that idea the theme of my feature! Singhalût Dilemma: Expand or Perish!''

"No, that would be inadvisable, inapplicable.''

Murphy was not convinced. "It sounds like a natural.''

The Sultan smiled. "I'll impart an item of confidential information—although Trimmer no doubt has preceded me with it.'' He gave his boots an irritated whack. "To expand, I need funds. Funds are best secured in an atmosphere of calm and confidence. The implication of emergency would be disastrous to my aims.''

"Well,'' said Murphy, "I see your position.''

The Sultan glanced at Murphy sidelong. "Anticipating your cooperation, my Minister of Propaganda has arranged an hour's program, stressing our progressive social attitude, our prosperity and financial prospects. . . .''

"But, Sultan. . . .''

"Well?''

"I can't allow your Minister of Propaganda to use me and *Know Your Universe!* as a kind of investment brochure.''

The Sultan nodded wearily. "I expected you to take that attitude. . . . Well—what do you yourself have in mind?''

"I've been looking for something to tie into,'' said Murphy. "I think it's going to be the dramatic contrast between the ruined cities and the new domed valleys. How the Earth settlers succeeded where the ancient people failed to meet the challenge of the dissipating atmosphere.''

"Well,'' the Sultan said grudgingly, "that's not too bad.''

"Today I want to take some shots of the palace, the dome, the city, the paddies, groves, orchards, farms. Tomorrow I'm taking a trip out to one of the ruins.''

"I see,'' said the Sultan. "Then you won't need my charts and statistics?''

"Well, Sultan, I could film the stuff your Propaganda Minister cooked up and I could take it back to Earth. Howard Frayberg or Sam Catlin would tear into it, rip it apart, splice in some head-hunting, a little cannibalism and temple prostitution, and you'd never know you were watching Singhalût. You'd scream with horror, and I'd be fired."

"In that case," said the Sultan, "I will leave you to the dictates of your conscience."

Howard Frayberg looked around the gray landscape of Riker's Planet, gazed out over the roaring black Mogador Ocean. "Sam, I think there's a story out there."

Sam Catlin shivered inside his electrically heated glass overcoat. "Out on that ocean? It's full of man-eating plesiosaurs—horrible things forty feet long."

"Suppose we worked something out on the line of Moby Dick? *The White Monster of the Mogador Ocean*. We'd set sail in a catamaran—"

"Us?"

"No," said Frayberg impatiently. "Of course not us. Two or three of the staff. They'd sail out there, look over these gray and red monsters, maybe fake a fight or two, but all the time they're after the legendary white one. How's it sound?"

"I don't think we pay our men enough money."

"Wilbur Murphy might do it. He's willing to look for a man riding a horse up to meet his spaceships."

"He might draw the line at a white plesiosaur riding up to meet his catamaran."

Frayberg turned away. "Somebody's got to have ideas around here. . . ."

"We'd better head back to the space-port," said Catlin. "We got two hours to make the Sirgamesk shuttle."

Wilbur Murphy sat in the Barangipan, watching mario-nettes performing to xylophone, castanet, gong and *gamelan*. The drama had its roots in protohistoric Mohenjo-Daro. It had filtered down through ancient India, medieval Burma, Malaya, across the Straits of Malacca to Sumatra and Java; from modern Java across space to Cirgamesç five thousand years of time, two hundred light-years of space. Somewhere along the route it had met and assimilated modern technology. Magnetic beams controlled arms, legs and bodies, guided the poses and posturings. The manipulator's face, by agency of clip, wire, radio control and minuscule selsyn, projected his scowl, smile, sneer or grimace to the peaked little face he controlled. The language was that of Old Java, which perhaps a third of the spectators understood. This portion did not include Murphy, and when the performance ended he was no wiser than at the start.

Soek Panjoebang slipped into the seat beside Murphy. She wore musician's garb: a sarong of brown, blue, and black *batik,* and a fantastic headdress of tiny silver bells. She greeted him with enthusiasm.

"Weelbrrr! I saw you watching. . . ."

"It was very interesting."

"Ah yes." She sighed. "Weelbrrr, you take me with you back to Earth?"

"Well, I don't know about that."

"I behave very well, Weelbrrr." She nuzzled his shoulder, looked soulfully up with her shiny yellow-hazel eyes. Murphy nearly forgot the experiment he intended to perform.

"What did you do today, Weelbrrr? You look at all the pretty girls?"

"Nope. I ran footage. Got the palace, climbed the ridge up to the condensation vanes. I never knew there was so much water in the air till I saw the steam pouring off those vanes! And *hot!*"

"We have much sunlight; it makes the rice grow."

"The Sultan ought to put some of that excess light to work. There's a secret process. . . . Well, I'd better not say."

"Oh come, Weelbrrr! Tell me your secrets!"

"It's not much of a secret. Just a catalyst that separates clay into aluminum and oxygen when sunlight shines on it."

Soek's eyebrows rose, poised in place like a seagull riding the wind. "Weelbrrr! I did not know you for a man of learning!"

"Oh, you thought I was just a bum, eh? Good enough to make picturama stars out of *gamelan* players, but no special genius. . . ."

"No, no, Weelbrrr."

"I know lots of tricks. I can take a flashlight battery, a piece of copper foil, a few transistors and bamboo tube and turn out a paralyzer gun that'll stop a man cold in his tracks. And you know how much it costs?"

"No, Weelbrrr. How much?"

"Ten cents. It wears out after two or three months, but what's the difference? I make 'em as a hobby—turn out two or three an hour."

"Weelbrrr! You're a man of marvels! Hello! We will drink!"

And Murphy settled back in the wicker chair, sipping his rice beer.

"Today," said Murphy, "I get into a space-suit, and ride out to the ruins in the plain. Ghatamipol, I think they're called. Like to come?"

"No, Weelbrrr." Soek Panjoebang looked off into a garden, her hands busy tucking a flower into her hair. A few minutes later she said, "Why must you waste your time among the rocks? There are better things to do and see. And it might well be—dangerous." She murmured the last word offhandedly.

"Danger? From the sjambaks?"

"Yes, perhaps."

"The Sultan's giving me a guard. Twenty men with crossbows."

"The sjambaks carry shields."

"Why should they risk their lives attacking me?"

Soek Panjoebang shrugged. After a moment she rose to her feet. "Goodbye, Weelbrrr."

"Goodbye? Isn't this rather abrupt? Won't I see you tonight?"

"If so be Allah's will."

Murphy looked after the lithe swaying figure. She paused, plucked a yellow flower, looked over her shoulder. Her eyes, golden as the flower, lucent as water-jewels, held his. Her face was utterly expressionless. She turned, tossed away the flower with a jaunty gesture, and continued on.

Murphy breathed deeply. She might have made picturama at that. . . .

One hour later he met his escort at the valley gate. They

were dressed in space-suits for the plains, twenty men with
sullen faces. The trip to Ghatamipol clearly was not to their
liking. Murphy climbed into his own suit, checked the oxygen pressure gauge, the seal at his collar. "All ready, boys?"

No one spoke. The silence lengthened. The gatekeeper, on
hand to let the party out, snickered. "They're all ready,
Tuan."

"Well," said Murphy, "let's go then."

Outside the gate, Murphy made a second check of his
equipment. No leaks in his suit. Inside pressure: 14.6. Outside pressure: zero. His twenty guards morosely inspected
their crossbows and slim swords.

The white ruins of Ghatamipol lay five miles across
Pharasang Plain. The horizon was clear, the sun was high, the
sky was black.

Murphy's radio hummed. Someone said sharply. "Look!
There it goes!" He wheeled around; his guards had halted,
and were pointing. He saw a fleet something vanishing into
the distance.

"Let's go," said Murphy. "There's nothing over there."

"Sjambak."

"Well, there's only one of them."

"Where one walks, others follow."

"That's why the twenty of you are here."

"It is madness! Challenging the sjambaks!"

"What is gained?" another argued.

"I'll be the judge of that," said Murphy, and set off along
the plain. The warriors reluctantly followed, muttering to
each other over their intercoms.

The eroded city walls rose above them, occupied more and
more of the sky. The platoon leader said in an angry voice,
"We have gone far enough."

"You're under my orders," said Murphy. "We're going
through the gate." He started his vidcam and walked under
the monstrous portal.

The city was frailer stuff than the wall, and had succumbed
to the thin storms which had raged a million years after the

passing of life. Murphy marvelled at the scope of the ruins.
Virgin archaeological territory!

There'd be tremendous prestige and publicity for *Know
Your Universe!* if Murphy uncovered a tomb, a library, works
of art. The Sultan would gladly provide diggers. They were a
sturdy enough people; they could make quite a showing in a
week, if they were able to put aside their superstitions, fears
and dreads.

Murphy sized one of them up from the corner of his eye.
He sat on a sunny slab of rock and if he felt uneasy he
concealed it quite successfully. In fact, thought Murphy, he
appeared completely relaxed. Maybe the problem of securing
diggers was a minor one after all. . . .

And here was an odd sidelight on the Singhalûsi character.
Once clear of the valley the man openly wore his shirt, a fine
loose garment of electric blue, in defiance of the Sultan's
edict.

Murphy felt his own skin crawling. How could he be alive?
Where was his space-suit? The man lounged casually on the
rock, grinning sardonically at Murphy. He wore heavy sandals, a black turban, loose breeches, the blue shirt. Nothing
more.

And where were the others?

Murphy turned a feverish glance over his shoulder. A good
three miles distant, bounding and leaping toward Singhalût,
were twenty desperate, dwindling figures, all wearing space-
suits. This man here. . . . A sjambak? A wizard? A hallucination?

The creature rose to his feet, strode haughtily toward Murphy. He carried a crossbow and a sword, like those of Murphy's fleet-footed guards. But he wore no space-suit. Could
there be breathable traces of an atmosphere? Murphy glanced
at his gauge. Outside pressure: zero.

Two other men appeared, moving with long elastic steps.
Their eyes were bright, their faces flushed. They came up to
Murphy, took his arm. They were solid, corporeal. They had
no invisible force fields around their heads.

Murphy jerked his arm free. "Let go of me, damn it!"

But they certainly couldn't hear him through the vacuum.

He glanced over his shoulder. The first man held his naked blade a foot or two behind Murphy's bulging space-suit. Murphy made no further resistance. He set his vidcam on automatic. It would now run for several hours.

The sjambaks led Murphy two hundred yards to a metal door. They opened it, pushed Murphy inside, slammed it shut. Murphy felt the vibration through his shoes, heard a gradually waxing hum. His gauge showed an outside pressure of 5, 10, 12, 14, 14.5. An inner door opened. Hands pulled Murphy in, unclamped his helmet.

"Just what's going on here?" demanded Murphy angrily.

Prince Ali-Tomás pointed to a table. Murphy saw a flashlight battery, aluminum foil, wire, a transistor kit, metal tubing, tools, a few other odds and ends.

"There it is," said Prince Ali-Tomás. "Get to work. Let's see one of these paralysis weapons you boast of."

"What do you want them for?"

"Does it matter?"

"I'd like to know." Murphy was conscious of his vidcam, recording sight, sound, odor.

"I lead an army," said Ali-Tomá, "but they march without weapons. Give me weapons! I will carry the sword to Hadra, to New Batavia, to Sundaman, to Boeng-Bohôt!"

"How? Why?"

"It is enough that I *will* it. Again, I insist you. . . ." He indicated the table.

Murphy laughed. "Suppose I don't make this weapon for you?"

"You'll remain until you do, under increasingly difficult conditions."

"I'll be here a long time."

"If such is the case," said Ali-Tomás, "we must make our arrangements for your incarceration on a long-term basis."

Ali made a gesture. Hands seized Murphy's shoulders. A respirator was held to his nostrils. He thought of his vidcam and he could have laughed. Mystery! Excitement! Thrills! Dramatic sequence for *Know Your Universe!* Staff man murdered by fanatics! The crime recorded on his own camera! See the blood, hear his death-rattle, smell the poison!

The vapor choked him. *What a break! What a sequence!* Slow fade to black.

"Sirgamesk," said Howard Frayberg, "bigger and brighter every minute."

"It must've been just about here," said Catlin, "that Wilbur's horseback rider appeared."

"That's right! Steward!"

"Yes, sir?"

"We're about twenty thousand miles out, aren't we?"

"About fifteen thousand, sir."

"Sidereal Cavalry! What an idea! I wonder how Wilbur's making out?"

Sam Catlin, peering squint-eyed out the window, said in a tight voice, "Why not ask him yourself?"

"Eh?"

"Ask him for yourself! There he is—outside, riding some kind of critter. . . ."

"It's a ghost," whispered Frayberg. "A man without a space-suit. . . . There's no such thing!"

"He sees us. . . . Look. . . ."

It was Murphy himself out there staring at them, and his surprise seemed equal to their own. He waved his hand. Catlin gingerly waved back.

Said Frayberg, "That's not a horse he's riding. It's a combination ram-jet and kiddie car with stirrups!"

"He's coming aboard the ship," said Catlin. "Through the entrance port down below. . . ."

Wilbur Murphy sat in the captain's stateroom, taking careful breaths of air.

"How are you now?" asked Frayberg.

"Fine. A little sore in the lungs."

"I shouldn't wonder," the ship's doctor growled. "I never saw anything like it."

"How does it *feel* out there, Wilbur?" Catlin asked.

"It feels awfully empty. And the breath seeping up out of your lungs, never going in—that's a terrifying feeling. And you miss the air blowing on your skin. I never realized it before. Air feels like—like silk, like whipped cream—it's got texture. . . ."

"But aren't you frozen? Space is supposed to be absolute zero!"

"Space is nothing. It's neither hot nor cold. When you're in the sunlight you get warm. It's better in the shade. You don't lose any heat by air convection, but radiation and sweat evaporation keep you comfortably cool."

"I still can't understand any of this," said Frayberg. "This Prince Ali, for example, he's some kind of rebel, eh?"

"I don't blame him in a way. A normal man living under those domes has to let off steam somehow. Prince Ali decided to go out crusading. I think he would have made it too—at least on Cirgamesç."

"Certainly there are many more men inside the domes. . . ."

"When it comes to fighting," said Murphy, "a sjambak can lick twenty men in spacesuits. A little nick won't hurt him, but a little nick bursts open a spacesuit, and the man inside comes apart."

"I see," said the Captain. "I imagine the Peace Office will send out a team to put things in order now."

Catlin asked, "What happened when you woke up from the drug?"

"Well, nothing very much. I felt this attachment on my chest, but didn't think much about it. Still kinda woozy. I was halfway through decompression. They keep a man there eight hours, drop pressure on him two pounds an hour, nice and slow so he don't get the bends."

"Was this the same place they took you, when you met Ali?"

"Yes, that was their decompression chamber. They had to make a sjambak out of me; there wasn't any other way they could keep me. Well, pretty soon my head cleared, and I saw this apparatus stuck to my chest." He poked at the mechanism on the table. "I saw the oxygen tank, the blood running through the plastic pipes—blue from me to that carburetor arrangement, red on the way back in—and I figured out the whole arrangement. Carbon dioxide still exhales up through the lungs, but the vein back to the left auricle is routed through the carburetor and supercharged with oxygen. A man doesn't need to breathe. The carburetor flushes his blood with oxygen, the decompression tank adjusts him to the lack of air-pressure. There's only one think to look out for; not to touch anything with your naked flesh. If it's in the sunlight it's blazing hot; if it's in the shade it's cold enough to cut. Otherwise you're free as a bird.''

''But—how did you get away?''

''I saw the rocket-bikes, and began figuring. I couldn't go back to Singhalût; I'd be lynched on sight as a sjambak. I couldn't fly to another planet—the bikes don't carry enough fuel.

''I knew when the ship would be coming in, so I decided to fly up to meet it. I told the guard I was going outside a minute and I absconded with one of the rocket-bikes. There was nothing much to it.''

''Well,'' said Frayberg, ''it's a great feature, Wilbur—a great film! Maybe we can stretch it into two hours.''

''One thing bothers me,'' said Catlin. ''Who did the steward see up here the first time? We got a flying horseman report, remember?''

Murphy shrugged. ''It might have been somebody up here skylarking. A little too much oxygen and you start cutting all kinds of capers. Or it might have been someone who decided he had enough crusading.

''There's a sjambak in a cage, right in the middle of Singhalût. Prince Ali walks past; they look at each other eye to eye. Ali smiles a little and walks on. Suppose this sjambak tried to escape to the ship. He's taken aboard, turned over to the Sultan and the Sultan makes an example of him. . . .''

''What will the Sultan do to Ali?''

Murphy shook his head. ''If I were Ali, I'd disappear.''

A loudspeaker turned on. ''Attention all passengers. We

have just passed through quarantine. Passengers may now disembark. Important: no weapons or explosives allowed on Singhalût!''

''This is where I came in,'' said Murphy.

The Augmented Agent

Over a period of some months, James Keith had undergone a series of subtle and intricate surgeries, and his normally efficient body had been altered in many ways: "augmented," to use the jargon of the Special Branch, CIA.

Looking into the mirror, he saw a face familiar only from the photographs he had studied—dark, feral and harsh: the face, literally, of a savage. His hair, which he had allowed to grow long, had been oiled, stranded with gold tinsel, braided and coiled; his teeth had been replaced with stainless-steel dentures; from his ears dangled a pair of ivory amulets. In each case, adornment was the secondary function. The tinsel strands in his headdress were multi-laminated accumulators, their charge maintained by thermo-electric action. The dentures scrambled, condensed, transmitted, received, expanded and unscrambled radio waves of energies almost too low to be detected. The seeming ivory amulets were stereophonic radar units, which not only could guide Keith through the dark, but also provided a fractional second's warning of a bullet, an arrow, a bludgeon. His fingernails were copper-silver alloy, internally connected to the accumulators in his hair. Another circuit served as a ground, to protect him against electrocution—one of his own potent weapons. These were the more obvious augmentations; others more subtle had been fabricated into his flesh.

As he stood before the mirror, two silent technicians wound a narrow *darshba* turban around his head, draped him with a white robe. Keith no longer recognized the image in the mirror as himself. He turned to Carl Sebastiani, who had been watching from across the room—a small man, parchment-pale, with austere cheekbones and a fragile look to his skull. Sebastiani's title, *Assistant to the Under Director*, understated his authority just as his air of delicacy misrepresented his inner toughness.

"Presently you'll become almost as much Tamba Ngasi as you are James Keith," said Sebastiani. "Quite possibly more. In which case your usefulness ends, and you'll be brought home."

Keith made no comment. He raised his arms, feeling the tension of new connections and conduits. He clenched his right fist, watched three metal stingers appear above his knuckles. He held up his left palm, felt the infrared radiation emitted by Sebastiani's face. "I'm James Keith. I'll act Tamba Ngasi—but I'll never become him."

Sebastiani chuckled coolly. "A face is an almost irresistible symbol. In any event you'll have little time for introspection. . . . Come along up to my office."

The aides removed Keith's white robe; he followed Sebastiani to his official suite, three rooms as calm, cool and elegant as Sebastiani himself. Keith settled into a deep-cushioned chair, Sebastiani slipped behind his desk, where he flicked at a row of buttons. On a screen appeared a large-scale map of Africa. "A new phase seems to be opening up and we want to exploit it." He touched another button, and a small rectangle on the underpart of the great Mauretanian bulge glowed green. "There's Lakhadi. Fejo is that bright point of light by Tabacoundi Bay." He glanced sidelong at Keith. "You remember the floating ICBM silos?"

"Vaguely. They were news more than thirty years ago. I remember the launchings."

Sebastiani nodded. "In 1963. Quite a boondoggle. The ICBM's—Titans—were already obsolete, the silos expensive, maintenance a headache. A month ago, they went for surplus to a Japanese salvage firm, warheads naturally not included. Last week Premier Adoui Shgawe of Lakhadi bought them, apparently without the advice, consent or approval of either Russians or Chinese."

Sebastiani keyed four new numbers; the screen flickered and blurred. "Still a new process," said Sebastiani critically. "Images recorded by the deposition of atoms on a light-sensitive crystal. The camera is disguised, effectively if whimsically, as a common housefly." A red and gold coruscation exploded upon the screen. "Impurities—rogue molecules, the engineers call them." The image steadied to reveal a high-domed council chamber, brightly lit by diffused sunlight. "The new architecture," said Sebastiani sardonically, "equal parts of Zimbabwe, Dr. Caligari and the Bolshoi Ballet."

"It has a certain wild charm," said Keith.

"Fejo's the showplace of all Africa; no question that it's a spectacular demonstration." Sebastiani touched a Hold button, freezing the scene in the council chamber. "Shgawe is at the head of the table, in gold and green. I'm sure you recognize him."

Keith nodded. Shgawe's big body and round muscular face had become almost as familiar as his own.

"To his right is Leonide Pashenko, the Russian ambassador. Opposite is the Chinese ambassador Hsia Lu-Minh. The others are aides." He set the image in motion. "We weren't able to record sound; the lip-reading lab gave us a rough translation. . . . Shgawe is now announcing his purchase. He's bland and affable, but watching Pashenko and Hsia like a hawk. They're startled and annoyed, agreeing possibly for the first time in years. . . . Pashenko inquires the need for such grandiose weapons. . . . Shgawe replies that they were cheap and will contribute both to the defense and prestige of Lakhadi. Pashenko says that the Soviet Union has guaranteed

Lakhadi independence, that such concerns are superfluous. Hsia sits thinking. Pashenko is more volatile. He points out that the Titans are not only obsolete and unarmed, but that they require an extensive technical complex to support them.

"Shgawe laughs. 'I realize this and I hereby request this help from the Soviet Union. If it is not forthcoming, I will make the same request of the People's Republic of China. If still unsuccessful, I shall look elsewhere.'

"Pashenko and Hsia close up like clams. There's bad blood between them; neither trusts the other. Pashenko manages to announce that he'll consult his government, and that's all for today."

The image faded. Sebastiani leaned back in his chair. "In two days Tamba Ngasi leaves his constituency, Kotoba on the Dasa River, for the convening of the Grand Parliament of Fejo." He projected a detailed map on the screen, indicated Kotoba and Fejo with a dot of light. "He'll come down the Dasa River by launch to Dasai, continue to Fejo by train. I suggest that you intercept him at Dasai. Tamba Ngasi is a Leopard Man, and took part in the Rhodesian Extermination. To win his seat in the Grand Parliament he killed his uncle, a brother, and four cousins. Extreme measures should cause you no compunction." With a fastidious gesture Sebastiani blanked out the screen. "The subsequent program we've discussed at length." He reached into a cabinet, brought forth a battered fiber case. "Here's your kit. You're familiar with all the contents except—these." He displayed three phials, containing respectively white, yellow and brown tablets. "Vitamins, according to the label." He regarded Keith owlishly. "We call them Unpopularity Pills. Don't take them yourself, unless you want to become *very* unpopular."

"Interesting," said Keith. "How do they work?"

"They induce body odor of a most unpleasant nature. Not all peoples react identically to the same odor; there's a large degree of social training involved, hence the three colors." He chuckled at Keith's skeptical expression. "Don't underestimate these pills. Odors create a subconscious backdrop to our impressions: an offensive odor induces irritation, dislike, distrust. Notice the color of the pills: they indicate the racial or cultural groups most strongly affected. White for Caucasians, yellow for Indo-Asian, brown for Africans.''

''I should think that a stench is a stench,'' said Keith.

Sebastiani pursed his lips didactically. ''These naturally are not infallible formulations. North Chinese and South Chinese react differently, as do Laplanders, Frenchmen, Russians and Moroccans. American Blacks are culturally Caucasians. But I need say no more; I'm sure the function of the pills is clear. A dose persists two or three days, and the person affected is unaware of his condition.'' He replaced the phials in the case, and as if by afterthought brought forth a battered flashlight. ''And this of course—absolutely top-secret. I marvel that you are allowed the use of it. When you press this button—a flashlight. Slip over the safety, press the button again—'' he tossed the flashlight back into the case ''—a deathray. Or if you prefer, a laser, projecting red and infra-red at high intensity. If you try to open it you'll blow your arm off. Recharge by plugging into any AC socket. The era of the simple projectile is at an end.'' He snapped shut the case, rose to his feet, gave a brusque wave of his hand. ''Wait in the outside office for Parrish; he'll take you to your plane. You know your objectives. This is a desperate business, a foolhardy business. You apparently like it or you'd have a job in the post office.''

At Latitude 6° 34′ N, Longitude 13° 30′ W, the plane made sunrise rendezvous with a wallowing black submarine. Keith drifted down on a jigger consisting of a seat, a small engine, four whirling blades. The submarine submerged with Keith aboard, surfaced twenty-three hours later to set him afloat in a sailing canoe, and once more submerged.

Keith was alone on the South Atlantic. Dawn ringed the horizon, and there to the east lay the dark mass of Africa. Keith trimmed his sail to the breeze and wake foamed up astern.

Daybreak illuminated a barren sandy coast, on which a few fishermen's huts could be seen. To the far north, under wads of black-green foliage, the white buildings of Dasai gleamed.

Keith drove his canoe up on the beach, plodded across sand dunes to the coast highway.

There was already considerable traffic abroad: women trudging beside donkeys, young men riding bicycles, an occasional small automobile of antique vintage; once an expensive new Amphitrite Air-Boat slid past on its air cushion, with a soft whispered *whoosh*.

At nine o'clock, crossing the sluggish brown Dasa River, he entered Dasai, a small sun-dazzled coastal port, as yet untouched by the changes which had transformed Fejo. Two- and three-storied buildings of white stucco, with arcades below, lined the main street, and a strip planted with palms, rhododendrons and oleanders ran down the middle. There were two hotels, a bank, a garage, miscellaneous shops and office buildings. A dispirited police officer in a white helmet directed traffic: at the moment, two camels led by a ragged Bedouin. A squat pedestal supported four large photographs of Adoui Shgawe, the "Beloved Premier of our Nation, the Great Beacon of Africa." Below, conspicuously smaller, were photographs of Karl Marx and Mao Tse-Tung.

Keith turned into a side street, walked to the river-bank. He saw ramshackle docks, a half-dozen restaurants, beer-gardens and cabarets built over the water on platforms and shaded by palm-thatched roofs. He beckoned to a nearby boy, who approached cautiously. "When the launch comes down the river from Kotoba, where does it land?"

The boy pointed a thin crooked finger. "That is the dock, sir, just beyond the Hollywood Cafe."

"And when is the launch due to arrive?"

"That I do not know, sir."

Keith flipped the boy a coin and made his way to the dock, where he learned that indeed the river-boat from Kotoba would arrive definitely at two P.M., certainly no later than three, beyond any question of doubt by four.

Keith considered. If Tamba Ngasi should arrive at two or even three, he would probably press on to Fejo, sixty miles down the coast. If the boat were late he might well decide to stay in Dasai for the night—there at the Grand Plaisir Hotel, only a few steps away.

The question: where to intercept Tamba Ngasi? Here in Dasai? At the Grand Plaisir Hotel? En route to Fejo?

None of these possibilities appealed to Keith. He returned to the main street. A tobacconist assured him that no automobiles could be hired except the town's three ancient taxicabs. He pointed up the street to an old black Citroen standing in the shade of an enormous sapodilla. The driver, a thin old man in white shorts, a faded blue shirt and canvas shoes, lounged beside a booth which sold crushed ice and syrup. The proprietress, a large woman in a brilliant black, gold and orange gown prodded him with her fly-whisk, directing his attention to Keith. He moved reluctantly across the sidewalk. "The gentleman wishes to be conveyed to a destination?"

Keith, in the role of the back-country barbarian, pulled at his long chin dubiously. "I will try your vehicle, provided you do not attempt to cheat me."

"The rates are definite," said the driver, unenthusiastically. "Three rupiahs for the first kilometer, one rupiah thereafter. Where do you wish to go?"

Keith entered the cab. "Drive up the river road."

They rattled out of town, along a dirt road which kept generally to the banks of the river. The countryside was dusty and barren, grown over with thorn, here and there a massive baobab. The miles passed and the driver became nervous. "Where does the gentleman intend to go?"

"Stop here," said Keith. The driver uncertainly slowed the cab. Keith brought money from the leather pouch at his belt. "I wish to drive the cab. Alone. You may wait for me under the tree." The driver protested vehemently. Keith pressed a hundred rupiahs upon him. "Do not argue; you have no choice. I may be gone several hours, but you shall have your cab back safely and another hundred rupiahs—if you wait here."

The driver alighted and limped through the dust to the shade of the tall yellow gum tree and Keith drove off up the road.

The country became more pleasant. Palm trees lined the riverbank; there were occasional garden-patches, and he passed three villages of round mud-wall huts with conical thatched roofs. Occasionally canoes moved across the dull brown water, and he saw a barge stacked with cord-wood, towed by what seemed a ridiculously inadequate rowboat with an outboard motor. He drove another ten miles and the country once more became inhospitable. The river, glazed by heat, wound between mud-banks where small crocodiles basked; the shores were choked with papyrus and acacia thickets. Keith stopped the car, consulted a map. The first town of any consequence where the boat might be expected to discharge passengers was Mbakouesse, another twenty-five miles—too far.

Replacing the map in his suitcase, Keith brought out a jar containing brilliantine, or so the label implied. He considered it a moment, and arrived at a plan of action.

He now drove slowly and presently found a spot where the channel swung close in under the bank. Keith parked beside a towering clump of red-jointed bamboo and made his preparations. He wadded a few ounces of the waxy so-called brilliantine around a strangely heavy lozenge from a box of cough drops, taped the mass to a dry stick of wood. He found a spool of fine cord, tied a rock to the end, unwound twenty feet, tied on the stick. Then, wary of adders, crocodiles, and the enormous clicking-wing wasps which lived in burrows along the river-bank, he made his way through the acacia to the shores of the river. Unreeling a hundred feet of cord, he flung stick and stone as far across the river as possible. The stone sank to the bottom, mooring the stick which now floated at the far edge of the channel, exactly where Keith had intended.

An hour passed, two hours. Keith sat in the shade of the acacia, surrounded by the resinous odor of the leaves, the swampy reek of the river. At last: the throb of a heavy diesel engine. Downstream came a typical boat of the African rivers. About seventy feet long, with first-class cabins on the upper deck, second-class cubicles on the main deck, the remainder of the passengers sitting, standing, crouching or huddling wherever room offered itself.

The boat approached, chugging down the center of the channel. Keith gathered in the slack of the cord, drew the stick closer. On the top deck stood a tall gaunt man, his face dark and feral under a *darshba* turban: Tamba Ngasi? Keith was uncertain. This man walked with head bent forward, elbows jutting at a sharp angle. Keith had studied photographs of Tamba Ngasi, but confronted by the living individual. . . . There was no time for speculation. The boat was almost abreast, the bow battering up a transparent yellow bow-wave. Keith drew in the cord, pulled the stick under the bow. He held up the palm of his right hand in which lay coiled a directional antenna. He spread his fingers, an impulse struck out to the detonator in the little black lozenge. A dull booming explosion, a gout of foam, sheets of mud and water, shrill cries of surprise and fear. The boat nosed down into the water, swerved erratically.

Keith pulled back and rewound what remained of his cord.

The boat, already overloaded, was about to sink. It swung toward the shore, ran aground fifty yards downstream.

Keith backed the taxi out of the acacia, drove a half-mile up the road, waited, watching through binoculars.

A straggle of white-robed men and women came through the acacia and presently a tall man in a *darshba* turban strode angrily out on the road. Keith focused the binoculars: there were the features he himself now wore. The posture, the stride seemed more angular, more nervous; he must remember to duplicate these mannerisms. . . . Now, to work. He pulled the hood of his cloak forward to conceal his face, shifted into gear. The taxi approached the knot of people standing by the roadside. A portly olive-skinned Indian in European whites sprang out, flagged him to a stop. Keith looked out in simulated surprise.

Keith shrugged. "I have a fare; I am going now to pick him up."

Tamba Ngasi came striding up. He flung open the door. "The fare can wait. I am a government official. Take me to Dasai."

The portly little Hindu made a motion as if he would likewise seek to enter the cab. Keith stopped him. "I have room only for one." Tamba Ngasi threw his suitcase into the cab, leapt in. Keith moved off, leaving the group staring disconsolately after him.

"An insane accident," Tamba Ngasi complained peevishly. "We ride along quietly; the boat strikes a rock; it seems like an explosion, and we sink! Can you imagine that? And I, an important member of the government, riding aboard! Why are you stopping?"

"I must see to my other fare." Keith turned off the road, along a faint track leading into the scrub.

"No matter about your other fare, I wish no delay. Drive on."

"I must also pick up a can of petrol, otherwise we will run short."

"Petrol, here, out in the thorn bushes?"

"A cache known only to the taxi drivers." Keith halted; alighted, opened the rear door. "Tamba Ngasi, come forth."

Tamba Ngasi stared under Keith's hood into his own face. He spit out a passionate expletive, clawed for the dagger at his waist. Keith lunged, tapped him on the forehead with his copper-silver fingernails. Electricity burst in a killing gush through Ngasi's brain; he staggered sidelong and fell into the road.

Keith dragged the corpse off the track, out into the scrub. Tamba Ngasi's legs were heavy and thick, out of proportion to his sinewy torso. This was a peculiarity of which Keith had been ignorant. But no matter; in this loose native garb, who would ever know that Keith's shanks were long and lean?

Jackals and vultures would speedily dispose of the corpse.

Keith transferred the contents of a pouch to his own, sought but found no money-belt. He returned to the taxi, drove back to the tall gum tree. The driver lay asleep; Keith woke him with a blast of the horn. "Hurry now, take me back to Dasai, I must be in Fejo before nightfall."

In all of Africa, ancient, medieval and modern, there had never been a city like Fejo. It rose on a barren headland north of Tabacoundi Bay. where twenty years before not even fishermen had deigned to live. Fejo was a bold city, startling in its shapes, textures and colors. Africans determined to express their unique cultural heritage had planned the city, rejecting absolutely the architectural traditions of Europe and America, both classical and contemporary. Construction had been financed by a massive loan from the Soviet Union; Russian engineers had translated the grandiose sketches of fervent Lakhadi students into space and solidity.

Fejo, therefore, was a remarkable city. Certain European critics dismissed it as a stage setting; some were fascinated, others repelled. No one denied that Fejo was compellingly dramatic. "In contrast to the impact of Fejo, Brasilia seems sterile, eclectic, prettified," wrote an English critic. "Insane fantasies, at which Gaudi himself might be appalled," snapped a Spaniard. "Fejo is the defiant challenge of African genius, and its excesses are those of passion, rather than of style," declared an Italian. "Fejo," wrote a Frenchman, "is hideous, startling, convoluted, pretentious, ignorant, oppressive, and noteworthy only for the tortured forms to which good building material has been put."

Fejo centered on the fifty-story spire of the Institute of Africa. Nearby stood the Grand Parliament, held aloft on copper arches, with oval windows and a blue-enameled roof like a broad-brimmed derby hat. Six tall warriors of polished basalt, representing the six principal tribes of Lakhadi, fronted a plaza; beyond, the Hotel des Tropiques, the most magnificent in Africa, and ranking with any in the world. The Hotel des Tropiques was perhaps the most conventional building of the central complex, but even here the architects had insisted on pure African style. Vegetation from the roof garden trailed down the white and blue walls; the lobby was furnished in *padauk,* teak and ebony; columns of structural glass rose from silver-blue carpets and purple-red rugs to support a ceiling of stainless steel and black enamel.

At the far end of the plaza stood the official palace, and beyond, the first three of a projected dozen apartment buildings, intended for the use of high officials. Of all the buildings in Fejo, these had been most favorably received by foreign critics, possibly because of their simplicity. Each floor consisted of a separate disk twelve feet in height, and was supported completely apart from the floors above and below by four stanchions piercing the disks. Each disk also served as a wide airy deck, and the top deck functioned as a heliport.

On the other side of the Hotel des Tropiques spread another plaza, to satisfy the African need for a communal bazaar. Here were booths with entertainers of every sort, and hawkers offering jujus, elixirs and talismans.

Through the plaza moved a cheerful and volatile mixture of people: negro women in magnificently printed cottons, silks and gauzes, Mohammedans in white *djellabas,* Tuaregs and Mauretanian Blue Men, Chinese in fusty black suits, ubiquitous Hindu shopkeepers, an occasional Russian, grim and aloof from the crowd. Beyond this plaza lay a district of stark white three-story apartment cubicles. The people looking from the windows seemed irresolute and uncertain, as if the shift from mud and thatch to glass, tile, and air-conditioning were too great to be encompassed in a lifetime.

Into Fejo, at five in the afternoon, came James Keith, riding first class on the train from Dasai. From the terminal he marched across the bazaar to the Hotel des Tropiques, strode to the desk, brushed aside a number of persons who stood waiting, pounded his fist to attract the clerk, a pale Eurasian who looked around in annoyance. "Quick!" snapped Keith, "Is it fitting that a Parliamentarian waits at the pleasure of such as you? Conduct me to my suite."

The clerk's manner altered. "Your name, sir?"

"I am Tamba Ngasi."

"There is no reservation, Comrade Ngasi. Did you—"

Keith fixed the man with a glare of outrage. "I am a Parliamentarian of the State. I need no reservation."

"But all the suites are occupied."

"Turn someone out, and quickly."

"Yes, Comrade Ngasi. At once."

Keith soon found himself in a sumptuous set of rooms furnished in carved woods, green glass, heavy rugs. He had not eaten since early morning; a touch on a button flashed the restaurant menu on a screen. No reason why a tribal chieftain should not enjoy European cuisine, thought Keith, and he ordered accordingly. Awaiting his lunch, he inspected walls, floor, drapes, ceiling, furniture. Spy cells might or might not be standard equipment here in intrigue-ridden Fejo. They were not apparent, nor did he expect them to be. The best of modern equipment was dependably undetectable.

He stepped out on the deck, pushed with his tongue against one of his teeth, spoke in a whisper for several minutes. He returned the switch to its former position, and his message was broadcast in a hundredth-second coded burst indistinguishable from static. A satellite, a thousand miles overhead, caught the signal, amplified and transmitted it to Washington.

Keith waited, and minutes passed. Then came the almost imperceptible click marking the arrival of the return message. It communicated itself in the voice of Sebastiani by way of Keith's jaw-bone to his auditory nerve, soundlessly, but with all of Sebastiani's characteristic inflections.

"So far so good," said Sebastiani. "But I've got some bad news. Don't try to make contact with Corty. Apparently he's been apprehended and brainwashed by the Chinese. So you're on your own."

Keith grunted glumly, returned to the sitting room. His lunch was served; he ate, then opened the case he had taken from Tamba Ngasi. It was similar to his own, even to the contents: clean linen, toilet articles, personal effects, a file of documents. The documents, printed in florid New African type, were of no particular interest: a poll list, various official notifications. Keith found a directive which read, ". . . When you arrive in Fejo, you will take up lodgings at Rue Arsabatte 453, where a suitable suite has been prepared for you. Please announce your presence to the Chief Clerk of Parliament as soon as possible."

Keith smiled faintly. He would simply declare that he preferred the Hotel des Tropiques. And who would question the whim of a notoriously ill-tempered back-country chieftain?

Replacing the contents of Tamba Ngasi's suitcase, Keith became aware of something peculiar. The objects felt—strange. This fetish-box for instance—just a half-ounce too heavy. Keith's mind raced along a whole network of speculations.

This rather battered ball-point pen. . . . He inspected it closely, pointed it away from himself, pressed the extensor-button. A click, a hiss, a spit of cloudy gas. Keith jerked back, moved across the room. It was a miniature gas-gun, designed to puff a drug into and through the pores of the skin. Confirmation for his suspicions—and in what a strange direction they led!

Keith replaced the pen, closed the suitcase. He paced thoughtfully back and forth a moment or two, then locked his own suitcase and left the room.

He rode down to the lobby on a twinkling escalator of pink and green crystal, stood for a moment surveying the scene. He had expected nothing so splendid; how, he wondered, would Tamba Ngasi have regarded this glittering room and its hyper-sophisticated guests? Not with approval, Keith decided. He walked to the entrance, twisting his face into a leer of disgust. Even by his own tastes, the Hotel des Tropiques seemed over-rich, a trifle too fanciful.

He crossed the plaza, marched along the Avenue of the Six Warriors to the grotesque but oddly impressive Grand Parliament of Lakhadi. A pair of glossy black guards, wearing metal sandals and greaves, pleated kirtles of white leather, sprang out, crossed spears in front of him.

Keith inspected them haughtily. "I am Tamba Ngasi, Grand Parliamentarian from Kotoba Province."

The guards twitched not a muscle; they might have been carved of ebony. From a side cubicle came a short fat white man in limp brown slacks and shirt. He barked, "Tamba Ngasi. Guards, *admit!*"

The guards with a single movement sprang back across the floor. The little fat man bowed politely, but it seemed as if his gaze never veered from Keith. "You have come to register, Sir Parliamentarian?"

"Precisely. With the Chief Clerk."

The fat man bowed his head again. "I am Vasif Doutoufsky, Chief Clerk. Will you step into my office?"

Doutoufsky's office was hot and stuffy and smelled sweet of rose incense. Doutoufsky offered Keith a cup of tea. Keith gave Tamba Ngasi's characteristic brusque shake, Doutoufsky appeared faintly surprised. He spoke in Russian. "Why did you not go to Rue Arsabatte? I awaited you there until ten minutes ago."

Keith's mind spun as if on ball bearings. He said gruffly, in his own not-too-facile Russian. "I had my reasons. . . . There was an accident to the riverboat, possibly an explosion. I hailed a taxi, and so arrived at Dasai."

"Aha," said Doutoufsky in a soft voice. "Do you suspect interference?"

"If so," said Keith, "it could only come from one source."

"Aha," said Doutoufsky again, even more softly. "You mean—"

"The Chinese."

Doutoufsky regarded Keith thoughtfully. "The transformation has been done well," he said. "Your skin is precisely correct, with convincing tones and shadings. You speak rather oddly."

"As might you, if your head were crammed with as much as mine."

Doutoufsky pursed his lips, as if at a secret joke. "You will change residence to Rue Arsabatte?"

Keith hesitated, trying to sense Doutoufsky's relationship to himself: inferior or superior? Inferior, probably, with the powers and prerogatives of the contact, from whom came instructions and from whom, back to the Kremlin, went evaluations. A chilling thought: Doutoufsky and he who had walked in the guise of Tamba Ngasi might both be renegade Russians, both Chinese agents in this most fantastic of all wars. In which case Keith's life was even more precarious than it had been a half-hour previous. . . . But this was the hypothesis of smaller probability. Keith said in a voice of authority, "An automobile has been placed at my disposal?"

Doutoufsky blinked. "To my knowledge, no."

"I will require an automobile," said Keith. "Where is your car?"

"Surely, sir, this is not in character?"

"I am to be the judge of that."

Doutoufsky heaved a sigh. "I will call out one of the Parliamentary limousines."

"Which, no doubt, is efficiently monitored."

"Naturally."

"I prefer a vehicle in which I can transact such business as necessary without fear of witnesses."

Doutoufsky nodded abruptly. "Very well." He tossed a key to the table of his desk. "This is my own Aerofloat. Please use it discreetly."

"This car is not monitored?"

"Definitely not."

"I will check it intensively nonetheless." Keith spoke in a tone of quiet menace. "I hope to find it as you describe."

Doutoufsky blinked, and in a subdued voice explained where the car might be found. "Tomorrow at noon Parliament convenes. You are naturally aware of this."

"Naturally. Are there supplementary instructions?"

Doutoufsky gave Keith a dry side-glance. "I was wondering when you would ask for them, since this was specified as the sole occasion for our contact. Not to hector, not to demand pleasure cars."

"Contain your arrogance, Vasif Doutoufsky. I must work without interference. Certain slight doubts regarding your ability already exist; spare me the necessity of corroborating them."

"Aha," said Doutoufsky softly. He reached in his drawer, tossed a small iron nail down upon the desk. "Here are your instructions. You have the key to my car, you have refused to use your designated lodgings. Do you require anything further?"

"Yes," said Keith, grinning wolfishly. "Funds."

Doutoufsky tossed a packet of *rupiah* notes on the desk. "This should suffice until our next contact."

Keith rose slowly to his feet. There would be difficulties if he failed to make prearranged contacts with Doutoufsky. "Certain circumstances may make it necessary to change the routine."

"Indeed? Such as?"

"I have learned—from a source which I am not authorized to reveal—that the Chinese have apprehended and brainwashed an agent of the West. He was detected by the periodicity of his actions. It is better to make no precise plans."

Doutoufsky nodded soberly. "There is something in what you say."

By moonlight the coast road from Fejo to Dasai was beautiful beyond imagination. To the left spread an endless expanse of sea, surf and wan desolate sand; to the right grew thornbush, baobabs, wire cactus—angular patterns in every tone of silver, gray and black.

Keith felt reasonably sure that he had not been followed. He had carefully washed the car with the radiation from his flashlight, to destroy a spy-cell's delicate circuits by the induced currents. Halfway to Dasai he braked to a halt, extinguished his lights, searched the sky with the radar in his ear-amulets. He could detect nothing; the air was clear and desolate, nor did he sense any car behind him. He took occasion to despatch a message to the hovering satellite. There was a five-minute wait; then the relay clicked home. Sebastiani's voice came sharp and distinct into his brain: "The coincidence, upon consideration, is not astonishing. The Russians selected Tamba Ngasi for the same reason we did: his reputation for aggressiveness and independence, his presumable popularity with the military, as opposed to their suspicion of Shgawe.

"As to the Arsabatte address, I feel you have made the correct decision. You'll be less exposed at the hotel. We have nothing definite on Doutoufsky. He is ostensibly a Polish emigrant, now a Lakhadi citizen. You may have overplayed your hand in taking so strong an attitude. If he seeks you out, show a degree of contrition and remark that you have been instructed to cooperate more closely with him."

Keith searched the sky once more, but received only a signal from a low-flying owl. Confidently he continued along the surreal landscape and presently arrived at Dasai.

The town was quiet, with only a sprinkling of streetlights, a tinkle of music and laughter from the cabarets. Keith turned along the river road and proceeded inland.

The country became wild and forlorn. Twenty miles passed; Keith drove slowly. Here, the yellow gum tree where he had discharged the taxi-driver. Here, where he had grounded the riverboat. He swung around, returned down the road. Here—where he had driven off the road with the man he had thought to be Tamba Ngasi. He turned, drove a space, then stopped, got out of the car. Off in the brush, a dozen yellow eyes reflected back his headlights, then swiftly retreated.

The jackals had been busy with the body. Three of them lay dead, mounds of rancid fur, and Keith was at a loss to account for their condition. He played his flashlight up and down the corpse, inspected the flesh at which the jackals had been tearing. He bent closer, frowning in puzzlement. A peculiar pad of specialized tissue lay along the outside of the thighs, almost an inch thick. It was organized in orderly strips and fed plentifully from large arteries, and here and there Keith detected the glint of metal. Suddenly he guessed the nature of the tissue and knew why the jackals lay dead. He straightened up, looked around through the moon-drenched forest of cactus and thorn-scrub and shivered. The presence of death alone was awesome, the more so for the kind of man who lay here, so far from his home, so strangely altered and augmented. Those pads of gray flesh must be electro-organic tissue, similar to that of the electric eel, somehow adapted to human flesh by Russian biologists. Keith felt a sense of oppression. How far they exceed us! he thought. My power source is chemical, inorganic; that of this man was controlled by the functioning of his body and remained at so high a potential that three jackals had been electrocuted tearing into it.

Gritting his teeth he bent over the corpse, and set about his examination.

Half an hour later he had finished, and stood erect with two films of semi-metalloid peeled from the inside of the corpse's cheeks: communication circuits certainly as sophisticated as his own.

He scrubbed his hands in the sand, returned to the car and drove back into the setting moon. He came to the dark town of Dasai, turned south along the coast road, and an hour later returned to Fejo.

The lobby of the Hotel des Tropiques was now illuminated only by great pale green and blue globes. A few groups sat talking and sipping drinks; to the hushed mutter of their conversation Keith crossed to the escalator, was conveyed to his room.

He entered with caution. Everything seemed in order. The two cases had not been tampered with; the bed had been turned back, pajamas of purple silk had been provided for him.

Before he slept, Keith touched another switch in his dentures, and the radar mounted an unseen guard. Any movement within the room would awaken him. He was temporarily secure; he slept.

An hour before the first session of the Grand Parliament, Keith sought out Vasif Doutoufsky, who compressed his mouth into a pink rosette. "Please. It is not suitable that we seem intimate acquaintances."

Keith grinned his vulpine unpleasant grin. "No fear of that." He displayed the devices he had taken from the body of the so-called Tamba Ngasi. Doutoufsky peered curiously.

"These are communication circuits." Keith tossed them to the desk. "They have failed, and I cannot submit my reports. You must do this for me, and relay my instructions."

Doutoufsky shook his head. "This was not to be my function. I cannot compromise myself; the Chinese already suspect my reports."

Ha, thought Keith, Doutoufsky functioned as a double-agent. The Russians seemed to trust him, which Keith considered somewhat naive. He ruminated a moment, then reaching in his pouch brought forth a flat tin. He opened it, extracted a small woody object resembling a clove. He dropped it in front of Doutoufsky. "Eat this."

Doutoufsky looked up slowly, brow wrinkled in plaintive protest. "You are acting very strangely. Of course I shall not eat this object. What is it?"

"It is a tie which binds our lives together," said Keith. "If I am killed, one of my organs broadcasts a pulse which will detonate this object."

"You are mad," muttered Doutoufsky. "I shall make a report to this effect."

Keith moved forward, laid his hand on Doutoufsky's shoulder, touched his neck. "You are aware that I can cause your heart to stop?" He sent a trickle of electricity into his copper-silver fingernails.

Doutoufsky seemed more puzzled than alarmed. Keith emitted a stronger current, enough to make any man wince. Doutoufsky merely reached up to disengage Keith's arm. His fingers were cold, and clamped like steel tongs. And into Keith's arm came a hurting surge of electricity.

"You are an idiot," said Doutoufsky in disgust. "I carry weapons you know nothing about. Leave me at once, or you will regret it."

Keith departed, sick with dismay. Doutoufsky was augmented. His rotundity no doubt concealed great slabs of electro-generative tissue. He had blundered; he had made a fool of himself.

A gong rang; other Parliamentarians filed past him. Keith took a deep breath, swaggered into the echoing red, gold, and black paneled hall. A doorkeeper saluted. "Name, sir?"

"Tamba Ngasi, Kotoba Province."

"Your seat, Excellency, is Number 27."

Keith seated himself, listened without interest to the invocation. What to do about Doutoufsky?

His ruminations were interrupted by the appearance on the rostrum of a heavy moon-faced man in a simple white robe. His skin was almost blue-black, the eyelids hung lazily across his protuberant eyeballs, his mouth was wide and heavy. Keith recognized Adoui Shgawe, Premier of Lakhadi, Benefactor of Africa.

He spoke resonantly, in generalities and platitudes, with many references to Socialist Solidarity. "The future of Lakhadi is the future of Black Africa! As we look through this magnificent chamber and note the colors of the tasteful decoration, can we not fail to be impressed by the correctness of the symbolism? Red is the color of blood, which is the same for all men, and also the color of International Socialism. Black is the color of our skins, and it is our prideful duty to ensure that the energy and genius of our race is respected around the globe. Gold is the color of success, of glory, and of progress; and golden is the future of Lakhadi!''

The chamber reverberated with applause.

Shgawe turned to more immediate problems. ''While spiritually rich, we are in certain ways impoverished. Comrade Nambey Faranah—'' he nodded toward a squat square-faced man in a black suit ''—has presented an interesting program. He suggests that a carefully scheduled program of immigration might provide us a valuable new national asset. On the other hand—''

Comrade Nambey Faranah bounded to his feet and turned to face the assembly. Shgawe held up a restraining hand, but Faranah ignored him. ''I have conferred with Ambassador Hsia Lu-Minh of our comrade nation, the People's Republic of China. He has made the most valuable assurances, and will use all his influence to help us. He agrees that a certain number of skilled agricultural technicians can immeasurably benefit our people, and can accelerate the political orientation of the back-regions. Forward to progress!'' bellowed Faranah. ''Hail the mighty advance of the colored races, arm in arm, united under the red banner of International Socialism!'' He looked expectantly around the hall for applause, which came only in a perfunctory spatter. He sat down abruptly. Keith studied him with a new somber speculation. Comrade Faranah—an augmented Chinese?

Adoui Shgawe had placidly continued his address. ''—some have questioned the practicality of this move,'' he was saying. ''Friends and comrades, I assure you that no matter how loyal and comradely our brother nations, they cannot provide us prestige! The more we rely on them for leadership, the more we diminish our own stature among the nations of Africa.''

Nambey Faranah held up a quivering finger. ''Not completely correct, Comrade Shgawe!''

Shgawe ignored him. ''For this reason I have purchased eighteen American missiles. Admittedly they are cumbersome and outmoded. But they are still terrible instruments—and they command respect. With eighteen intercontinental missiles poised against any attack, we consolidate our position as the leaders of black Africa.''

There was another spatter of applause. Adoui Shgawe leaned forward, gazed blandly over the assembly. "That concludes my address. I will answer questions from the floor. . . . Ah, Comrade Bouassede."

Comrade Bouassede, a fragile old man with a fine fluffy white beard, rose to his feet. "All very fine, these great weapons, but against whom do we wish to use them? What good are they to us, who know nothing of such things?"

Shgawe nodded with vast benevolence. "A wise question, Comrade. I can only answer that one never knows from which direction some insane militarism may strike."

Faranah leapt to his feet. "May I answer the question, Comrade Shgawe?"

"The assembly will listen to your opinions with respect," Shgawe declared courteously.

Faranah turned toward old Bouassede. "The imperialists are at bay, they cower in their rotting strongholds, but still they can muster strength for one final feverish lunge, should they see a chance to profit."

Shgawe said, "Comrade Faranah has expressed himself with his customary untiring zeal."

"Are not these devices completely beyond our capacity to maintain?" demanded Bouassede.

Shgawe nodded. "We live in a swiftly changing environment. At the moment this is the case. But until we are able to act for ourselves, our Russian allies have offered many valuable services. They will bring great suction dredges, and will station the launching tubes in the tidal sands off our coast. They have also undertaken to provide us a specially designed ship to supply liquid oxygen and fuel."

"This is all nonsense," growled Bouassede. "We must pay for this ship; it is not a gift. The money could be better spent building roads and buying cattle."

"Comrade Bouassede has not considered the intangible factors involved," declared Shgawe equably. "Ah, Comrade Maguemi. Your question, please."

Comrade Maguemi was a serious bespectacled young man in a black suit. "Exactly how many Chinese immigrants are envisioned?"

Shgawe looked from the corner of his eye toward Faranah. "The proposal so far is purely theoretical, and probably—"

Faranah jumped to his feet. "It is a program of great urgency. However many Chinese are needed, we shall welcome them."

"This does not answer my question," Maguemi persisted coldly. "A hundred actual technicians might in fact be useful. A hundred thousand peasants, a colony of aliens in our midst, could only bring us harm."

Shgawe nodded gravely. "Comrade Maguemi has illuminated a very serious difficulty."

"By no means," cried Faranah. "Comrade Maguemi's premises are incorrect. A hundred, a hundred thousand, a million, ten million—what is the difference? We are bound together, striving toward a common goal!"

"I do not agree," shouted Maguemi. "We must avoid doctrinaire solutions to our problems. If we are submerged in the Asiatic tide, our voices will be drowned."

Another young man, thin as a starved bird, with a gaunt face and blade-like nose, sprang up. "Comrade Maguemi has no sense of historical projection. He ignores the teachings of Marx, Lenin, and Mao. A true Communist takes no heed of race or geography."

"I am no true Communist," declared Maguemi coldly. "I have never made such a humiliating admission. I consider the teachings of Marx, Lenin and Mao even more obsolete than the American weapons with which Comrade Shgawe has unwisely burdened us."

Adoui Shgawe smiled broadly. "We may safely pass on from the subject of Chinese immigration, as in all likelihood it will never occur. A few hundred technicians, as Comrade Maguemi suggests, of course will be welcome. A more extended program would certainly lead to difficulties."

Nambey Faranah glowered at the floor.

Shgawe spoke on, in a soothing voice, and presently adjourned the Parliament for two days.

Keith returned to his room at the des Tropiques, settled himself on the couch, considered his position. He could feel no satisfaction in his performance to date. He had blundered seriously with Doutoufsky, might well have aroused his suspicions. There was certainly small reason for optimism.

Two days later Adoui Shgawe reappeared in the Grand Chamber, to speak on a routine matter connected with the state-operated cannery. Nambey Faranah could not resist a sardonic jibe: "At last we perceive a use for the cast-off American missile-docks: they can easily be converted into fish-processing plants, and we can shoot the wastes into space."

Shgawe held up his hands against the mutter of appreciative laughter. "This is no more than stupidity; I have explained the symbolic importance of these weapons. Persons inexperienced in such matters should not criticize."

Faranah was not to be subdued so easily. "How can we be anything other than inexperienced? We know nothing of these American cast-offs; they float unseen in the ocean. Do they even exist?"

Shgawe shook his head in pitying disgust. "Are there no extremes to which you will not go? The docks are at hand for any and all to inspect. Tomorrow I will order the *Lumumba* out, and I now request the entire membership to make a trip of inspection. There will be no further excuse for skepticism—if, indeed, there is now."

Faranah was silenced. He gave a petulant shrug, settled back into his seat.

Almost two-thirds of the chamber responded to Shgawe's invitation, and on the following morning, trooped aboard the single warship of the Lakhadi navy, an ancient French destroyer. Bells clanged, whistles sounded, water churned up aft and the *Lumumba* eased out of Tabacoundi Bay, to swing south over long blue swells.

Twenty miles the destroyer cruised, paralleling the wind-beaten shore; then at the horizon appeared seventeen pale humps—the floating missile silos. But the *Lumumba* veered in toward shore, where the eighteenth of the docks had been raised on buoyancy tanks, floated in toward the beach and lowered to the sub-tidal sand. Alongside was moored an

Egyptian dredge which pumped water below the silo, dislodging sand and allowing the dock to settle.

The Parliamentarians stood on the *Lumumba*'s foredeck, staring at the admittedly impressive cylinder. All were forced to agree that the docks existed. Premier Shgawe came out on the wing of the bridge, with beside him the Grand Marshal of the Army, Achille Hashembe, a hard-bitten man of sixty, with close-cropped gray hair. While Shgawe addressed the Parliamentarians Hashembe scrutinized them carefully, first one face, then another.

"The helicopter assigned to this particular dock is under repair," said Shgawe. "It will be inconvenient to inspect the missile itself. But no matter; our imaginations will serve us. Picture eighteen of these impressive weapons ranged at intervals along the shores of our homeland!"

Keith, standing near Faranah heard him mutter to those near at hand. He watched with great attention. Two hours previously, stewards had served small cups of black coffee, and Keith, stationing himself four places above Faranah had dropped an Unpopularity Pill into the fourth cup. The steward passed along the line; each intervening Parliamentarian took a cup and Faranah received the cup with the pill. Now Faranah's audience regarded him with fastidious distaste and moved away. A whiff of odor reached Keith himself: American biochemists, he thought, had wrought effectively. Faranah smelled very poorly indeed. And Faranah glared about in bafflement.

The *Lumumba* circled the dock slowly, which now had reached a permanent bed in the sand. Aboard the dredge, the Egyptian engineers were disengaging the pumps, preparatory to performing the same operation upon a second dock.

A steward approached Keith. "Adoui Shgawe wishes a word with you."

Keith followed the steward to the officers' mess, and as he entered met one of his colleagues on the way out.

Adoui Shgawe rose to his feet, bowed gravely. "Tamba Ngasi, please be seated. Will you take a glass of brandy?"

Keith shook his head brusquely: one of Ngasi's idiosyncrasies.

"You have met Grand Marshal Hashembe?" Shgawe asked politely.

Keith had been briefed as thoroughly as possible but on this point had no information. He evaded the question. "I have a high regard for the Grand Marshal's abilities."

Hashembe returned a curt nod, but said nothing.

"I take this occasion," said Shgawe, "to learn if you are sympathetic to my program, now that you have had an opportunity to observe it more closely."

Keith took a moment to reflect. In Shgawe's words lay the implication of previous disagreement. He submerged himself in the role of Tamba Ngasi, spoke with the sentiments Tamba Ngasi might be expected to entertain. "There is too much waste, too much foreign influence. We need water for the dry lands, we need medicine for the cattle. These are lacking while treasures are squandered on the idiotic buildings of Fejo." From the corner of his eye he saw Hashembe's eyes narrow a trifle. Approval?

Shgawe answered, ponderously suave. "I respect your argument, but there is also this to be considered: the Russians lent us the money for the purpose of building Fejo into a symbol of progress. They would not allow the money to be used for less dramatic purposes. We accepted, and I feel that we have benefited. Prestige nowadays is highly important."

"Important, to whom? To what end?" grumbled Keith. "Why must we pretend to a glory which is not ours?"

"You concede defeat before the battle begins," said Shgawe more vigorously. "Unfortunately this is our African heritage, and it must be overcome."

Keith, in the role of Ngasi, said, "My home is Kotoba, at the backwaters of the Dasa, and my people live in mud huts. Is not the idea of glory for the people of Kotoba ridiculous? Give us water and cattle and medicine."

Shgawe's voice dropped in pitch. "For the people of Kotoba, I too want water and cattle and medicine. But I want more than this, and glory is perhaps the wrong word to use."

Hashembe rose to his feet, bowed stiffly to Shgawe and to Keith, and left the room. Shgawe shook his round head. "Hashembe cannot understand my vision. He wants me to expel the foreigners: the Russians, the Hindus, especially the Chinese.''

Keith rose to his feet. "I am not absolutely opposed to your views. Perhaps you have some sort of document I might read?" He took a casual step across the room. Shgawe shrugged, looked among his papers. Keith seemed to stumble and his knuckles touched the nape of Shgawe's plump neck. "Your pardon, Excellency," said Keith. "I am clumsy."

"No matter," said Shgawe. "Here: this and this—papers which explain my views for the development of Lakhadi and of the New Africa." He blinked. Keith picked up the papers, studied them. Shgawe's eyes drooped shut, as the drug which Keith had blasted through his skin began to permeate his body. A moment later he was unconscious.

Keith moved quickly. Shgawe wore his hair in short oiled clusters; at the base of one of these, Keith attached a black pellet no larger than a grain of rice, then stepped back to read the papers.

Hashembe returned to the room. He halted, looked from Shgawe to Keith. "He seems to have dozed off," said Keith and continued to read the papers.

"Adoui Shgawe!" called Hashembe. "Are you asleep?"

Shgawe's eyelids fluttered; he heaved a deep sigh, looked up. "Hashembe . . . I seem to have napped. Ah, Tamba Ngasi. Those papers, you may keep them, and I pray that you deal sympathetically with my proposals in Parliament. You are an influential man, and I depend upon your support."

"I take your words to heart, Excellency." Leaving the dining area Keith climbed quickly to the bridge. The *Lumumba* was now heading back up the coast toward Fejo. Keith touched one of his internal switches, and into his auditory channel came the voice of Shgawe: "—has changed, and on the whole become a more reasonable man. I have no evidence for this, other than what I sense in him."

Hashembe's voice sounded more faintly. "He does not seem to remember me, but many years ago when he belonged to the Leopard Society, I captured him and a dozen of his fellows at Engassa. He killed two of my men and escaped, but I bear him no grudge."

"Ngasi is a man worth careful attention," said Shgawe. "He is more subtle than he appears, and I believe, not so much of the back-country tribesman as he would have us believe."

"Possibly not," said Hashembe.

Keith switched off the connections, spoke for the encoder: "I'm aboard the *Lumumba*, we've just been out for a look at the missile docks. I've attached my No. 1 transmitter to the person of Adoui Shgawe; you'll now be picking up Shgawe's conversations. I don't dare listen in; they could detect me by the resonance. If anything interesting occurs, notify me."

He snapped back the switch; the pulse of information whisked up to the satellite and relayed down to Washington.

The *Lumumba* entered Tabacoundi Bay, docked. Keith returned to the Hotel des Tropiques, rode the sparkling escalator to the second floor, strode along the silk and marble corridor to the door of his room. Two situations saved his life: an ingrained habit never to pass unwarily through a door, and the radar in his ear-amulets. The first keyed him to vigilance; the second hurled him aside and back. A shower of glass needles shot past his face, exploded against the far wall, tinkled to the floor in fragments.

Keith picked himself up, peered into the room. It was empty. He entered, closed the door. A catapult had launched the needles, a relatively simple mechanism. Someone in the hotel would be on hand to observe what had happened and remove the catapult—necessarily soon.

Keith ran to the door, eased it open, looked into the corridor. Empty—but here came footsteps. Leaving the door open, Keith pressed against the wall.

The footsteps halted. Keith heard the sound of breathing. The tip of a nose appeared through the doorway; it moved inquiringly this way and that. The face came through; it turned and looked into Keith's face, almost eye to eye. The mouth opened in a gasp, then a crooked wince as Keith reached forth, grasped the neck. The mouth opened but made no sound.

Keith pulled the man into the room, shut the door. He was

a light-skinned African, about forty years old. His cheeks were fleshy and expansive, his nose a lumpy beak. Keith recognized him: Corty, his original contact in Fejo. He looked deep into the man's eyes; they were stained pink and the pupils were small; the gaze seemed leaden.

Keith sent a tingle of electricity through the rubbery body. Corty opened his mouth in agony, but failed to cry out. Keith started to speak, but Corty made a despairing sign for silence. He seized the pencil from Keith's pocket, scribbled in English: "Chinese, they have a circuit in my head, they drive me mad."

Keith stared. Corty suddenly opened his eyes wide. Yelling soundlessly he lunged for Keith's throat, clawing, tearing. Keith reluctantly killed him with a rush of electricity, stood looking down at the limp body.

Heaven help the American agent who fell into Chinese hands, thought Keith. They ran wires through his brain into the very core of the pain processes; then instructing and listening through transceivers, they could tweak, punish, or drive into a frantic frenzy at will. The man was happier dead.

The Chinese had identified him. Had someone witnessed the placing of the tap on Shgawe? Or the dosing of Faranah? Or had Doutoufsky passed a broad hint? Or—the least likely possibility—did the Chinese merely wish to expunge him, as an African Isolationist?

Keith looked out into the corridor, which was untenanted. He rolled out the corpse, and then in a spirit of macabre whimsy, dragged it by the heels to the escalator, and sent it down into the lobby.

He returned to his room in a mood of depression. North vs. East vs. South vs. West: a four-way war. Think of all the battles, campaigns, tragedies: grief beyond calculation. And to what end? The final pacification of Earth? Improbable, thought Keith, considering the millions of years ahead. So why did he, James Keith, American citizen, masquerade as Tamba Ngasi, risking his life and circuits inserted into the pain centers of his brain? Keith pondered. The answer evidently was this: all of human history is condensed into each individual lifetime. Each man can enjoy the triumphs or suffer the defeats of all the human race. Charlemagne died a great hero, though his empire immediately split into fragments. Each man must win his personal victory, achieve his unique and selfish goal.

Otherwise, hope could not exist.

The sky over the fantastic silhouette of Fejo grew smoky purple. Colored lights twinkled in the plaza. Keith went to the window, looked off into the dreaming twilight skies. He wished no more of this business; if he fled now for home, he might escape with his life. Otherwise—he thought of Corty. In his own mind a relay activated. The voice of Carl Sebastiani spoke soundlessly, but harsh and urgent. "Adoui Shgawe is dead—assassinated two minutes ago. The news came by your transmitter No. 1. Go to the palace, act decisively. This is a critical event."

Keith armed himself, tested his accumulators. Sliding back the door, he looked into the corridor. Two men in the white tunic of the Lakhadi Militia stood by the escalator. Keith stepped out, walked toward them. They became silent, watched his approach. Keith nodded with austere politeness, started to descend, but they halted him. "Sir, have you had a visitor this evening? An African of early middle-age?"

"No. What is all this about?"

"We are trying to identify this man. He died under strange circumstances."

"I know nothing about him. Let me pass; I am Parliamentarian Tamba Ngasi."

The militia-men bowed politely; Keith rode the escalator down into the lobby.

He ran across the plaza, passed before the six basalt warriors, approached the front of the palace. He marched up the low steps, entered the vestibule. A doorman in a red and silver uniform, wearing a plumed head dress with a silver noseguard, stepped forward. "Good evening, sir."

"I am Tamba Ngasi, Parliamentarian. I must see His Excellency immediately."

"I am sorry, sir, Premier Shgawe has given orders not to be disturbed this evening."

Keith pointed into the foyer. "Who then is that person?"

The doorman looked, Keith tapped him in the throat with his knuckles, held him at the nerve junctions under the ears until he stopped struggling, then dragged him back into his cubicle. He peered into the foyer. At the reception desk sat a handsome young woman in a Polynesian *lava-lava*. Her skin was golden-brown, she wore her hair piled in a soft black pyramid.

Keith entered; the young woman smiled politely up at him.

"Premier Shgawe is expecting me," said Keith. "Where may I find him?"

"I'm sorry sir, he has just given orders that he is not to be disturbed."

"*Just* given orders?"

"Yes, sir."

Keith nodded judiciously. He indicated her telephone. "Be so good as to call Grand Marshal Achille Hashembe, on an urgent matter."

"Your name, sir?"

"I am Parliamentarian Tamba Ngasi. Hurry."

The girl bent to the telephone.

"Ask him to join me and Premier Shgawe at once," Keith ordered curtly.

"But sir—"

"Premier Shgawe is expecting me. Call Marshal Hashembe at once."

"Yes sir." She punched a button. "Grand Marshal Hashembe from the State Palace."

"Where do I find the Premier?" inquired Keith, moving past.

"He is in the second-floor drawing room, with his friends. A page will conduct you." Keith waited; better a few seconds delay than a hysterical receptionist.

The page appeared: a lad of sixteen in a long smock of black velvet. Keith followed him up a flight of stairs to a pair of carved wooden doors. The page made as if to open the doors but Keith stopped him. "Return and wait for Grand Marshal Hashembe; bring him here at once."

The page retreated uncertainly, looking over his shoulder. Keith paid him no further heed. Gently he pressed the latch.

The door was locked. Keith wadded a trifle of plastic explosive against the doorjamb, attached a detonator, pressed against the wall.

Crack! Keith reached through the slivers, slammed the door open, stepped inside. Three startled men looked at him. One of them was Adoui Shgawe. The other two were Hsia Lu-Minh, the Chinese Ambassador, and Vasif Doutoufsky, Chief Clerk of the Grand Lakhadi Parliament.

Doutoufsky stood with his right fist clenched and advanced slightly. On his middle finger glittered the jewel of a large ring.

Steps pounded down the corridor: the doorman and a warrior in the black leather uniform of the Raven Elite Guard.

Shgawe asked mildly, "What is the meaning of all this?"

The doorkeeper cried fiercely. "This man attacked me; he has come with an evil heart!"

"No," cried Keith in confusion. "I feared that Your Excellency was in danger; now I see that I was misinformed."

"Seriously misinformed," said Shgawe. He motioned with his fingers. "Please go."

Doutoufsky leaned over, whispered into Shgawe's ear. Keith's gaze focused on Shgawe's hand, where he also wore a heavy ring. "Tamba Ngasi, stay if you will; I wish to confer with you." He dismissed the doorkeeper and the warrior. "This man is trustworthy. You may go."

They bowed, departed. And the confusion in Keith's mind had disappeared. Shgawe started to rise to his feet. Doutoufsky sidled thoughtfully forward. Keith flung himself to the carpet; the laser beam from his flashlight slashed across Doutoufsky's face, over against Shgawe's temple. Doutoufsky croaked, clutched his burnt-out eyes; the beam from his own ring burnt a furrow up his face. Shgawe had fallen on his back. The fat body quaked, jerked and quivered. Keith struck them again and they both died. Hsia Lu-Minh, pressing against the wall stood motionless, eyes bulging in horror. Keith jumped to his feet, ran forward. Hsia Lu-Minh made no resistance as Keith pumped anesthetic into his neck. Keith stood back panting, and once again the built-in radar saved his life. An impulse, not even registered by his brain, convulsed his muscles and jerked him aside. The bullet tore through his robe, grazing his skin. Another bullet sang past him. Keith saw Hashembe standing in the doorway, the terrified page cringing behind.

Hashembe took leisurely aim. "Wait," cried Keith. "I did not do this!"

Hashembe smiled faintly, and his trigger-finger tightened. Keith dropped to the floor, slashed the laser down over Hashembe's wrist. The gun dropped, Hashembe stood stiff, erect, numb. Keith ran forward, hurled him to the floor, seized the page, blasted anesthetic gas into the nape of his neck, pulled him inside, slammed shut the door.

He turned to find Hashembe groping for the gun with his left hand. "Stop!" cried Keith hoarsely. "I tell you I did not do this."

"You killed Shgawe."

"This is not Shgawe." He picked up the gun. "It is a Chinese agent, his face molded to look like Shgawe."

Hashembe was skeptical. "That is hard to believe." He looked down at the corpse. "Adoui Shgawe was not as fat as this man." He bent, lifted the thick fingers, then straightened up, "This is not Adoui Shgawe!" He inspected Doutoufsky. "The Chief Clerk, a renegade Pole."

"I thought that he worked for the Russians. The mistake almost cost me my life."

"Where is Shgawe?"

Keith looked around the room. "He must be nearby."

In the bathroom they found Shgawe's corpse. A sheet of fluoro-silicon plastic lined the tub, into which had been poured hydrofluoric acid from two large carboys. Shgawe's body lay on its back in the tub, already blurred, unrecognizable.

Choking from the fumes, Hashembe and Keith staggered back, slammed the door.

Hashembe's composure had departed. He tottered to a chair, nursing his wounded arm, muttered, "I understand nothing of these crimes."

Keith looked across to the limp form of the Chinese Ambassador. "Shgawe was too strong for them. Or perhaps he learned of the grand plan."

Hashembe shook his head numbly.

"The Chinese want Africa," said Keith. "It's as simple as that. The lands of Africa will support a billion Chinese."

"If true," said Hashembe, "it is monstrous. And Shgawe, who would tolerate none of this, is dead."

"Therefore," said Keith, "we must replace Shgawe with a leader who will pursue the same goals."

"Where shall we find such a leader?"

"I am such a leader. You control the army; there can be no opposition."

Hashembe sat for two minutes looking into space. Then he rose to his feet. "Very well. You are the new premier. If necessary, we shall dissolve the Parliament. In any event it is no more than a pen for cackling hens."

The assassination of Adoui Shgawe shocked the nation, all of Africa. When Grand Marshal Achille Hashembe appeared before the Parliament, and announced that the assembly had the choice either of electing Tamba Ngasi Premier of Lakhadi, or submitting to dissolution and martial law, Tamba Ngasi was elected without demur.

Keith, wearing the black and gold uniform of the Lion Elite, addressed the chamber.

"In general, my policies are identical to those of Adoui Shgawe. He hoped for a strong united Africa; this is also my hope. He tried to avoid a dependence upon foreign powers, while accepting as much genuine help as was offered. This is also my policy. Adoui Shgawe loved his native land, and sought to make Lakhadi a light of inspiration to all Africa. I hope to do as well. The missile docks will be emplaced exactly as Adoui Shgawe planned, and our Lakhadi technicians will continue to learn how to operate these great devices."

Weeks passed. Keith restaffed the palace, and burned every square inch of floor, wall, ceiling, furniture and fixtures clear of spy-cells. Sebastiani had sent him three new operatives to function as liaison and provide technical advice. Keith no longer communicated directly with Sebastiani; without this direct connection with his erstwhile superior, the distinction between James Keith and Tamba Ngasi sometimes seemed to blur.

Keith was aware of this tendency, and exercised himself against the confusion. "I have taken this man's name, his face, his personality. I must think like him, I must act like him. But I cannot *be* that man!" But sometimes, if he were especially tired, uncertainty plagued him. Tamba Ngasi? James Keith? Which was the real personality?

Two months passed quietly, and a third month. The calm was like the eye of a hurricane, thought Keith. Occasionally protocol required that he meet and confer with Hsia Lu-Minh, the Chinese Ambassador. During these occasions, decorum and formality prevailed; the murder of Adoui Shgawe seemed nothing more than the wisp of an unpleasant dream. "Dream," thought Keith, the word persisting. "I live a dream." In a sudden spasm of dread, he called Sebastiani. "I'm going stale, I'm losing myself."

Sebastiani's voice was cool and reasonable. "You seem to be doing the job very well."

"One of these days," said Keith gloomily, "you'll talk to me in English and I'll answer in Swahili. And then—"

"And then?" Sebastiani prompted.

"Nothing important," said Keith. *And then you'll know that when James Keith and Tamba Ngasi met in the thorn bushes beside the Dasa River, Tamba Ngasi walked away alive and jackals ate the body of James Keith.*

Sebastiani made Keith a slightly improper suggestion: "Find yourself one of those beautiful Fejo girls and work off some of your nervous energy."

Keith somberly rejected the idea. "She'd hear relays clanking and buzzing and wonder who she was kissing."

A day arrived when the missile docks were finally emplaced. Eighteen great concrete cylinders, washed by the Atlantic swells, stretched in a line along the Lakhadi coast. Keith ordained a national holiday to celebrate the installation, and presided at an open air banquet in the plaza before the Parliament House. Speeches continued for hours, celebrating the new grandeur of Lakhadi: "—a nation once subject to the cruel imperial yoke, and now possessed of a culture superior to any west of China!" These were the words of Hsia Lu-Minh, with a bland side-glance for Leon Pashenko, the Russian Ambassador.

Pashenko, in his turn, spoke with words equally mordant. "With the aid of the Soviet Union, Lakhadi finds itself absolutely secure against the offensive maneuvers of the West. We now recommend that all technicians, except those currently employed in the training programs, be withdrawn. African manpower must shape the future of Africa!"

James Keith sat only half-listening to the voices, and without conscious formulation, into his mind came a scheme so magnificent in scope that he could only marvel. It was a policy matter; should he move without prior conference with Sebastiani? But he was Tamba Ngasi as well as James Keith. When he arose to address the gathering, Tamba Ngasi spoke.

"Comrades Pashenko and Hsia have spoken and I have listened with interest. Especially I welcome the sentiments expressed by Comrade Pashenko. The citizens of Lakhadi must perform excellently in every field, without further guidance from abroad. Except in one critical area. We still are unable to manufacture warheads for our new defense system. I therefore take the happy occasion to formally request from the Soviet Union the requisite explosive materials."

Loud applause, and now, while Hsia Lu-Minh clapped with zest, Leon Pashenko showed little enthusiasm. After the banquet, he called upon Keith, and made a blunt statement.

"I regret that the fixed policy of the Soviet Union is to retain control over all its nuclear devices. We cannot accede to your request."

"A pity," said Keith.

Leon Pashenko appeared puzzled, having expected protracted protest and argument.

"A pity, because now I must make the request of the Chinese."

Leon Pashenko pointed out the contingent dangers. "The Chinese make hard masters!"

Keith bowed the baffled Russian out of his apartment. Immediately he sent a message to the Chinese Embassy, and Hsia Lu-Minh appeared shortly.

"The ideas expressed by Comrade Pashenko this evening seemed valuable," said Keith. "I assume you agree?"

"Wholeheartedly," declared Hsia Lu-Minh. "Naturally the programs for agricultural reform we have long discussed would not come under these restraints."

"Most emphatically they would," said Keith. "However a very limited pilot program might be launched, provided that the People's Republic of China supplies warheads, immediately and at once, for our eighteen missiles."

"I must communicate with my government," said Hsia Lu-Minh.

"Please use all possible haste," said Keith, "I am impatient."

Hsia Lu-Minh returned the following day. "My government agrees to arm the missiles provided that the pilot program you envision consists of at least two hundred thousand agricultural technicians."

"Impossible! How can we support so large an incursion?"

The figure was finally set at one hundred thousand, with six missiles only being supplied with nuclear warheads.

"This is an epoch-making agreement," declared Hsia Lu-Minh.

"It is the beginning of a revolutionary process," Keith agreed.

There was further wrangling about the phasing of delivery of the warheads *vis-a-vis* the arrival of the technicians, and negotiations almost broke down. Hsia Lu-Minh seemed aggrieved to find that Keith wanted actual and immediate delivery of the warheads, rather than merely a symbolic statement of intent. Keith, in his turn, experienced surprise when Hsia Lu-Minh objected to a proviso that the incoming "technicians" be granted only six-month visas marked TEMPORARY, with option of renewal at the discretion of the Lakhadi government. "How can these technicians identify themselves with the problems? How can they learn to love the soil which they must till?"

The difficulties were eventually ironed out; Hsia Lu-Minh took his leave. Almost at once Keith received a call from Sebastiani, who had only just learned of the projected China-

Lakhadi treaty. Sebastiani's voice was cautious, tentative, probing. "I don't quite understand the rationale of this project."

When Keith was over-tired, the Tamba Ngasi element of his personality exerted greater influence. The voice which answered Sebastiani sounded impatient, harsh and rough even to Keith himself.

"I did not plan this scheme by rationality, but by intuition."

Sebastiani's voice became even more cautious. "I fail to see any advantageous end to the business."

Keith, or Tamba Ngasi—whoever was dominant—laughed. "The Russians are leaving Lakhadi."

"The Chinese remain in control. Compared with the Chinese, the Russians are genteel conservatives."

"You make a mistake. I am in control!"

"Very well, Keith," said Sebastiani thoughtfully, "I see that we must trust your judgment."

Keith—or Tamba Ngasi—made a brusque reply, and took himself to bed. Here the tension departed and James Keith lay staring into the dark.

A month passed; two warheads were delivered by the Chinese, flown in from the processing plants at Ulan Bator. Cargo helicopters set them in place, and Keith made a triumphant address to Lakhadi, to Africa, and to the world. "From this day forward, Lakhadi, the Helm of Africa, must be granted its place in the world's counsels. We have sought power, not for the sake of power alone, but to secure for Africa the representation our people only nominally have enjoyed. The South no longer must defer to West, to North or to East!"

The first contingent of Chinese "technicians" arrived three days later: a thousand young men and women, uniformly clad in blue coveralls and white canvas shoes. They marched in disciplined platoons to buses, and were conveyed to a tent city near the lands on which they were to be settled.

On this day Leon Pashenko called to deliver a confidential memorandum from the Premier of the U.S.S.R. He waited while Keith glanced through the note.

"It is necessary to point out," read the note, "that Soviet

Russia adversely regards the expansion of Chinese influence in Lakhadi, and holds itself free to take such steps as are necessary to protect the interests of the U.S.S.R.''

Keith nodded slowly. He raised his eyes to Pashenko, who sat watching with a glassy thin-lipped smile. Keith punched a button, spoke into a mesh. ''Send in the television cameras, I am broadcasting an important bulletin.''

A crew hurriedly wheeled in equipment. Pashenko's smile became more fixed, his skin pasty.

The director made a signal to Keith. ''You're on the air.''

Keith looked into the lens. ''Citizens of Lakhadi, and Africans. Sitting beside me is Leon Pashenko, Ambassador of the U.S.S.R. He has just now presented me with an official communication which attempts to interfere with the internal policy of Lakhadi. I take this occasion to issue a public rebuke to the Soviet Union. I declare that the government of Lakhadi will be influenced only by measures designed to benefit its citizens, and that any further interference by the Soviet Union may lead to a rupture of diplomatic relations.''

Keith bowed politely to Leon Pashenko, who had sat full in view of the camera with a frozen grimace on his face. ''Please accept this statement as a formal reply to your memorandum of this morning.''

Without a word Pashenko rose to his feet and left the room.

Minutes later Keith received a communication from Sebastiani. The soundless voice was sharper than ever Keith had heard it. ''What the devil are you up to? Publicity? You've humiliated the Russians, perhaps finished them in Africa— but have you considered the risks? Not for yourself, not for Lakhadi, not even for Africa—but for the whole world?''

''I have not considered such risks. They do not affect Lakhadi.''

Sebastiani's voice crackled with rage. ''Lakhadi isn't the center of the universe merely because you've been assigned there! From now on—these are orders, mind you—make no moves without consulting me!''

''I have heard all I care to hear,'' said Tamba Ngasi. ''Do not call me again, do not try to interfere with my plans.'' He clicked off the receiver, sighed, slumped back in his chair.

Then he blinked, straightened up as the memory of the conversation echoed in his brain.

The following day he received a report from a Swiss technical group, and snorted in anger, though the findings were no more than he had expected.

The Chinese Ambassador unluckily chose this moment to pay a call, and was ushered into the premier's office. Round-faced, prim, brimming with affability, Hsia Lu-Minh came forward.

He takes me for a back-country chieftain, thought the man who was now entirely Tamba Ngasi—a man relentless as a crocodile, sly as a jackal, dark as the jungle.

Hsia Lu-Minh was full of gracious compliments. "How clearly you have discerned the course of the future! It is no mere truism to state that the races of the third world share a common destiny."

"Indeed?"

"Indeed! And I carry the authorization of my government to permit the transfer of another group of skillful, highly trained workers to Lakhadi!"

"What of the remaining warheads for the missiles?"

"They will assuredly be delivered and installed on schedule."

"I have changed my mind," said Tamba Ngasi. "I want no more Chinese immigrants. I speak for all Africa. Those already in this country must leave, and likewise the Chinese missions in Mali, Ghana, Sudan, Angola, the Congolese Federation—in fact in all of Africa. The Chinese must leave Africa, completely and inalterably. This is an ultimatum. You have a week to agree. Otherwise Lakhadi will declare war on the People's Republic of China."

Hsia Lu-Minh listened in astonishment, his mouth a doughnut of shock. "You are joking?" he quavered.

"You think I am joking? Listen!" Once again Tamba Ngasi called for the television crew, and again issued a public statement.

"Yesterday I cleansed my country of the Russians; today I expel the Chinese. They helped us from our post-colonial chaos—but why? To pursue their own advantage. We are not the fools they take us to be." Tamba Ngasi jerked a finger at

Hsia Lu-Minh. "Speaking on behalf of his government, Comrade Hsia has agreed to my terms. The Chinese are withdrawing from Africa. They will leave at once. Hsia Lu-Minh has graciously consented to this. Lakhadi now has a stalwart defense, and no longer needs protection from anyone. Should anyone seek to thwart this purge of foreign influence, these weapons will be instantly used, without remorse. I cannot speak any plainer." He turned to the limp Chinese ambassador. "Comrade Hsia, in the name of Africa, I thank you for your promise of cooperation, and I shall hold you to it!"

Hsia Lu-Minh tottered from the room. He returned to the Chinese Embassy and put a bullet through his head.

Eight hours later, a Chinese plane arrived in Fejo, loaded with ministers, generals and aides. Tamba Ngasi received them immediately. Ting Sieuh-Ma, the leading Chinese theoretician, spoke vehemently. "You put us into an intolerable position. You must reverse yourself!"

Tamba Ngasi laughed. "There is only one road for you to travel. You must obey me. Do you think the Chinese will profit by going to war with Lakhadi? All Africa will rise against you; you will face disaster. And never forget our new weapons. At this moment they are aimed at the most sensitive areas in China."

Ting Sieuh-Ma's laugh was mocking. "It is the least of our worries. Do you think we would trust you with active warheads? Your ridiculous weapons are as harmless as mice."

Tamba Ngasi displayed the Swiss report. "I know this. The detonators: ninety-six percent lead, four percent radioactive waste. The lithium hydride—ordinary hydrogen. You cheated me; therefore I am expelling you from Africa. As for the warheads, I have dealt with a certain European power; even now they are installing active materials in these missiles you profess to despise. You have no choice. Get out of Africa within the week."

"It is disaster either way," said Ting Sieuh-Ma. "But ponder: you are a single man, we are the East. Can you really hope to beat us?"

Tamba Ngasi bared his stainless-steel teeth in a wolfish grin. "That is my hope."

Keith leaned back in his chair. The deputation had departed; he sat alone in the conference chamber. He felt drained of energy, lax and listless. Tamba Ngasi, temporarily at least, had been purged.

Keith thought of the last few days, and felt a pang of terror at his own recklessness. The recklessness, rather, of Tamba Ngasi, who had humiliated and confused two of the great world powers. They would not forgive him. Adoui Shgawe, a relatively mild adversary, had been dissolved in acid. Tamba Ngasi, author of absolutely intolerable policies, could hardly expect to survive.

Keith rubbed his long harsh chin and tried to formulate a plan for survival. For perhaps a week he might be safe, while his enemies decided upon a plan of attack. . . .

Keith jumped to his feet. Why should there be any delay whatever? Minutes now were precious to both Russians and Chinese; they must have arranged for any and all contingencies.

His communication screen tinkled; the frowning face of Grand Marshal Achille Hashembe appeared. He spoke curtly. "I cannot understand your orders. Why should we hesitate now? Clear the vermin out, send them back to their own land—"

"What orders are you talking about?" Keith demanded.

"Those you issued five minutes ago in front of the palace, relative to the Chinese immigrants."

"I see," said Keith. "You are correct. There was a misunderstanding. Ignore those orders, proceed as before."

Hashembe nodded with brusque satisfaction; the screen faded. There would be no delay whatever, thought Keith. The Chinese already were striking. He twisted a knob on the screen, and his reception clerk looked forth. She seemed startled.

"Has anyone entered the palace during the last five minutes?"

"Only yourself, sir. . . . How did you get upstairs so quickly?"

Keith cut her off. He went to the door, listened, and heard the hum of the rising elevator. He ran to his private apartments, snatched open a drawer. His weapons—gone. Betrayed by one of his servants.

Keith went to the door which led out into the terrace garden. From the garden he could make his way to the plaza and escape if he so chose. To his ears came a soft flutter of sound. Keith stepped out into the dark, searched the sky. The night was overcast; he could see only murk. But his radar apprised him of a descending object, the infra-red detector in his hand felt heat.

From behind him, in his bedroom, came another soft sound. He turned, watched a simulacrum of himself step warily through the door, glance around the room. They had done a good job, thought Keith, considering the shortness of time. This version of Tamba Ngasi was perhaps a half-inch shorter, the face was fuller, the skin a shade darker and not too subtly toned. He moved without the loose African swing, on legs thicker and shorter than Keith's own. Keith decided that to simulate an African, it was best to begin with a black man. In this respect at least the United States had an advantage.

The new Tamba left the bedroom. Keith slipped over to the door, intending to stalk him attack with his bare hands but now down from the sky came the object he had sensed on his radar: a jigger-plane, little more than a seat suspended from four whirling air-foils. It landed softly on the dark terrace; Keith pressed against the wall, ducked behind an earthenware urn.

The man from the sky approached, went to the sliding door, slipped into the bedroom. Keith stared. Tamba Ngasi once more, leaner and more angular than the first interloper. This Tamba from the sky looked quickly around the room, peered through the door into the corridor, stepped confidently through.

Keith followed cautiously. The Tamba from the sky jogged swiftly down the corridor, stopped at the archway opening onto the tri-level study. Keith nearly laughed out loud at the farce of deadly misconceptions which now must ensue.

Sky-Tamba leapt into the study like a cat. Instantly there was an ejaculation of excitement, a sputter of deadly sound. Silence.

Keith ran to the doorway, and standing back in the shadow, peered into the study. Sky-Tamba stood holding some sort of gun or projector in one hand and a polished disc in the other. He sidled along the wall. Tamba Short-legs had ducked behind a bookcase, where Keith could hear him muttering under his breath. Sky-Tamba made a quick leap forward; from behind the bookcase came a sparkling line of light and ions. Sky-Tamba caught the beam on his shield, tossed a grenade which Tamba Short-legs thrust at the bookcase; it toppled forward; Sky-Tamba jerked back to avoid it. He tripped and sprawled awkwardly. Tamba Short-legs was on him, hacking with a hatchet, which gave off sparks and smoke where it struck.

Sky-Tamba lay dead, his mission a failure, his life ended. Tamba Short-legs rose in triumph. He saw Keith, uttered a guttural expletive of surprise. He bounded like a rubber ball down to the second landing, intending to out-flank Keith.

Keith ran to the body of Sky-Tamba, tugged at his weapon, but it was caught under the heavy body. A line of ionizing light sizzled across his face; he fell flat. Tamba Short-legs came running up the steps; Keith yanked furiously at the weapon, but there would be no time: his end had come.

Tamba Short-legs stopped short. In the doorway opposite stood a lean harsh-visaged man in white robes—still another Tamba. This one was like Keith, in skin, feature, and heft, identical except for an indefinable difference of expression. The three gazed stupefied at each other; the Tamba Short-legs aimed his electric beam. New Tamba slipped to the side like a shadow, slashing the air with his laser. Tamba Short-legs dropped, rolled over, drove forward in a low crouch. New Tamba waited for him; they grappled. Sparks flew from their feet as each sought to electrocute the other; each had been equipped with ground circuits, and the electricity dissipated harmlessly. Tamba Shortlegs disengaged himself, swung his hatchet. New Tamba dodged back, pointed his laser. Tamba Short-legs threw his hatchet, knocked the laser spinning. The two men sprang together. Keith picked up hatchet and laser and prepared to deal with the survivor. "Peculiar sort of assassination," he reflected. "Everyone gets killed but the victim."

Tamba Short-legs and New Tamba were locked in a writhing tangle. There was a clicking sound, a gasp. One of the men stood up, faced Keith: New Tamba.

Keith aimed the laser. New Tamba held up his hands, moved back. He cried, "Don't shoot me, James Keith. I'm your replacement."

SCIENCE FICTION AT ITS BEST!

MORE SCIENCE FICTION ADVENTURE!